REFuGEE

C.A. HARTMAN

5280 PRESS

Published by 5280 Press
PO Box 12477, Denver, CO 80212
www.5280Press.com

ISBN 10: 0984826297
ISBN 13: 978-0-9848262-9-2

Printed in the United States of America

Cover design by Chris Voeller (chrisvoeller.com)

ACKNOWLEDGEMENTS

I want to thank my friends at LittleSpec (Littleton Area Speculative Fiction Writers) for all their suggestions and encouragement in turning a tentative manuscript into a published novel. Kudos to Jeff Stover for creating such a supportive environment for science fiction and fantasy writers.

I especially want to thank Nick Stasnopolis and Ken Roberts for their critique and support. In your very different ways, you've helped me create a better book... and made me a better writer.

CHAPTER 1

Choose carefully who you associate with during the first six months of a long-term space mission; these individuals will become your closest companions for the next three years… if not for the rest of your life.
                                          – old Space Corps adage

Thursday, Catherine walked into the ship's mess. As she stood in line, she tried to make a quick decision about what to eat. The mess usually served up a few options, including at least one alternative for those otherworld crewmembers who disliked human food. Catherine often wavered between the usual fare and the otherworld option. Today she chose otherworld—a bowl of sea vegetables with ornon, the white gooey flesh of the ubiquitous sea creature that swam in the waters of Derovia's northern hemisphere.

She looked around for Tom and Snow. Crewpersons in black uniforms occupied the mess, eating and filling the large room with the din of conversation. Catherine spotted Tom's curly blonde hair and headed in his direction.

It was Tom Kingston who'd convinced her to sign up for the longest mission the Space Corps allowed. Across from him sat Jebediah Snow, Tom's childhood friend. But nobody who knew Jebediah called him by that name. He was known only as Snow. If someone referred to him otherwise, Snow would correct that person, even if that person were Admiral Scott. Tom loved to tell that story.

"What do you think, Finnegan?" Tom asked as she sat down. "You up for playing some poker tomorrow night?"

Catherine dug into her meal. She was starving. "Possibly," she replied between bites. "I have a project to finish for Steele and it's due tomorrow, so I'll be working late. Are you playing for sure?"

Tom and Snow both nodded.

"Let's start later, say twenty-one hundred," Tom said. He turned to greet a couple of women who happened to walk by their table, briefly discussing their plans for that evening. Once the girls left, Tom turned his attention back to Catherine. "You should be finished by then. It's Friday night. We'll get a little…" he made a drinking gesture with his hands, "and make it a late morning."

Catherine smiled. "Okay."

Snow eyed her meal and made a face. "How can you eat that?"

"How can you eat the same thing every day?" she said, eyeing the beef and potatoes he'd almost finished. His serving of vegetables sat untouched.

"Because it's good."

Tom shook his head. "It's the same shit we ate growing up in the service. And he hasn't eaten veggies since his folks forced him to. I'd drop by his house after dinner and he'd still be sitting there at eight thirty with a pile of broccoli on his plate. I'd eat it when his mom left the room."

Snow shrugged. Suddenly, he looked around him. "Whoa."

"What?" Tom also looked around, but saw nothing to clue him in.

"We just dropped out of FTL."

"How can you tell?" Catherine asked.

"I'm an engineer," Snow replied with a crooked smile, gathering his dishes. "If the fuel ratio is off by even a tenth of a percent, I lie awake at night."

Catherine started laughing.

"You're so full of shit," Tom said.

Snow stood up to leave. Duty called.

After eating, on the way back to her lab, Catherine passed a small window with several crewpersons crowded around it. She halted. They had no scheduled stops that day, or even that week. They weren't close to any star system of significance or known phenomena. She searched for an opening among the others and found a tiny one, spotting what appeared to be the aft end of a small ship, the rest of which was out of view. Captain Ferguson would eventually send a bulletin to the crew; until then, they must satisfy themselves with speculation.

After her crew completed their duty shifts, Catherine worked alone in her lab and finished writing up the results from a project Commander Steele had assigned her. She forwarded the write-up to Steele, leaving her to one last odious task—the weekly progress report he required, detailing how she, and the two crewmen who reported to her, spent each hour of each shift. She slumped in her chair.

Where she came from, such progress reports were unheard of. Grants and publications were the hallmarks of a scientist's progress—you either got them, or you were out of a job.

Catherine fabricated half of her progress report anyway. Once she learned what Steele expected, she would craft the report according to those parameters. She sent the report to Steele and walked back to her quarters.

Having her own quarters, as cramped as they were, was a key factor in Catherine's decision to take the three-year mission. Those with the rank of lieutenant or higher got a window. She couldn't see much more than dark space from her small window, but it still gave her a feeling of freedom. In her limited bulkhead space, Catherine had hung photographs: skiing with her friends, her parents, her and Tom when they graduated from the Academy, a trip she'd taken to the Himalayas. She left one bulkhead space empty, hoping to eventually fill it with some otherworld art or artifact, acquired during their mission.

She changed out of her uniform, grabbed her cup, and headed to Tom's. She arrived a few minutes early, and often did so intentionally, hoping for the rare chance to chat with Tom without interruption.

Tom organized the poker games and they always took place in his quarters. Due to his rank, Tom's larger quarters could accommodate a second table that, when combined with his table, fit ten people. He decorated his quarters with a series of weapons, most of which were antiques. Over many years in the Corps, Tom had assembled a nice collection of artifacts, only a sampling of which he brought on board with him. The remainder were stored back in Chicago with his other belongings.

"Beer?" Tom said.

"Sure." She gave him her metal cup. He filled it from a vessel stored in the large cooling bucket he routinely borrowed from Soren, a bartender they were chummy with. Tom turned his chair backward and sat down at the table.

"Did you finish it?" he asked, referring to her report.

Catherine scowled. "Yes."

"Why that face?"

"I don't like working for him."

He waved a dismissive hand at her. "Long-term missions aren't about work, Finnegan. They're about adventure and seeing what's around the corner. Work is just something you do because you have to." He smiled, his blue eyes crinkling. "How many people back on the rock get to see what's out there?" he said, gesturing out his window. "This is awesome."

She smiled. Tom's enthusiasm was hard to ignore.

"You should've become a soldier," he admonished. "It's better than sitting in that lab, staring into a microscope, surrounded by a bunch of whitecoats."

"Come on, Tom, don't start the soldier-scientist shit. I get so tired of that. And you're starting to sound like my dad," she added.

"You'd make a good soldier. How is Jimmy, by the way?" Tom had worked under Catherine's father, Captain Jim Finnegan, on several brief missions.

"He's good. We holo-chatted pretty regularly until we got out of range." She shifted in the hard chair, trying to get comfortable. "How's Weapons?"

He grinned. "We have a good time down there. The only problem is there are no women." He shook his head in disbelief. "Did you know that Weapons is the only section on this damned ship with no women? Even Engineering has women. Even a cranky bastard like Snow gets more female proximity than I do. I'm telling you, it's wrong."

Catherine laughed. "You're the boss now, Kingston. You couldn't date them anyway."

He shrugged. "I know. Life's just better with girls around." He rapped his hand on the table. "Speaking of which, how'd your date go with Kovsky?"

She shook her head.

"You don't like him, either? Why not?"

"He talks too much."

He shrugged. "Yeah, he's kind of cocky, but he's alright. Give him another chance."

She shook her head again, tucking her auburn hair behind her ear.

"Stubborn. You're running out of options, Finnegan. You're stuck on this ship for three years. There's only so much porn I can loan you."

Before she could think of a good response to Tom's crack, the door sounded.

They turned their attention to the display—it was Snow. Once Tom called for the door to open, Snow walked in. He wore a t-shirt, revealing arms covered in tattoos, and he'd put earrings back in both ears.

Following Snow was the remainder of the invite list, which included the other poker regulars, plus three newbies. The regulars included Private Javier Zander, the youngest of the bunch and part of Tom's Weapons crew, Petty Officer Mackey Middleton—friend of Zander's—and Petty Officer Shanti Patel, who worked in the communications center. All the players carried their own cups, and two of the three newbies carried beer under their arms.

"You forget something, newb?" Tom asked the empty-handed newbie.

"You didn't tell me to bring beer, LC! I swear!" he said. "You started talkin' to that blonde girl from Supply... and..." The newbie, a brand new Private Recruit, took a couple of steps back.

Hearing Snow snort in disapproval and seeing his glare, Tom relented. "Alright, alright," he told the newbie. "Bring it next time."

Snow and the others filled their cups with the brown murky beer and began chatting. It was, by some standards, an unusual mix of people. On a starship, social groups often formed in predictable ways. Many banded together based on the department they reported to. And those from Derovia—about twenty percent of the 507 crewmembers—often associated with their own kind. Soldiers and scientists typically socialized with their own. However, the most important social divider was rank—officers ate in a separate area from enlisted crew, and the two groups rarely fraternized.

But that night, their poker game represented several departments, ranks from Private Recruit to Lieutenant Commander, one scientist, and one Derovian newbie. Tom's view was that once they were off duty and in his quarters, things like rank, department, and race no longer mattered. He didn't allow his guests to wear uniforms, salute, or address by rank. If anyone didn't like it, they weren't invited back.

Everyone sat down and Tom dealt the first hand. The conversation began as mostly idle chatter about growing accustomed to life on a starship and estimating when they would arrive on Derovia, their first encampment.

"So what's the story with those aliens we picked up yesterday?" Zander said, posing the question to anyone.

A few of them, Catherine included, looked up from their cards. That's what she'd caught a glimpse of yesterday—an otherworld ship. The Captain still hadn't sent out a bulletin, and they hadn't yet resumed their course.

Everyone looked to Tom. Recently promoted to Lieutenant Commander, Tom was the highest-ranking officer in the group, and a well-informed one due to his wide acquaintance. If anything interesting happened, Tom usually knew before most people.

"Were they Calyyt?" Middleton said. "They had to be with that piece of shit little cruiser."

"You didn't hear?" Tom said, taking a peek at his cards.

Snow looked at Tom impatiently, tossing in his folded cards. "No, LC, we didn't hear. We aren't in the know, part of the privileged few."

Tom grinned at Snow's sarcasm and placed a large bet into the pot. "They weren't Calyyt." He paused. "They were Korvali."

A silence fell over the table.

"Korvali?" Catherine said.

"Way the hell out here?" Snow said.

Tom nodded. "They were a group of ten or so. They'd been stranded in this region for weeks, and we were the first to pick up their SOS."

"Where are they?" Catherine asked, looking around.

"They're dead."

Catherine felt her blood run cold. "All of them? What happened?"

Tom shook his head. "I don't know. That's all I got. This has never happened before, so it's anybody's guess."

"Wow," Shanti said. "I only know one person who's even seen a Korvali. Why didn't the Captain make an announcement?"

"Don't know that either," Tom replied. "They're probably still trying to figure out how to handle ten dead Korvali. Think about it: what are we going to do with them? Bring them all the way back to the Forbidden Planet, where they'll wage war on us? Dump them into space like garbage? It puts the Alliance in a tough position."

"I say dump the Mutants," Middleton said. "They hate us anyway."

"Don't call them that, Mackey," Shanti said, frowning. "It's mean. And what do you know about them? You've never even met one."

Middleton glanced at his cards. "I don't have to meet one. I've heard the stories. When the Sunai entered their space, the Korvali killed them all with some kind of virus."

"The Sunai didn't *enter* their space, Mackey, they invaded it," Shanti said. "After being warned to stay away. What would you do if a bunch of aliens stormed your house?"

Middleton shook his head. "It's been ten years since we discovered them. They still refuse to join the Alliance and still look down their noses at us." A few of the others nodded.

Catherine rolled her eyes, but said nothing. She'd heard it all before.

"Wait, I don't get it," young Zander said. "If it only takes three days to get from Korvalis to Suna, why were they stranded for so long?"

"They don't have FTL drives, dumbass." Middleton peered at his cards and tossed in his bet. "Their technology is last century. They could get FTL technology in exchange for their genetic technology if they joined the Alliance, but they refuse. How stupid can you be? Who gives a shit about genetics when you can travel to other worlds?"

Catherine looked up at Middleton. Before she could retort, Tom spoke.

"Watch your mouth, Middleton," Tom warned. "Doc Finnegan here is a geneticist."

All eyes were on Middleton.

"Sorry," Middleton said to Catherine, fiddling with his chips. He paused, a confused look on his face as he glanced down, then back at Catherine. "I thought you were a soldier, like us."

Tom started to laugh. Catherine elbowed him. "I'm a scientist," she said.

Middleton and the other enlisted crew laughed nervously.

"The Korvali don't want to travel to other worlds, Middleton," Snow said. "They don't like outsiders. Especially tatted-up losers like you," he added, putting his fist up. Middleton, also heavily tattooed under his clothing, raised his fist and bumped it with Snow's.

"You're both dumbasses." Shanti threw in her folded hand. "They're a different species. Just because the Derovians are so friendly," she motioned to the Derovian newbie, who produced a big smile, "and the Sunai are explorers, the Korvali have to be the same way? The Calyyt aren't friendly, and I don't hear you bitching about them."

"The Calyyt are part of the Alliance," Middleton argued. "And it's hard to be friendly with them because nobody understands their stupid sign language." A few others laughed at this.

"But the Korvali have never tried to harm us, Mackey. And think about it—why were they so far from home, adrift in space? For a vacation?"

Catherine nodded in agreement.

"I don't know," Middleton grumbled. "Who cares?"

"Alright," Tom said. "You kids quiet down. Let's play some poker, damn it!" He held up his beer cup. "To poker!"

Everyone followed suit and raised their cups. "To poker!"

At 0300, after numerous games and one too many beers, Catherine made her way back to her quarters. Tom had a tricky way of keeping your cup full without you realizing it. She undressed, climbed into bed, and fell right to sleep.

A loud beep woke her. Startled, she looked for the source of the offending noise—it was her contactor. She glanced at the time: 0610. Grabbing her contactor, she wondered who the hell would wake her up this early on a Saturday.

It was Dr. Vargas, Chief of Medicine.

"Yes, Doctor," Catherine said, her voice thick with sleep.

"Lieutenant Finnegan, report to sick bay immediately," a gruff voice barked at her.

"On my way, Sir."

She stumbled a little as she got up, still feeling a little drunk. She quickly donned her uniform, threw her long hair back into a ponytail, and gulped a big cup of water. In her groggy state, Catherine wondered if she'd missed a sick bay duty shift, required of all officers once per month, regardless of rank or position. She hadn't had hers in a while.

She walked swiftly to the stairwell and descended four decks, mentally preparing her apology. After only three months, *Cornelia*'s crew quickly learned that missing sick bay duty, or otherwise angering Dr. Vargas, was unwise. When one science officer missed his duty, Vargas yelled at him in front of the other medical staff and assigned him to work *both* of his off-duty days in sick bay.

Catherine arrived at sick bay, squinting from the bright lights. When she spotted Vargas near his office on the far side of the main chamber, he didn't accost her, yell, or even appear angry. Instead, he impatiently gestured for her to join him.

As she crossed the chamber to where Vargas stood, she noticed a body on one of the medical beds, a tiny, almost transparent IV attached to its hand. She stopped and took a closer look.

He was an otherworlder. He was Korvali.

CHAPTER 2

"I thought they were dead," she said in wonder, staring at the Korvali.

He was fair-skinned with short, light brown hair. She noticed the webbing between his long fingers, the absence of fingernails, and his small, almost non-existent ears... all characteristic of the Korvali. His clothing, the traditional Korvali robe, was slightly dirty. Otherwise, he appeared peaceful and unharmed.

"They are dead," Vargas replied, joining her at the bedside. "And I thought this one was too until my scanner picked up some very faint vital signs. He's in some type of... stasis, and I can't revive him. I've tried, believe me. His heart and respiratory rates are so slow they're barely detectable. But he's alive." He turned to face Catherine. "When I scanned him, I found some irregularities in his DNA. They could explain why he's in a coma, but I'm no geneticist. I need some answers." Vargas, with his thick mustache and heavy build, looked at Catherine expectantly.

Catherine stood up straight, doing her best to absorb everything Vargas told her. "I'll do what I can, Doctor," she said, hoping she sounded more coherent than she felt. She glanced at his viewer. "I've never seen one of their genomes before."

Dr. Vargas pulled the remote from the pocket of his white coat and scrolled to the scan results, which listed the four anomalies he'd found.

"I need to see his entire genome, at chromosomal resolution," she said.

He handed her the remote. "The boy has twenty-three pairs of chromosomes, like we do."

I knew it, she thought with some excitement. "Some believe they're the most similar to us, genetically speaking." She instructed the computer to conduct a series of scans, each at increasing resolution. "How did the others die?"

"Dehydration. I've got them chilling like popsicles in the cold chamber until I know what the hell to do with them."

She rolled her eyes, knowing he couldn't see her. Catherine rarely got sick, but told herself if she ever did come down with something, it must wait until evening, when Vargas was typically off duty.

Once the scans finished, she took a look at the results. "Interesting. Those four irregularities you mentioned—on chromosomes six, seven, and eighteen—they're anomalous because his DNA has been altered there…"

"Altered? As in, intentionally changed? How can you tell?"

She ordered the computer to project a three-dimensional image of the genome. "You can see the markers," she said, pointing at them. While Vargas walked around the image, she connected to her own network, entered her password, and uploaded the file of the Korvali patient's genetic material. She reran her scans and cross-referenced each alteration with her human genomic library. One by one, the viewer displayed the names and descriptions of the four altered loci. Two of the altered loci were in a region involved in visual processing. The other two, on different chromosomes, appeared to have some regulatory function.

She shook her head. "This couldn't possibly explain his coma. Let me try something else." Catherine conducted a different scan, again repeating her scans at increasing levels of resolution. It wasn't until the third scan that she saw something strange. "What the hell?" she muttered to herself.

"What do you see?"

"I don't know," she said, staring at the viewer. "I'm picking up something, but the results don't make sense. It almost looks as if the epigenome has been tampered with."

"The epigenome?" Vargas said, confused.

"Yeah. It includes all the proteins and stuff the DNA is packaged in."

"Why does that matter?"

"Because it controls the regulation of the DNA... which genes are turned on and off."

"Nothing like that showed up when I scanned him..." Vargas said, skeptical.

Catherine shook her head. "A medical scanner wouldn't detect something like this." She continued to look, fascinated.

"How could this explain why he's in a coma? Was he attacked by a bioweapon? Or did they experiment on him like some kind of lab rat?"

"I'm not sure." Perplexed, she examined the remaining readout from her analyses. Suddenly, she sat back in her chair. "Holy shit."

"What do you see?" Vargas said, not noticing her use of profanity.

She turned to look at him. "How long have the others been dead?"

"Two weeks or so."

She nodded in excitement. "He hasn't been attacked. They've engineered his epigenome. I think these alterations are the very thing that's keeping him alive, like some sort of... epigenetic therapy!"

"Wait, slow down," Vargas said, putting his hands up. "Epigenetic therapy?"

"Yeah... instead of altering the DNA, you alter how the genes are regulated. Think about some of those cancer therapies, and how they use those drugs to turn off the tumor genes. It's like that... but far more sophisticated!"

Vargas gave her a look. "Sounds pretty farfetched, Lieutenant."

"I know. But what else can explain this?" She gestured at the young man lying on the bed.

Vargas shook his head. "The kid's been in a coma for two weeks, and hooked up for nearly two days. He's probably brain dead by now."

Catherine sighed, trying to hide her annoyance. Maybe Vargas was right. But she refused to believe it until she had a chance to investigate further, until there was no hope of his survival.

"If what you say is true," Vargas said, "why didn't the others survive?"

"Did you scan them?"

Vargas didn't answer. He immediately walked away, returning minutes later with scanned samples from the nine deceased. "I picked up genetic irregularities for three of them."

Catherine analyzed the samples. When finished, she shook her head. "That's just a few DNA changes. I don't see anything unusual in their epigenomes."

She stood up and approached the Korvali, looking at him closely. Then she noticed something: a mark on his left hand, just peeking out from the edge of his long sleeve. She leaned down for a closer look, and then slowly nudged his sleeve up, careful not to touch him. The marking was a tattoo, a fan-shaped form with irregular edges, appearing almost like a leaf, with an intricate design. It consisted of one strange color that Catherine couldn't easily describe... like dark magenta.

"Doctor," she said, showing him.

"A tattoo?"

Catherine examined it for a moment. There was something familiar about it... then it hit her. "He's Shereb."

Vargas just looked at her.

"He's a member of the Shereb clan, the clan that includes their monarchy."

"How do you know that?"

"That's the Shereb crest. I've seen it before, in graduate school."

Vargas motioned for her to follow him as he walked to the rear chamber. He entered a code into a heavy, secure door, opened it, and walked in. Catherine did the same, hugging her arms to herself as the frigid air engulfed her. *The cold chamber.* Narrow metal shelf-like protrusions lined three of the four chamber walls. Nine shelves were occupied, each corpse covered in a dark shroud. Several of the corpses hung partially over the end of their respective shelves, due to their great height.

A hollow feeling came over her.

"Lieutenant." Vargas's voice woke her from her internal reverie. He gestured at her to come closer, and lifted a shroud to reveal a long, thin, webbed hand, so pale in color that it didn't appear real. It had no tattoo.

"Left hand," Catherine said. Vargas reached over and found the other hand.

And there it was. The tattoo differed from their patient's—it had many dark gray vines, or perhaps branches, spreading out from a common origin. Six of the bodies shared this crest, while the remaining three displayed a third crest, circular in shape and simpler in design. It had the appearance of a biological thing, but Catherine couldn't decipher it.

"This makes no sense," she said, following Vargas back to the main chamber. "Why would a Shereb be on a ship with these other people who aren't Shereb? Where were they going?"

Vargas didn't answer. Instead, he contacted the Captain.

"Yes, Doctor," Captain Ferguson's voice rang through on Vargas's contactor.

"Captain. The boy is still comatose, but our geneticist has identified a tattoo on his hand that she claims is a crest of the…" Vargas glanced at her, "… the Shereb clan. The dead ones don't appear to be Shereb."

"Are you sure?" the Captain replied in an obviously puzzled tone.

"Yes. His genes have been altered too, and—"

"Order two Masters-at-Arms to report to sick bay immediately. Contact me the moment the boy wakes up."

"Yes, Captain."

Catherine looked at Vargas, waiting for an explanation. But none came.

"Please, continue," he said. Vargas went back to the cold chamber. Upon returning, he remarked that the deceased Korvali wore robes of gray. "The boy's is blue."

"Well, he's male but he isn't a boy," Catherine said, eyes glued to the viewer. "His telomeres indicate that he's around twenty-two years old."

"In Earth years? I don't think so, Lieutenant. He has no facial hair."

"The Korvali don't have facial or body hair, Doctor."

Vargas started to make another point, but was interrupted by another voice speaking to them.

"My age is twenty-three, in Earth years," the male voice said in a thick accent.

She and Dr. Vargas turned around in unison.

The Korvali was sitting up, conscious and alert, staring at them with pale, sea-colored eyes. The two Masters-at-Arms still hadn't arrived.

"Where am I?" he inquired coldly, his face expressionless. He looked primarily at Catherine as he spoke. She was standing now, inadvertently staring back at the Korvali's unusual, penetrating gaze.

Catherine waited for Vargas to answer. As the higher-ranking officer, it was his duty to speak, not hers. After recovering from his surprise, Vargas called for the Captain to report to sick bay.

"You're on the Starship *Cornelia*," Vargas finally replied. "We represent the Space Corps, from Earth. We responded to your vessel's SOS and brought you aboard close to two days ago. I am Doctor Vargas, the ship's Chief Medical Officer. This is Doctor Lieutenant Finnegan, a science officer." He paused. "I've been trying to wake you up."

There was a long pause. Then, the Korvali replied, "Attempting to 'wake' me would be impossible without the correct conditions."

Dr. Vargas glanced at Catherine, then looked back at the Korvali. "So once we supplied you with adequate levels of hydration and nutrition, you woke up on your own."

"Yes," he replied, elaborating no further. He sat perfectly still on medical bed.

Just then, two MAs entered sick bay, their weapons in hand as they advanced toward the bed where the Korvali sat. Dr. Vargas put up his hand, and the soldiers ceased their approach and stood aside.

Vargas approached the Korvali with his scanner. The Korvali immediately recoiled. Vargas froze, unsure of what to do next.

"Does the doctor have permission to scan you?" Catherine offered. "He won't touch you."

The Korvali relaxed slightly, not taking his eyes off Vargas. "Yes."

Vargas raised the bed to a full sitting position and began scanning his patient. The Korvali looked uncomfortable but said nothing. Although it didn't register initially, Catherine realized that he spoke English, and rather well, as though he'd interacted with humans before. He must be a scientist or government official, on his way to make a rare appearance at an Alliance function.

Vargas finished his scan. "Lieutenant here believes that your ability to enter this stasis was due to some intentional mucking with your… genetic material."

The young man turned his attention back to Catherine, his unblinking gaze peering at her for a moment before he answered. "She is correct."

"You're not recovered yet," Vargas said. "Your heart and respiratory rates are better but they're still pretty low, and you're running a little hot."

"Let me view your instrument." Vargas, eyebrows knitted, rotated the medical scanner so that the Korvali could see the readout. After examining it for a few moments, he said, "Each result is within normal range for my people."

Bewildered, Vargas looked at the readout again. He asked more questions. The Korvali kept his answers quite brief, appearing uninterested in conversing and, on one or two occasions, he simply offered no answer at all. Finally, Vargas gave up and went to download his scanner data. The Korvali turned his attention to Catherine.

"The doctor is unaware of your customs," she said once Vargas stepped out of earshot. "You will find that we all are." The Korvali continued to watch her, signaling her to continue. "Are you willing to talk about your genome?" It was risky to ask him about genetics. The Korvali rarely shared information, especially about that. But something made her ask anyway.

"Ask me anything."

Catherine, not expecting that response, scrambled to choose her most pressing questions. "So my hypothesis was correct? The epigenomic changes I saw were responsible for your stasis?" She spoke in her most scientific tone, which she used when she was nervous.

"Yes."

"And your epigenome has been altered so you could survive?"

"Yes."

Unfathomable.

He looked at her, encouraging her to continue.

"The alterations aren't enough. What initiated this stasis?" Then the answer came to her. "A drug."

"Yes." He looked almost pleased.

"What kind?"

"You know this. You have a... publication... that discusses a class of related drugs."

Catherine stared at him.

"Are you not Catherine Finnegan, the geneticist who authored the publication on the six classes of methylation inhibitors?" As he spoke, his speech seemed to suddenly grow more fluid, his accent softer.

"You know my work?"

"Yes. We study all publications from Earth's geneticists."

"Wha… why? Isn't our work a bit rudimentary to you?"

He thought for a moment. "Perhaps. It can also be… interesting."

Catherine couldn't help but smile at his attempt at diplomacy.

The Korvali smiled in response. It wasn't a big smile or, really, much of a smile at all. It was a subtle change in his expression that somehow conveyed pleasure.

"That's an old paper," she finally replied, recovering from her surprise. "Anyway, that's as far as I got before you came to life… rather suddenly."

"Yes, you both appeared… what is the word?"

"Surprised."

"Yes. Surprised. I am familiar with your language, but unaccustomed to speaking with… outsiders." The word came out strange, like he was uncomfortable with it.

"You haven't spoken to otherworlders before?"

"No."

Catherine, again torn between the many, many questions she wanted to ask, decided to stick with the most important ones.

"If you don't mind my asking, which designer did this level of work on you? Was it Othniel? We have so little information on Korvali genetics, but Othniel's work seemed to be heading in this direction."

His expression changed, and he broke his strong eye contact, if only momentarily.

Catherine felt a chill. She'd gone too far, asked too many questions. "Have I offended you?"

"No. It is my work. I was the designer."

Catherine stared again. "You were."

"Yes." He paused. "Othniel… provided guidance with the initial design."

"Othniel is your mentor?"

"He was my father."

Catherine nodded, unsure of what to say. Sensing she was in dangerous waters, she dropped it.

"You again appear… surprised," he said.

"You aren't what I expected."

He looked at her with his sea gaze. "Neither are you." He then held out his webbed hand to her. "I am Eshel."

Catherine, completely taken aback by the unexpected offering, stared at the long-fingered, webbed hand before she finally put her hand in his and shook it. She was embarrassed that he, the outsider, had to offer his name, rather than she or Vargas asking for it. "Catherine," she replied.

Before either could say anything more, Eshel's powerful gaze was redirected elsewhere. When Catherine followed his glance, she saw that Captain Ferguson had arrived. She'd been so absorbed by the Korvali that she hadn't heard Vargas announce her arrival. She quickly turned and stood at attention.

Ferguson walked over to them, her graying raven hair pulled back into a bun. Her blue eyes had their usual gleam, her posture its usual confidence. "At ease," she said, faintly waving her arm, not taking her eyes off the Korvali. "Welcome aboard. I'm Janice Ferguson, Captain of this ship. What's your name, young man?"

"I am Eshel," he said, his manner once more aloof.

"Eshel, our first priority is to make sure you're well. Doctor, what's Eshel's status?"

Vargas replied with some trepidation that Eshel appeared to be healthy and functioning normally.

"Good," Ferguson said. "How can we help you?"

"I seek asylum from Korvalis."

Stunned at the Korvali's request, Catherine turned to see Ferguson's reaction.

Ferguson could not contain her surprise either. "You want asylum? To live with us… to live under our protection?"

"Yes."

"That's no small request." She eyed the Korvali for a moment before she shifted to a softer tone. "Your crewmates didn't survive your journey."

His expression clouded over. "Yes."

"They also sought asylum?"

"Yes."

"What happened to them?"

"The Korvali Guard aimed their weapons at our water supply when they could not catch us. The others did not have the capacity to survive under such conditions."

"But you did," the Captain said, her tone skeptical.

Dr. Vargas chimed in. "We can explain that at the briefing, Captain."

"Why aim for the water supply, rather than the entire ship?" Ferguson pressed.

"That is not how it is done," Eshel replied, offering no further explanation.

"We'll consider your request for asylum," she said. "For now, we'll need your assistance in handling the deceased. You'll remain under guard until further notice." She turned to Catherine and Vargas. "I want you two at the meeting at eighteen hundred. I expect a full report beforehand."

"Yes, Captain," they replied.

Ferguson turned and left sick bay.

Dr. Vargas turned to Catherine. "Thank you for your assistance, Dr. Finnegan. You're dismissed."

Catherine, disappointed at her dismissal and wishing she could stay, saluted Dr. Vargas. She then turned to Eshel and nodded. He returned her nod. With that, she left sick bay.

But back in her quarters, Catherine couldn't sleep. She had too many questions. And there was only one person who could answer them.

September 28th

Hi Dad,

You're not going to believe this. On what has (so far) been a rather uneventful mission, the most amazing thing has happened. I don't know if I'm allowed to discuss it, but you're going to find out anyway when you go back to Headquarters, and for once I'm too excited to keep this to myself.

The other day, the ship dropped out of FTL. We're way out past the Katara system, nowhere near civilization. I'm the last to know anything around here, being a scientist and all, but the guys leaked at the poker game that we'd chased down an SOS. They found a small ship with ten dead Korvali on it. But... it turns out one of them was ALIVE and in some kind of stasis. Vargas woke me out of a dead sleep to help him figure out some genetic oddities with the patient. While he and I were blathering about the particulars, we heard a voice—it was the Korvali, sitting up and fully alert! Even Vargas—who we both know is prone to talking more rather than less—was temporarily stunned into silence!

Dad: he survived with no food or water—for more than two weeks—because he altered his own epigenome. GENETICS, Dad! No one's ever done anything like this before. I know you aren't especially confident in medical genetics because of Mom and all, but think about the potential implications of this!

You wouldn't believe his skill with our language. And he was forthcoming with me, and even offered his hand. His hand, Dad, for shaking! I knew it. I knew they weren't like people say. I knew they didn't hate us. Admittedly, he was really cold to Dr. Vargas and didn't seem intimidated by anyone, even Ferguson. I found that funny. Oh, and his name is Eshel.

But on to my main point. I don't understand, Dad. I assumed these Korvali were on their way to Suna for a scientific meeting and something went wrong... but then he asked Ferguson for asylum from Korvalis! They escaped Korvalis and nine of them died, all because they wanted to leave. Do you know anything about this? Why would a scientist from the most powerful clan of a people who shun outsiders want to leave and live among strangers?

Love,
C

P.S. I hope you don't mind my sending this over FTLcom. We're out of range and I don't know when that will change. I'll reimburse you for it…

CHAPTER 3

"Mail," Catherine said. A moment later, a brief response from her father, along with two attached documents, appeared on her viewer. *Keep them to yourself,* her dad said. She scanned the first document, a brief report from the Alliance. The report, dated over a year ago, was written by an official from Suna's military government.

One of our patrol vessels, on exploratory detail 0.77 kpc 240 degrees from our Katara solar system, discovered a vessel adrift in space. The ship, very small in size and quite unimpressive in design, was distinctly Korvali. It barely qualifies the title of ship! The vessel was similar to others encountered previously. Our best men very quickly and easily gained entry to the vessel. The vessel contained six Korvali persons, all deceased. The bodies will be handled in the usual way.

Signed,

Gro Karo, 4th Class, Rank 2
3rd Regiment, Jula

Catherine sat back in her chair. *This has happened before?*

Reading over the report again, Catherine's lip curled at the officer's tone. She'd heard that Sunai males were full of themselves. She glanced at the officer's class and rank: he was only a Gro and not especially high up on the Sunai military totem pole. If this report were any indication, others' accounts of Sunai men were not unfounded.

Catherine moved on to the second, longer document. She could find no insignia or other sign of its origin, which meant it couldn't have come from any planetary government or from the Alliance. A quick glance over the first several lines revealed that the English was acceptable, although choppy enough to indicate that either an other-worlder had written it or an interpreter had translated the document into English. But after reading the first of many long paragraphs, Catherine realized that the document's author was not Sunai, human, or even Derovian. The author was Korvali, one of their Guard.

Catherine read the entire lengthy document in one sitting. It offered a first person narrative of the unsettling political situation in the industrialized region of Korvalis, and all the historical events that led to it. After scrolling down more, she found an appended report from the Alliance that summarized the document's important points. She chuckled; the brass, especially if not scientists, never wanted to read a long, detailed document.

Summary:

- *Korvalis's industrialized region had known peace at one time under the rule of the previous monarchial line, all of whom were descended from the Osecal clan. However, the young Osecal malkaris (monarchial leader) died unexpectedly. His only sibling, a sister, also died at a young age, and both passed before either married or bore any heirs. Next in line for the throne was the eldest cousin, who took her place as ruler.*

- *In an unusual turn of events, the new malkaris severed her bond with her current mate and instead chose a mate from the Shereb clan. Such an unjoining and rejoining is an extremely rare occurrence among the Korvali. This began the shift in power to the Shereb clan after fifteen generations of Osecal rule.*

- *Together, the malkaris and her mate eradicated the Osecal representatives from their government seats and appointed a new kunsheld (non-monarchial political leader). The new kunsheld, a Shereb and former assembly member called Elisan, usurped most of the assembly's power. The people protested this violation of Doctrine; but nothing changed. Korvalis has experienced turmoil since.*

- *The political upset had its far-reaching consequences for their social and economic structure, and it created unrest among the clans and fostered occasional rebellions of minor scale. Escape attempts by non-Shereb citizens became a challenge for the Korvali Guard. Korvali Doctrine forbids its citizens to leave their planet without permission from the kunsheld. However, until the shift in power to the Shereb clan, attempts to leave without permission were unheard of.*

- *With these escape attempts, the Korvali Guard retrieved the rogue vessel and took its passengers to prison. No outsiders knew of these attempts that got no further than ~300 parsecs from Korvalis. Lack of FTL technology and the planet's isolated location made successful escape extremely difficult. Those few ships managing to avoid the Guard's detection lacked the ability to reach Suna—the closest inhabited planet—in a timely fashion; the Guard eventually found them. If not caught, their resources were fired upon or otherwise sabotaged, ensuring the escapees did not survive the long journey to Suna.*

After finishing the appended report, Catherine considered writing her father again. *Who is this guy? Some sort of mole, leaking information from Korvalis to the Alliance? If so, why do we still know so little about the Korvali?* But after scrolling down more, Catherine got her answer.

The long report, written nearly four Earth years ago, was the word of the first Korvali citizen to escape Korvalis and survive. He delivered the report to numerous Alliance representatives; then he disappeared. Nobody knew how he escaped, where he was, or even whether he was still alive. This escapee—known only as Ashan—sparked some controversy among the Alliance delegates, who argued over the handling of any future escapees. However, years passed without another incident.

For Catherine, the report generated more questions than it answered. But they would have to wait. She had a report of her own to write.

At 1800, Commander Yamamoto, the ship's Executive Officer, stood in the bridge ready room. He looked briefly out the large window that offered a spectacular view of the space they travelled through, as each department head took his place at the rectangular table. When Catherine Finnegan walked in, she hesitated, as if unsure where to sit among the command team. She looked to him and he motioned for her to take the unoccupied seat next to Dr. Vargas.

Captain Ferguson sat down at the head of the table, scanned the group to ensure everyone had arrived, and began. "As you've read in your reports, we now have a Korvali citizen aboard *Cornelia*, the only survivor of ten." She paused and looked at them. "And he has, if you can believe it, requested asylum with us. He made it clear he doesn't want to go to Suna, Derovia lacks the resources to protect him, and Calyyt-Calloq doesn't allow immigration. He's only the second to successfully escape Korvalis... you've all read the Ashan Report... but, unlike Ashan, he has no plans to disappear."

There was silence, followed by numerous reactions of surprise. When they began asking questions all at once, Ferguson put up her hand. "One thing at a time. Commander Ov'Raa has spoken with our refugee." She turned to Ov'Raa.

Ov'Raa, Chief of Administration and a highly respected inter-species relations expert from Derovia, smiled his most pleasant smile, making his large almond eyes gleam. His small frame almost engulfed by the large black chair and one thick six-digit hand gently resting on the other, he addressed the group. "Our new refugee, who declares his name to be Eshel, requests asylum with the Space Corps, under the auspices of the Orion Interplanetary Alliance. Eshel read the Ashan Report; even before reading it, he confirmed Ashan's claims about the unrest on Korvalis."

"Did Eshel know Ashan, or offer any information about Ashan's escape or whereabouts?" Yamamoto asked.

"No, Commander," Ov'Raa replied, clasping his thick hands. "Eshel belonged to Korvalis's very powerful Shereb clan and did not associate with members of the Korvali Guard. However, Commander, you will be interested to know that Eshel knew nothing of Ashan's successful escape, and took a most eager interest in the report!"

"How was he able to survive when the others didn't?" Ferguson asked, aiming her question at Dr. Vargas.

Dr. Vargas, who looked tired, cleared his throat. "When we found him, he was in some kind of stasis. His vital and metabolic functions were reduced so much that my scanner didn't pick up his life signs at first. He was as cold as a damned iceberg. After almost two days of hydration, he came to. Dr. Finnegan, our geneticist, can explain the rest."

Everyone looked at Catherine. "Eshel was able to survive weeks without food or water because he's been genetically altered to stay alive in low-resource situations. When I asked him who designed these alterations, he admitted that he did."

"And the other refugees don't show these alterations," Ferguson surmised.

"No, Captain," Catherine said. "We checked."

Ferguson nodded. "So we've not only picked up a Korvali, we've gotten ourselves a genetic scientist, one who appears to live up to Korvali lore. I'm starting to understand why they're called 'Mutants.'"

A few laughed nervously at this.

"Why was I not contacted when this refugee was in stasis?" The question came from Commander Steele, Chief of Research and Catherine's commanding officer. The group looked at Dr. Vargas, to whom the questioned was aimed.

"I scanned his DNA and found some irregularities, and wondered if they were related to his comatose state," Vargas said. "The logical person to contact is a geneticist." He motioned to Catherine.

"The logical person to contact is the Chief of Research," Steele corrected him.

Vargas's tired face scowled in annoyance. "This was a medical problem, James, not a research problem. I had a half-dead kid lying in my sick bay. I needed a geneticist."

"I'm a geneticist," Steele said.

"And when was your last genetics paper published?" Vargas said.

Yamamoto saw Catherine press her lips together, as if stifling a smile. Steele's expression hardened further as he began to retort.

"Enough!" Ferguson interrupted. The men quieted down. "We didn't anticipate this turn of events. We have no protocol for handling comatose Korvali with genetic… changes." She resumed talking to the group. "So this… Eshel… when I addressed him, he was very aloof. But he came up clean during interrogation, and he's been forthcoming so far."

"Of course he's been forthcoming, Captain. He wants something from us," said Chief Operations Officer Marks, whose square jaw and tight haircut gave him a tough, stubborn appearance.

"Let's not think the worst of him yet, Commander," Ferguson said.

"He's an oddball," Vargas said. "Getting information out of him is like trying to squeeze water from a stone. And although he was perfectly calm interacting with us, the moment I got too close to him… only to check his damned vitals… he shrank back from me like I was going to slice him open."

"Yes," Ov'Raa interjected. "The Korvali do not tolerate anyone unfamiliar touching them, even to shake hands. It is best to give them much space, in my experience."

"How are we supposed to know that?" Marks complained. "Most of us have never even seen one of them in person."

"Such information was included in the report given to each member of this crew at the start of this mission, Commander Marks," Ov'Raa said with a smile. "It is quite important that we learn the customs of other peoples, including the Korvali."

Marks scowled and gave no reply.

Vargas glanced at Catherine. "He seemed to warm up around Dr. Finnegan. He had plenty to say to her… hell, he even shook her hand."

All eyes turned to Catherine again, who appeared embarrassed.

"Perhaps we'll send her when we need information from him," Ferguson said with a half smile. There was a bit of laughter.

"And how the hell did he learn such good English?" Vargas added.

"I asked Eshel that very question, Doctor!" Ov'Raa said. "I too wondered after briefly conversing with two Korvali government officials with remarkable English skill years ago. Eshel stated only that he learned from his father, and that our language was, 'very easy to learn.' He speaks Derovian and primary Sunai as well. I was *very* impressed with his Derovian," he added with a smile.

"He could serve as a diplomat," Ferguson added dryly, "if he had any people skills." More laughter. "Moving on… the implications of offering asylum to a Korvali. Commander?"

"The implications are many," Yamamoto said. "The most substantial one is that the Korvali don't allow their citizens to emigrate under any circumstances. Our willingly offering a home to one of them, especially one with such scientific abilities, will not sit well with their kunsheld. It is imperative that we institute protections."

"Agreed," Vargas said, as a few others nodded.

"Protections?" Marks said. "You're actually thinking about letting him live on this ship? You can't be serious! He comes from a people who've spent ten years hiding themselves from us and killing people who enter their space!"

"They killed *one* group of Sunai soldiers, *one* time, after numerous warnings to stay out of their space," Yamamoto said. "Otherwise, the Korvali haven't said so much as a bad word to anyone."

Marks shook his head. "Even if this… Eshel… isn't some agent of death, he's from their ruling clan. If they don't let the average citizen leave, what will they do when they find out we have someone so valuable?" He looked around at the group. "They'll funnel resources to retaliate, that's what! Offering asylum to one boy may not be worth the consequences."

"I agree," said Chief Engineer Commander O'Leary in his quiet, deep voice. "He shouldn't be forced to return to Korvalis, but Suna is a better choice for his asylum, whether he likes it or not. The Sunai would love to show the Korvali that they have one of theirs."

"I discuss this further with Admiral Scott once we're back in satellite range," Ferguson said. "But I have the distinct feeling we'll be taking him on, regardless of the consequences. The political and other strategic advantages of this offset the risks."

There were a variety of reactions from the group, some surprised, some disapproving.

"Nothing is decided yet," Ferguson continued. "But if we take him, we'll have a lot to do, so start preparing yourselves." She glanced down at her pad. "Next issue: what, if anything, to report to the Korvali."

"I say we report nothing," Marks said. "Then they have no reason to start trouble."

"And what happens when they find out the truth?" Yamamoto said.

"What can they do about it?" said O'Leary. "The Forbidden Planet is 500 parsecs from here. They have limited technology and resources, and they lack the ability to take us to task when off their turf. It's that simple."

The Captain shook her head. "Deception will bite us in the ass later. What else?"

Ov'Raa spoke up. "Captain, we must consider our relationship with the Korvali. The Korvali do not trust otherworlders and deception will hurt our efforts to earn Korvali trust, or to persuade the Korvali to join the Alliance—"

"Since when is the Korvali joining the Alliance a priority?" Marks argued, looking around the table again. "They're never going to."

"I do not agree," Ov'Raa replied, unruffled. "The Korvali now attend more Alliance summits than ever before, and they have much to offer the Alliance—"

Ferguson stepped in again. "Persuading the Korvali to join the Alliance, fruitful or not, is the Alliance's concern, not ours." She sat back in her chair. "We'll report the truth without specifying Eshel's identity. That will buy us time to create a plan for handling any future inquiries from them. Once I communicate with Admiral Scott, we'll take the next step."

Sensing that Ferguson was about to adjourn the meeting, the group began pushing their chairs back.

"There is another issue that needs addressing," said Commander Steele. The officers reluctantly sat back to hear what the scientist had to say. "We need to establish how we'll handle Eshel's scientific expertise. He has advanced knowledge that will prove extremely valuable to virtually every scientist, human engineer, and genetic technologist that ever existed in this galaxy. We need to gain control over such powerful information, lest it be abused in some way."

"Yeah," Marks added. "Who knows what he could do with that knowledge."

"The topic of Eshel putting this ship at risk has already been covered at length," Steele replied coldly to Marks. "I am referring now to protecting Eshel from us."

Just as Marks was to retort, the Captain put her hand up to silence him. "Ov'Raa?"

"Yes, Captain. The Korvali guard their genetic technology even more closely than their citizens, and they have shared very little of their knowledge."

"Don't the Korvali attend those scientific summits on Suna?" Ferguson said.

"They do," Steele said. "On rare occasion. But they never share their methods. This refusal has ruffled the feathers of the interstellar scientific community and contributes to preventing the Korvali from inclusion in the Alliance. However, it is their knowledge, and their choice. We cannot expect Eshel to violate Korvali Doctrine simply because we gave him asylum. Even if he chose to, without necessary regulations the implications could be far-reaching and disastrous."

Ferguson let out an exasperated sigh. "So he shares what he knows. Isn't the entire purpose of science to share one's discoveries for the betterment of society?"

"Manipulating genetic material doesn't always result in the 'betterment' of society, Captain, which is why we have an extensive body of laws governing it," Steele said. "The Korvali appear to be more advanced than us in genetics. They deserve dominion over their intellectual property. They may forgive our housing one of their scientists, but stealing their innovations will bring certain retaliation." He paused. "However, if that does not convince you, may I remind all of you of the Nystrom incident that occurred five years ago? A genetic technologist—not to be confused with a genetic scientist— sold ninety-two people a gene therapy that would purportedly make them taller. All ninety-two died. When the authorities investigated, they found that the therapy came from Korvali sources."

Ferguson nodded. "Yes. I recall that incident."

"What the hell is a genetic technologist?" Vargas asked. "A fancy name for a lab worker?"

"They're known as 'biocrackers'," Catherine said. "They hack into others' information systems, steal their biological patents, and attempt to recreate and sell them illegally—"

"The point is," Steele interrupted, "that such powerful information in the wrong hands could lead to similar incidents. And with Eshel aboard, any misuse of genetic material would have Alliance and Korvali authorities questioning you and myself, Captain."

Ferguson sighed again, glancing at the time. "We've opened Pandora's Box here. Until we can discuss this in detail, Eshel must refrain from sharing any of his knowledge with anyone, until further orders. In addition, the proceedings from this meeting shall not be discussed with anyone, until further orders. You're dismissed."

Catherine sat at the desk in her tiny office, reading a new paper on epigenetic engineering methods. She heard a double chirp, which meant that the Captain or XO had sent an alert. She checked her contactor:

Attention all crewpersons:

Three days ago, we responded to an SOS from a ship with 10 Korvali citizens aboard. Nine didn't survive the journey from Korvalis, but one is alive and has requested asylum with our organization. His request has been approved.

This Korvali citizen, whose name is Eshel, will live and work among us. You are expected to treat him with the same respect afforded any other member of this organization.

Commander Yamamoto
Executive Officer

A few minutes later, her contactor gave a single chirp. A message, from Commander Steele.

My office. Immediately.

A glimmer of anticipation rose in her. Someone needed to advise the brass on Eshel's knowledge and to ensure it wasn't misused or exploited. And there was no one more qualified to do so than her. Steele was a geneticist, but he'd stepped away from his own research 15 years ago when he accepted his position as Chief. The field had changed dramatically since then. Steele would want to manage everything, but he needed her for the details. She smiled and quickly walked to his office.

Once arrived, she saluted and stood before her commanding officer. Steele glanced up at her, but didn't ask her to sit. Steele's thin frame and narrow face, along with his age, gave him a gaunt, mean appearance.

"Because of Eshel's knowledge and the risks that come with it," he began, "I am to oversee protection of Eshel's genetic knowledge and provide the Captain and the Alliance with guidance on how to proceed with this challenge in the future."

"Yes, Sir."

"As such, I will need you to furnish any and all analyses, scans, or any other work you've conducted regarding Eshel. I will also need the file with his genetic information, as well as any and all emails or other exchanges you've had with Eshel. Once you give me this information, you must permanently remove it from your network and VirNet. That's an order."

Catherine blinked a few times. "You don't... Sir, you don't want me to help with this?"

"Did I request your help?"

"No, Sir."

"Then address my requests."

Catherine, speechless for a moment, tried to recall what he'd asked for. "I have no analyses or scans, Sir. I didn't save those I conducted while Eshel was in stasis. I don't have Eshel's genetic file either, but Dr. Vargas probably does. And I've had no contact with him since talking with him in sick bay."

Steele gave her a hard look. "You are aware that withholding such information could end your career with the Space Corps."

Catherine felt anger spread through her. "Yes, Sir." She knew he expected her to elaborate or to rephrase her answer in order to sound more reassuring. But she had no intention of doing either.

"Don't make me repeat myself, Lieutenant."

"I am withholding nothing, Sir."

"You are the head of your lab. No one shall discuss genetics with Eshel, question Eshel in any way, or pursue any of the information you found when you examined Eshel. You are responsible for ensuring that you and your subordinates obey this order. If you violate any of it, you will be finished here and sent back to Earth. Is that understood?"

"Yes, Sir."

Steele turned away. "Dismissed."

CHAPTER 4

Eshel descended the aft stairwell to the second deck and proceeded to the living quarters that Ov'Raa's administration had assigned him. All non-commissioned crew shared their quarters, anywhere from two to four per room, depending on rank. Eshel's bunkmates included one human, Private Suzuki, and two Derovians, Private Coran Mel'Ri and his brother Dorel.

Ov'Raa had told Eshel he'd chosen his bunkmates intentionally; Derovians, with their highly forgiving natures, would be least bothered by Eshel's aloofness. Ov'Raa had warned him that his communication style seemed "quite unfriendly" at times. Eshel didn't understand the purpose of being "friendly," even after Ov'Raa explained what the word meant. He only knew that sleeping in such tight quarters with others, particularly otherworlders, was going to be difficult.

Nonetheless, Eshel did as his father taught him and prepared himself to greet his bunkmates according to their native traditions. He would shake hands with the human and perform the meron with the two Derovians. The meron was similar to the handshake, but with both hands and without the shake, where one clasps the other's hands for a longer duration. Eshel took a deep, long breath in preparation, a small discomfort beginning to spread through his long fingers.

As Eshel approached the door of his quarters, he heard laughter and talking. When Coran spotted him in the doorway, he leapt up from his bunk. Dorel did the same, with just as much zest, while Suzuki slowly stood up, staring at him.

None offered their hands. *Ov'Raa must have warned them,* Eshel thought with some relief. From what he'd heard, Derovians especially could not resist offering their thick hands in friendship. The diminutive brothers greeted him, staring up at him with their wide eyes.

Not expecting a fourth, they'd spread out in the small space, their belongings stowed in what would be Eshel's storage area.

"Many, many apologies, Eshel!" said Coran. "We've taken your space here with our things. Never did we expect to have a new crewmember, especially one who's Korvali!" Coran shuffled over and began the hasty removal of his things, as did the others.

"You need not make much space," Eshel said. "I own no more than what you see here." He laid out his personal items on his bunk. Other than his robes, which he was told he could wear when off-duty, he had only one metal box. The men stared at the box.

Recognizing their curiosity, Eshel put two fingers on the box's console. The lid snapped open. The others crowded around him; Eshel let them look inside, quickly backing away from their close proximity. The two brothers showed expressions of mild disappointment at the box's contents, which were technical in nature.

"Do you not have images, or art, from Korvalis?" Coran asked.

"I do not. No piece of art would fit in this case. And we do not take images where I am from, as you do."

Dorel, eager to chime in, said, "No images? Why not?"

"It is unnecessary."

"How so, Eshel?" Coran said.

Eshel paused. "We do not need to take images. I recall all that I have seen."

"What do you mean you recall all you've seen?" Suzuki asked him. "Don't you forget details, or doesn't the picture in your mind get... fuzzyish... until you see it again?"

"Fuzzyish?"

"Less clear, Eshel," Dorel said.

"No."

Coran and Dorel looked at one another, then back at Eshel.

"We can change the image, if you wish," Coran said.

Eshel, not understanding at first, realized Coran referred to large digital image of a Derovian woman, who stood nude on a beach. The image took up the remaining bulkhead space between their two bunks. He then noticed that next to Suzuki's bunk hung a similar image of a human woman.

"There is no need," Eshel replied.

The men chuckled.

"You may not require all your space now, Eshel," Coran said, "but you will collect things once we visit all the planets. We go to Derovia first," he glanced at his brother with a big smile, "then Suna, then Calyyt-Calloq!"

Eshel hung his robes, put away his things, and sat down on his bunk.

Eshel woke to the sound of his contactor. He felt tired, his circadian rhythm still not quite adjusted to the length of a human day. Just as he emerged from what the others referred to as the "head," the door sounded.

"Eshel... good morning!" Ov'Raa said, a big smile on his face as he entered.

Eshel did not reply.

"I see your bunkmates are on duty, Eshel. Is everything fine with Coran, Dorel, and Private Suzuki? How about with your new post?"

"Yes. Sir," he added, having learned from his new CO, Chief Selway, that one must always properly address one's superiors. "I begin duty soon."

"Of course, Eshel! I will not keep you. I wanted to tell you that should any problems arise, any problems at all, Eshel, you must come to me." When Eshel didn't respond, he added, "The practical aspects of integrating an unfamiliar species are not so simple!"

Eshel agreed to Ov'Raa's request, still not understanding why Ov'Raa bothered him. Once Ov'Raa left, Eshel changed into his uniform, which still felt constricting compared to the comfort of his robe. He reported for duty at the maintenance section of Engineering.

All maintenance crew reported to Master Chief Petty Officer Selway, a 35-year Space Corps "old-timer" who could keep a starship running efficiently under nearly any conditions. Such information had come from Selway himself. Selway had also taken it upon himself to teach Eshel the way things worked on a starship—where things were, and who did what and why. He had especially emphasized the importance of proper addresses.

Eshel found the use of salutes and such wordy addresses absurd. However, even more perplexing was Selway's propensity to tell stories, particularly tales of past maintenance challenges and how he tackled them. Selway's stories were extremely detailed and often quite long; it wasn't unusual for him to devote as much as sixty minutes to a given story. Eshel, utterly baffled by this, said little, and often nothing, in response.

Eshel went to the engine room to complete his newest assignment. Eshel disliked the engine room, as it often reached temperatures that were too warm for him. When he arrived, the Engineering crew was undergoing engine maintenance, crowding the area with more people and causing the temperature to rise further. Discomfort set in as he felt the heat consume him. After working for a while, Eshel realized he could tolerate no more. But just as he decided to leave the area, his vision blurred and he became weak. Unable to walk, he knelt down.

"You alright?" said a flat, male voice. An officer, whose expression showed a mixture of hesitation and concern, knelt down as well, his unusually dark eyes studying him closely. Eshel recognized the face from the ship's roster: Lieutenant Jebediah Snow.

"I am not," Eshel replied, his voice faint. "I believe I am having difficulty adjusting to the temperature."

"Middleton!" Snow shouted across the crowd. A man with a shaved scalp looked up upon hearing his name. "Toss me my canteen." Snow caught the canteen that soared his way. "Drink this."

Eshel drank, the cool water offering him some relief. When he was able to stand up, he realized people were staring at him. Middleton, the canteen-thrower, whispered something to another man.

"Leave the engine room and cool off," Snow told him. "If you don't feel better in a few minutes, go to sick bay. That's an order." He paused. "And tell Selway you're better off working here during redeye shift. Few of us are here then."

Eshel turned and left. Feeling recovered enough, Eshel decided against sick bay and the unpleasant prospect of encountering Dr. Vargas again. Instead, he went to Selway's tiny, cramped office, where Selway stood at his equipment locker, his back to Eshel.

"Chief Selway… Sir. I request that I complete my maintenance detail in the engine room during the late hours, when there are few crewpersons on duty—"

Selway shook his head, still facing his locker. "We don't change the maintenance schedule, Korvali."

"It is too hot in the engine room when occupied by so many," Eshel said. "Such temperatures are nearly intolerable for my physiology."

Selway turned to face Eshel, his portly, round body bumping into the locker door. "Your physiology?" Selway scoffed in his gravelly voice, laughing his gravelly laugh. "Such excuses! Your physiology!"

"It is the truth," Eshel replied, his tone bordering on a sneer.

"It is the truth, *what?*"

Eshel stared down at Selway. He repeated the sentence, adding the address that Selway so valued.

"And don't forget it, Korvali," Selway warned, wagging his finger at Eshel. "Next time, bring water. If you say anything more about it again, you'll be cleaning toilets." He slammed his locker door shut.

"You choose to disregard the truth," Eshel said. "And I will clean toilets if it will free me of your stupidity."

Selway's face turned red, his jowls shaking. "You're out of line, Private!" He ordered Eshel out of his office.

Just as Eshel arrived at his quarters, Ov'Raa contacted him. "Eshel," said Ov'Raa's high, melodious voice. "You are needed in sick bay immediately for examination! Do you remember where sick bay is?"

"Of course, Commander." Selway had shown him a schematic of the entire ship. He knew exactly where to go.

Once at sick bay, Eshel felt a sense of dread at the sight of Dr. Vargas.

"Have a seat," Vargas ordered.

Eshel sat on the medical bed. When Vargas reached up and touched his forehead, Eshel felt fury spread through him as he withdrew from the offending contact. "Do not touch me."

Vargas's face showed exasperation. "I have to examine you. Captain's orders."

"Then do so without touching me. Did you not learn the first time?"

"You'd better watch that mouth, kid," Vargas threatened in a loud voice. "Touching people is part of my job. I don't do it because I like it, believe me. Why does it bother you so damn much?"

"Why do you not have webbed hands?"

Vargas held up the scanner. "Shut your mouth and let me do my goddamn job. I won't touch you, for Christ's sake."

Eshel did as he was told but refused to make eye contact as Vargas scanned him several times. When finished, Vargas said, "You're fine. Get out of my sick bay."

Yamamoto, having just finished teaching his intermediate self-defense course, received a meeting request from Ov'Raa. *We must speak about Eshel.* Yamamoto smiled. He'd been expecting this. He changed into his uniform and made his way to Ov'Raa's office.

Ov'Raa smiled with chagrin, clasping his thick hands together. "There's been an… incident… between Eshel and Chief Selway."

"Yes, I heard. Are you surprised?"

Ov'Raa twittered a little. "Perhaps not. Dr. Vargas reports that Eshel does indeed have true difficulty tolerating warm environmental conditions. Chief Selway has been informed of this. I issued Eshel a formal warning and explained that such disrespectful behavior is not tolerated. I suggested that Eshel offer apology to Chief Selway, and Eshel did so once I taught him what an apology was!" He paused. "However, Eshel still has difficulty addressing his superiors properly and with other social… niceties."

Yamamoto nodded. "Dr. Vargas said Eshel was very impatient with him during the medical exam."

"Is that so? Shall I call Eshel in again?"

Yamamoto shook his head dismissively. "The doctor knew to avoid touching him and still chose to. Make sure Eshel gets one of the cold-water canteens to keep with him at all times." He paused. "Is he getting along with his bunkmates?"

"I've heard no complaints yet, Commander. However, I've had numerous complaints from others, particularly his superiors. Eshel has insulted his commanding officer, spoken insubordinately to many others, and can be very rude! Eshel does not seem to be integrating well and seems quite unhappy!" Ov'Raa clasped his hands tighter.

"This is the first time he's interacted with those who are different from him, Niri. He will learn."

"Many enlisted crewmembers have begun making jokes at Eshel's expense. They call Eshel 'Mutant.' Eshel does not react, which seems only to anger them! I fear he may be harmed." Ov'Raa's skin flushed a dark bluish color, and then faded.

Yamamoto hadn't seen Ov'Raa turn that dark in a long time. Ov'Raa disliked when crewmembers fought with one another, particularly if from different species. "Do not worry yourself, Niri. These problems should abate with time." He paused. "I'd like one of your people to administer the Corps test battery to Eshel."

"Yes, of course. Yes. What idea have you developed, Commander?"

"Humor me."

Yamamoto sat down with Commander Ov'Raa. A minute later, Captain Ferguson joined them and Ov'Raa briefed the Captain on Eshel's conduct.

"How did the test results turn out?" Yamamoto asked, before the Captain could respond.

"Eshel's scores ranged from the ninety-fifth to the ninety-ninth percentile in most of the sciences," Ov'Raa said. "Many of our science officers don't score that high! Eshel also scored above the seventy-fifth percentile in many of the technical subjects, which is most impressive considering that Eshel comes from a technologically modest homeworld. There were large deficits in other areas... however, Eshel's general intelligence scores were extremely high."

Yamamoto gave Ferguson a slight smile.

The Captain leaned back in her chair. "So Eshel's abilities are going to waste working in maintenance."

"Perhaps so... " Ov'Raa said.

"Why was he assigned there?" she demanded. "Just because he can't work in genetics doesn't mean he can't be of some use to us."

Ov'Raa briefly flushed a pale blue. "Many new crewpersons work in maintenance, Captain. It's an excellent way to learn how the ship operates. Also, Eshel is a new enlistee, so it is most unfair to place Eshel in coveted positions. Eshel must earn such a privilege, as the other crew have."

"Fine," Ferguson relented. "But there must be a more appropriate choice for him."

"Perhaps with a more challenging station, he'll integrate better," Yamamoto said. "In my experience, a soldier working too far below his ability is the most difficult to deal with.

"Where shall I place Eshel?" Ov'Raa said. "Let us avoid Engineering, given Eshel's sensitivity to heat. One of the science labs, perhaps?"

"No," Ferguson said. "Steele is already managing this genetics mess. I want someone I can trust looking over Eshel's shoulder."

"How about Weapons?" Yamamoto suggested.

Ferguson gave him an amused look. "You want to put a security risk in Weapons?"

"With Tom Kingston to look after him, yes."

Ov'Raa looked uncomfortable. "Commander, I would reconsider such a choice. Tom can be quite—"

But Ferguson nodded. "Yes. Tom's perfect. And we need to get Eshel integrated socially. Find someone to help him, someone he won't offend." She pushed her chair back and stood up.

After Ferguson left, Ov'Raa sat for a moment, until his face lit up. "When Eshel first came aboard, Dr. Vargas said Eshel enjoyed speaking with Lieutenant Finnegan!" His face fell. "But Lieutenant Finnegan is a geneticist, and not a good choice."

Yamamoto shook his head. "As long as they avoid the topic of genetics, it should be fine. Yes, excellent idea, Niri. I will speak to Catherine about it."

Eshel's contactor chirped. The display showed Catherine Finnegan's name and a message. *Are you free to eat third meal with me tonight?*

His contactor offered him a yes or no. *Yes.*

Meet me at the mess. 1830.

Despite arriving three minutes early, Eshel found that Catherine was waiting for him outside the mess. He felt relief at the sight of her, and the feeling surprised him. She smiled at him and they exchanged nods. Instead of her uniform, she wore garments he did not recognize.

Eshel followed Catherine through the line and retrieved the one option he was willing to eat, one his father had told him about: Derovian ornon and sea vegetables. As they headed to the dining area for enlisted crew, they chose two empty seats at the far end of a long table filled with people. Many turned to look at them as they sat.

"I see you like ornon," Catherine commented as she sat down. She'd chosen the same dish as he.

"Yes. I find Derovian food palatable. I cannot digest your terrestrial animals." He picked up his fork, awkwardly wrapping his hand around it.

"You aren't used to using utensils."

He looked down at his fork. "I am not." Coran and Dorel warned him that they'd been severely chastised for not using utensils when they joined the Corps. He ignored their warning, seeing utensils as pointless, only to be chastised himself.

"Do you know why I requested we meet?"

"Yes," he replied. "The XO asked you to."

"He did. But I was hoping to talk to you anyway. I haven't seen you since your arrival."

"It is unfortunate we did not speak more at that time. We had much to discuss about our work, and now we cannot."

She looked down, appearing angry. She tucked her long hair behind her ear.

Eshel was still struck by the strangeness of her hair—the length of it, and the color... unusual even for humans.

"Have you talked with Commander Steele?" she asked him. A strange expression crossed her face, one he didn't understand.

"Only once. His knowledge of genetics is... disappointing." Eshel immediately wished he'd refrained from such a comment. Commander Steele was Catherine's CO and research collaborator. If what Ov'Raa had taught him was correct, the comment could offend her. However, to his surprise, his comment seemed to have the opposite effect; she appeared pleased.

"Are you familiar with the Nystrom incident?" she asked.

"The Nystrom incident?"

Catherine told him about the 92 human deaths resulting from a gene therapy designed to increase stature, and that the therapy was believed to be Korvali. "The Nystrom incident was the argument that convinced the Captain to bar you from sharing your knowledge."

Eshel felt himself grow angry. "That is ridiculous. We would never waste resources developing something that does not benefit us. And if we did, we would not share it with... with humans."

"I thought as much. But if you want to overturn that decision, you must find a way to convince them that your knowledge won't be exploited in a similar fashion. They must see that the benefits of allowing you to work as a geneticist outweigh the costs."

"What costs, other than protecting the information from exploitation?"

"The costs of angering your people," she said.

"It is my own work. They have no claim on it."

"Perhaps not. But you trained with them; you'd be sharing their way of thinking."

Eshel realized she was correct. "I will consider what you've said. The XO has informed me that I must meet with this... Alliance... very soon."

"When we're in satellite range?"

"No. They will come here."

Catherine stared at him in surprise. "They're coming here?"

"Yes."

They ate in silence for a bit longer. Finally, Catherine spoke again. "Has being here, with us, been more difficult than you anticipated?"

"Yes," Eshel admitted. "My father attempted to prepare me for what I would encounter among the outsiders. But perhaps his training was incomplete."

"Your father was permitted to leave Korvalis, then."

"Yes."

She paused again, as if considering what to say. "I'm told you're transferring to Weapons."

He nodded.

"Tom talks a lot. And he's loud. But he's smart... and the kind of person you want on your side." She put her napkin down. "It will take time to grow accustomed to life here. It could take a year. Be patient. And, with some persuasion, the Alliance should loosen up their rule and allow you to do what you do best."

Eshel, not entirely convinced, said only, "I am glad we spoke."

"Me, too. Drop by the lab sometime and I'll give you a tour."

"I will."

CHAPTER 5

Eshel arrived at Weapons three minutes before he was to report to duty. A human male with well-developed musculature and curly fair hair immediately spotted him. "You must be Eshel," he called out in a loud voice, striding over to him.

Based on Ov'Raa's description, and the ship's roster, Eshel guessed the man was Lieutenant Commander Tom Kingston, his new CO. When Eshel started to salute, Tom shook his head.

"No saluting allowed. Unless the brass is here." He offered his hand instead.

Eshel hesitated, then slowly produced his hand. The handshake seemed a small price to pay for not having to salute.

Tom, seeing his reaction, withdrew his hand and put both hands up. "Ahhh, forgot about that. I heard you don't like being touched. It's good that you wound up with us and not the Sunai. They're the touchy ones. I'm fine with people touching me, but that took some getting used to."

Eshel kept watching Tom, waiting to see if he had more to say.

"Welcome to Weapons," Tom said, gesturing around him. "This is where the magic happens. I'm Tom Kingston... you can call me Tom. I'll be training you."

Eshel, who stood nearly a full head taller than Tom, remained still as Tom looked him over.

"Jesus," Tom remarked. "You Korvali are tall, aren't you?" He pointed at Eshel's webbed hand. "May I?"

Eshel, confused, produced his hand again.

Tom leaned in to get a closer look. "Webbed hands." He studied them with some fascination. "Pretty interesting, man. You swim well?"

"Of course."

"How many kilometers can you swim, at one time?"

"It depends on the conditions. Many."

"How many? Five? Fifty? Five hundred?"

Eshel made a few mental calculations. "Fifty without problem. Five hundred is more difficult, but possible."

"No shit," Tom said, impressed. He looked down at Eshel's shoes. "Webbed feet, too?"

"Yes."

"Anything else webbed?" Tom asked with a grin.

"Not to my knowledge."

He motioned for Eshel to follow him. "Let's give you a tour of my domain." Tom introduced him to the Weapons crew. "No handshakes, guys," he told them. He toured Eshel around Weapons control and small arms storage, then took him down to the deck below, where the missiles and warheads were stored.

Finally, Tom led him into a small, lab-like cold room. "You aren't supposed to be in here," he said in a hushed voice. "But no Weapons tour would be complete without seeing the bioweapons."

Eshel approached one of the shelves, carefully studying the various vials and canisters.

"Does bioweaponry interest you?" Tom asked.

"Yes." Eshel examined the items on the adjacent shelf. "It is a Korvali... specialty." He turned back to Tom.

"Is it, now? We'll have to talk about that over beers."

"Beers?"

"Drinks. Leisure time. Fun." Tom looked around before ushering Eshel out the door, shutting it behind him.

Back in the control room, Tom motioned for Eshel to sit. He excused himself to talk to a human female, one who smiled a lot and who appeared to be called "Greta." After she left, Tom pulled up a chair next to him, turned it backward, and sat. "I know you can't work with the whitecoats like you wanted. But you'll get used to being in our camp."

"Your camp?"

Tom nodded. "There are two kinds of people in the Corps: soldiers and scientists. You're either in one camp or the other. And on this ship, with Ferguson running things, you're better off being a soldier. From my standpoint, Weapons is the place to be," he added, gesturing around him.

"Catherine Finnegan believes I will find it tolerable here."

Tom chuckled. "I guess I'll take that as a compliment. Finnegan knows me better than almost anyone… she's one of my best friends." He picked up a remote and turned on a viewer.

"Dr. Finnegan is your friend, and Greta is your girlfriend," Eshel surmised.

Tom turned toward Eshel again, a stern look on his face. "Greta is *not* my girlfriend. She's someone I'm seeing."

"Seeing?"

"Spending time with. A girlfriend is a woman you're serious about. You only get involved with *her*, and no other girls. I like my options." He grinned. "What about you? Did you have a girlfriend on Korvalis? You do like women…?"

Eshel didn't answer.

"Why the silence?" Tom pressed, eyeing him. "There are females on your planet, right?"

"Yes. We are dimorphic, like humans."

Tom's attention was diverted when Private Zander called out and asked if Tom were going to the fights. "Yup. Let's get a drink first." He looked at Eshel. "Come with us. You'll like it."

Eshel refilled his cold-water canteen and walked to the ship's port bar. "*Not* the starboard bar," Tom had told him twice. "That's only for officers." As he entered the bar, he heard Tom call his name, and he joined the table where Tom sat with Zander, Kovsky, Portino, and another male with a shaved head. Eshel recognized the shaved male; he'd thrown Lieutenant Snow the water canteen that day in Engineering, and had whispered what Eshel learned later was an insult. *Middleton.* Middleton stared at him with the same strange look as he had that day.

Tom had already ordered Eshel a beer. Eshel picked up the cold cup and took a sip. A disgusting taste spread through his mouth as he felt a wave of nausea come over him. He quickly turned his head and spat the beer on the floor, hoping the feeling would pass. Fortunately, it did.

When he looked up, the men watched him in silence. Tom quickly glanced around, then at the bartender, who chatted animatedly with two females. Once their initial shock wore off, Tom and the other guys erupted into laughter. Except Middleton.

"Man, what's wrong with you?" Middleton said. "You can't spit on the floor. You're gonna get us kicked out of here."

"Shut it, Middleton," Tom said. "No one saw."

Middleton scowled, shaking his head.

Eshel looked at them. "You cannot tell me you enjoy this taste," he said in wonder, looking inside the cup, the horrible taste still in his mouth. "Repulsive." He reached for his canteen and took a drink.

"It's an acquired taste, man," Tom said. "Just keep sipping it."

"Not everyone likes beer when they first try it, but I've never seen anyone react like that!" Zander said. "Maybe I should drink yours for you."

Eshel pushed his cup toward Zander.

"Get him a girl's drink, LC," Portino suggested.

The other men watched him. He sensed they were looking for some kind of reaction to Portino's remark, but he didn't know what.

"If a girl's drink is palatable, then I will try one."

Tom rapped his hand on the table and went to the bar. He returned with a new cup filled with a green beverage, but a green he'd never seen before, even in the gardens of his homeworld. Eshel eyed it skeptically and took a sip. It had a very pleasant taste. "That is better."

"Girl's drink it is!" Tom concluded. He raised his cup.

"Here, here," the other men said, raising their cups. They looked at Eshel, so he followed suit and raised his cup.

Once the men finished their beers, and Eshel his Derovian green-berry liqueur, they descended a few decks to the gymnasium and took a seat on the bleachers with all the other spectators. He recognized Commander Yamamoto standing on the gym floor, surrounded by a group of people in loose black outfits.

The crowd quieted down as Eshel watched a pair of human males—one fair and one dark—face one another on a large mat. They circled each other. Then, the dark man attempted to strike at the other with his leg, but was blocked. They swung at one another with their arms, each blocking the other's hits. They continued to block one another's strikes until, suddenly, the dark one managed to tangle his leg with his opponent's and take him to the mat. They grappled on the mat, each struggling to gain control over the other, until the dark one seemed to dominate. There were shouts from the crowd. Commander Yamamoto intervened by separating the two men, who stood up, bowed to one another, and left the mat. Another pair of men took position on the mat.

Eshel, who observed the proceedings with fascinated uneasiness, suddenly felt a painful sensation on his right side. Tom had elbowed him.

"Sorry, buddy," Tom said upon seeing Eshel's annoyance. "I said your name three times. What do you think of the fights?"

"They are… interesting. What is the purpose of their combat?"

"It's friendly competition, training for those who take self-defense. You try to get the other guy to submit, or give up."

After several pairs of men competed, two females entered the competition circle.

"This is my favorite part," Zander said. He whistled, and Portino joined in, as did some other spectators.

When the two women finished their session, one subduing the other by pinning her on the mat, each bowed and exited. Another woman and man walked onto the mat. The woman's hair was arranged in knots on her head, and something seemed familiar about her. Once he saw her face, Eshel realized why. "That is Catherine Finnegan."

"Go Doctor F!" Zander called out.

"Yep, that's her. And her opponent, Holloway, works for her," Tom said with a chuckle. "Take him out, Finnegan!"

Eshel watched as Catherine calmly waited for her opponent to make his move. Once he did, she easily blocked his series of attacks before she hugged both his legs and took him to the mat, her long-limbed figure performing the task with a grace that Eshel found strangely admirable. After wrestling with one another for a time, she managed to trap her opponent with her legs around him and her arm around his neck until he seemed to have no option for escape. When he rapped his hand on the mat twice, Yamamoto called for them to stop. They untangled themselves, stood up, and bowed.

Once the fights finished, the guys disbanded while Eshel went the ship's library.

Eshel arrived at the bridge ready room at 1350. As he walked in, Yamamoto immediately greeted him and told him where to sit. He pulled out the chair at the far end of the long empty table and sat down. When Ov'Raa and Commander Steele walked in, Yamamoto pointed out their seats and each sat on the long side of the table to Eshel's left.

A minute later, Captain Ferguson arrived, her usual uniform adorned with a sash that crossed her torso. The sash had an insignia containing four different symbols, each with a different color. Eshel recognized it; it was the Alliance's insignia, each color and symbol representing the four Alliance worlds: Suna, Derovia, Calyyt-Calloq, and Earth. In Ferguson's wake were two people he didn't recognize.

The first was Derovian, a female dressed in a bright orange and red printed gown beneath her sash. Yamamoto grasped her thick hands for the meron; she smiled profusely, her almond eyes lighting up as she offered a warm greeting to Yamamoto. Yamamoto motioned to a chair to Eshel's right. Following her was a large, formidable looking male who made the Derovian delegate appear even smaller by comparison.

Sunai.

The Sunai wore an elaborate rust-colored uniform covered in a series of metallic adornments, which Eshel had learned were military decorations. He recognized the decorations of a Gronoi. The Gronoi's very dark skin had a rough, almost scaly quality to it and his eyes were obscured by dark eyeshades. There was something feral, almost animalistic about the Sunai. Eshel disliked him immediately.

The Gronoi looked around until something caught his eye. Despite the eyeshades, Eshel knew the Gronoi stared at him. Eshel returned his stare.

The Gronoi turned his attention to Yamamoto, who raised his palm, and the Gronoi placed his large hand against Yamamoto's before putting his hands on Yamamoto's shoulders in what Eshel's father had described as a gesture of friendship. Yamamoto walked over and pulled out the chair on the right side of the table, furthest away from Eshel. Eshel sensed that the XO offered the Sunai that particular seat not because he wanted the Sunai to sit there, but because the Sunai somehow required it.

Finally, once everyone was seated, Yamamoto took his place next to Ov'Raa. Captain Ferguson, after greeting each of the Alliance delegates, sat down at the other end of the table and began. "Thank you, Gronoi Sansuai, and thank you, Tallyn, for coming all this way.

Toq, of Calyyt-Calloq, won't be joining us and has informed us that we may decide on this issue without Calyyt vote. For the sake of convenience, Admiral Scott has asked me to represent Earth on this matter," she added, briefly placing her hand on the sash. She glanced down at her electronic pad and set it aside.

"As you all know," she continued, "we have granted Eshel asylum from Korvalis. He brings with him an advanced scientific knowledge that could prove beneficial to the Alliance. However, for reasons that Commander Steele can elaborate on, Eshel has been banned from discussing genetics. Today we will decide whether this ban shall remain… or be lifted with the proper regulations." She looked over at Steele and nodded.

"The issues are many," Steele said. "As previously discussed, the Korvali do not permit sharing of their scientific methods or innovations with outsiders. To allow Eshel to freely share his knowledge brings up many concerns. First, Eshel, being the only of his kind among us, is vulnerable to scientists or genetic engineers who may exploit him for his knowledge. Second, Eshel's knowledge, in the wrong hands, has the potential for detriment." Steele reiterated the events surrounding the Nystrom incident and added a few more points concerning the relationship with, and potential retaliation from, the Korvali.

"Eshel," Ferguson said, finally addressing him. "Do you have anything to add, anything you'd like to say before we cast our votes?"

"Yes. Captain," he added, recalling that now, of all times, he must be sure to use the formal addresses with everyone. "I request that I be allowed to work in my area of expertise, as a geneticist. My most recent work, which is mine alone, and which allowed me to survive escape while my shipmates perished, may be of great use to the Alliance peoples, particularly for the survival of their militaries during warfare, or for those who must survive during droughts or other times of want. Exploitation or theft will be no concern—my work, like all our work, is stored and coded so that no outsider could decipher it without training."

"If Korvali work is stored so carefully," Commander Steele said, "how do you explain the Nystrom incident and the deaths of nine-ty-two people?"

"It is impossible for such a therapy to have come from Korvali sources, Commander," Eshel replied. "We would not waste valuable resources on a genetic patent that increased stature. We place no value on stature. Even if created, no thief could decode it."

"Perhaps it was created and used as barter, to trade for valuables," Sansuai Gronoi said in a thick accent, his voice deep and guttural.

"Impossible," Eshel said. "There is no item of greater value to a Korvali than our scientific discoveries, Gronoi Sansuai."

Some of the others nodded in understanding.

Ferguson spoke again. "Are you saying that, if approved to work in your chosen profession, you will share this... treatment... with us, but not share how you created it?"

"That is correct. Such a decision will greatly minimize the risk of angering my people and will guarantee the information remains safe. However, I hope to share some of my methods in the future, after conditions on Korvalis change, at which time I would choose an appropriate collaborator."

"Change?" Yamamoto asked. "Change how?"

"The power of the assembly must be restored according to our Doctrine, requiring removal of the current leadership. When this happens, much will change."

The others glanced at one another.

"You believe it's this Elisan," Ferguson said, "and the monarchy, who are responsible for the relationship we have with the Korvali, for their non-participation in the Alliance."

"It is not my belief, Captain. It is the truth."

Ferguson raised her eyebrows at him. "But you also said that no Korvali would share their methods with outsiders."

"That is also true. However, those who oppose the current leadership and respect Doctrine recognize the value of limited sharing, Captain."

Tallyn spoke up. "Are you saying, Eshel, that with different leadership, the Korvali will share some of their technology and join our Alliance?"

"Yes, Tallyn."

He saw the Derovian official's smile grow large and sensed a change in the others. *I have convinced them.*

"Do you have any other comments, Eshel?" Ferguson asked him.

"No, Captain."

Ferguson turned to Sansuai. "Gronoi Sansuai, what is your opinion?"

The Gronoi sat with his back straight, his chin high, and his arms resting on those of the chair. "This is a difficult dilemma, Captain. The Sunai value scientific exploration; one must only view our excellent scientific program to see this! We see many benefits of such knowledge. The Korvali leadership will be angry at such a decision… yet, it is their policies that created this problem! I vote that your refugee exploit his knowledge and take his position as scientist."

"Tallyn?" Ferguson said.

Tallyn smiled as she brought her clasped, six-digit hands closer to herself. "It is with much respect that I acknowledge my brother planet's point of view," she began, glancing at Gronoi Sansuai. "Such knowledge would be quite valuable to so many." She paused, a faint blue coloring her briefly. "However, I feel great concern that sharing Eshel's knowledge will cause the Korvali much anger, and harm the relationship we have built with them. It is, perhaps, too soon? Therefore, I vote we postpone until we negotiate agreement with the Korvali."

Everyone looked to Ferguson, whose vote would serve as tiebreaker. She sat back in her chair, tapping her index finger on the table. "The Space Corps was created to defend our people beyond the limits of our atmosphere. It was also created to foster scientific discovery and develop relations with those from beyond our world. This very mission is both scientific and diplomatic in nature. I believe Eshel should be able to share his knowledge however he chooses." She paused. "However, at this time, I believe the costs of allowing him to work as a scientist outweigh the benefits. Peace, and Eshel's safety, come first, and keeping his knowledge tucked away greatly reduces risk of Korvali retaliation. Until the Korvali agree, I vote no."

Eshel, frustrated, resisted the urge to speak his true thoughts. He glanced at the delegates, then looked back at the Captain. "Until the change in leadership occurs, they will never agree, Captain. Nor will this decision placate them."

"Then so be it," she replied, her blue eyes looking back at him. "Choosing to leave Korvalis means giving up the life you had there, Eshel. You may still speak with Commander Steele about genetics, as before." She stood up. "This topic is closed. You are dismissed, Eshel."

Eshel looked away from her. And without a word, he left.

Catherine finished turning off the automatic light sensors in her laboratory. The lab would remain dark except for one small light in her office, and no passersby would notice that someone was inside unless they purposely looked in the window. Such a possibility was unlikely, as Research was in a quiet area of the ship and typically deserted at that late hour.

She fired up her viewer. "File, epigenetic engineering techniques two," she said. The file's contents appeared. She glanced around, somewhat paranoid that Steele would awaken and discover her late night forays in the lab. Meeting Eshel had sparked a series of new ideas and she had to explore them, one way or the other. While undertaking nothing nearly as ambitious as what Eshel had done, she'd begun examining the epigenomic data she had at her disposal. Such research required no bench work and could be accomplished from her quarters, except for one problem: the data belonged to the Space Corps, which she could only access from her lab.

Suddenly, Catherine heard something. The door. Feeling trapped as she heard footsteps approach her tiny office, Catherine felt herself get into a defensive posture.

It was Eshel.

Catherine breathed a sigh of relief. "You scared the hell out of me."

"I am… sorry," Eshel said. His apology sounded odd, as if he were as unaccustomed to offering apology as he was to using utensils. "My duty shift just ended. Tom said you work here late at night."

"What happened today?"

His expression grew cold. "My arguments did not succeed."

She sighed. *Shit.* She sat for several moments, until something occurred to her. But before she could speak, she realized the laboratory lights had come on. Her heart began to pound as she waited to see who would emerge through her doorway this time.

It was Steele, his gaunt face looking right at her.

November 18th

Hi Dad,

Happy Thanksgiving. I know it's still a week away, but we're in and out of satellite range and I don't know when this will get to you. Are you going to Aunt Cora's this year? I hope so. I hate the idea of you spending the holidays alone in the mountains. Whatever you do, eat some turkey for me. Something went wrong with one of the meat freezers, so all the turkey spoiled, leaving us with a vegetarian Thanksgiving. Tom and Snow are not happy.

Work isn't good. I am quite sure that Commander Steele hates me. He assigns me projects that a graduate student could do; and now, after finding me working on a side project late at night, he's forbidden me to work on any projects he doesn't assign. I can't even enter my own lab after hours without setting off an alert! What's worse is that Eshel happened to be there with me when Steele showed up. It took multiple meetings with the brass and Technology searching our personal messages to convince them that Eshel and I aren't defying the Alliance and threatening the galaxy with our genetic plots.

This isn't what I signed up for, Dad. This is supposed to be a scientific mission, too. Commander Edelstein and I talked about the projects we'd do. I know he's struggling with his health and there was only Steele to replace him at the last minute, but Steele sees no reason to live up to Edelstein's promises. What's worse is that Eshel, the one person whose knowledge might help me make the breakthrough I've sought for so long, still can't discuss genetics at all with anyone but Steele. How's that for irony?

Maybe I'm just irritable. Nearly five months of being ship-bound is getting to me, and I think it's getting to the rest of the crew, too. People seem testier than usual.

According to Tom's sources, the Korvali haven't reacted to one of their people living with us. Some of the brass seemed pretty concerned about it. I did some digging and found out that the Korvali made quite a stink when Ashan escaped years ago, and it was only his disappearance that quelled the rising conflict. Some believe the Korvali found him and killed him; others say his disappearance was staged, that he's alive and well and only hiding to prevent conflict.

Eshel has decided to stay with us and—you won't believe this—he's now a midshipman, training to become an officer! Apparently he works extremely hard and easily passed all the entrance exams. From what Tom said, his promotion is provisional, at least until Headquarters feels secure he's not some Korvali spy. To be honest, I'm surprised they approved his request at all, considering the anti-Korvali sentiment that's still prevalent around here. Tom must have had something to do with that. He gets a kick out of Eshel and seems to have taken him under his wing.

A lot of people still keep their distance from Eshel. He still won't tolerate anyone touching him, even if the contact is accidental. And he's not much for socializing; even Tom's powers of persuasion aren't enough to drag him away from his studies. He recently asked me about the meaning of "Mutant." Apparently he overheard a couple people mutter the term when they didn't realize he was nearby. When I explained, he seemed more curious than offended.

Not much else to report. We'll arrive at Derovia in 4-5 weeks. Talk to you soon, Dad.

Love,
C

CHAPTER 6

Captain Ferguson removed her canteen from its small holster and set it down on her desk. She sat down in her large black chair and turned on her viewer, giving Yamamoto a quick glance. Upon seeing his expression, she stopped what she was doing.

"What's wrong?"

"We have company."

"Company?"

"The on-duty helmsman just contacted me," Yamamoto said. "A small ship has positioned itself near our starboard landing bays."

"Let me guess," she said, sitting back in her chair, a gleam in her eye. "The fueling station manager miscalculated the currency conversion and believes we owe him money." She shook her head. "It's amazing that no station manager ever sends armed workers to refund ships that overpaid."

"It's not the fueling manager this time."

Ferguson's expression changed. "Who are they and what do they want?"

"They're Korvali. And they want to speak with you."

Ferguson began to speak, but said nothing. She sat up straight, gazing out her window, as if hoping to see them. "Show them in."

Yamamoto nodded and turned to leave.

"Scan them thoroughly," she added as the door shut behind him.

"Ensign," he spoke into his contactor. "Send four Masters-at-Arms to join me on the hangar deck. Right now."

"Yes, Sir."

He contacted the communications center. "Shanti, clear the visiting ship to land. Starboard bay two. I will arrive momentarily."

"Yes, Commander," Shanti's voice replied.

Waiting behind the glass barrier, Yamamoto ordered one of the MAs to open the bay door. A Sunai ship entered the bay and set down as the bay door closed behind it. After a few moments, two very tall robed figures emerged from the craft, while the Sunai pilot remained. They had very short hair, as Eshel did, but theirs was paler in color. Their robes differed from those Yamamoto had seen in the past, and from Eshel's. They were black and plain, with a crest near the right side of the upper torso. They also wore belts around their thin middles, presumably to store weapons. The MA asked them to remove their belts; they did so without argument. Yamamoto realized the men represented the Korvali Guard.

One of the MAs ordered the Korvali to stay put, as he scanned them for weapons and biological agents. The scans were clear, giving the two men permission to enter the ship.

Yamamoto looked up at the tall Guardsmen, making eye contact with both and offering them a nod. "I am Commander Yamamoto, Executive Officer of the *Cornelia*. Welcome." He didn't offer his hand. The two men looked at Yamamoto with their pale eyes. "I understand you desire a meeting with the Captain."

"That is correct," the older of the two men replied, his accent thick.

Yamamoto led them, with the four MAs in tow, to Ferguson's office. Two MAs remained outside her door while the others followed Yamamoto inside and stood on the periphery.

Ferguson emerged from behind her desk to greet the Guardsmen. She nodded to them and each Guardsman offered a slight nod in return. Yamamoto gestured for the two men to sit in the two available chairs. Ferguson resumed her seat, while Yamamoto stood aside.

"I'm Captain Ferguson," she said. The two men remained silent, offering no names. "How can we help you?"

The elder Guardsman spoke. "We have come to inquire about a group of our citizens you reported to have found." The Captain nodded, and waited for him to continue. "The Korvali appreciate your report of the dead, and also your candor about offering asylum for our surviving citizen. Is he well?"

A look of almost pleasant surprise crossed her face. "Yes… yes, he is quite well, thank you."

"If you are expecting that we came here to make threats regarding our citizen, or otherwise try to retrieve him by force, that is not our goal."

"Then what is?"

"The Korvali prefer to keep accurate death records, for our government's purposes, and for those clanspeople with whom the escapees share genetic bonds. We request the identities of the deceased, as well as the survivor."

Ferguson nodded. "I see. Why make the long trip here, rather than simply ask for that information?"

"We felt a personal meeting was preferable, for many reasons," the younger Guardsman said, speaking for the first time. "The Korvali devote much time and energy to caring for all of its citizens. We are… concerned… about one of our people wandering the galaxy with none of his own kind to guide him. It is our way."

"I understand. But with all due respect," Ferguson said, sitting back in her chair, "if that's the case, why didn't you pursue and retrieve the escapees after you launched your attack against them? Why did you let them go?"

The younger Guardsman gazed at her with grayish eyes, the intense stare that was similar to Eshel's. The room seemed to quiet. Yamamoto watched as Ferguson worked to maintain the Guardsman's stare. Other than a couple of blinks, she didn't break eye contact. He finally spoke, his voice a hair colder than before. "We live in a technologically simple society, Captain. We lack the resources to chase a ship across such a distance. As you know, our customs differ from yours. Again, we request the identities of our citizens."

"I will get you the information you request," Ferguson replied, glancing at Yamamoto. "Give me a moment." A small viewer arose from the top of her desk. She browsed through several directories and pressed the pads of her fingers to the screen when necessary. The document, written up by Vargas, with Eshel's input, listed the names of the nine dead, including the clans to which they belonged. "Do you want to see the list here, or shall I send it to you?"

"We need only to view it," the elder replied.

Ferguson's screen rotated until it faced the two Guardsmen. They peered at it briefly.

"And the surviving citizen?"

"He is mentioned in the report, below the list."

The Guardsmen shifted their gazes down to the report. They glanced at one another, speaking a couple of words in their native language.

"We must speak to him," the younger said.

"Unfortunately, I can't allow that," Ferguson said. "He's in the Alliance's custody, by his own request." She grabbed her water canteen and took a swig from it. "If you tell me your concerns, perhaps I can help you or find some way to accommodate you."

The elder Guardsman, who sat motionless, spoke up. "The one you hold on your ship, Eshel, is what humans refer to as a scientist. He is expert in our genetic technology." He paused. "You have your policies, but we have ours. We do not share our technology with outsiders."

"I understand. Our policy is that he's forbidden to share any of his knowledge about genetics, an imperative he has upheld. The Alliance agrees with this policy, and violation of it would violate the terms of his asylum."

"Why were we not informed of this information, and of his identity, at an earlier date?" the younger Guardsman asked, his tone still chilly.

"He has revealed little about himself. We didn't know his importance to your people. Our concern was providing him asylum, while still respecting your traditions. It isn't the Alliance's intent to obtain Korvali technology without it being willingly offered." She paused. "Since you've come all this way, I suggest you meet with the Alliance delegates on Derovia about this issue. I can arrange the meeting from here, if you prefer…"

"That will not be necessary," the elder Guardsman said. "Eshel is… very intelligent. He is also quite treacherous. His father was a traitor and a most untrustworthy individual. You have chosen to let Eshel live among you, but be warned that you have placed yourselves in great danger." He stood up, and the other did the same.

Ferguson, not expecting the sudden end to the meeting, awkwardly stood up, nodding at Yamamoto. Yamamoto nodded at the MAs, who followed him and the two Guardsmen out of Ferguson's office.

Back at the hangar deck, with little ceremony and no verbal exchange, the Guardsmen retrieved their weapons belts and returned to their ship.

"What a couple of freaks," one MA muttered to his comrade, who snickered. When he saw that Yamamoto watched him, the MA cleared his throat, muttered an apology, and resumed his silence.

Once the ship left and the bay door shut, Yamamoto returned to Ferguson's office, where she would be waiting for him.

"What do you think?" Ferguson said, turning away from the window and facing him. Before he could answer, she offered her own commentary. "Maybe it was unwise to be straight with them. Perhaps I should've sent them to the Alliance. Let them deal with it."

"Perhaps," Yamamoto replied. "But we, not the Alliance, are Eshel's caretakers. They must deal with the political implications of Eshel's asylum, but we must deal with Eshel."

She made a face. "Yes, which means we must deal with the Korvali. It's as if they're focusing on every word, looking to pick apart anything you say. But they were more reasonable than I thought they'd be, considering."

"Agreed." He sat down. "But something doesn't add up. Their making such a long voyage, visiting in person... "

"Yes, and that speech about Eshel wandering the galaxy...." Ferguson shook her head.

"It's more than that. I suspect the entire conversation was a ruse. They wanted something."

"Such as?"

"I don't know."

"Do I have reason to be concerned, Suko?"

"I know one way to find out. Ask Eshel's opinion."

She scowled. "For what? So he can refute what they said? I don't trust him any more than I trust them."

"He may offer useful information about this unexpected visit."

She nodded in consent.

When Eshel arrived at the Captain's office, he stood at the door and saluted, his gaze shifting from Ferguson to Yamamoto.

"At ease, Eshel," Yamamoto said. "Please sit down. We were just paid a visit by two people from your homeworld. They were Guardsmen, seeking the identities of the deceased refugees, and yourself."

Eshel's eyebrows went up.

"Unfortunately," Yamamoto went on, "we're unaccustomed to interacting with your people. We suspect some level of deception on their part."

"Deception is a possibility, if not a likelihood," Eshel replied.

"We will show you a video of the conversation. Any observation you can offer would be useful." Yamamoto used the remote to pull up the video on Ferguson's large viewer, locating the point at which the two Guardsmen entered her office. Eshel watched the video from start to finish, his expression showing no reaction to anything he saw.

When finished, he turned to Yamamoto.

"As you suspect, you were deceived. They wore the robe of the Guard, but they are not Guardsmen."

"Do you know them?"

"I recognize them. They work for the kunsheld. The younger is Minel. I do not know the elder's name."

"Why would they pretend to be Guardsmen?"

"To confuse you."

"Is there any way to detect such deception?"

"Yes," Eshel said. "Skill with your language always indicates one who associates with those in power. The Guard do not speak other languages."

"I thought other languages came easy for the Korvali," Ferguson said.

"They do. But one cannot learn without exposure to the new language."

"And the Korvali Guard aren't exposed to outside languages?"

"No."

"Why not?"

"The Korvali are forbidden to learn the languages of outsiders, Captain. Only those given permission to leave Korvalis may learn them."

"You said your father taught you," Ferguson said. "He was one of these people given permission?"

Eshel's face clouded over. "At one time, yes."

"Why at one time, Eshel?"

Eshel paused, his eyes shifting elsewhere momentarily. "The kunsheld did not like my father and began refusing to let him attend scientific meetings on Suna."

"And why didn't the kunsheld like your father?"

"My father did not agree with many of the kunsheld's policies."

Ferguson sighed impatiently, pushing her water bottle away from her. "Eshel, why do I need to ask one thousand questions to get information out of you?"

Eshel stared at her. "You ask me questions, Captain; I answer you in truth. It is not our custom to provide superfluous information unnecessarily, nor is it our custom to obtain information by such detailed questioning."

"Detailed questioning is something you'd better get used to if you're going to be part of this organization." She paused, watching Eshel. "Is your father a traitor?"

Eshel sat still in his chair, gazing at Ferguson. He said nothing.

"Answer me, soldier," Ferguson insisted.

"I will not discuss my father. *Captain.*" The address came out with a bite, almost as if he were mocking her.

Yamamoto could see Ferguson's temper beginning to flare, so he took his cue. "I hope you aren't concerned about our having revealed your identity. You're still under our protection, and I believe they strongly suspected that you were the one who survived."

"It does not matter that you revealed my identity. They knew I was here the moment they stepped onto this ship."

"How?"

"We have extremely sensitive instruments that can detect DNA fragments from shedding skin and hair. The instruments can scan large areas within minutes. I have been here long enough to leave traces of myself, including on the hangar deck, where Tom and I have visited on several occasions."

The Captain's face showed a flash of anger as she looked at Yamamoto. "These men were supposed to be scanned and their weapons removed."

"They were," Yamamoto said.

"The instrument can work passively, once initiated," Eshel said.

"I thought your people were technologically 'simple,'" Ferguson said. "Isn't that the word I keep hearing? *Simple?*"

Eshel didn't reply.

"Tell me this, Eshel," she said. "Other than trying to find out if you're the one who survived, why did these men come here?"

"To gain information about you."

"What information?"

"Any information that will help them to reclaim me."

"Reclaim you?" she said. "They can't reclaim you. You're under our protection now, and there's nothing they can do about it."

"You underestimate them, Captain."

Ferguson's lip curled. "And you underestimate us. You're dismissed." After Eshel left, she rose from her chair and looked out the window. "God damn it, he irritates me."

"Is it Eshel who irritates you, or that we've been had by his people?"

Ferguson threw up her hands. "We don't know what we're dealing with, Suko. We don't know what these people are about. Their defining characteristic, other than their arrogance, is their unwillingness to share their homeworld or their technology with us. Now we have one of them on my ship, forcing a relationship with them that they don't want and we aren't prepared to deal with." She shook her head. "The Derovians are concerned we'll offend the Korvali, the Sunai want to know why Eshel chose us over them, the Calyyt refuse to take a position, and I've been hounded by the press for weeks. And now we've weakened our position by allowing those people on my ship."

"We're in uncharted territory, Janice. We will make mistakes. We need to be glad the consequences were no more severe than our having been hoodwinked." He paused. "Thus far, we've had the luxury of avoiding these issues."

Ferguson sat back down. "We've put ourselves at risk by giving him a home here. All this trouble for a kid who talks to us like we're his goddamn inferiors!"

"That's just his way," Yamamoto reasoned. "Besides, you're the one who approved his application for officer's training."

She gave a wry smile. "How could I refuse? He's bright and hardworking, and at least he's not squandering his abilities in the science labs. The Corps wants more otherworlders. They'll reward us for recruiting the first Korvali officer in history and the Alliance will love us for it." She shrugged. "And the sooner we train him, the more control we have over him. The rewards are worth the risks… if he can manage to get along with people."

"Tom likes him."

"Thank God." She gave a throaty laugh. "Ov'Raa was so worried when we assigned Eshel to Weapons, expecting he would clash with Tom… and somehow the opposite has happened." Her smiled faded. "Suko, what if they're right? What if he's dangerous?"

"I've had Eshel under my personal surveillance since he arrived. I've watched his every move and seen no sign of duplicity yet. But I do have several safeguards installed in case I am wrong."

Ferguson grabbed her water canteen. "Twenty-five years we've known each other. What would I do without you?"

"You would succeed, as always," he replied, rising from his chair to make his exit.

"A bottle of Derovian red tefuna says he won't last with us," she said, leaning back in her chair.

Yamamoto looked at her for a few moments, lightly stroking his chin. "I'll take that bet."

CHAPTER 7

Catherine shook her head. *Fifty-four.* Fifty-four messages enquiring about Eshel. Did he speak English? Did he reveal information about Korvalis? Was he working with her? Is it true that the Korvali have gill slits? She laughed at that one. Word had gotten out.

She left her small office and pulled up a chair. Waiting for her were her two crewmen, Ensign Patrick Holloway and Private First Class Varan Mel'Kavi. Holloway, a recent PhD recipient who handled most of the lab's information processing, often had messy hair and a somewhat wrinkled uniform. Another lab head might have upbraided him for his disheveled appearance, but Catherine didn't mind. From her standpoint, Holloway could show up in his underwear as long as he performed his duties.

Varan kept track of records and supplies, performed any necessary bench work, and generally made sure the lab ran smoothly. Varan, having struggled with sharing his workspace with two quiet humans, eventually found solace working alongside a fellow Derovian from Anka Henriksen's lab next door. Catherine didn't mind this arrangement either, as Varan always completed his duties.

"Any agenda items?" Catherine asked them.

Both shook their heads.

"I've got a couple," she said. "The first is that Commander Steele has assigned a new project. We'll use our current data sources to conduct a comparative analysis of a fifty-thousand kilobase region across chromosome 12… chromosome 14 for Derovian and Sunai data." She looked at Holloway. "Will you compile the data and send Varan the ID codes?" He nodded. She turned to Varan. "Once Holloway gives you the IDs, I need you to pull their samples. We're going to be sequencing."

Varan smiled. "Yes, Catherine!" It took a while, but Catherine had finally convinced Varan it was okay to call her by her first name.

"That's it?" Holloway asked.

Catherine recognized Holloway's tone. The project was far from difficult, and anything but innovative, but would still take a significant amount of time. "I'm afraid so."

"Balls," Holloway muttered. "What was the second agenda item?"

"Oh, yes… we arrive on Derovia in a few weeks. And," she smiled, "I'm told we'll collect new samples there."

Both crewmen perked up at this—Varan at the prospect of spending several months on his homeworld, and Holloway at the prospect of collecting new data.

"Helloooo…" a female voice rang out.

The three of them turned toward the door. Lieutenant Anka Henriksen stood there, her grinning blonde self appearing a bit embarrassed. "Sorry to interrupt," she said in a Germanic accent.

"Come on in, Anka," Catherine said.

Anka, a molecular biologist from the neighboring lab, waved to Holloway and Varan. "Do you have a pipette I can borrow?" she asked Catherine. "The robot's down and I'm in the middle of an assay."

Before Catherine could respond, Varan jumped up. "I'll get the pipette for you, Lieutenant Henriksen!" He scurried off and returned quickly, pipette in hand.

She gave him a big smile. "You're the best, Varan." She looked Holloway up and down. "Did you sleep in your uniform, Ensign?"

Holloway only laughed, his complexion reddening.

She held the pipette up to Catherine. "Thanks. Let's catch up later."

Catherine nodded. "That's it... meeting adjourned," she said to her crewmen." She glanced at Holloway. "Good effort the other night. I had to work harder to submit you this time."

"Thanks," Holloway said. "I still hate grappling."

"I don't like it either, but it's a crucial skill—" Her contactor chirped. It was a message from Tom: *Poker. Friday. 1900. Newbs bring beer.* Just as she was about to continue, the lab door opened again. She smiled and turned around, ready to offer up more equipment to Anka. But it was Eshel, his strong gaze making eye contact with her.

Eshel wore the uniform of a midshipman: it had the gray sleeves that soldiers wore but lacked any banding. It was immaculate.

"I do not mean to interrupt your work," he said. "I came here to ask you about... self-defense."

"What do you want to know?"

"I would like to learn the discipline. Is that possible?"

"Do you have any self-defense experience?"

"No. Hand-to-hand combat is not permitted on Korvalis."

"Why not?"

"It is considered... primitive," Eshel replied. "It is also forbidden to touch another without their permission."

Catherine hesitated in surprise. "Wait... I thought the Korvali didn't like being touched by outsiders. You're saying you don't even touch each other?"

"Not without permission."

"Huh." She stepped back slightly. "Eshel, self-defense training means a lot of physical contact with others. Do you think you can handle that?"

"I do not know. I would like to try."

Catherine walked back to her office, motioning to Eshel to follow her. She ordered the computer to send a document to Eshel's contactor. "I just sent you a schedule for the basic self-defense course. Start with that. I teach one two Saturdays from now. Anyone can take the basic course, but if you're interested in formal training, talk to Commander Yamamoto."

Eshel nodded, and turned to leave.

"Eshel." He turned back to face her. "Tom is hosting a poker game in his quarters Friday night. If you're not on duty, do you want to join us?"

"You play this game?"

She nodded. "You might like it."

When Eshel hesitated, Catherine knew he'd probably say no.

"Yes, I will join you." He turned away again, but this time stopped and looked around. Her crewmen, no longer pretending they weren't listening in, watched him as he studied every corner of the lab. "Your lab is small."

"Space is limited on a starship. The labs at home are much bigger. Do you have time for a quick tour? My crew has wanted to talk to you since you arrived."

Eshel agreed and Catherine showed him the high-res and 3D viewers as well as the cold storage areas. Eshel looked with great curiosity at everything, asking more questions than usual and taking an interest in all her answers. She introduced him to Holloway and Varan and let each explain his duties.

Eshel looked at Holloway. "You competed with Catherine at the fights."

Holloway chuckled. "Thanks for saying I competed with her, rather than lost to her." Eshel kept his eyes on him, so Holloway took his cue and kept talking. "I heard that you altered your genome somehow to survive the long trip to Suna. How did you do that? Did you alter the epigenome?"

"Holloway." Catherine shook her head. "No questions."

A look of annoyance crossed Holloway's face. "It's disappointing that you can't work with us." He glanced at Catherine. Varan eagerly seconded Holloway's statement.

Eshel took another glance around the lab. "'Disappointing' is an inadequate word," he replied. He checked the time, and left to return to duty.

When Catherine returned to her office, she realized Holloway had followed her. He closed the door.

"Why can he talk with Steele about genetics, but not us?" Holloway said. "Doesn't that seem rather strange to you?"

She shrugged. "Steele's head of Research and he's been around a long time. And Ferguson doesn't care much about science, so she relies on his judgment."

"He's an idiot. He doesn't even know the new analytic techniques."

Catherine pulled up a batch of data files on her viewer and began sorting them. "This isn't about techniques, Holloway. It's about politics. Alliance officials came all the way here to meet him, but they refused to change their minds on this. They don't want to anger the Korvali."

"Then what's to stop us from pursuing the issue on our own?"

Catherine stopped sorting and looked at him. "What are you suggesting?"

"You must have some data from when Eshel woke up in sick bay… or something to work with?" Holloway's face flushed a little.

She couldn't help but smile. "You're going to get us in a lot of trouble, talking like that. Unfortunately, I didn't save the files I generated. I recall ideas, not specifics. And the specifics are important."

Holloway sighed. "Let me know if you decide to pursue it. I can keep quiet, you know."

"Get back to work."

When Catherine arrived at the studio on Saturday, Commander Yamamoto stood quietly at the front of the room, waiting for the rest of his advanced students. She bowed to him. He would begin promptly at 0900, and not a moment after. In the studio, Yamamoto ceased being the ship's XO and became its self-defense master. While on the small side, Yamamoto was quite possibly the most physically fit person on the ship. This was no small distinction, as many of their soldiers were fresh out of training and Yamamoto was older than most of the crew.

After Yamamoto dismissed class, everyone bowed to him. Catherine went to grab her towel, until she heard her name. "I need to speak with you," Yamamoto said.

Yamamoto encouraged mentoring for all students who trained beyond the basic levels. Because of her advanced skill, Yamamoto was Catherine's mentor. She wondered if she'd done something wrong, as they were not scheduled to talk that day. With Yamamoto, it was difficult to tell.

Once everyone left the studio, he addressed her. "After taking your course, Eshel has requested to train in our discipline and has recently begun formal instruction. He still shows discomfort with physical contact, but he is determined. Given his limitations, I believe he would benefit greatly from private tutelage. I would like you to take him as a student and provide mentorship to him." He paused. "He must learn to defend himself, especially once we arrive at Derovia, where looking after him will prove more difficult."

She hesitated, surprised at the request. "Why me?"

"Eshel seems to feel more at ease with you than he does with others."

"What if he prefers someone else?"

Yamamoto shook his head. "I already asked him. He prefers you." He paused, studying her. "Does the prospect of working with Eshel make you uncomfortable?"

"No. I've just never mentored anyone. It's… intimidating."

"You will do fine. I will provide you with guidelines and suggested curricula, should you need them. He will continue class instruction twice per week, and I would like him to meet once per week with you, at a time agreed upon by you both. He preferred a more ambitious schedule, but it is better that he focus on his studies."

Catherine shook her head. "He's tireless."

"Consider it your job to tire him out a little."

She smiled. "Consider it done."

Catherine met with Eshel Sunday morning at 1000. When she arrived, Eshel was already in the studio, dressed in training apparel. Upon seeing her, he bowed.

"How do you want to handle contact?" she asked him.

"Contact?"

"Touching."

"You have my permission. I will adapt."

"Don't worry," she said. "Most of your early training won't involve a lot of contact anyway."

They spent their time working on self-defense fundamentals: punches, blocks, and kicks. By the end of their session, which ran way over their 90-minute window of time, Catherine was starving and Eshel, to her delight, looked tired. Instead of grabbing a shower, she decided to head straight for the mess. When Eshel learned that was her plan, he asked to join her.

Once they got their meals, Eshel walked to the officer's section of the mess. Catherine halted, confused, until she realized Eshel's midshipman status allowed him to eat there now. When they sat down, Eshel gazed at her as if looking at something specific.

"Your hair color... it is highly valued on Korvalis."

"Really?" Catherine said, surprised. "Why?"

"Such a pigment is extremely rare among my people, and is considered genetically superior. There is a group among the Osecal that specializes in breeding children with red hair."

"Are there a bunch of redheaded kids running around Korvalis now?"

Eshel finished chewing his food. "No. It is an expensive procedure. Most cannot afford it. And we could not reproduce your color red... what do you call it?"

"Auburn."

"We can only produce fairer shades."

"Breeding for physical attributes was banned on Earth years ago," she told him, tucking her hair behind her ear. "But even before the ban, nobody wanted red hair."

"Why?"

"A lot of people don't like it. There's still a very old prejudice that redheads are temperamental."

"Temperamental?"

"That they have angry, difficult temperaments."

"That makes little sense. The genes for hair color show no linkage with those responsible for one's character. And you do not seem 'temperamental,'" he added.

She smiled. "I have my moments."

He studied her hair once more. "It is not accurate to label red hair as red. There are many versions of this color."

She shrugged. "Humans like simplicity, not accuracy. And I can't comment... I can't see reds."

It was Eshel's turn to be surprised. "You are colorblind?"

She nodded.

"I have read about this. It is absurd. A scan of your X chromosomes would identify the nature of the anomaly, and could be easily fixed. Have you surveyed the region around the receptor genes?"

"I have. The problem I ran into..." She stopped herself, glancing around. "We better not talk about this."

Eshel, a look of recognition on his face, surreptitiously glanced around as well. "Obeying the Alliance's rule is easy with others. There is no... temptation... as they know nothing of genetics."

Catherine nodded, but said nothing.

"Why do you appear concerned?" Eshel asked her. "It is I who is sanctioned, not you."

Catherine hesitated, fiddling with her fork. "It was made clear to me that discussing that, with you, would result in my being discharged and sent back to Earth."

Eshel raised his eyebrows. "Did the Captain offer this warning?"

Catherine shook her head. "Commander Steele did. That's why he made such a fuss about us talking in my office that night."

Eshel did not reply.

After a long silence, Catherine noticed Eshel's hand. "I have a question, Eshel. You don't have to answer if you don't want to." Eshel looked at her, indicating for her to continue. "Your tattoo… the others who escaped with you… they had tattoos as well. Two other kinds. Who were they?"

Eshel looked down for a moment. "Six of them, those with the branches of the tree… they were from the Osecal clan. They were people of science, seeking to associate with outsiders. The others were Moshal, one of whom was a Guardsman."

"He helped you escape."

"She," Eshel corrected. "Yes. One has no chance of escaping Korvalis without the help of the Guard."

She. "Were there other females in your group?"

"Two others," Eshel said. "We are not as dimorphic as humans… but you could not tell they were female?"

"They were enshrouded when I saw them. But Vargas didn't notice it. He didn't even notice the tattoos until I pointed them out."

Eshel scowled slightly. "How does such a person become a physician?"

Catherine laughed and moved on to a different topic. "I've received a lot of inquiries about you."

"From whom?"

"Journalists. Scientists. Other people. They're dying for information about you. Some of them offered me money. A lot of money."

"Why do they come to you?"

"They know the brass will only give them limited information, so they try to wheedle it out of the rest of us. I guess word got out that I know you."

Eshel's expression grew cold. "What did you tell them?"

"Everything I knew," she replied. "I even made some stuff up."

Eshel stared at her.

She smiled. "That's a joke. I didn't respond to any of them. I wouldn't share anything about you unless you asked me to."

Eshel said nothing for a moment. "Perhaps they contacted you because they learned that you are my friend."

Catherine looked up from her plate, a little taken aback at Eshel's words. She realized he was right. They were friends, and she felt a sense of honor at having earned the title. "Perhaps you're right."

They finished their meals, cleared their trays, and left. Just as they reached the intersection that would send them in separate directions, they came upon a series of shelves built onto the bulkhead. Eshel stopped and examined the shelves, which were filled with a variety of random items, mostly clothing and computer equipment. Next to the shelves was a viewer with digital images of other items.

"What is this?" Eshel asked. "I have wondered since I arrived."

"This is the Free Box. When you're on a ship for three years, you tend to acquire things you don't want, or need things you can't get, so people dispose of their stuff here and other people take it."

He peered at the stuff piled on the shelves. "A good idea."

"Most of the time it's junk, but once in a while you can score something good."

"And the images?" he asked, looking at the photo display.

"That's stuff people don't want to give away, but want to sell or barter for a trade. Look through it," she said. "You could probably find some things you need."

"I will."

They said their goodbyes, and Catherine left Eshel to the Free Box.

Catherine finished her shower, dressed, and turned on her viewer. An alert told her the ship was back in satellite range, so she sat down to see if her father was available for a holo-chat. She'd found a couple of brief articles on epigenetic therapy, written for a lay audience, that she wanted to show her dad. Since Steele had prevented her from working in the lab, she'd begun doing research in her quarters. She couldn't accomplish nearly as much there, but she could still make headway by reading. Steele couldn't prevent her from reading.

When she called up one of her directories to find the two articles, the computer misheard her command and took her to the wrong directory. She shook her head in annoyance. Just as she was about to restate the command, a series of files caught her attention. She didn't recognize the numeric filenames. She never used numeric filenames. So she opened one of them.

The file contained the results of a genome scan, including a list of genetic loci. Confused, she examined the list and realized she recognized it; it was from her scan of Eshel's genome, while he was in stasis. She examined the next file, then the next. The files contained the results of every scan she'd conducted when Eshel arrived. And, finally, she opened the last one: a large, multi-terabyte file. There, staring at her from her viewer, was Eshel's genetic material.

Catherine's face grew hot. *How did this happen?* Then she recalled accessing her network to cross-reference the four genes that Dr. Vargas's initial scan had identified. She'd conducted every scan on her network; the software must have automatically saved each result. All the information Steele accused her of having, the information Holloway wished she'd had, she'd actually had all along.

She immediately pulled the files from her network and saved them on a portable drive. If Steele knew she had them, he would've spoken up by now. And he wouldn't find them now unless he had Technology search the VirNet... the VirNet! She logged in and checked everything she'd backed up last time they were in range. And there they were, the incriminating files. She deleted them all.

Once off the networks, she opened the files again. How did Eshel conceive of such a design? How did he test it to make sure it would work? On Earth, doctors used gene therapy for single gene disorders like hemophilia and Huntington's disease, and for treatment of certain cancers. But epigenetic therapy? They'd had partial success with one type of breast cancer and a few other rare conditions, but that's it. To accomplish what Eshel had, to engineer the epigenome for preventative purposes, to ensure survival in extreme circumstances… no one, *no one*, had done anything like it.

"Open EpiGenomix," she said. Her computer did as she asked. "Load file Finnegan Two." Finnegan 2 was her new name for the file with Eshel's genetic data. "Run methylation analysis."

When the analysis completed, Catherine examined the results. She sat back in her chair; sure enough, the results showed numerous signs of hypermethylation, a clear sign of intentional alteration. She made a list of the other analyses she would conduct. She knew Eshel had altered his epigenome; he'd told her so. Now she sought to discover what he wasn't free to tell her: *how* he'd done it.

Countless hours later and long after she should've gone to bed, Catherine had conducted every scan and analysis she could think of. What she needed now was to analyze a current copy of Eshel's genetic material, for comparison. Eshel had created some of the epigenomic changes she saw… but so would the drug Eshel took to initiate his stasis. Now, the drug was out of his system. With a fresh sample from Eshel, she could clearly see the effects of the changes he'd made and begin to work backward.

Could she obtain such crucial information?

Asking Eshel for a sample, assuming he would even allow it, was too risky. If they were found out, Eshel would lose his asylum and she would be discharged. Even if Eshel were willing to maintain secrecy, she couldn't put him in such a position.

She could obtain the sample without Eshel's knowledge—an accidently pulled hair or some scratched skin cells under her nail from training, or perhaps a quick onceover with a medical scanner for other reasons…. No. She couldn't do that. The Korvali were extremely guarded with their genetic code and took careful measures to prevent others from obtaining it. Some scientists even speculated that the Korvali robe, which almost completely covered the wearer when the hood was pulled up, was designed not to prevent outsiders from touching them, but to prevent others from obtaining their DNA. To go behind Eshel's back would be far worse than collaborating with him secretly.

Catherine sighed, shut everything down, and put away her portable drive.

December 25th

Hi Dad,

Merry Christmas! Thanks for the old Christmas tunes—I haven't heard those since Mom used to play them. Growing up, they always seemed kind of silly; now I cherish them.

Is the snow good enough for skiing yet? What I wouldn't give to be off this ship and out there in the backcountry with you right now.

At Yamamoto's request, I've been training Eshel in self-defense. It's gone well so far—he's still uncomfortable with the physical contact, but he handles it well. Because he didn't grow up fighting or wrestling like most human boys, he's pretty awkward. But he's very hard-working and has surprisingly little difficulty handling the ineptness of learning a new skill. He makes no excuses and expresses no frustration. His height is an obstacle at times; but I assured him that once his training advances, his height, and the long reach that comes with it, will eventually become an asset to him. To be honest, I wasn't sure how good he'd be at taking instruction from me (he doesn't have much respect for authority), but it hasn't been a problem.

Once Tom found out that Eshel eats second meal with me after training, he insisted that Eshel also eat second meal with us once in a while during the week. Eshel finds the idea of socializing over a meal odd, and he doesn't need to eat more than once a day, but he was willing to rearrange his schedule to accommodate Tom, probably because he knew Tom would keep bugging him if he didn't.

Oh, Dad, you missed a great poker tournament, one of the most exciting I've played in a long time. Ten of us started the game (including Eshel, who reluctantly decided to give poker a try). After seven players got eliminated, it came down to Tom, Eshel, and me. Between his expressionless face and his ability to calculate probabilities quickly, Eshel has become a formidable poker player. The others groan when he shows up to play. But most of them seem to have accepted him, although they're still baffled by the fact that he refuses to answer certain kinds of questions and that he has, on one or two occasions, gotten up and left without a word. Tom gave him a hard time about that latter thing; apparently Eshel didn't know that it's customary to announce one's exit from a social gathering. I still laugh when I think about it. The only one who seems to genuinely dislike Eshel is Mackey Middleton—Eshel and Middleton have exchanged tense words on several occasions, at least until Tom intervened. From what I can tell, Middleton is what Holloway would call a "twat."

Anyway, Tom, as usual, started playing aggressively. I suspected he had a high flush, but he clearly didn't suspect I was holding a full house. I pushed him all in and next thing you know, Eshel pushed his entire stack in and showed us four of a kind! Tom and I never saw it coming.

That's not all. Tom had talked us into betting sick bay duty, and now I have to serve two of Eshel's! You know I hate sick bay, Dad! What's worse is they're redeye shifts (didn't you tell me that Vargas assigns redeye duty to people he doesn't like?). Eshel doesn't mind the shifts, as he dislikes Vargas as much as Vargas dislikes him. Anyway, I was the big stack at the table; instead of beating a drunken Tom and an otherworld newb, I wind up working redeye! To his credit, Eshel tried to take one of the shifts back, but I wouldn't let him. He's got studying to do and, well, I agreed to the stakes. It serves me right for letting Tom rope me into a high risk game.

We had another exciting poker game as well, although this time the excitement wasn't due to the game itself. A couple of officers showed up to play, both new to Tom's game but both experienced players. They were pretty aggressive players, especially a Lieutenant Haus, who I'd never met before. Turned out he's a sore loser—Private Zander (who's smarter than he seems) bluffed Haus out of a big pot with a lousy hand. Haus wouldn't let it go and resorted to calling Zander a "service kid." Needless to say, Tom lost his temper and he and Haus came to blows. Snow stepped in and they tossed Haus and his buddy out.

The irony is that Zander isn't even a service kid like Tom and Snow are; he didn't grow up on the base and he isn't adopted. Tom has no problem admitting he grew up in military social services, but he's still pretty sensitive about the service kid stereotypes and the common belief that they get preference when it comes to promotions. I don't blame him. Tom has earned every promotion he's gotten, and I'd bet more redeye sick bay duty that he'll be Captain Kingston before he turns 40.

I'm counting the hours until we reach Derovia.

Love,
C

CHAPTER 8

As the number of days spent in space travel increases, the morale of one's crew shall proportionately decrease.

— Commander Retan Ov'Raa, Space Corps, retired

When *Cornelia* set down on the surface of Derovia, Catherine felt palpable relief. At six months, this was their mission's longest period of travel. Catherine read through the brief document Ov'Raa had sent, reminding them of the rules of conduct when on Derovia, none of which were remotely unreasonable. The document offered a few facts about Derovia:

- *Derovia is one of 19 moons that orbit Suna, the ringed third planet of the Katara solar system.*

- *Derovia is the only moon of the 19 that sustains an atmosphere.*

- *Derovia's population resides on its two continents: the northern, Ovlon, and the southern, Mellon. Due to its more favorable climate, Ovlon is the most densely populated.*

- *Those from Ovlon have the "Ov" prefix in their family names. Likewise, those from Mellon have the "Mel" prefix.*

- *The western coast of Ovlon, at the capital city of Ronia, will be the location of* Cornelia*'s arrival and encampment.*

Gaining entry to Derovia and landing at Ronia's spaceport was an uncomplicated affair, as Derovian security measures were the most relaxed of the Alliance worlds. It didn't hurt that a significant proportion of *Cornelia*'s crew was Derovian. In a matter of what seemed like minutes, the Captain had ordered them to recalibrate their contactors for a 25.6-hour day and cleared them to debark the ship. With permission to take three days leave, all but essential crew deserted the ship and scurried in various directions.

Catherine, Tom, and Snow couldn't manage to agree on where to go first and ended up heading three different ways: Snow to Ronia to see live music, Tom (and a date) to hike up one of Ronia's cliffs and enjoy libations at the summit, and Catherine to the beach with Anka.

Eshel would spend the morning aiding Dr. Vargas in the burial of his homeworlders, stored all those months in the ship's cold chamber. Eshel had told Catherine about the sher memeshar, or rite of death, which required that they release the dead into the ocean. The bodies could not be released until showing early signs of decay; thus, a grumbling Vargas removed the bodies from the cold chamber several days before arrival at Derovia.

When Catherine debarked the ship with Anka, she was struck by two things: how bright the Katara sun seemed after living in artificial light conditions for so long, and how dense and humid the air was.

They boarded the crowded train heading north to the closest beach. The train, filled with din of chatty Derovians in brightly colored clothing, felt remarkably slow compared to those she was used to. They peered out the window at the stucco-like, multi-unit Ronian homes and the sunny, grassy hills in the distance. When they arrived at the beach, it was filled with people, most of whom were tourists. There were many humans, especially couples and families with young children.

"My God," Anka commented in surprise. "Such wealth they must have to afford a family vacation on Derovia!"

Catherine nodded.

Catherine took off her shoes and felt the warm, pinkish sand on her feet as she looked out at the tranquil ocean, its blue so blue that it appeared almost surreal. The beach was peppered with odd looking trees: short and stout, with white-flowered foliage on branches that splayed out, providing the shade that Derovians enjoyed but someone as fair as Catherine required.

Anka pointed to a tree with no inhabitants. "Will that one work for you, whitey?"

Catherine smiled. As they sat down, Catherine spotted a man out in the water. He seemed familiar, until she realized the man was Eshel. He dove into the water and began to swim away. Eshel's form was smooth and powerful, and his progress swift. She'd never seen anyone swim like that. Before much time passed, she could no longer see him.

Catherine and Anka went for a swim in the cool water. If breathing fresh air and absorbing real sunlight hadn't felt sublime enough, swimming in the sea did the trick. She forgot any memory of having been ship bound so long.

Back at their tree, they pulled out the sandwiches they'd packed and began comparing notes about their CO.

"You like the weekly progress reports?" Anka said. "Zero eight hundred: centrifuged my samples. Zero nine hundred: took a pee and borrowed more equipment from Catherine." They erupted in laughter.

"I'm glad I'm not the only one who thinks they're stupid," Catherine said. "Does he give you boring assignments too?"

"No. That part hasn't been bad. The old man's been nice to me."

"Really? He hates me."

"Oh, yes! He told me he hates your red hair. And he doesn't like your small boobs either."

They laughed again at Anka's jest.

"Is that Eshel?" Anka asked, squinting as she looked past Catherine.

Catherine turned and saw Eshel walking their way. Not having seen them, he sat down under a nearby tree. "I saw him go for a swim when we first got here."

"He swam that entire time?" Anka said. She glanced at her contactor. "It's been two hours! I suppose those webbed hands are good for something."

"I'll be back," Catherine said, getting up. "I need to ask him a quick question."

She approached Eshel's tree. "Hey, Esh."

"Catherine," he replied.

"Tom told me to ask you if you want to hike up Danal Cliff tomorrow with us. He needs to make a reservation at the restaurant on top, which I'm told offers 360-degree views and good Derovian seafood. If you want to go, we'll have to skip our training… or start earlier."

"I will go, but I prefer to train first."

"Okay. See you at zero eight hundred."

When Catherine and Eshel boarded the train to Ronia, Eshel hunched over to avoid hitting his head. Too tall to stand fully upright, and with no available seats, Eshel found an unoccupied corner where he seated his lanky body on the floor. Just then, a Derovian man stood up in excitement, speaking spiritedly to them in his native language, and motioned to his seat. Eshel, eyebrows raised, spoke a single word in Derovian and took the seat. Catherine also thanked the man, and gave him a smile.

Other than the filled seats, the train wasn't as crowded that day. This was fortunate, as Catherine had noticed that Eshel seemed to get uncomfortable when too many people stood near him. When their stop came, they got off and walked along a dirt path to the trailhead, where they would meet Tom and Snow. Both peered at the calm sea to the west, and Catherine could smell the faint sweet scent of the beach tree blooms.

As they neared the trailhead, the shrubs that lined their path grew larger and denser, obscuring their ocean view. Occasionally a small creature with patchy brown and white fur would scurry across the trail, startling Eshel and making Catherine laugh. Further along, Catherine heard rustling in some trees to their left. It sounded like a much larger creature, although she was under the impression that Ronia had no animals to fear. She looked past Eshel, half expecting another animal to emerge, wondering what it would be this time.

Suddenly, a large humanoid male appeared from behind the greenery and rapidly approached them. Before she could react, the man grabbed Eshel, wrapping his large arms around him to constrain him. Catherine went to strike the attacker, but found herself unable to move. Two large, dark arms had encircled her from behind.

They were Sunai.

Trapped by the Sunai's strong grip, Catherine purposely let her body relax. It had the desired effect—her captor relaxed slightly and she was able to grab his hand and twist the fingers until at least two of them broke. He growled in pain, further loosening his grip. She delivered an elbow to his face and then turned and punched him in the throat. He began to wheeze—a loud rasping noise that she hadn't expected—as he backed away from her, his hands on his throat.

Catherine went after Eshel's assailant, who struggled to keep Eshel in his clutches.

"Stay back, nonaii," the Sunai said in a thick guttural voice.

Nonaii. Woman.

Catherine rapidly approached him, knowing he must choose between holding on to Eshel or protecting himself from her. He chose to keep Eshel, and Catherine punched him squarely in the eye, cracking his eyeshades and causing him to release Eshel, who broke free and backed away. She went to strike again, this time aiming for his throat. He managed to block part of her punch and then grabbed her ponytail and jerked it down.

Catherine felt a surge of anger spread through her at having her hair pulled. She delivered a kick to his abdominal region, disabling him for the time being. She whipped around to check for the other Sunai. He was gone.

She turned back toward her opponent, ready for any retaliation, until she heard a shout. Another male voice. Catherine hoped Eshel could run. She couldn't take on more of them.

It was Tom and Snow.

Tom began to run. Catherine watched him run past her, confused, until she realized he was chasing Eshel's fleeing attacker. After a short time, Tom returned, completely out of breath.

"Jesus," he gasped. "That Sunai can run. Who knew someone that large could run so fast?"

"What the hell happened?" Snow asked her.

"They jumped us…. there were two of them… the other one ran away, too." She looked over at Eshel, who stood aside. He looked pale. She began walking toward him, but something told her to leave him be, so she stopped. "Are you injured?"

"No." He turned away from her.

Catherine turned back to Tom and Snow, who looked at her with questioning faces. She shrugged, perplexed.

Snow contacted the Derovian authorities. A short while later, two officers in orange uniforms arrived. Catherine, Tom, and Snow pulled their Space Corps IDs for the officers. The small, friendly officers listened patiently as Catherine told them what happened.

"They didn't try to take our belongings or anything," she told them. "I don't know why they attacked us. Other than pulling my hair, they didn't even retaliate when I hit them."

"A Sunai male does not strike any female of any race, even if attacked," one of the officers told them, his accent strong. "He will attempt to subdue the female with his great strength. But your skill made that difficult, Miss!"

"The attack was… how do you say… motivated by race, Miss Finnegan," the other authority added. "Sunai gumiia males may want fight with otherworld males." He looked over at Eshel, who still stood aside, but within earshot. "He is Korvali!" He glanced at the other authority with widened eyes. "How did this Korvali come to be on your Space Corps ship?"

"He's a refugee," she said.

"Does this Korvali need medic?"

"No. I think he's just in shock."

"Will this Korvali speak to us?"

"Yes. Just avoid touching him."

"Of course, Miss."

The two authorities walked toward Eshel, who turned to face them, handing them his ID. He towered over the two Derovian men, who looked up at him in awe. When Eshel answered all their questions in their native language, their awe turned to glee. After they finished, the authorities told Catherine they must report the incident to Captain Ferguson.

"We are most sorry for this very unfortunate incident. Our brothers, the Sunai, are good peoples, but some gumiia males may be… what is word… aggressive?" The authority smiled. "May we offer you transport to final destination, or back to spaceport?"

"No thanks, officers," Tom told them, gesturing toward the trail-head. "We're hiking up Danal Cliff."

"Oh, yes, you will most enjoy it!"

"I will not join you," Eshel told them. "I would prefer to swim."

"I recommend you no go alone, Eshel," the authority said. "These Sunai may wait and attack again."

"Exactly," Tom said. "You need to stay with us. We'll hike up, get you a few greenberry liqueurs, and you'll forget all about this."

Eshel shook his head. "These men cannot catch me in the water."

The other authority smiled. "That is true, Eshel! The Sunai do not like water! You will be safe in water. We will transport you to beach."

Tom sighed. "I'm only agreeing to this if you wait for us at the beach, and come back to the ship with us."

"That is fine." He looked at Catherine. "You will find me where you saw me yesterday."

Eshel turned to the authorities, who escorted him down the path and out of sight.

The three of them resumed their journey to the trailhead and began the steep climb up Danal Cliff. Catherine realized her knuckles bled a little. The eyeshades must have cut her.

"I should've made him come with us," Tom said, shaking his head. "I'm telling you, he can't be doing stuff alone all the time. He's a target. Did I not say he'd be a target?"

"He looked shook up, man," Snow said. "Besides, you know how stubborn he is."

"Yeah, wait until Ferguson finds out," Tom said. "She's gonna shit. I take it you didn't have any weapons on you?" he asked Catherine.

"Uh, no, Tom. They're illegal here, remember?"

Tom reached into the side pocket of his pants and retrieved a device made of black alloy. "Yup. I remember," he said with a grin.

"Maybe you should give Eshel one of those," Snow muttered.

When, they reached the cliff's peak, they could see the ocean to the west, more steep cliffs to the north, and Ronia to the east. The restaurant host greeted them and took them to a shaded table overlooking the ocean. Tom and Snow drank beer and chatted, but Catherine said little. She was worried about Eshel. When they descended the cliff and made their way to the beach, Catherine led them to the area she and Anka had gone to.

They searched the entire area. Eshel was nowhere to be seen. When they tried to contact him, they got no response.

Catherine felt a sense of panic as she looked around for Sunai. Tom cursed.

"Whoa… wait a minute…" Tom said. He studied his contactor. "I've got him. The signal's pretty weak, but he's out in the water somewhere."

Relief flooded her. "He's swimming." She looked at Tom's contactor. "He gave you permission to track him?"

Tom grinned. "He didn't have much of a choice."

And within minutes, Eshel emerged from the water.

Catherine sat down as Tom finished shuffling the cards and dealt the first hand.

"So how'd your date with Kate go?" Shanti asked Tom.

"We had a good time," Tom replied.

"And?" Shanti pressed.

"Does there have to be an 'and'?" Tom peeked at his cards.

"Are you going out with her again?"

He shrugged. "I don't know. I haven't thought about it yet." He leaned back in his chair and took a sip of beer. "I have another date tomorrow."

"You're a jerk," Shanti said, shaking her head.

"I'm not a jerk," Tom argued politely, with a hint of cockiness. "I'm a guy with options. I don't like to rush into anything." Zander and Middleton laughed at this.

"You're so full of shit," Snow said, flinging a poker chip at Tom.

The others tossed down their cards when they realized Shanti had beaten them. After Shanti scooped up her pot, Tom gathered the cards and began shuffling them again.

"Where's Eshel tonight?" Shanti asked.

"He didn't want to play," Tom said with a shrug.

"Still shook up over the Sunai thing?" Snow asked.

"Nah. But Ferguson is. Word has it she's so afraid of the shit she'll get if something happens to him that she almost banned him from leaving the ship at all. Now one of us has to go with him anytime he leaves." Tom looked at Shanti with a grin. "Why do you ask about Esh? You interested in gettin' a little alien love?"

The others laughed while Shanti reached over and smacked Tom. "No!" she cried. "And I don't date otherworlders!"

"Oh come on! It's not that big a deal," Tom said, peeking at his cards.

"My parents would kill me," Shanti said, a look of embarrassment on her dark face. "And I have nothing against anyone, but I just can't imagine… that."

"Me neither," Middleton said, shaking his head. "Nasty."

"I can," Tom said. "Sunai females. Any day, any time."

"You would?" Zander asked, fascinated. "Isn't that banned?"

"You would really do that?" Middleton added. "You would do it with an alien?"

"Middleton, unlike yourself, I'll try anything once." Tom tossed a stack of chips into the pot. "Yes, Z, it's banned. And that's exactly why I want to do it. The more the males try to protect them from us, and the more the Alliance says to leave them alone to avoid pissing off the males, the more I want to do dirty, dirty things with them."

The guys laughed.

"Tom!" Shanti cried, smacking him again.

Catherine stifled a laugh as she peeked at her cards. *A pair of twos. In bad position.* She folded.

"You sure you don't want me to set you up with Esh?" Tom asked Shanti. "He could use… something."

"Does Eshel like girls?" Zander asked. "I've never seen him even look at one. He barely noticed when Kate dropped by last week. And she is beauuuuuutiful." He called Tom's bet.

"Your guess is as good as mine," Tom said. "He goes mute if I bring up that topic. I've introduced him to girls, and… nothing. No matter what their looks, personality, rank, or cup size… he doesn't care." He looked around at the others. "Zander even showed us an image of this gorgeous woman… human, of course… it showed *everything.* No response. I've never seen anything like it."

"He's probably a fag," Middleton said with a sly grin.

"Shut up, Mackey," Shanti told him.

"What?" Middleton cried. "He could be!"

Tom shook his head. "I can spot a homo anywhere. He's not gay."

"Maybe he's kind of… asexual," Zander said.

Catherine shook her head. "Impossible. They're too similar to us to reproduce asexually."

Zander shook his head. "No, not like that. I mean maybe he's not into girls like we are. Maybe they just do it to have kids or something."

Catherine wondered what Eshel would think of people speculating about his sexual tendencies. Anthropologists had attempted to observe the Korvali from afar, while hovering just outside the border of Korvali space, but even state-of-the-art instruments lacked adequate power to capture anything useful. Attempts to allow ships to observe at a closer distance were vetoed by the Alliance, despite numerous objections from Sunai and human groups… including the Space Corps.

After playing for a couple of hours, Catherine folded her cards and stood up. "I have to go," Catherine said.

"Why?" Tom asked. "Where do you have to be at this hour?"

She smiled. "A little side project I've been working on." She said her goodbyes and left.

Catherine sat down for second meal. Tom and Snow had half devoured their chicken and dumplings; Eshel's full plate of ornon indicated that he'd just sat down. She was glad they were all there. She had news.

"What's up, Finnegan?" Tom asked her, his words muffled from his full mouth.

"I'll tell you what's up. I found out that the CCFs will be here—*in Ronia*—in a couple of months."

The three men looked up from their plates, their attention on her.

"What?" Tom said. "Are you sure? The Calyyt-Calloq Fights are coming here? Why didn't I hear about this?"

"They haven't announced it yet. The authorities who handled

the assault case told me. I think they assumed I'd be interested," she added with a smile.

"About damn time we get to see the fights live," Snow said. "Which days? I need to make sure O'Leary will let me off duty."

Catherine checked her contactor. "April sixth through eighth."

"Alright," Tom announced, rapping his hand on the table. "I'm ordering tickets for all three days, the best seats we can get. Who's in?"

"I'm in," Snow said.

"I am as well," Eshel said, "if my CO will allow it."

Tom grinned. "No need to worry, Esh. I'll set it up so all the guys get to go. We'll run a skeleton crew on those days. And Marks loves the CCs too, so he won't give me any shit about it. Man, how lucky is this? Right here in Ronia!" He looked at Catherine. "Will the old man give you the time off? You never take leave, so you must have some time accrued."

"I do," she replied. "But I only need a ticket for Day Three."

"Why?" Tom said. "You only want to watch the famous guys? Days One and Two are when you get the otherworlders and the crazy, unexpected stuff."

"I know, Tom. I'll be busy the other two days." She paused. "I'm going to compete."

The guys looked at Catherine, her news registering on their faces. Tom reacted first. "What do you mean, you're going to compete?"

"I'm an official competitor. They told me I'll probably compete on Day Two."

"I thought you didn't like competing," Snow said in disbelief.

"I don't. But I want to try it."

"No," Tom said, shaking his head. "No. The CCFs are dangerous, Finnegan. You could get hurt. You know how the Calyyt fight."

"I know. But I may never get this opportunity again. And you said yourself I should seek out more adventure," she added, stirring her food with her fork.

"Yeah," Tom said, "through soldier training. *Soldier training.* Not getting the shit beat out of you by some mute Neuter with a mean streak."

Snow laughed. Catherine, despite herself, chuckled a little at the insult.

"I'm serious, Catherine," Tom said.

Catherine stopped laughing. When Tom called her by her given name, she knew he wasn't kidding around. Eshel and Snow said nothing, waiting to see what Tom would say next.

"This isn't one of your little grappling competitions," Tom went on. "It's dangerous. I've watched the CCFs for years and they're insane."

"Tom, I know what they're like. I've watched them, too."

He gave her a disapproving look. "I've seen countless men a lot bigger than you sustain serious head injuries. What about that guy last year? Same training as you... in the martial arts... it took two days of surgery to repair the damage. Two days!"

"I'm doing it," she said, her tone resolute.

Tom shook his head. "Stubborn as a mule." He paused. "What's Jimmy going to say? He won't want his only daughter fighting in the CCFs."

"I'm not telling him until afterward. And you better not say anything to him," she warned.

Out of arguments, Tom waved his hand at her as if done trying to talk sense into her.

Then it was Snow's turn. "Don't get mad, alright? But I think I've seen two, maybe three females fight in the CCFs. It wasn't pretty. They don't have the strength to keep up with those guys."

She took a forkful of food. "Strength helps. But skill determines who's victorious, Snow. Why do you think the Calyyt can beat the Sunai, who are so much larger? And the reason there are so few females in the CCFs is because most of them can't pass the assessments."

Eshel chose that moment to speak. "Assessments?"

"If you've never competed in the CCs, they have to evaluate your skills before they'll allow you to get in the ring."

"You have passed them?"

She nodded.

"What did Commander Yamamoto say about your decision?" Eshel asked.

"I haven't told him either," she admitted with some chagrin. "He won't approve. He hates the CCFs."

Tom sighed. "Alright, alright." He held up his cup. "Here's to the CCs."

The others raised their cups and clinked them with Tom's.

Eshel turned to Tom. "What is the meaning of 'Neuter?'"

Tom grimaced slightly. "Ah, it's just a joke. You know... because the Calyyt don't have male and female."

"Do you also have disparaging names for Derovians and Sunai?"

"Absolutely," Tom said. "Derovians are Smileys... that one's obvious. To me, that's the least insulting of the bunch, but they detest it... they'll turn as blue as the ocean if you even come close to saying it. As for the Sunai..."

"Don't say it, man," Snow warned.

Catherine shook her head as well.

"What is the purpose of such names?" Eshel asked.

"What," Tom said, "the Korvali don't have insulting ways of labeling us?"

Eshel remained silent.

CHAPTER 9

If you want to start a fight, bring in a Sunai.
If you want to break up a fight, bring in a Derovian.
If you want to win a fight, bring in a Calyyt.

– author unknown

Once committed to compete, Catherine spent much of her spare time training for the event. She asked Holloway to practice Calyyt-style grappling with her; he was her best option on the ship. Holloway's thick build and greater strength were good practice for her, and solid grappling skills were key to fighting the Calyyt. Eshel, whose interest in self-defense had continued to increase, asked if he could observe her and Holloway as they trained. He even offered up their Sunday morning training time, where Catherine would practice with Holloway and then use some of their training as a way to show Eshel new techniques.

Calyyt fighters were famous... and feared. Nearly everyone remotely skilled in boxing, wrestling, or the martial arts hoped for the opportunity to fight them. However, those opportunities were rare, as the CCFs only took place on Calyyt-Calloq, Suna, and Derovia, and most humans couldn't afford to travel that far to compete. As such, the CCFs didn't see many humans. Earth had its own version of the fights; but much of the enjoyment of watching the CCFs came from the unusual pairings of otherworld fighters.

Despite being slightly smaller than humans, the Calyyt were like bundles of unpredictable and highly skilled power, often beating opponents larger than themselves, including the Sunai. Legend had it that the Calyyt learned their skills wrestling a dangerous predator on their planet: the moyyt-toq, large reptile-like creatures that resided in the rocky outcrops of the planet's arid regions. Most notably, when a Calyyt fighter got in the ring with an otherworlder, the Calyyt usually won.

To match up fighters for competition, the Calyyt organizers utilized algorithms that they'd refined over centuries, based on information they gleaned during the assessments. After assessing her skills, Catherine had stood in puzzlement as two silent Calyyt poked, sniffed, scanned, and measured her, their pungent but not unpleasant bodily odor wafting up to her.

As the CCFs approached, Catherine received her match assignment: she would compete with a Calyyt on Day 2 of the three-day event. In the past, Catherine had no desire to compete in the CCFs, to subject herself to injury and humiliation. But something had changed.

The night before her match, Catherine slept poorly. She woke often, feeling like she hadn't slept at all, and was awake well before her alarm sounded. She took a hot shower and wondered why she'd chosen to do this when no one expected her to, or even wanted her to.

She went to the mess to get something to eat, bringing it back to her quarters so she could be alone. Her appetite was dull, but she forced herself to eat nonetheless. Contactor messages from Tom, Snow, and Eshel all wished her luck. She put her hair into tight braids, knotting and extensively pinning them to keep her long hair from hindering her. She attempted to read, but found that she'd scrolled through several pages of text without having any idea of what she'd read. Finally, she gathered her things, including her white competition uniform, and headed to the arena.

After checking the schedule three times to ensure she had the correct train, she boarded and sat down in one of the seats, putting her pack on her lap. The train was crowded that day as passengers continued to board, all heading to the arena to see the fights. But as Catherine glanced around, something seemed off. She noticed that the Derovians, usually talking and laughing amongst themselves, were quieter than usual, and their gazes showed that something had caught their attention.

Catherine looked over. Not too far away, two very tall figures wearing blue robes sat quietly, their hoods pulled up so one could barely see their faces. *Korvali.* While the Derovians stared at the Korvali, she realized the Korvali didn't stare back at them. They stared at her. Catherine felt the hair on her arms stand up. She looked away from the two Korvali. But she never let them out of her peripheral vision for the entire ride.

It occurred to her that her pre-fight anxiety had made her jumpy, so she took a deep breath and relaxed. She reminded herself that while no Korvali ever came to Earth—the Space Corps forbade them to visit—it was not so unusual for them to occasionally come, always in pairs, to Derovia and Suna.

The train stopped and everyone stood up, the brightly dressed Derovians excitedly clamoring to get off the train. Catherine stood up as well and followed the crowd. When she glanced over her shoulder nervously, wondering if the hooded figures would follow her, they were gone.

At the arena, the organizers checked her in and sent her to the holding area, an underground network of plain concrete rooms where she spent an hour warming up. She visualized her opponent and all the maneuvers he could try on her, as she'd been taught.

"Catherine."

She jumped. When she turned around, Yamamoto stood before her. She quickly bowed, and before she could remember her etiquette, she said, "I thought you didn't like the CCs."

"Is that why you didn't tell me you were competing?"

Embarrassed, she nodded.

"I cannot fulfill my role as mentor if you hide the truth from me."

She looked down. "Sorry."

"Do you feel prepared?"

"I did until about an hour ago…"

"That is okay. What do you fear most?"

She took a deep breath, looking down again. "Looking like a fool. Everyone thinks I'm going to get crushed out there."

He put his finger under her chin and nudged it up until her eyes met his. "If you agreed with them, you wouldn't be here." He paused. "Be prepared for the unexpected. Your opponent may bend the rules, and get away with it because the crowds like it. Do not let it distract you. Also, Calyyt are not accustomed to fighting females, so you should expect a very poor welcome."

"Thank you, Commander."

"Good luck," he said, offering a slight bow. She bowed in return, and he left.

"Catherine Finnegan," said a high, loud voice. She jumped again. This time it was the announcer, an older Derovian man with a big smile. Next to him stood a Calyyt, one of the fight organizers, who looked at her through slit-like eyes. He inhaled through his nasal orifice, as if sniffing her from a distance. The Calyyt communicated something in sign language. She looked at the Derovian announcer, who said, "Miss Finnegan, time for your scan."

After being scanned for weapons and performance enhancing substances, Catherine proceeded to the waiting area. Her heart palpitated as she waited, until another Calyyt led her up the stairs. He stopped. She heard the Derovian announcer speaking in another language over the arena's sound system. She understood nothing except "Space Corps" and her name. The Calyyt gave her a nudge, indicating for to proceed.

As she emerged from below and entered the circular ring, she squinted in the extremely bright light and headed to her side of the ring as the ref motioned her to. The massive crowd above and everything else around her was a blur. Her opponent was already there, in position on the other side of the ring. She held her head up to the point of arrogance, to counteract the pounding of her heart and the cold sweat developing in her armpits. Once on her side, she locked eyes with her opponent. She felt a knot in her stomach.

The Calyyt, slightly shorter than Catherine but compact with sinewy musculature, watched her with slitted, black, lashless eyes. When a match was ready to begin, a Calyyt always stood in ready position. However, her opponent stepped out of ready position. She'd seen such a maneuver before; it signaled that the Calyyt didn't believe she was a worthy opponent. Catherine ignored the display of insolence and maintained eye contact with him, staring him down and trying to look as mean as possible.

The bell rang.

When the Calyyt advanced toward her, and she toward him, she immediately knew she'd have to give her all to stay afloat. The Calyyt, true to form, wasted no time trying to take her to the mat with one of the common maneuvers she'd shown Eshel, where he suddenly grabbed her leg. She saw the attempt coming and shifted just enough to prevent takedown and free her leg. She then took advantage of his unprotected head and delivered a solid face punch that drew blood, followed by another punch. The crowd went crazy.

The Calyyt very quickly recovered. They circled for a bit before he took several punches at her, all of which she blocked, until he attempted another takedown. She saw this one coming as well, knowing almost instinctively that he would aim for her other leg. She punished him again, this time with a knee to his face that forced him to retreat. They continued to circle, each eyeing the other, each taking the occasional shot and missing. Then, the bell rang. Round one was over.

Catherine retreated to her side and sat down, grateful for a chance to catch her breath. She glanced over and noticed the line of judges, all Calyyt, seated along the rim of the ring. All had their eyes on her, not her opponent. She wiped the sweat off her brow with her towel, and looked over at her opponent. He watched her too, until each turned away to drink some water and prepare for the next round. Catherine concentrated on slowing down her breathing and centering herself, until the bell rang for round two.

They circled a bit again until the Calyyt made his move and put her in a clinch. Catherine recognized this maneuver as well, but was unprepared for it as the Calyyt coiled his leg around hers and took her to the mat with a thud. She knew he could submit her, and quickly, and that she could lose in the second round. He took a few shots at her—she felt a stabbing pain in her ribs and took another punch to her cheek, both of which quickly went numb from shock. He tried for a choke submission, but she managed to reorient herself to a more advantageous position, where he couldn't hit her again without making himself vulnerable to counterattack. And while she was unable to completely free herself from his grasp, she knew she could fend him off for as long as necessary.

At one point, in their stalemate grappling position, Catherine could smell the Calyyt's pungent smell, could feel his rough, sticky skin on hers and his dense body pressing upon her. She felt a momentary sensation of fear at being so physically close to a stranger, to a hostile stranger, and she strained to turn her head away. She then noticed the Calyyt's exposed ankle. It had a small scar, indicating that he'd sustained some type of injury there at one time. She knew she should attack; but it was too risky at that time, so she put her remaining energies into avoiding submission. Just as she felt herself weakening, the bell rang, and each retreated to their respective corners.

Fatigue set in. She felt slower and less coordinated as the energy she'd had at the start began its inevitable decline. As she sipped her water and calmed herself, she began to wonder if she would make it through the third round. She felt worn out. Her ribs hurt and her cheek felt swollen. But after a minute's rest, she made up her mind that she must finish the round.

Once the bell rang, each approached the other. Fatigue had set in for her opponent as well, and he didn't attack as often or with as much ferocity as before. But he continued to throw punches, and her tired state rendered her slower to block them. She took a couple more hits and could feel herself losing ground. She faltered, and took one vicious hit to her cheek that sent her crashing into the side of the ring. She saw stars and felt almost as if she'd gone deaf.

At that moment, while protecting herself from another blow to the head, the Calyyt's ankle came into her line of sight. She delivered a kick to it. It had the desired effect—the Calyyt stumbled. She took a shot at his face and followed up with several more before she dove for his hips, took him down to the mat, and maneuvered to trap him between her legs. As she attempted to lock his elbow, he wrangled out of his compromised position and she didn't get the submission she'd hoped for. They grappled for what seemed like endless minutes, each attempting to best the other, both exhausted but both refusing to relent.

The bell rang and the Calyyt refs separated them. Catherine felt relief as she tried to catch her breath. It was over. She survived. After a few minutes of deliberation, the judges made their announcement.

It was a draw.

Catherine couldn't believe it. A draw was extremely rare in the CCFs. It meant the competitors were too close in ability and performance to select a winner from that match, and would be scheduled for a rematch if they chose.

She finally noticed the crowd noise; there was a lot of high-pitched cheering and yelling, and she couldn't tell if they were happy or angry about the decision. She didn't care. She'd survived the fight. She didn't win, but she didn't lose, and that made her smile.

And then she saw something from the corner of her eye; suddenly, she felt a terrible pain on the side of her head. The Calyyt had blind-sided her with a punch, knocking her sideways. She felt tears come to her eyes from the shock of it, and everything seemed to get quiet again, as if she could no longer hear.

Catherine's shock quickly turned to rage. She delivered a hook to the Calyyt's head, where the ear would be if the Calyyt had ears. It was where the Calyyt people perceived sounds and vibrations, and was an area of substantial sensitivity. The Calyyt stumbled back, grimacing in pain, his hands clutching the side of his head. She hit him again, aiming for the same sensitive region, but in her rage she missed and her strike landed on his face. He began to bleed from his nasal orifice again.

Suddenly Catherine felt arms around her, restraining her. They restrained her opponent as well. He signed to her—she recognized it as a common Calyyt insult. She spat at him as she strained against the refs who held her back.

They dragged her down the steps and thrust her into one of the warm-up rooms, shutting and locking the door after they left. She found herself alone in the room, where the roar of the shouting crowd was replaced by a glaring silence. The silence made her aware of her rapid breathing and the ringing in her ears. She paced the room, trying to calm her agitated state. Her eye stung as sweat dripped from her brow. She wiped it away; but when she looked at her white sleeve, it was stained bright red. Bewildered, Catherine realized she was bleeding. And it only made her angrier.

Catherine heard the door unlock. As the door opened, she prepared herself to lash out at whoever came to taunt her.

It was Eshel.

CHAPTER 10

Eshel halted at the sight of Catherine's bloodied face and infuriated expression. But once she recognized him, her anger seemed to dissipate. She turned away and sat down on the hard bench. Eshel walked over to her and kneeled down to get a closer look at her injuries.

She breathed rapidly and trembled a bit. "Take deep breaths," he told her. She did so. But when he tried to examine her head wound, she shrank away. Just then, Tom arrived. Before Tom could say anything, Eshel said, "I need to get her to sick bay. Will you get a transport?"

"They're already here," Tom replied, a worried look on his face.

"Catherine, we must go to sick bay," Eshel said. He led Catherine to the transport vessel; a medic had her lie down while Eshel climbed in and directed them to the *Cornelia*. Within a few minutes they reached the external entrance to sick bay. When Catherine stood up, she lost her balance and stumbled. Eshel caught her and helped her regain her footing.

Once they entered sick bay, Eshel heard Catherine mumble something. He didn't understand at first, until he realized she'd said, "Not Vargas." Eshel took a brief look around and assured her that Vargas wasn't there. The physician on duty, who he recognized from his redeye sick bay duty, approached them. "She has sustained a head injury in the CCFs. She is... disoriented."

The doctor led Catherine to a medical bed. "Lieutenant, what day is it today?"

"Day Two of the fights," she replied absentmindedly. By then, her face grimaced in pain.

Eshel stood aside while the doctor scanned Catherine, retrieved a small tube from a drawer, and gave her an injection. He gave orders to the nurse, who treated her and cleaned her up. After they finished, Eshel approached her again. To his relief, her grimace had faded and she looked better.

Catherine looked at him and smiled. "You're so handsome, Esh," she said, her words somewhat slurred.

Eshel, surprised, found himself unsure of how to respond.

"I think they were watching me on the train," Catherine went on, seeming almost pleased with herself.

"Who was?" Eshel replied, amused at Catherine's altered state.

"Those two Korvali," she said dreamily.

Eshel stared at her. "What do you mean, Catherine?" But before she could offer any response, she went unconscious. "Doctor."

The doctor turned, a smile on his face as he glanced at Catherine. "She's fine. It's the medication. She'll be in and out for a while."

Eshel heard the doors open. Tom and Snow walked in.

"How is she?" Tom asked. "Is she unconscious?"

"The medication has sedated her," Eshel said.

"Let me guess," Snow said. "Concussion?"

Eshel nodded.

Tom walked over to the doctor and spoke with him for a moment. When he returned, he said, "Looks like Vargas will be in later, so we should get her out of here before then. We'll all get redeye duty forever if Vargas finds out she willingly submitted herself to the CCFs and is using his resources for treatment. We can look after her. Doc will contact us when it's time."

Eshel nodded and they left sick bay.

When Eshel received the doctor's page and returned to sick bay, Catherine was sitting up while the doctor scanned her head wound.

"The swelling has gone down quite a bit," the doctor told her. "Your injury could've been much worse, but you seem to have a hard head."

"So I'm told," she replied.

The doctor chuckled. "Rest for two days before resuming any work, and no training until the wounds heal and the symptoms are completely gone. That's an order," he added. Catherine nodded and thanked him for his care. He turned to Eshel. "So, Handsome, you know what to look for, right?" He handed Eshel the scanner.

Eshel nodded, ignoring the jest. "I... must thank you, Doctor. For your assistance." The doctor's expression turned to genuine surprise. Eshel turned his attention to Catherine, who seemed more coherent than before.

"Hey Esh."

"You're smiling."

"It's the painkillers."

"We need to leave," he told her. "Dr. Vargas will be here soon."

Even in her haze, Catherine understood. She slowly sat up, grimacing in pain, and turned until her feet touched the ground. Eshel put out his arm to help her up.

As they left sick bay, Eshel's contactor chirped. "I have her," he said to Tom.

"Sorry, I got hung up," Tom's voice said. "How about bringing her here?"

"I will take her to her quarters. I can care for her there."

There was a pause. "Are you sure? You know what to look for?"

"Yes," Eshel replied.

Once at Catherine's quarters, Eshel explained that, per the doctor's suggestion, he must stay with her to monitor her concussion. She didn't argue. Instead, she began fumbling around, looking for something.

"What are you looking for?"

"Tea."

"I will make it," Eshel told her. "Lie down."

Catherine gave up her search and proceeded to her bed. "Don't turn around," she said.

Not understanding, he turned toward her. She'd begun peeling off her dirty, bloodstained uniform, revealing bruising on her pale skin. He turned back around to make tea. When she gave him the okay to look, he watched her grimace as she got into bed, propping herself up against the bulkhead. Eshel set her tea down on her small bedside shelf. He moved a chair near her bed and sat down, removing his cold-water container and taking a drink from it.

"How are you feeling?" It was an expression he'd learned during his sick bay duty. He still found it strange to ask such a question.

"Better," she said, blowing on the hot tea and taking a small sip.

"I did research; it is possible to get your opponent banned from competing."

She shook her head. "We'll both be penalized. We were both angry little idiots. Yamamoto will be so proud of me." She sighed with a bit of laughter. "He'll be so proud of the example I am for you!"

"I don't understand."

"I lost my temper, Eshel. People in our discipline aren't supposed to do that."

Eshel gave a small scowl. "What other solution is there? You cannot let a coward harm you and still respect yourself. He must be punished." Catherine, appearing surprised by his remark, only smiled. "Your opponent used two of the maneuvers that you and Ensign Holloway demonstrated," he said. "I recognized them."

She nodded in approval. They discussed the details of the fight for a while, until Eshel noticed that Catherine's face no longer looked happy, that she said little.

"You are experiencing pain again?"

She nodded.

Eshel got up and retrieved her small container of medication. He handed her a pill, which she drank with her tea. He quickly scanned her with the medical scanner the doctor had loaned him. Her readings had improved slightly, but still weren't acceptable.

"You don't have to take care of me, Esh," Catherine said. "I'm fine."

"You are not fine."

"I am. I feel much better."

Reminded of Tom's failed attempts to persuade Catherine when she was resolute, Eshel, despite knowing he was in the right, tried a different tactic. "Perhaps. But it is better to be cautious."

She argued no more, only resting with her eyes closed for a few minutes.

"Catherine."

"Mmm," she replied, her eyes still closed.

"You said you saw two Korvali on the train."

She opened her eyes and blinked a couple of times. "That's right. I did see them." She cocked her head. "When did I say that?"

"In sick bay. What did you see?"

Catherine recounted what she saw.

"Did you take an image?"

"No."

Eshel looked at her. "Catherine, if you see any Korvali again, do not speak to them, do not let them near you, and never let them isolate you from others. Do you understand?"

"Yes," she said, her expression curious. Her relaxed look returned as the medication began to work. "How is Commander Steele treating you, Eshel?"

Not expecting the question, Eshel hesitated. "He is… it is fine."

"Good," she replied in a soft voice, her pace of speech about half its normal speed, a faint smile on her face. "When he became your genetics liaison, he was so concerned… so concerned about you and me. He wanted analyses I'd done… scans… emails between you and I… the file with your genetic material… I told him I had none of that, that we hadn't talked after that morning in sick bay… but he didn't believe me. He even threatened me, saying that if I were lying, or if I or Holloway or Varan ever questioned you, he'd send me back to Earth!" She didn't sound angry, but merely relayed the information as if it amused her. "Nystrom incident, my ass. It was almost as if he wanted that information for himself… not that he'd know what to do with any of it…" She looked at him, a gleam in her eye and her smiling broadening. "I have permission to be mean about him, you know. He's mean to me. After catching us at the lab that one night, he banned me from going to the lab after hours. I was working on an exploratory epigenetics project… it's your fault for inspiring me…" She smiled at him. "Don't tell him I said that. I have a concussion, fractured ribs, and pains in places that shouldn't hurt… I don't need more trouble."

Eshel did not respond.

"Did I stumble onto the wrong topic again, Eshel? You looked away… like the time I mentioned Othniel… your father… when we first met. I'm not in everyone's business, like our good friend Tom. I just want to know more about you, whatever you want to share."

"You may ask me anything."

She giggled. "You said that too, when we first met."

Surprised, Eshel said, "Your memory is very good."

"It's not like yours… but, yes, it's good. When Tom and I argue about past events, he always believes I'm being stubborn. But it's not stubbornness… I just remember everything better than he does." She paused. "Did something happen to your father, Eshel, on Korvalis?"

Eshel was silent for several moments. "Yes. He was murdered."

"By whom?" Catherine asked, her sleepy eyes narrowed.

"By someone powerful."

"Someone from your own clan," she surmised.

Eshel nodded.

"Does this powerful person know that you know?"

"He does not," Eshel replied. "But he will."

Catherine looked away, staring up at the ceiling. "Hard to say which is more unjust," she mused. "Losing a parent at the hands of a horrible person, or losing a parent at the hands of a horrible disease with a genetic origin."

Eshel, not understanding what she meant, waited for her to elaborate.

"My mother," she said. "She died, during my first year at the Academy. Breast cancer." She briefly touched her left breast. "I can tell you which therapies they tried and recount every protein, chromosome, locus, and nucleotide they targeted … but I don't want to put either of us in jeopardy, or anger the old man who controls my every move as a scientist."

"You may tell me," Eshel said. "I will say nothing to the Commander."

Catherine told him the details about her mother's cancer, from the initial genotype screening to the failed attempts at gene therapy. Eshel listened, Catherine's story making clear sense, even in her current state.

As afternoon moved into evening, and evening into night, they talked. At some point during a conversational lull, Eshel saw that Catherine had fallen asleep. He scanned her, used the head, and lay down on the deck. He nodded off, waking every few hours to scan her and ensure she was recovering. At 0400, satisfied with the scan's results, he returned to his quarters.

As the starting time for the Day 3 fights grew near, Eshel hadn't heard from Catherine. He knew she'd prefer attending the fights to sleeping, no matter how tired, so he went to her quarters to wake her. When he walked in, she was dressed in her personal apparel and she had wet hair. She must have just finished bathing. He looked closely at her; her face appeared worse than it had previously, as the bruising had grown darker. And while she seemed more lucid than she had, she looked tired. He pulled out his borrowed medical scanner and scanned her.

"Am I all better, Doc?"

"You are improved, but not yet well. What do you feel?"

"Foggy. The shower helped. I ran over my allotment, which means no shower tomorrow, but it was worth it."

"Do you have your ticket?"

"Ticket?"

"For the fights." He noted her forgetfulness, making sure to monitor it over the next several days.

"Oh. Yes. It's stored on my contactor. But I need to eat, Esh. I'm starving."

Eshel hesitated. "We will be late."

"I'll grab something at the arena."

On their way out, they saw two male crewmen heading toward them. One struck the other with his elbow and pointed at them. Eshel ignored it, until he realized they pointed at Catherine, not him. One crewman flashed a sign that Eshel did not understand, while the other said, "Nice fighting, LT," as they passed. When Eshel turned to observe her reaction, he saw that she smiled.

Once on the train, Eshel scanned the area carefully before finding a corner in which he could kneel down. He saw nothing of concern. At the arena, they joined 30,000 others as they filled the seats surrounding the circular ring. Higher up in the stands, several very large screens projected a larger image of the ring to the audience.

When they found their seats, Catherine looked at him. "They're in awe of you."

"Who is?"

"Everyone. They're staring."

"Today, they stare at you, not me."

When Tom, Snow, Middleton, and Zander arrived, Eshel and Catherine stood up to let them pass. Tom smiled at Catherine, shaking his head and putting his arms around her in what Eshel had learned was a "hug."

She cried out. "Watch the ribs!"

"Ah, quit your whining," Tom chided, as he sat down in the seat next to hers.

"Nice shiner," Snow said.

Middleton gave him a wary glance and nodded at Catherine as he passed by. Finally, when it was Zander's turn to pass them, he spread his arms out.

Catherine smiled. "Not too hard, Z."

Zander gave her a gentle hug. "Nice fighting, Dr. F. When you took that Neuter to the mat… that was awesome!" He looked at Eshel and grinned. "You want a hug too?"

Eshel only smiled.

"Hey, C," Tom said. "You made the news!"

"What?" she said in disbelief.

Before he could finish, Zander had pulled Tom's attention elsewhere.

After numerous rounds of fights, some exciting and some very exciting, Eshel waited until much of the crowd had dissipated before leaving the arena. The others assumed he did so because he disliked crowds. While that was true, he had a more compelling reason: smaller crowds meant fewer people to keep track of. Tom and the other men waited as well, to honor the Captain's wish that he be protected, especially on that particular day, when Catherine was unprepared to do so.

As they exited the arena, large crowds of Derovians still gathered outside in the large stone courtyard, enjoying the waning sun. Some excitedly talked about the fights, while others moved their bodies about in strange ways to music, something Catherine called dancing. Derovians often seemed to be dancing. He spotted a few Sunai, but they were not watching him. Instead, they held instruments, creating the music that the Derovians danced to. Others stood by drinking rallnofia, a beverage that Eshel found palatable but that made him feel strange if he drank too much of it.

In an eager desire to be near the music, many Derovians darted around Eshel, separating him from the others. Eshel felt his temperature rise and his vision blur slightly. He reached for his canteen; it was empty. He quickly moved away from the crowd, feeling a small bit of fresh air circulate past him as he spotted a water station nearby with a circular blue symbol, indicating it contained a dispenser for the water humans needed. After filling his canteen, he took a long drink and felt himself cool. He knew he must hurry and find the others, as they couldn't see him behind the water station and would worry about him.

When he turned to leave, he was surprised to find two people standing behind him. They were Sunai males dressed in black trousers with pale rust vests, exposing their dark arms. *Gumiia. Non-military Sunai males of low status.* Eshel immediately recognized one of them from the day he and Catherine were attacked. He did the first thing that came to mind, something Catherine had taught him: he took his fist and aimed for the Sunai's eyeshades, hoping to catch him by surprise and escape in that direction, where only five paces would render him visible to the crowd.

The attack did surprise the Sunai; his eyeshades didn't break, but having them jammed into his eye temporarily disabled him. However, the other Sunai reacted quickly and encircled Eshel with strong arms. Eshel expected the first Sunai to strike him, but he didn't; instead he angrily growled something Eshel didn't understand and fumbled with an object he didn't recognize.

They had a weapon.

Eshel felt the small metal disk in his own hand, which he'd retrieved from his pocket upon sight of the two Sunai. He pressed the release button.

After mere seconds, the Sunai he'd struck stopped fumbling, appearing dazed. The strong arms that imprisoned him became slack and he easily released himself from the Sunai's grip. Eshel turned and looked at him, presumably the one who'd grabbed him from behind before, whose face he hadn't seen until now. He wore the same dazed expression.

Eshel emerged from behind the water station. The crowd had thinned somewhat, but still contained enough people heading in the direction of the train station to offer him some protection. He couldn't see Catherine's red hair or Tom's fair curls anywhere. He followed the others, taking another drink from his canteen.

"Eshel!"

Eshel saw Catherine and Tom emerge from behind a cluster of trees. He scanned the area to see if the gumiia had followed him. But they were nowhere to be seen.

April 8th

Hi Dad,

So I guess you heard about the CCFs. I'm sorry I didn't tell you about it ahead of time. I never thought the fight would make the news, and I didn't want you to worry. Please don't give Tom a hard time either; he did his best to talk me out of it and even used you as an argument, but I told him to keep his big mouth shut. I promise I'm still alive and—other than some broken ribs and a concussion—healthy.

But I have to say, Dad, you taught me well. Your street fighting tricks kept my head above water, probably more than my martial arts training did. No one expected me to even survive out there, and not only did I survive all three rounds, the judges called a draw. A DRAW, Dad! The Calyyt have certainly earned their reputation—I had to use every weapon in my arsenal just to stay alive out there, and my opponent wasn't even one of the best fighters.

Yes, he (He? Why haven't we come up with a gender-neutral pronoun for these people by now?) took a shot at me after the final bell. I thought that kind of thing didn't happen anymore, so I didn't see it coming. It was a pretty cheap shot, resulting in the worst of my injuries, and, as you probably saw, it made me madder than you can imagine. I punished him for it, but even though it satisfied my ego at the time, it didn't make me feel better. The organizers penalized us for fighting after the bell and for engaging in illegal maneuvers. We're banned from the CCFs for six Earth months. People are already talking about a rematch after the ban lifts (we'll be encamped at Suna then, so easy enough to get a transport), but I've already decided I'm not interested. I got it out of my system and proved I could do it, so I have no need to do it again. Tom and Snow, who were both very resistant to the idea of my competing at all, now can't understand why I won't take the rematch and beat him for good! Eshel understands, though.

Oh... I just got a message from Commander Steele. He wants me in his office immediately. That can't be good.

Let me know what's happening with you…

Love,
C

P.S. The emitters are down, so no holo-chat for a while.

CHAPTER 11

Catherine braced herself as she approached Steele's office. She was tired, injured, and bruised... maybe Steele would go easy on her. She entered, saluted her commanding officer, and stood in her usual spot in front of his desk, knowing that he wouldn't ask her to sit. Steele glanced up at her, but continued reading something on his electronic pad. Several minutes passed; Catherine waited, refusing to speak or otherwise indicate her presence. She knew this game and was prepared to stand there all day, if necessary.

Finally, Steele spoke. "You may recall, Lieutenant, my rather stern warning about the consequences of discussing genetics with our Korvali crewmember, Eshel."

"Yes, Sir."

"You may also recall that violation of that order would result in your being sent back to Earth."

"Yes, Sir."

"Then perhaps you don't value your position here, on this ship," he said, staring at her with cold blue eyes.

"How so, Sir?"

"I have reports that you violated this order."

Catherine felt her stomach jump, a slightly sick feeling coming over her. Her mind flashed back to a somewhat foggy memory of the previous evening, of her conversation with Eshel. Catherine began to speak, but hesitated, unaware of any response that wouldn't make things worse.

Steele continued. "I've reported your infraction to Captain Ferguson and Commander Yamamoto. They will deal with you." He leaned back in his chair. "I knew from the moment Eshel arrived on this ship that you couldn't be trusted. You don't deserve your post." He turned away. "Dismissed."

Catherine left, fury building in her as she walked back to her quarters. Her contactor chirped again. Yamamoto.

Fuck.

Catherine slowly made her way up to the seventh deck, her stiff and tired body resenting having to climb the stairs, her mind too preoccupied to acknowledge those she passed. She arrived at the XO's office, pausing before she walked in. She took a couple of deep breaths. Finally, she entered and saluted.

"At ease, Catherine. Sit down." Once she eased herself into the chair, he began. "Your commanding officer has spoken with the Captain and myself about his concerns that you've potentially violated the Alliance's rule about discussing genetics with Eshel."

"Yes," she replied, doing her best to keep the anger out of her voice. "The Commander just told me as much."

"Did you discuss genetics with Eshel?"

She sighed. "Last night, when I was on pain meds, I told Eshel the details of my mother's cancer diagnosis and failed treatment, which... which were genetic in nature."

Yamamoto asked her to elaborate. Her mind still foggy, she did her best to recount what she'd said during her medicated and fatigued state.

"Did you talk about other topics pertaining to genetics?"

"No."

"What did Eshel say in response to what happened with your mother?"

She thought for a moment. "Nothing at all. He just listened."

It struck her how cold that seemed. She realized that Eshel hadn't encouraged her to speak about her mother out of friendship, but did so merely out of scientific curiosity. And now, when under fire, he'd broken his promise to her, divulging what she'd told him in order to protect himself and his own interests.

"What else was discussed?" Yamamoto asked.

She shrugged. "The fight. Normal stuff. Perhaps a little about my frustration with Commander Steele."

Yamamoto sat in his chair, studying her. "What brought up the topic of your mother?"

She could tell that Yamamoto was looking for something. "I don't recall…" Then it came to her. "Wait. I do recall. He lost a parent too. His father."

"Ah," Yamamoto said, nodding in acknowledgement. "That may explain his sensitivity about that topic."

Catherine held her breath, afraid that Yamamoto would probe her for more information about Eshel's father. Her instinct was not to repeat it; but given the situation, she may have to. And why shouldn't she? Fortunately, Yamamoto didn't pursue it.

"And Eshel didn't talk of his own knowledge of genetics, or attempt to pry information out of you?"

"No. He hardly talked at all."

"And that is your sworn word, to your mentor and XO?"

"Yes, Sir, that is my sworn word." She paused. "Will I be discharged for this?"

Yamamoto shook his head. "I see no violation in talking about what happened with your mother, even in such scientific detail. I do, however, highly recommend you avoid the topic of genetics with Eshel in the future, if you want to avoid further scrutiny."

She sighed in relief. "I will, Sir. Thank you." She paused. "Why did Commander Steele seem so convinced I would be sent home?"

Yamamoto was silent for a moment as he stroked his chin. "Catherine, I must ask you a question that is personal in nature. However, there is good reason for my prying." He paused. "Are you romantically involved with Eshel?"

Catherine felt her face grow hot. "Are you serious?"

"When have you known me to be silly, Catherine?"

"Sorry, Sir," Catherine replied quickly. "No. We are *not* involved in any way. But with all due respect, even if we were, why is that anyone's business? He doesn't report to me."

"Given the situation, such an involvement would create suspicion among many, especially Commander Steele, who must oversee the protection of highly sensitive information."

Catherine could tell from Yamamoto's tone that his statement wasn't merely a justification for suspicion. It was a warning. She nodded in acknowledgment. "We're only friends, Sir. He shares very little about himself. And he shows no interest at all in... in any of that. I don't understand why anyone would think otherwise."

"Apparently, it is known that Eshel was in your quarters last night, and that he didn't return to his own quarters until a very early hour this morning. Reports from several crewmembers were such that suggested a romantic connection between you."

She shook her head again, recalling Middleton's complaining that everyone knows everyone else's business on a starship. She wondered if perhaps he wasn't quite so whiny after all. "I see Tom and Snow nearly every day and no one says anything about that. Eshel was in my quarters last night, but only because he insisted on making sure I recovered from my concussion, as the doctor asked him to."

Yamamoto smiled. "And how often does Eshel tear himself away from his studies to spend time with others, much less spend twelve hours tending to someone's bedside?"

She let out an exasperated sigh. What could she say? Yamamoto and these other people didn't understand. They didn't know Eshel, that he'd ratted her out to cover his own ass, that he'd come close to getting her discharged.

"I will let the Captain and Commander Steele know we have spoken. However," he added, "I strongly urge you to be cautious, Catherine."

"Yes, Sir."

Catherine left Yamamoto's office and walked back to her quarters, praying she would hear no more chirps for a while. She lay on her bed, exhaustion suddenly overcoming her. Her head hurt. While relieved that her talk with Eshel hadn't landed her in any real hot water, she couldn't shake the uneasy feeling that Eshel had betrayed her. People said the Korvali weren't trustworthy, that they were calculating. Perhaps, in her friendship with Eshel, she'd forgotten that, had let down her guard too much.

Just as she rose to get a pain pill, her door sounded. She scowled. Eshel. She voiced him in.

"Why did you do it?" she demanded.

Eshel didn't reply. She could tell he knew exactly what she referred to.

"Don't pull that goddamn silent treatment with me, Eshel," she hissed at him. "I know you ratted me out! Tell me why you call yourself my friend and ask me to tell you about my mother's illness, promise to say nothing to Steele or to anyone else, and then go right out and tell him."

"It was necessary."

"Necessary? I could have been discharged!"

"You weren't."

Catherine shook her head at Eshel's annoyingly cold response. She felt her head throb again, and sat down on her bed, her weariness catching up with her again.

"You look unwell," Eshel said. "Do you require your pain medication?" He began walking to her table, where the small dispenser sat.

"Don't."

He ignored the medication and faced her. "My betraying you was necessary to convince Commander Steele that he can trust me, that I do not keep secrets from him regarding you."

"You couldn't have told me that before I shared what happened with my mother?" she shot back, feeling herself get angrier. "If I'd known you required Steele's good opinion, I would've kept my mouth shut instead of telling you something so personal. That wasn't just a lesson in cancer genetics, Eshel! She was my mother, and she's dead, and she's a big reason I do what I do … and you revealed that information to the one person who seems determined to hold me back! I'm losing years of progress on this ship and you just made it worse!" She stopped herself, realizing she was nearly shouting.

"Be calm, Catherine…"

"Don't tell me to be calm!"

Eshel was silent, and remained so for some time, as if waiting for her to settle down on her own. Finally, he spoke. "You do not understand. If you and I are to achieve our aims, one of us must gain Commander Steele's trust. He does not like you, so it is I he must trust."

Catherine looked up at Eshel. "What aims?"

"For you, to conduct your research as you should be."

"And for you?"

He hesitated. "I have projects as well."

"Genetics projects?"

"No. That is too risky for me." He paused. "Catherine, it was important that I betray you in this way. The information about your mother was enough to convince the Commander that I show no loyalty to you, but not enough to result in your discharge."

A realization came over her. "You did this on purpose."

"Yes."

"And what happens next time you need to do that? The consequences may be more severe."

"They won't."

"How do you know?" she said.

"There will be no next time."

"Why should I believe you?"

He stared at her with his pale sea eyes. "It is like your poker game. The stakes are much higher for me, should you choose to betray me."

He was right. He had far more to lose than she did. Catherine felt her anger dissipate. "I'm on your side, Eshel. And I have nothing to betray you with, anyway."

"No. But you will." He walked over to her table, retrieving one tablet from her pill dispenser and handing it to her. He gave her his canteen to drink from.

After a bit of hesitation, she placed the pill on her tongue and drank Eshel's chilly water. "I'm sorry if I was…" She handed his canteen back to him, trying to think of the right word.

"Temperamental," he offered.

She chuckled, shaking her head, too tired to rebut.

"You are tired," he said. "Rest. I am off duty on Saturday and will swim. Since you cannot yet train, perhaps you will go with me to the coastline."

Catherine replied that she would. After Eshel left, she lay down and slept.

Saturday, Eshel and Catherine boarded the train and sat down among chattering Derovians, many of whom looked at them in curiosity. Catherine's black eye had diminished quite a bit, her bandages had been removed, and her other injuries were only mild aches. But even with her almost-normal appearance, she and Eshel stood out.

Eshel conducted his usual scan, probably looking for Sunai. There were none to be found. Tom and Snow had told her at second meal that week about Eshel's attack at the water station. Catherine shook her head, chastising herself for having let him out of her sight. They told her he'd managed to defend himself by going for the eyeshades and escaping back into the crowd. She wondered why Eshel hadn't told her about the attack. Then, with some chagrin, she realized why; the evening the Sunai accosted him was the same evening she'd been called up by Steele and had accused Eshel of selling her out.

"You should've told me the other night about being attacked again," she said.

"There were more important things to discuss," Eshel replied.

She considered reminding him to stay close to them when off the ship, but she refrained. Eshel already knew he shouldn't wander off alone, but struggled with it nonetheless. The Korvali were a clanspeople, but Eshel said they tended to go about their business alone or in pairs, free to splinter off in their own direction at will, without a word. "Did you talk with Yamamoto or the Captain? It seems strange that it was the same guys who attacked us before."

"Yes. They will speak with the Sunai, but there is little to be done if the attacks do not occur on Suna."

When they reached their stop, Catherine stood up but Eshel remained seated, stating that he'd found a "far superior" location than their usual tourist's beach. Although 20 minutes farther away, Eshel's new find was a small cove that required them to descend a long, narrow staircase from the top of one of the steep cliffs. There were a couple of portions where the stairs turned into a ladder, forcing them to climb down with their belongings on their backs, with nothing but a long fall to the cove below. The cove had few people and far more trees, providing the privacy Eshel craved and the shade both their fair skins required.

Eshel had barely set his things down before he began stripping down to his swim trunks. He walked gracefully into the ocean, dove into the water, and swam away. Catherine read. Later, she took out a picnic she'd packed for herself, making sure to bring enough in case Eshel decided to eat.

When Eshel returned hours later, he saw the spread and said, "I have berrywine."

She smiled. "Perfect."

He retrieved the canister from his pack and opened it. Catherine put out her cup, and Eshel poured some for her, then some for himself.

"Cheers." She raised her cup and clinked it with Eshel's. She took a sip; it was delicious. "Is this red tefuna? Where did you get this?"

"My sources."

She laughed. "Your sources? You're beginning to sound like Tom."

He smiled at that.

"Esh, does it feel strange to be so far away from your people?"

Eshel looked at her with his sea gaze. She'd begun to know his different gazes, and knew he would answer her question. "Yes. But I still have half of one year to complete my adjustment."

Catherine was unsure of what he meant. Then she recalled telling him it could take a year for him to grow used to living among them. And he'd been with them six months already.

"What about your family, your… clan?" she asked. "Do you miss them?"

"Miss them?"

"Long for them… or wish you were near them."

He thought for a moment. "That is not the correct word. It is more that a Korvali must face the difficulty of a broken… bond… when separated from those he has joined with. It can be difficult. Who do you… miss?"

Not expecting the question, Catherine thought about it. "My dad, mostly. And my mom… but she's been gone a long time. And you?"

"My mother and father. It is different with my father," he added, his expression getting colder. "And Elan."

"Elan? Who's Elan?"

"He is a geneticist. And my friend."

"He's Shereb?"

"Yes. He is the eldest son of the malkaris."

Catherine stared at him, not sure what to say.

"You appear surprised," Eshel said.

"I thought you hated them."

Eshel took a sip from his cup. "Elan is not like the others. The second eldest, Ivar, is the worst of them. The two youngest, Moeb and Vashar… they are less vile, but growing to be more like Ivar." He paused. "Elan would chastise me for not continuing my work, for not having convinced the Alliance. He would not understand the world outside Korvalis. But my father would understand. My father desired that I have opportunity to explore offworld."

"That's why he helped you with your epigenetic design."

"Yes. But he taught me much more than that. He taught me what he knew about the other worlds. He wanted me to learn the language of the outsiders, and when we worked alone in the lab, he would speak in English, in primary Sunai, in Derovian… to ensure I learned." He paused. "If he lived, he would be pleased."

"Does your mother, or Elan, know you're alive?"

"Elan must know. If my mother does not, she will discover the truth. She is a member of our assembly, and she is… clever."

Catherine nodded, turning to look out at the sea. The water had darkened to a deeper blue under the fading sun.

"I will swim," Eshel said after a while, standing up. "I believe you are safe here," he added, glancing around him. The cove's other visitors had left.

"It's going to get dark soon," she warned.

"Do not worry." He departed, entered the sea once more, and disappeared.

Catherine took a quick dip in the sea and then lay on her mat, relaxed from the red tefuna and the quiet surrounds. *Eshel had found the perfect spot,* she thought to herself. She imagined what it would be like to live in such a place, to do what a small number of human ex-pats had done and set up residence on Derovia. She smiled, imagining how she would stick out among Derovia's citizens, how they would call her "Miss Catherine" and "Dr. Finnegan" instead of just "Catherine," and ask her lots of questions about Earth. She imagined a life free of research, of genetics, of Commander Steele and technology and glutted cities, with days spent reading in quiet coves….

She jumped when something cold touched her leg. It was a water droplet. A dark figure stood silhouetted above her. She gasped and within a moment she was on her feet.

It was Eshel. She let out a sigh of relief.

"If you must sleep," Eshel said, "I will stay here. It is not safe otherwise."

She looked around. The Katara sun had set, their small cove illuminated only by the reflected light from Suna's rings. No one else was around.

"I don't remember falling sleep." She hugged her arms around her, chilled from the breeze, the long leaves of their tree swaying above them.

"You are cold," Eshel said.

Catherine nodded, goose bumps forming on her skin. Eshel's skin showed no such bumps, as the water droplets seemed to bead up and evaporate from his pale body.

She knew it was time for them to return to the ship, so she reached for her pack. "I need to change," she said. She twirled her hand, indicating for Eshel to turn around. As she stripped off her clammy suit and dropped it on her mat, she dug through her bag for her dry clothing. Just as she pulled out a t-shirt, she felt something touch her hair. A quiver ran through her. She turned around quickly, shielding her nudity with her shirt.

Eshel stood close to her, far closer than he ever had.

CHAPTER 12

Catherine stood motionless as Eshel stared at her with an unfamiliar gaze. Eshel often watched things or people, observing some minor behavior or thing he found unusual. But despite her familiarity with Eshel, and despite the length of their acquaintance, his proximity to her unnerved her. Instinctively, she backed away.

"I do not mean to startle you," he said. "I should have asked first."

"Asked what?"

"To touch you."

Catherine looked at him in surprise, attempting to discover some sign of his intent, but finding none. "You want to touch me?"

"Yes."

"Why?"

Eshel peered at her with his unblinking eyes. "I do not know." Catherine still didn't move, seeing only the strange expression on Eshel's face. He stepped toward her, and she felt her heart begin to pound. Eshel reached up and touched her hair, taking a handful at its roots and gently following it to its ends. He did the same with another handful of her hair, seeming almost fascinated by its existence, staring at it as he let it run between his webbed fingers.

After letting go of her hair, he placed both hands on her shoulders, their heat warming her. She'd noticed the warmth of his hands during training—it was the only skin-to-skin contact they'd ever had—but she assumed the warmth was due mostly to heat generated from their workout. But even in their stillness, the heat of his hands was intense.

He moved his hands to her chest, and she wondered if he could feel her heart, which still pounded. She realized her t-shirt no longer covered her. It lay in a heap at her feet, leaving her completely nude. She didn't know if she'd dropped it, or if Eshel had removed it.

Eshel touched her breasts, almost as if afraid to harm them. Then his hands travelled down to her stomach, and further downward. Just as Catherine began to wonder if she should back away, he withdrew his hands and took two steps back. He looked down, his expression clouded.

"Never speak of this," he said, his voice almost a whisper.

She nodded, agreeing to his request. She bent down to retrieve her shirt.

But just before she picked it up, Eshel stopped her, encircling her arm with his hand. She stood up and faced him, her heart thumping once again. He looked down at her, taking two steps toward her, until he was next to her.

Eshel placed his hand between her legs. She froze, until he began exploring the area with his fingers. He touched softly, again almost as if afraid of harming her, his smooth nail-less fingers stroking her. She felt lightheaded suddenly and almost backed away, but realized the tree they'd sat under was right behind her. Eshel saw her expression and stopped. She put her hand on his and guided it back to her, leaning against the tree for support. He continued until she was so overwhelmed by the sensation that she grabbed Eshel's other arm to steady herself.

After, she sank down onto her mat as she tried to recapture her breath. Eshel kneeled down next to her. She glanced up at him, and his faced showed raised eyebrows and another expression she'd never seen before. Not knowing what to say, she sat there, the lightheaded-ness passing but her sense of nervousness returning.

Before she could make any move, Eshel took her hand and placed it on his chest, palm down. She looked back up at him, and when he saw she didn't protest, he slowly moved her hand across his chest, down to his abdominal area, then back up. He let go of her hand.

She rearranged herself closer to him so she could comfortably touch him, not daring to look up at his face. She felt her hand grow a little shaky, but kept stroking him. Despite its smooth, hairless appearance, his skin wasn't soft. It felt tougher, thicker, than human skin. Not knowing if she were doing it right, she kept going. She finally peeked up at him, wondering if he'd still be gazing at her. But to her surprise, his eyes were closed, his face expressionless. For the first time, Catherine took a quick glance around, hoping they were still alone. They seemed to be. She felt a bit foolish; but with no sign of resistance from Eshel, she continued stroking him.

Suddenly, Eshel shoved her hand away, a slight scowl on his face. It was the most unpleasant expression she'd ever seen on him, worse than even his disgust at the small sip he'd once taken of Snow's coffee. His eyes opened.

"I hurt you," she said, feeling guilty for whatever offense she'd given.

"No," he said, looking down.

She looked down as well, but saw nothing. Then, she looked more closely—there, near the top of his swim shorts, was a small bit of brownish liquid. Catherine stared at it, wanting to touch it. But before she could, Eshel stood up.

"I will be gone only a brief time." And he headed toward the water, light reflecting off of Suna's rings and shining on his pale skin. He dove in, disappeared, and then reappeared, standing up where the water reached his torso. Catherine watched Eshel bend over and fumble with something; he'd removed his shorts to rinse them in the sea. He disappeared under the water again, only to reemerge closer to the shore, swim shorts on.

"You are cold again," he said when he returned.

She nodded, realizing she'd developed goose bumps. She turned away to retrieve her clothing, and began dressing herself.

"Catherine."

She looked up, Eshel's tone making her apprehensive.

"Never speak of this. With anyone."

It was the first time Eshel had ever repeated himself. "I won't," she reassured him. "But people will suspect, Eshel. They already do. Commander Yamamoto asked if we were… involved. I told him we weren't," she added quickly. As awkward as the conversation was, it was a welcome relief from their previous interaction.

Eshel's eyes narrowed. "Why did you lie?"

"It wasn't a lie," she replied, baffled.

"Wasn't it?"

She looked aside, considering what he'd said. *Was it?*

Eshel continued. "I refer not to our… involvement, but to our… sexual activity. That can never be shared."

"What can't? The specifics, or the fact that we did… what we did… at all?"

"Neither."

"Why?"

"You said you would not speak of it," he said, his tone colder.

"And I won't. But if I'm going to lie, to contradict everyone's assumptions, it would help if I understood why you want me to be so secretive." The moment she said it, she knew why. He was secretive about everything, but especially about anything having to do with sex. No one knew about the mating habits of the Korvali, about their procreative ability, about their reproductive morphology. Eshel never discussed it, and he would remain silent if Tom or someone else asked a question of that nature or made a drunken, inappropriate quip. And Eshel's response only confirmed the conclusion she came to.

"It is difficult to explain, Catherine. It is… how I am."

Before she could say more, she heard a chirp. She looked around before realizing it was her contactor, and reached for her bag. There was another chirp; Eshel reached into his bag.

"They're worried about you," Catherine said.

Eshel checked his contactor. He spoke Yamamoto's name and waited until he heard the XO's voice. "Yes, Commander. I am fine. Catherine is with me. We are returning to the ship now."

Yamamoto had contacted her as well. *We're on our way back, Sir,* she replied.

Catherine and Eshel packed up their things. They walked toward the narrow stairway and climbed it, carefully ascending the ladder portions of the climb, with only Suna's ring shine to illuminate their journey. Once reaching the top, they waited for the train to arrive and take them back to *Cornelia*.

Catherine arrived at Yamamoto's office and sat down for their scheduled meeting, feeling more nervous than usual. A lot had happened recently. Yamamoto knew all that transpired on the ship, and it was difficult to predict how he'd react to any of it.

"You look uncomfortable today," Yamamoto said.

She shrugged. "I guess I'm nervous about what you thought of the fight… and its encore."

"You fought well. To result in a draw is a good outcome for anyone in the CCFs, particularly a female."

"Thank you, Sir." She paused, sensing that a "however" was to follow.

"However…" he began.

Her heart began to pound.

"You should have won the match. If you choose to take the rematch, you will need to train with me to prepare."

Catherine sat there for several moments. *Won the match?* "I… I wasn't planning on taking the rematch."

"You aren't required to. But if you do, you will need to prepare properly next time. You had inadequate endurance from inadequate training. With proper training, you will overtake your opponent in the final round." Yamamoto's contactor chirped. He glanced at it. "And you were too passive, Catherine. As we've discussed before, you should not wait for your opponent to make a move; he will see your hesitation and exploit it."

"Yes, Sir," she replied, nodding. "What about what happened afterward?"

He sat back in his chair. "I imagine you will guard yourself more carefully if you choose to compete again."

Despite his criticisms, Catherine felt relief that Yamamoto didn't chastise her for her retaliation against the Calyyt. However, she still felt nervous. And she knew exactly why.

"You were right," she blurted out. "About Eshel."

Yamamoto gave a slight nod.

"I didn't see it before. But we are now... involved. I... I don't know what it is. I don't know anything." She paused, overwhelmed with self-consciousness. "We don't talk about genetics," she added. "I just... I don't know what to say. Eshel is very private. But I wanted you to know." She finally stopped talking and looked down, too embarrassed to say more.

"You seem happy, when you're with him. So does he."

Catherine looked up again. "You approve of this?"

"I understand it." He paused. "As I told you before, be cautious. You will be scrutinized even more now."

She nodded. "Yes, Sir."

"You are aware that Eshel was attacked again."

Catherine nodded, grateful for the change in topic. "It was pretty crowded in the arena courtyard. When I turned around, he was gone. He does that sometimes... just disappears."

"I want you to concentrate more on Sunai defense techniques with Eshel," he said. "This has happened twice, and may occur again. Since he is comfortable with you now, I encourage you to teach him full contact methods, including the more aggressive ones." He stood up, indicating that their time was up.

She did the same. "Yes, Sir. Thank you." She bowed and left.

Yamamoto glanced at his schedule, then at the time. The Captain had called a meeting. Once he saw it was in the bridge ready room, he knew the meeting would involve the rest of the command team. He had a very good idea of what was on the agenda and he prepared himself for more than the usual amount of questions.

He arrived at the ready room a few minutes early and nodded at Ov'Raa, who was the only attendee present. Commanders Marks and O'Leary came in a minute later, Marks talking in his usual loud voice about the CCFs. Commander Steele followed the two men and sat down, acknowledging no one. Finally, Ferguson walked in with Dr. Vargas.

Ferguson looked down at her electronic pad before setting it down and glancing around the table to see that everyone had arrived. "Let's have the updates," she said.

Marks informed them of a couple of minor changes to their itinerary. O'Leary discussed the engine efficiency estimates and their maintenance work on the FTL drive. Ov'Raa briefed them on who was up for review or promotion. Vargas gave a longer synopsis of sick bay activity, the shortage of scanners, and the intermittent warming of the cold chamber. And Steele offered a brief summary of the scientific activities on the ship, most of which was focused on molecular biology and astrophysics.

Ferguson nodded, pulling her electronic pad closer to her. Yamamoto saw this as a promising sign that she would adjourn the meeting. Instead, she paused and sat back in her chair. A wary look crossed her face.

"There are a couple of issues with our newest crewmember," she said. "Eshel has had two confrontations with Sunai gumiia in Ronia. In both cases, they attacked him; the first time he was protected by the geneticist, who happens to be one of Suko's students," she nodded at Yamamoto, "and the second time he managed to defend himself. I've spoken to Gronoi Sansuai about this, but even he has limited reach on Derovia. I've warned Eshel more than once about staying close to the others." She glanced over at Ov'Raa.

Ov'Raa took his cue. "Yes, Captain, the gumiia can be trouble-some at times, especially with otherworld males."

"Yes," Steele said. "But why did they target Eshel on two occasions, when there have been no other attacks on our human crew?"

Before Ov'Raa could respond, Marks jumped in. "It's because he's Korvali. The Sunai don't like them because of what happened when they breached the Korvali border years ago. Wait until we go to Suna," he added with a smirk.

Ov'Raa shook his head. "I do not believe the attacks are related to Eshel's race. The gumiia often display such behavior, and Eshel is a novelty for them."

"What if they're more serious than that?" Yamamoto said. "Eshel said Catherine Finnegan saw two Korvali on the train, staring at her. This was just hours before he was attacked."

Ferguson shook her head. "The Korvali are allowed on Derovia. And they stare at everyone. It's probably a coincidence. Just be aware, all of you. He's enough trouble as it is without creating more friction with the Sunai over him. Which leads me to my final agenda item," she said, looking over at Yamamoto. "Eshel and the geneticist, Lieutenant Finnegan, have developed some sort of romantic relationship."

After a moment of silence, they looked around at one another, their expressions a mix of surprise, amusement, and disapproval.

"Wait… what are we talking about here, Captain?" Commander Marks asked, his expression half displeasure, half puerile fascination. "Are they in love or are they just nailing each other?" His smile got larger. Once O'Leary began to laugh, Marks joined in.

Ferguson gave him a stern look. "Stow it, Commander."

Yamamoto was somewhat grateful for Marks's gaffe, since it would take some of the heat off of him.

Ferguson looked at him. "What is this?"

"I don't know the intimate details of their connection," Yamamoto replied. "Nor is it our business. I am of the understanding that it's a recent development and that their relationship is tentative."

"I don't know what shocks me more," Vargas chimed in. "That she'd put up with him, or that he's capable of any kind of relationship." More laughter ensued.

"This is not a situation that exists for our amusement!" Steele said, his voice raised. The laughter ceased. "Eshel is a refugee from a planet that has very strict rules about protecting their genetic expertise, and he is intimately involved with a human geneticist! This must stop, and it must stop immediately! Lieutenant Finnegan has already broken my strict code regarding talking about genetics with Eshel, which I still believe wasn't taken nearly as seriously as it ought to have been. Do you believe they will obey the order now, considering that they've already broken it, that they've been having a secret affair? Do you have any idea how dangerous such knowledge is?"

"Their relationship isn't secret, James," Yamamoto said. "Catherine told me about it herself. And she made it clear they do not discuss genetics."

"And you believe her," Steele said, "despite her already having breached the rules."

"She didn't breach the rules," Yamamoto argued. "Her mother died of cancer despite numerous attempts at genetic treatment, and she told Eshel the details. That breaks no rule."

"You're missing the point," Steele said angrily. "I instructed her to not discuss genetics of any kind. It's a slippery slope to more involved conversations. I have found Lieutenant Finnegan to be untrustworthy, and if sensitive information gets into her hands, it could be disseminated in ways that will cause significant problems with the Korvali. You're in charge of beds and heads—it's your job to put an end to this relationship."

"You do *not* tell me what my job is," Yamamoto said, his voice raised. "I will handle this the way I believe it should be handled. And if you question my authority again, Commander, you will find yourself on your way back to Headquarters by the end of the week."

The room quieted. Steele's gaunt, angry face paled. "You don't have the authority to make that decision."

"I will get it."

Steele glanced at Ferguson, who returned his look in silence. Steele gave Yamamoto a withering look, but said nothing.

Ferguson spoke, aiming her comment at Yamamoto. "You have to admit that, given our relationship with the Korvali and the Alliance's rule, those two getting involved does create complications."

"It may," Yamamoto said. "But it is my opinion, and I believe Niri would agree," he glanced at Ov'Raa, "that we have no grounds to prevent their involvement. She is not his commanding officer. We have no edicts preventing relations with otherworlders, with the exception of human males involving themselves with Sunai females, and that rule only came about to mollify the Sunai. All we can do is make it very clear that breach of our rules about the discussion of genetics will have severe consequences."

The others nodded, while Steele didn't respond.

"We have no formal rules about interspecies relationships, other than no hitting on Sunai females?" Marks asked in disbelief. He was about to continue, but instead glanced at Ov'Raa and kept quiet.

"It is acceptable for Space Corps enlistees to involve themselves with members of other species, and even to inter-mate," Ov'Raa replied somewhat defensively. He flushed a brief shade of blue. "Such interactions are good for interplanetary relations."

"Times have changed." Vargas smiled and stroked his mustache. "They weren't so liberal back in my day."

O'Leary nodded. "I think the Alliance had a lot to do with that. They're very... idealistic." He too glanced at Ov'Raa, and said nothing else.

Yamamoto understood O'Leary's hesitance to speak more on the subject. He knew what they were all thinking, save Ov'Raa. Despite being permitted to involve oneself with otherworlders, it was still considered strange, perhaps even deviant, to do so.

"Alright," Ferguson said, eager to wrap up the discussion. "Keep your eye on those two," she said to Yamamoto. "If you find out there's been a breach of classified information, or anything that puts Eshel or any of us in jeopardy, I will separate them and send the geneticist home," she added, glancing at Steele. "Dismissed."

July 7th

Hi Dad,

How are you? Did you get up to the high country to fish last week? The wildflowers must be gorgeous by now. Did you see any gentians? Those were Mom's favorite.

Yes, the rumors are true about Eshel and me. It's been going on for a few months now. I was going to tell you but didn't want to speak too soon. You don't need to be concerned. He's really not all that different from us, you know, and it would be nice if you soldiers would back off about the Korvali for once. He's been nothing but good to me. I think you'd find him interesting if you actually met him. And if you don't trust me, trust Tom, who treats Eshel like he's one of us now.

Work is about the same. Steele still hates me, perhaps more than ever. I went to Anka's lab to see if she wanted to get a drink, and she was talking with Steele. He was a different man with her—he spoke more softly, and was almost smiling. Anyway, I still do my own research in my quarters when I can. Did you ever read those papers I sent? I feel strongly that we can do so much more with epigenetics, Dad. If Eshel can alter his epigenome to survive weeks without water or food, we can find a way to regulate the expression of the necessary genes to prevent tumor formation. If only I could get even a little data to work with, I could run a few simulations and answer some questions…

I'm thinking of paying a visit to the Peloni Institute during our mid-mission leave. I sometimes wonder if I should've taken that job offer instead of going on this mission. But who knew Commander Edelstein would become ill? I heard from him recently; he did his best to encourage me, but it sounds like his health is still a challenge for him. It made me sad. Anyway, I'm hoping I can get a few answers at Peloni that can sustain me for the remainder of the mission.

Tom's doing well. He's still spending time with lots of different women, although several have taken issue with his non-committal ways. I don't know what these women expect; everyone knows Tom isn't the type to settle down. His birthday passed recently and we all went out to celebrate. We had to explain to Eshel the significance of a birthday, something the Korvali don't observe. Eshel and I got him a great gift, a small biological agent dispenser (with no agent in it, of course), custom made based on a Korvali design. Tom was thrilled and he mounted the tiny thing up on his bulkhead.

I miss you, Dad. Talk to you soon.

Love,
C

CHAPTER 13

Once off duty, Eshel left Weapons. He nodded at the two soldiers he passed on the way to the stairwell, having learned from Tom that doing so might make him seem less unfriendly. He still didn't understand the purpose of such a gesture, since he didn't know the men and the men didn't seem inclined to speak. But he'd learned that Tom was often correct about such things, whether or not they made sense. He contacted Catherine.

"Hey, Esh," said Catherine's voice on his contactor.

"Are you in your quarters?" Eshel asked. "I want to propose to you."

There was a pause. "You mean you want to propose something *to* me," she corrected.

"That is different?"

"Yes."

When Eshel arrived at Catherine's quarters, he used the code Catherine had given him and entered. She was unclothed and looking in a drawer, her uniform in a heap on the deck.

"You are just returning from duty?" he asked her, glancing at the time. It was almost 2100.

"Long day." She dressed herself and hung up her uniform.

He walked to her and put his hand on the back of her head. She followed suit, placing her hand on the back of his head, as they touched their cheeks together. The first time Eshel had tried the leshe with Catherine, she appeared startled, much like the first time he touched her hair. But she'd grown accustomed to using the Korvali greeting with him—in private, of course.

He sat down. "Because of the ship's change in itinerary, I can get off duty for two consecutive days. We can take leave."

The time had come for the crew to finish its business on Derovia and head to nearby Suna. However, Yamamoto sent an announcement to the crew that day, one that would change their schedule:

Attention all crewpersons:

The Captain received an urgent message from the Sunai government this morning; Gronoio Vahara, one of Suna's top military leaders, has passed away unexpectedly.

We will postpone business with the Sunai to allow them to honor the death of their leader and to rearrange their military leadership to compensate for the loss.

The Captain paid her condolences on behalf of the crew.

We will convene with the Sunai AFTER we return from the mid-mission visit to Earth. As such, our encampment on Derovia will continue for at least several more weeks.

Commander Yamamoto
Executive Officer

Catherine joined Eshel at the table, her face showing surprise. "Take leave?"

"I want to go to Mellon," Eshel continued. "Coran and Dorel have urged me to visit that part of Derovia. There is a place that will make a good setting for something I want us to do, if you are willing."

Catherine's eyes narrowed. "Do what?"

"It is a Korvali rite. I would rather reveal more about the rite, and why I am asking you to participate in it, when we arrive there."

Catherine hesitated, waiting to see if he would offer more information. When he didn't, she agreed and said no more about it.

Friday evening, Eshel and Catherine took a transport to Mellon. Coran and Dorel saw them off, each offering advice about their native land, excited that Eshel would choose to visit the more remote continent of Mellon rather than popular Ovlon. Eshel gave the two brothers credit for correctly identifying what sort of place he sought. At that time of year, Mellon's weather wasn't too cold for Catherine to swim without discomfort if she wore a protective suit. The location he'd chosen was quite isolated and had limited services, two things he looked forward to. The truth was, Eshel secretly found Derovian hospitality tiresome, and preferred taking care of himself.

Eshel chose accommodations not far from the town of Viorov. Their wooden hut was small, quiet, and primitive by modern standards, and even better than he'd hoped for. When Catherine remarked how much she liked it, he felt some relief, not because he'd feared she wouldn't like it, but because he hadn't considered whether such simple accommodations would suit her.

The hut contained a small cooler, which he had stocked with Derovian food for their first meal there. Eshel saved his appetite for then, knowing Catherine would want to eat dinner and would prefer him to do so with her. He took out the food—a spread that included ornon, four other kinds of sea flesh, a variety of sea vegetables, bowls of the bright pink berries they'd eaten on Tom's birthday, and a large canister of rallnofia. Eshel poured two glasses and they ate together.

Afterward, tired from a long week of studying late, Eshel lay down on the large, comfortable bed. When he awoke, he saw daylight. He looked over; Catherine lay asleep next to him, the white sheet covering her nudity. He reached for his contactor: 0715. He'd slept the entire night, in his clothing, on top of the bedding.

Catherine stirred. Her eyes opened. "You're finally awake," she said, smiling.

"I do not recall falling asleep," he admitted.

She leaned over to him and put her lips on his cheek. "Good morning."

Startled, Eshel backed away slightly, then recalled that he'd seen Shanti do the same thing to Zander at poker and Tom meet lips with a woman he was "seeing." He'd seen it in some of the videos from the ship's library, and among the Derovians, and had heard the Sunai observed the custom as well. "That is a kiss," he said.

"Yes, that is a kiss."

"What is its purpose?"

"It's like your leshe," she said. "It's an expression of affection. It can be for family, or it can be more romantic, or arousing, depending on how it's done. There's no kissing on Korvalis?"

"No."

"None at all?" she asked, appearing possibly disappointed.

"None at all."

"Does it bother you, the kiss?"

Eshel hesitated. "It is more that I am unfamiliar with it, and do not know if I could ever become accustomed to it." He watched her expression, wondering if his admission would bother her. But instead, she smiled.

"There's one way to find out, Esh. Are you ready?"

Eshel braced himself. "Yes."

Catherine leaned over and gave him a brief peck on his mouth, then backed away, waiting for his reaction. "Well?"

"It is... strange. But not arousing."

"It's not arousing when it's done that way." She got up, peered into the cooler, and pulled out a canister of pink juice. "Want some?"

He nodded as she poured two cups of the juice and gave one to him. She propped up her pillows and sat back against them. "So. Are you going to tell me anything about this rite you mentioned?"

"You are curious."

"Yes. I am curious."

Eshel recognized Catherine's tone. It was the one she used with him when he stated something that, to her, was obvious.

"I will explain tonight. If you agree, we will perform the rite tomorrow."

Catherine sighed. "Are you going to swim?"

"Yes. Are you coming?"

She shook her head. "Too cold. I'll wait until later."

Eshel got up from bed and changed into his swim trunks. He'd just begun to grow used to being unclothed in front of Catherine, something he hadn't believed possible. He knew, from seeing Tom and the other men swimming nude on Tom's birthday, and from the videos, how he differed from the human males. But they didn't know. He knew they were curious. They were always curious. But he would reveal himself to none of them.

He'd tried, undoubtedly with only moderate success, to explain to Catherine that while nudity is common among his people, especially when swimming, exposing one's genitalia to outsiders was… it was not done. He was relieved that she didn't question him further. He didn't even reveal himself to Catherine until… until it became necessary. She didn't appear all that surprised upon finally seeing him fully nude; she had seemed almost… relieved. She was perhaps even impressed by his internal testicles, calling it "advantageous."

"Advantageous?"

"You lack a major area of vulnerability," she'd said. "If you ever get attacked by a human male, always go for the testicles. But it only works on humans…"

Once he finished dressing, Eshel told Catherine when he would return from his swim, something she'd begun asking him to do. Eshel knew she worried when he went out alone, even into the water, and so he indulged her by offering her a time frame in which he would always return.

Eshel left their hut and looked around. He saw no one in any direction, which only confirmed that he'd made a wise choice in selecting their accommodations. The sky was overcast and the temperature cooler than in Ronia. The gray-blue ocean produced large waves that crashed noisily upon the shore, and for a mere moment a vision of his homeworld passed through his mind. He entered the cool, refreshing water, dove beneath the waves, and began to swim. He could now swim 30 strokes before needing a breath, close to where he was before leaving Korvalis. At his first swim on the beach in Ronia, after not having swum in so long, he was greatly bothered by his need to come up for air after a mere 12 strokes.

He swam out for some time until, glancing at his contactor, he saw he needed to turn around. He could no longer see land and looked up at the sky in order to reorient himself. As he swam back, he went under again to look for more sea creatures, finally coming upon a school of fish that divided in order to continue their path past him. They were bright yellow and much smaller than the fish he was used to on his homeworld. He also saw, from a short distance, a much larger bluish creature, one that looked far more imposing than Eshel's research said it was.

Once back, Eshel and Catherine explored the shore caves Coran and Dorel had told him about and spent time examining sea creatures in the tide pools. Later on, Catherine put on a wetsuit and they went swimming. He gave her more lessons in proper swim form, as her form was, at best, inefficient. However, at one point during the lesson, Catherine stopped him.

"Eshel, you're being rude."

"Rude?"

"Yes. You keep telling me what I'm doing wrong." She treaded water, slightly breathless from her efforts. "You sound like my father."

"I don't understand. If I am to teach you, I must correct you when you are wrong."

She sighed. "Yes. But it's *how* you do it. It's better to say, 'instead of this, try this,' like I do when I train you. Be encouraging."

"Are you learning?"

"Yes."

"Then why does it matter how I teach you?"

"Because one way will anger me, and the other won't."

Eshel still didn't understand Catherine's protest. But he couldn't argue with her reasoning, and did his best to avoid teaching her in what was, in his opinion, the most efficient way for her to learn.

Later that day, they went into town. Viorov had a small enclave of Derovian artists, so at Catherine's suggestion they went to look at the art. There were many large, flat shells that had been painted with plant-based dyes in visually interesting ways. Catherine searched for something to hang in her remaining bulkhead space. There were several pieces she admired, but she couldn't decide, and eventually gave up looking.

Afterward, they ate dinner at a café that contained numerous plants and several tall trees within it, as if they'd built the café around the vegetation. One could look up and see the evening sky through the foliage. During their meal, a Derovian male played a stringed instrument that Catherine called a "guitar."

"I love the guitar," she told Eshel. "I've always wanted to learn how to play."

"Why don't you?"

"No one to teach me."

"Snow cannot?"

She shook her head. "Snow plays bass guitar. It's totally different. And I don't have a guitar."

"Can you not purchase one?"

"I might, when we get to Suna. The Sunai will have many to choose from."

"But will you be able to decide on one?" he asked, hoping she would understand his meaning.

Catherine smiled in surprise. "Did you just make a joke at my expense?"

"I believe it is a valid question," he replied, pleased that his attempt at humor had succeeded.

Catherine giggled. "Tom would've loved that one. He still gives me a hard time about how long it takes me to decide what to eat."

Eshel said nothing.

"What?" she asked him, seeing his expression.

"I have noticed that, as well."

"Unlike you guys, who eat the same thing all the time, I like variety and it's hard to choose!" she cried, laughing.

"That is fair," he replied, still quite pleased with himself.

Later, they went back to the beach and sat down on the sand, up against the cool rocks. Recognizing that Catherine was getting cold, Eshel brought himself close to her to warm her. He brought his cheek to hers, and began to stroke her hair.

Afterward, Catherine rested against Eshel. But after a while, she disengaged herself from him, her skin glistening with perspiration. "I'm hot," she said, resuming her place sitting next to him.

"And very soon you will be cold again."

She laughed. She reached for her dress, shook out the rosy sand, and put it back on.

Eshel sat down on the porch and poured two glasses of rallnofia. Catherine wrapped herself in a blanket and joined him.

"The rite," Eshel began. "It is called the sher mishtar, or the rite of secrets."

He explained that the sher mishtar was one of many Korvali rites. Its purpose was to enter into a bond of secrecy, never to be broken, with a trusted person. To break secrecy would cause a permanent rift in the relationship, a rift that could never be repaired, and could result in being ousted from one's clan, or worse. He explained that the sher mishtar was, in some ways, a lifetime obligation. "I brought you here because I want to perform the sher mishtar with you."

Catherine shifted in her seat. "Eshel, this sounds... serious. What if... what happens when the mission is over? We may not be able to remain... tied."

"No. With the sher mishtar, you are not bound to the person; you are bound to the secrets you share. I have performed the rite with others." She nodded in understanding. "If you choose to do the rite, you cannot share what I tell you with anyone. You also cannot tell anyone that we performed the rite."

"Is there something I must do, other than listen?"

"No."

"Am I allowed to talk, or ask questions?"

"Yes."

She tucked her hair behind her ear, pondering what Eshel had proposed. She sat for some time, her expression unreadable. "Okay," she finally said.

"We will go tomorrow."

Sunday morning, Eshel got up early and swam, returning sooner than usual. They gathered their things, left their hut, and began walking along the coastline. Heavy clouds blocked the mild sun, muting the blue of the calm sea and darkening the inland hills. Eshel walked briskly as Catherine made an effort to keep up with him. Once having walked for the better part of an hour, Eshel found a location he liked.

It was a small tide pool deep enough to cover them up to their middles, surrounded by rocks and sheltered from the break. Although there were hidden tide pools, Eshel chose one that was exposed, where he could see all that was around him. He set down their things on the smooth pink rocks, and turned toward Catherine, who stood at the edge of the pool, as if afraid to go in the water.

"You appear nervous," Eshel said to her.

"I am."

"There is nothing to fear. The sher mishtar is always performed in water. And in complete privacy." She stepped into the tide pool and faced him. "Catherine, what is said until we emerge from the sea today must never be repeated to anyone. You must promise."

"I promise."

"You know it is against Korvali Doctrine to leave Korvalis without permission, to live among outsiders. The Korvali have not retaliated against what I have done, but they will not tolerate it. Just as Ashan offered secret information before he vanished, I must do the same."

Catherine's expression turned to one of horror. "You're leaving us?"

"No. I am only preparing for the occasion in which I am killed. I am, as Tom would say, a target."

Catherine's face paled as she looked away.

"It is a precaution, Catherine. I am protected by your people, and I have developed my own methods of defense. But if I am killed, it is important that I contribute to the betterment of the Korvali, just as Ashan did." He paused. "When the Sunai attacked me the second time, after the Calyyt-Calloq Fights, my form of defense was not as I told others."

Catherine looked at Eshel again. "You didn't go for the eyeshades?"

"I did, but it was not enough to create opportunity for escape."

She raised her eyebrows. "What did you do?"

"I deployed a weapon."

"What kind of weapon?"

"A biological weapon."

"Did it harm them?" she asked.

"No. It temporarily subdued them."

"Which allowed you to get away."

"Yes," Eshel said. "The weapon worked even more effectively than I had envisioned."

"How did you design it? Did you use the same casing as the one we made for Tom?"

"It is better that you don't know how the weapon works." Catherine scowled a little as she looked away again. "You are offended."

"Not that you won't tell me. That you lied, about the attack."

"It was a necessary deception, Catherine. Using such a weapon is illegal. It is also… it is my technology and I am not prepared to share it at this time. When I developed it, I didn't yet know I could trust you."

She nodded in understanding. "They'll anticipate that maneuver next time."

"I have other options," he replied.

Catherine, appearing satisfied with Eshel's responses, said no more.

Eshel went on. "The first secret is my developing weapons to defend myself. The second… is the reason I left Korvalis. I was carefully watched on Korvalis because I am the son of my father." He paused for a moment. "My father, who you know as Othniel, was not Shereb by birth. He gained inclusion to our clan through joining with my mother. My father, along with others, openly opposed many of the kunsheld's policies, especially those pertaining to going offworld and interacting with outsiders. Despite his remarkable scientific achievements and proper behavior while offworld, Elisan revoked one of my father's requests to leave Korvalis and attend a scientific summit on Suna. When my father made his next request, Elisan rejected that one as well, as he did any future requests. Soon after, funding for my father's research began to diminish.

"One evening, my father, along with several other scientists, was invited to dine with the malkaris and her family at Fallal Hall. We had dined with them before, although such invitations had become very infrequent." Eshel looked down. "Later that night, my father was found dead in the gardens at Fallal Hall, killed by a bioweapon." Eshel remained still for several moments. "Despite my father's significant achievements, the kunsheld, the kunsheld's aides, and the malkaris's family did not attend the sher memeshar... the rite of death. Only Elan attended. Elan had learned from my father, had respected him."

Eshel briefly scanned the area around them before continuing. "My father's murder was the fourth in a series of similar murders. The dead... they each offered opposing opinions to Elisan's policies, and each had become Shereb through joining with a Shereb mate. I began a detailed investigation of my father's murder in secret. Only my mother knew. Weeks into my investigation, a messenger, an Osecal merchant who sold us some of our research equipment, visited me at my lab and told me of an opportunity to leave Korvalis. They would leave in three days."

Catherine nodded. "So you had to abandon the investigation to take the opportunity to escape."

"It was what my father would have wanted." He paused again. "The loss of a family member is... difficult. You know this. But murder... on Korvalis it is extremely rare. It is not our way."

Eshel noticed that the bumps had resurfaced on Catherine's skin, so he walked to her and warmed her. "Finally," Eshel said after releasing her, "the last secret. You know I am sanctioned from sharing my scientific knowledge. However, my father is dead, other scientists are dead, and if something happens to me, knowledge will vanish. Such knowledge is irreplaceable and cannot be lost. To do so would dishonor my father, my mother, and my people." He stared at her. "You are the proper candidate to receive some of this knowledge. I will not provide you with answers; but I will, and believe it my duty to, offer you tools with which to find the answers yourself."

Catherine's face lit up. However, the look of pleasure on her face faded, to be replaced by a more troubled expression.

"What bothers you?" he asked her.

"I have a secret too, and I'm not sure you'll like it."

Eshel's eyebrows went up. "You want to divulge a secret to me?"

"Is that allowed?"

"Yes."

Catherine hesitated for several moments. "I've been studying your epigenome," she finally said. She told him about the files she'd discovered, about the work she'd done.

Eshel showed no reaction. "Commander Steele does not know?"

"I don't think so. He hasn't said anything, which he would have because he'd assume I'd lied to him. But I'm surprised he didn't have someone scan my network, and—"

"Did you remove the files from your network and the VirNet?"

Catherine, taken aback by Eshel's uncharacteristic interruption, said, "Of course."

"Where are they stored?"

"On one of my portables."

"Is it well-hidden?"

"Yes." She looked a little ashamed. "Are you angry?"

"No. Continue studying them, without getting caught. Commander Steele must never see those files, Catherine."

She nodded. "I know."

Eshel paused, his expression softening. "Have you examined the files carefully?"

She smiled a little. "I have."

"What have you discovered?"

"Lots of alteration to the methylation patterns. And some of the proteins have been altered."

"And what conclusions have you come to?"

"Well… that I couldn't come to any useful conclusions without viewing a new sample of your epigenome."

"Why do you need a new sample?"

Catherine was reminded of her dissertation defense, where her committee asked her questions not because they didn't know the answers, but to ensure she knew them. "I need to compare the two samples."

"Why compare them?"

Catherine wrapped her arms around herself, as if chilled again.

"Well… to see which of the changes were engineered and which were a result of having taken the drug to initiate the stasis…"

Eshel's expression changed. It was, perhaps, the most pleased he'd ever looked. His intense gaze remained on Catherine, and then he finally spoke. "Perhaps it is fortunate that I am forbidden to work as a geneticist."

"Why is that?"

"I would want you to work with me, but you could not."

"Why not?"

"I am very… rude, as you say, when I work. You do not like that, and I would not like angering you."

Catherine grinned and, unable to contain herself, gave Eshel a big kiss on the lips.

Eshel, while surprised at first, smiled his small smile. "The rite is complete. We have revealed our secrets. Now, we seal it." He looked at her closely. "Are you ready?"

Catherine's grin subsided and she appeared serious again. She nodded.

Eshel reached out and put his hand behind her head and brought his cheek to hers. Then, he put his hand on her shoulder and gently pressed down. Catherine, confused, finally realized he wanted her to submerge herself in the sea. She sank down, leaning back and letting the cool water envelop her. Before she surfaced, she saw that Eshel had done the same.

They emerged from the tide pool, dressed themselves, and walked back to their hut in silence.

Later, Catherine read while Eshel slept. He was a quiet sleeper, his breathing slow and barely perceptible. However, later on, a noise awakened Catherine. She looked around her, realizing the noise had come from Eshel. He sat up, his breathing erratic.

"What's wrong?" she asked.

"It is nothing."

Back at her quarters, Catherine unpacked her bag. A short while later, Eshel arrived. He carried a flat package.

"What's that?"

"It is for you."

She couldn't help but smile, taking the package and removing its linen wrapping. She gasped. It was a shell painting, an abstract design, mottled in color with vivid blues and greens. It was one of the pieces she'd admired in Viorov.

"Eshel," she said in wonder, staring at it. "It's beautiful. You remembered that I liked this one."

He nodded. "Since you could not decide, I hope you don't mind my choosing for you."

"That makes it even more special. I love it."

He motioned to her photo display. "It is the correct size for the empty space."

She looked over at the bare spot she'd hoped to fill with something special from their long mission. Eshel helped her mount the painting; the mounting process took a while when done correctly, as the object had to be secure enough to handle any turbulence or other challenges of space travel. As Eshel had predicted, the piece fit perfectly.

When finished, Eshel reached into his pocket, retrieved two portable drives, and handed them to her. "This one," he said, pointing with his long finger to the black one, "is one you must never look at unless something happens to me."

"And the blue one?"

"The blue one has something you need."

After Eshel left to go study, Catherine tucked the black portable away and examined the contents of the blue one. It contained only one multi-terabyte file, created just minutes before Eshel arrived at her quarters.

It was an image. It was a new copy of Eshel's genetic material.

CHAPTER 14

Eshel walked through the hallway, glancing out one of the windows. Once again, its view offered little more than the quiet darkness of space. They'd wrapped up their business with the Derovians and left the Katara system. With their revised itinerary, *Cornelia* journeyed through a region that was far from anywhere habitable and thus out of satellite range. Such conditions left the crew with little to do but work, eat, and sleep. At first, Eshel had difficulty with the confinement after months of freedom to roam and swim on Derovia. But he soon settled into his space routine.

And that day had brought interesting news: a double chirp on his contactor announced the exact dates of their upcoming mid-mission 30-day leave, which everyone called the "Thirty."

Once at Catherine's quarters, Eshel sat down at the table and took a drink from his canteen. He felt considerable anticipation at the prospect of seeing Earth, the place he'd been most curious about since his father told him about the other worlds. Eshel had only two wishes: to swim as much as possible, preferably in water that was cooler than Derovia's, and to visit one of the "Big Three" genetics institutes.

Catherine joined him at the table. "Aren't you worried about getting in trouble for visiting one of the Big Three? You know the brass will find out."

"The rule is that I cannot talk about what I know. They didn't say I could not learn what you know."

"They may not agree with your reasoning, Esh," Catherine warned.

"They do not have to. I studied your legal system. Without more specific sanctions, they have no valid argument."

Catherine smiled at Eshel's resourcefulness. "Earth will be different from what you're used to, and different from Derovia."

Eshel nodded. Despite his curiosity about Earth, he was intimidated to go to the most populous and advanced of the Alliance planets. The Sunai viewed themselves as more technologically advanced, but Eshel knew better. He didn't fear the humans—he'd grown somewhat familiar with their ways—but he was hesitant to face the vast number of people, the noise, and the other assaults on his senses. The videos he'd seen were overwhelming enough. But Catherine would mitigate much of that. She would know what he needed.

"We'll visit my hometown in Colorado," she said. "You'll like the mountains."

He nodded. "I want to see the mountain flowers, like those in your images.

She shook her head. "Wrong time of year. We'll be there in December, when the mountains are covered in snow."

Snow. Another thing Eshel had never experienced. Korvalis only had snow in the uninhabited polar regions. Catherine voiced a series of commands to her computer, and a video appeared on her viewer and began to play. The video showed a human female, possibly an adolescent, descending a white slope on what Eshel had learned were skis. "That is skiing."

She grinned. "That is *me* skiing. When I was twelve."

Eshel looked more closely, realizing the child did look like Catherine.

She called out a few more commands and a series of images appeared on her viewer: steep peaks blanketed in white, a dwelling made of tree trunks, and Catherine in a forest.

"What is wrong with those trees?" he asked.

"What do you mean?"

"Some of them lack foliage. Do they absorb energy through their branches?"

"No. They're dormant. When it gets cold, they lose their foliage and regrow it when it warms up again in springtime." She paused, her expression changing. "Esh... I want you to meet my father."

"Of course."

She smiled. "And I can arrange for a tour of the Peloni Institute. Given that we only have thirty days, I recommended we restrict our remaining travels to only one other continent besides North America. Since it will be wintertime, southern Europe might be good. The water will be nice and cool for you. Good wine, too."

They talked more about the Thirty before it was time for Eshel to leave. Just as he rose from his seat, his contactor chirped.

"Tom?" Catherine asked.

"No. The XO."

Eshel left and headed in the direction of Yamamoto's office. And thirty minutes later, he returned.

"There is a problem," Eshel said.

She put her reading pad down and sat up.

"If I am to obtain my commission, I must spend my Thirty at boot camp."

At Tom's quarters, Catherine filled her cup with beer, sat down at the table, and listened with detachment while the others discussed their Thirty plans. Tom hadn't committed yet; he preferred to play things by ear, to see where opportunity and inspiration would take him. Snow would go to California to visit friends before meeting up with Tom. Zander and Middleton would visit family for the holidays before they went dog sledding in Alaska. Shanti would split her time between India and Indonesia. Catherine said nothing, hoping they'd get carried away and forget to ask her. She hadn't realized how much she looked forward to her plans with Eshel, until they were taken away from her.

"And," Tom said, grinning and taking a swig of beer, "guess who gets to spend his Thirty in West Virginia… at boot camp?"

Everyone looked up from their cards at Eshel, offering reactions of surprise and sympathy for him.

"How'd you work that out?" Snow asked Eshel. "We're only off thirty days and boot camp is six weeks."

"I am told I may miss the first five days," Eshel said. "Boot camp will finish seven days after the *Cornelia* leaves Earth, after which I will obtain a transport back to the ship."

"Ferguson had to pull some strings to arrange that," Tom said, tossing in his bet. "Marks said she even tried to get them to let you skip that last week, but they weren't having it."

Snow folded his cards. "Damned right. Be glad you'll miss those five days, you lucky bastard." He shook his head. "The most miserable six weeks of my life, man."

"It's not that bad," Zander said, placing his bet. "The first week is the worst. Maybe they'll go a little easier on you since you're not human…"

"Just remember to use the proper addresses, Esh," Tom said. "No matter what. And for Christ's sake, don't correct your commanding officers. Don't even argue with them. I know that'll be tough for you."

The others, who all knew Eshel's character by now, laughed at this. But Middleton, who sat with a scowl on his face, offered no laughter.

He slapped down his cards. "He gets five days less than the rest of us? Man, that's such bullshit."

"Ah, quit your whining, Middleton," Tom said, rummaging through his chips to gather up another bet. "There's nothing important during those first few days that he hasn't already learned here."

Middleton, who'd become increasingly immune to Tom's rebukes, pressed on. "That's not the point, man. They're doing it because he's Korvali. They give special favors to the alien enlistees. Did you know that?" He posed the question to Eshel, one of the rare times he spoke directly to him. "Did you know they treat aliens special?"

"I do not recall having received special treatment," Eshel replied, unruffled.

"What do you call gettin' five days shaved off your boot camp time?" Middleton said. "What do you call gettin' transferred from Maintenance to Weapons after, what, a few weeks?"

Eshel stared at Middleton. "I call them things that will never replace my work as a scientist, or those I left on Korvalis."

Middleton shrugged, fiddling with his chips, looking at no one. "If those things are so important to you, maybe you should go back to where you came from."

"Mackey!" Shanti said.

Middleton continued playing with his chips, his scowl deepening. The room quieted.

"I believe it would be better if you returned to your homeworld," Eshel replied.

Middleton pointed at his own chest. "This ship comes from *my* homeworld. I belong here."

Eshel put down his cards. "This ship visits three other inhabited planets, each populated by an alien people. What is the purpose of your joining this organization, since it is clear that you dislike aliens?"

"What?" Middleton cried. "I never said I disliked aliens! It's your goddamn people who hate outsiders, not us! I don't dislike aliens at all, man. All I said is they get special favors, and that's bullshit."

People began shifting in their seats. Catherine and a few others glanced at Tom, wondering when he was going to put a stop to the argument.

Eshel continued to stare Middleton down. "You disliked me before I received this 'special treatment.' You called me 'Mutant' when you thought I couldn't hear you. It is true that the Korvali do not trust outsiders. But we acknowledge that about ourselves. You are no different from us, but you pretend you are."

Catherine felt a smile reach her lips. She looked back at Middleton, knowing he could have no worthwhile response.

Middleton's face reddened as he stood up and gestured at Eshel with tattooed arms. "You think you're better than everyone. You don't belong here! You haven't earned the privilege to be here!"

Eshel stood up as well. "And how have you earned that privilege? With your whining and stupidity?"

Middleton lunged at Eshel, bumping the table hard enough that beer sloshed from their cups and their chips slid to the deck. Tom yelled out as he pushed to intervene, and Catherine leapt up from her chair. The table blocked her from stopping Middleton's attack. But before they could do anything, Eshel made one swift move and pressed his webbed hand on Middleton's throat, pinning him against the bulkhead. Middleton swung his arms at Eshel, thrashing them about until completely red-faced. But Eshel's long arm rendered Middleton's efforts fruitless. Once the pressure of Eshel's hand pushed against his larynx, Middleton stopped flailing. A look of fear crossed his face.

"Eshel," Tom warned.

Eshel ignored him. "Never come near me again," he said, his chilly stare boring into Middleton. He released his hand.

"I'll kill you, motherfucker," Middleton warned in a raspy voice. But his threat sounded empty, like that of an infuriated child who didn't get his way.

Tom stepped closer to Middleton and pointed to the door. "Out. And don't come back until you're done being an asshole."

"Why should I leave?" Middleton complained. "I was here first. Everything was fine until he came around."

"Get the fuck out," Tom said, giving Middleton a shove. Middleton shook Tom off and stomped out the door. "How much did he drink?" Tom asked no one in particular.

"No more than usual," Zander said.

"What's his problem?" Shanti asked, her dark face a mixture of shock and concern.

Zander shrugged, looking sheepish over his friend's outburst. "He gets like that sometimes."

Tom looked at Eshel, who stood silent. "Nice move, Esh."

Eshel gave no reply.

Only a few weeks out from arriving at Earth, they stopped at Station 3 to refuel. As such, they had satellite again and were able to holo-chat with those on Earth and watch interactive entertainment, and would retain this luxury for the majority of the journey back.

When Catherine sat down to second meal with Tom and Snow, she was somewhat surprised that Eshel hadn't shown up yet, as he usually arrived before she did. Then she recalled that he'd been preparing for an exam, and that Eshel often skipped second meal on exam days. However, Eshel didn't show up the following day either. Nor the day after that. She hadn't heard from him, either. He disappeared from time to time when he had much to do, but would always surface eventually. And while it took longer than usual, he did finally make an appearance, paying her a visit after their duty shifts were over.

Eshel walked into her quarters, his eyes clouded. She knew something was on his mind, something likely related to what had kept him so busy. Catherine approached one of her chairs, ready to sit down and listen to whatever Eshel had to say.

But Eshel didn't sit.

"What's wrong?"

He looked at her with his sea eyes. "We can no longer have a relationship, Catherine."

Catherine felt a chill go through her. "What do you mean?"

"Our... involvement. It must end."

She maintained eye contact with him, waiting for clarification. But none came. "Are you angry at me?"

"No."

"Did the brass come down on you?"

"No."

She put her hands up in puzzlement. "Then why?"

Eshel hesitated. "There is no explanation that I can offer."

"There is no explanation you can offer, or none you want to offer?" Eshel said nothing, his gaze appearing almost as if he looked right through her. It was the first time Eshel hadn't responded to a direct question from her in longer than she could remember. "No matter what question I ask, I'm not going to get a satisfactory answer, am I?"

"No."

She could find no words. Her mind was blank. She only knew that trying to coax information out of Eshel would further alienate him. Finally, she took a deep breath. "Okay." She paused. "Can we remain friends, at least?"

"Of course."

Softening slightly, she nodded.

Eshel broke eye contact with her. Then he turned and left.

For several days, Catherine felt a strange, hollow feeling as she worked and slept. She didn't talk to anyone about what had happened; she didn't know what she would say. The others wouldn't understand what it meant for her and Eshel to be separated because they didn't understand what it meant for them to be together. That's how Eshel had wanted it. She hoped he'd offer her some sort of explanation for his decision. But it never came. So, now, they would be friends. That's what they'd been before, and that's what they'd be again.

Catherine worked late that day, with Steel's permission. At 2130 she realized she'd missed third meal, so she grabbed a quick snack, swung by her quarters to pick up her water bottle, and headed back to her office to do some more work. She veered from her usual route to drop by the Free Box; she had an extra beach mat from Derovia that she no longer needed. After Derovia, the Free Box contained far more items, which made her smile, recalling Eshel's fascination with it.

On her way back, she passed a couple of crewpersons and gave them a brief nod. She glanced at the time again, but as she looked up, she saw Eshel coming her way. He didn't see her yet. Once he got closer to her, he made eye contact. She smiled, slowing her pace a bit.

Eshel nodded at her briefly, looked away, and kept walking.

Catherine stopped and turned around. She watched as Eshel's long strides took him further and further away from her, until he was out of sight.

A couple of days later, Catherine left her lab at nearly 2230, surprised Steele had allowed her to remain so late again. As she walked to the mess to get a snack, she rather improbably saw Eshel in the hallway again, heading toward her. Catherine watched him as he approached; Eshel made brief eye contact with her, and, as before, gave a brief nod as he continued walking.

She halted. "Eshel."

Eshel ceased his walk, turning to face her, his expression cold as he waited for her to speak. Catherine walked over to him and slapped his face as hard as she could.

Eshel's webbed hand immediately went to his cheek as he attempted to balance himself from her unexpected assault. The expression on his face was one she'd never seen before.

"You don't want to be involved with me, that's fine," Catherine said, her voice shaking. "But don't you ever, *ever* nod at me again."

She turned and walked away, the stinging feeling dissipating from her hand.

Holed up in her office, the sound of a knock made Catherine jump.

"Where've you been?" Tom asked her, looking at her with some concern.

"Working."

"You coming to eat today?"

"No."

"Come eat. It's just me and Snow. You gotta eat sometime, right?"

She sighed. "Okay. I'll be there shortly."

When she arrived at the mess, she got herself a plate of spaghetti and joined Tom and Snow. She took a few bites; it tasted as dull as it looked.

"Why so mopey?" Tom chided her.

"I'm not mopey. I'm tired."

"Leave her alone, dumbass," Snow said.

Tom ignored him. "Oh, come on, C! You can't be that upset over Esh. I'm telling you, it's always weird when things don't work out, especially on a starship where everyone knows about it, but that passes."

She nodded, fiddling with her noodles. "I know, Tom. I'm fine."

"Could've fooled me," Tom said. "Look, even Jimmy will tell you that getting involved with otherworlders is a bad idea. Eshel's a weird guy. I don't think he's capable of… what we're capable of."

"Who asked you, man?" Snow said, giving Tom a look. "It's not your business."

"I know it's not my business," Tom said to Snow, stabbing a meatball with his fork. He looked back at Catherine. "But I know Eshel. He had a few cups of rallnofia one night and admitted he'd never do that kind of thing, that getting it on with otherworlders is one of the strongest taboos the Korvali have. And it was pretty plain that he found the entire idea disgusting." He glanced at Snow. "It's just the way he is and she should know that. It's not like they were serious, anyway. See, I told you he wasn't gay," he added, shoveling the forkful of spaghetti and meatball into his mouth.

Catherine's throat tightened and a sick feeling came over. She lowered her head, concentrating on her food, hoping the tears that welled up in her eyes would quickly go away. She ate some more spaghetti and forced herself to chew it slowly, but could barely swallow it. After slowly gathering another forkful, she managed to recover herself from what Tom had told them.

When she finally looked up, Tom had turned his attention to some women who walked by, but Snow's eyes were on her. Catherine forced a smile, hoping it would convince them she wasn't shocked at the news. Too many thoughts running through her mind, she glanced at her contactor. "I have to go. Boss is expecting me." She stood up, walked her tray to the dish area, and slammed it down, her barely-eaten spaghetti spilling off the plate. Back at the lab, she ignored Holloway and Varan and shut her office door behind her.

It all made sense. Eshel unexpectedly touching her on the beach, and looking as surprised as she was that he'd done so. The hesitation that immediately followed, like he was wrestling with some part of himself that believed it was wrong. His repeated requests for secrecy, with his remarkably vague explanation for why secrecy was so important to him. Eshel had broken a fundamental edict of his own culture, had done something that not only went against his people, but against his personal beliefs. He was ashamed of what they'd done. Ashamed of her.

After her duty shift ended, she went back to her quarters and pulled up the epigenetic data she had, including the file Eshel had given her. She sat there staring at it, but made no move to begin working again. Then, something caught her eye.

The painting. The one Eshel had given her after their trip to Mellon.

She turned away, refocusing on her data, on the progress she'd made. But she could still see the piece of art hovering in her peripheral vision.

Finally, she stood up and walked over to the painting, loosening the mountings and removing it from the bulkhead. She left her quarters and walked fore to the nearest stairwell, climbed up one deck, and proceeded aft again. Once she arrived at the Free Box, she carefully set the piece down amongst the plentiful clothing, computer parts, and other junk. And with that, she turned and walked away.

November 20th

Hi Dad,

I finally got your messages now that we're back in range. We just left Station 3, and it looks like we land on December 6th. Unless re-entry takes longer than they said it would, or something unexpected happens, I should be at the house by dinnertime.

I'm really looking forward to seeing you, Dad. I miss you a lot.

But, I have bad news. You won't like it. I'm not returning to the mission when the Thirty is up. I'll explain more when I get there.

Have a nice Thanksgiving and say hello to Aunt Cora.

C

CHAPTER 15

Captain Ferguson's voice rang out over the Com at 0900: in one hour, *Cornelia* would land at the Space Corps shipyards in Virginia.

Tradition dictated that all officers met in the starboard bar before leaving the ship. They would each receive one shot—typically whiskey but not always—and drink to a good Thirty. But instead of attending, Catherine grabbed her bag and headed to the exit, where Yamamoto stood with two MAs. He hadn't yet announced that they could debark, but she'd requested to leave early. He'd approved her request so that she could elude the press, who would hound her about Eshel. But she got the feeling that wasn't the entire reason.

Yamamoto signaled for the two MAs to step aside. "I will see you back here in thirty, Lieutenant," he said. "That's an order."

Catherine nodded. "Yes, Sir."

When she'd told Yamamoto her decision, she knew her career with the Corps would, in many ways, come to an end. Yamamoto had refused to honor her decision until Day 30 of her leave. She'd told him she was resolute, but he'd insisted. She could have ignored his order to return; once resigned from the mission, she was no longer under his command. And if it were anyone but Yamamoto, she would have.

Catherine left the hangar, crossed the tarmac, and exited the Space Corps shipyard. Being first off the ship, her scans went quickly, and they let her through once she tested negative for biological agents and illegal substances. Back in the civilian world, she walked to the train station that would take her to the airport in Washington D.C. Once seated on the train, she heard a chirp.

Her contactor. She'd forgotten to remove it. The message was from Tom, probably giving her a hard time for not showing up to the starboard bar. She ignored the message and put the contactor away. She heard another noise and sighed in annoyance. It was her phone this time—Tom again. She ignored it. But after sitting for a few minutes, she tucked the detachable earpiece into her ear and listened to her voice mail.

"Finnegan," Tom's loud voice began. "Hey. Listen… I just went to your quarters and all your photos are gone. What the hell is going on? I can only assume the worst, and… and I damned well refuse to." He paused. "Look… I'm sorry if I was an asshole, alright? Snow told me… well, we can talk about that later. I'm sorry, alright? Please call me back."

She sent him a message. *It's okay, Tom. Let's talk in a couple of weeks. Have a great time.*

At the airport, she waited in line for scanning, looking around at the other people. Couples with young children, elderly people, professionals in suits. All human. It felt like she'd been gone longer than 18 months.

Aboard the next flight to Denver, she sipped her beer and felt the weight of the ship, her duties, and the cloud of negative associations lift. The further the aircraft travelled west, the quieter it all seemed, as if she'd left the clamor of the city for the stillness of the country. She peered out the window for the entire flight, happy to have something to look at besides dark space. There were densely populated cities, rectangles of agricultural land blanketed in white snow, forests, and lakes, all glowing in the waning light of a winter's day. She felt better than she had in a long time. Even the prospect of her father's disapproval couldn't dent her mood.

Forty-five minutes later, when Catherine exited the plane, she found herself surrounded by people, all talking to her at once. She heard familiar clicking sounds as they took photos of her, and ahead she spotted reporters with their serpent-like self-tracking cameras.

"Lieutenant Finnegan, did Eshel alter his own DNA to survive his escape from Korvalis?"

"Dr. Finnegan, is it true that you defended Eshel from numerous attacks on Derovia…"

"Ms. Finnegan, did Eshel end your relationship because you wanted children with him?"

Catherine, unprepared for the onslaught, focused her attention one thing: the sign with the picture of a train. She walked toward it, keeping her eyes on it as they followed her through the airport. Finally, she flashed her ID and entered the waiting area for the train, leaving the madding crowd behind her.

Once on the train, the sight of the Rocky Mountains to the west put her at ease. She watched Denver go by, all the urban sprawl of six million people. She saw the rise of downtown's exceptionally tall buildings in the distance, reminding her of the place she'd lived before she accepted the mission and put most of her things in storage. The winterscape was peaceful and quiet, with its dormant trees and the ground covered in snow, leftover from a recent storm. The approaching mountains glowed under a fading sky.

When the train arrived at the Evergreen Station, she grabbed her bag and stepped out into the cold, dry mountain air. Her phone registered -7 Celsius, 13% humidity. She smiled at the conditions; she was home. She walked; despite lugging her heavy bag, it felt great to walk, to be outside on firm ground, near real trees, in her hometown on the planet Earth. She smelled the pine and spruce trees and heard the dry snow crunch beneath her shoes. She walked past the restaurants and bars and shops, a couple of which she didn't recognize. Five kilometers later, she arrived at a modest log home, where she input the security code and walked into the warm house.

"Dad?" she called out, dropping her bag in the foyer and removing her shoes and coat. She felt herself grow nervous suddenly, bracing herself for a lecture.

A tall man with a lean physique and neatly cut gray hair emerged from around the corner, a Space Corps t-shirt on and a freshly opened beer in his hand. His cold look only made her more nervous. But as she went to hug him, a tiny smile reached his face. Catherine was surprised at how relieved she was to see him. As they released one another, she took a deep breath.

"How'd you get here?" he inquired, looking around as if searching for her means of transportation.

"Walked."

He nodded in approval. Jimmy Finnegan was an outdoorsman and preferred walking to transports.

"The press found me at the airport," she said. "They'll probably come here, too."

"So give 'em a little something. Then they'll leave you alone."

Catherine took a good look around the cabin that had been in their family for so many generations. It smelled like home, a faint woody smell that pleased her.

"You hungry?"

She nodded. "Starving."

They walked to the Little Bear, a historic local tavern and a favorite of Jimmy's. They ordered two cheeseburgers and a couple of beers. Finally, Catherine broached the topic that weighed on her.

"Dad, don't you want to lecture me about leaving the mission?"

Jimmy finished chewing his food, set his burger down, and wiped his hands on his napkin. He took a sip of his beer. "Yamamoto's a smart guy, C. Take his advice and don't make any decisions until it's necessary."

"I don't want to go back. I know it will get me in trouble, but I don't care anymore—"

"Tom told me what happened."

"What happened?"

"With the Korvali."

She sighed. *Damn Tom's big mouth.*

"He called me today. He's worried about you. Said you wouldn't talk to him." Catherine remained silent. "Why are you mad at Tom?"

"He pissed me off. He… he doesn't understand. He thinks Eshel and I were just having fun, goofing off… like he does."

"You weren't?"

"No."

Jimmy looked at her. She could tell he wanted to give her a stern lecture, but chose not to. "Ship romances are risky, C. Triple that when it's with an otherworlder. I've been on enough missions to know."

"I know. It was stupid." She paused, setting her burger down. "It's not just that. It's all of it, Dad. I feel useless on that ship. And bored. I'm doing stupid work no decent journal would publish and I'm making no progress."

"Then do something more interesting, something people do care about."

"Such as?"

"Cross training."

"You sound like Tom."

He shrugged. "You committed to a three-year mission. You've completed half that. Instead of throwing it all away, why not make the most of the remaining time you have? Learn something new, seek a new challenge. We always let the whitecoats try out the life of a soldier and they get a lot out of it… the few that try."

She picked up her burger. "That's not what I want."

"Not what you want? Refusing to complete a mission won't earn you a dishonorable discharge, but your career with the Corps will be over. Is that what you want?"

Catherine said nothing. There was no point in arguing when neither of them would give up their position.

Jimmy changed the subject. "So who's Tom with these days? Anyone special?"

"Nah. You know Tom."

"How about a little skiing tomorrow?"

"I'd love to, but my gear's in storage, down in Denver," she said. "Day after?"

"Done."

After finishing their beers, they walked back home. Sure enough, a small band of warmly dressed, camera-laden people waited at the bottom of her father's driveway. So Catherine did as her father suggested and stood with them for a few minutes, answering the questions she could answer and not answering those she couldn't. When they asked her about her relationship with Eshel, she said they were friends. It wasn't a true statement—they'd been more than friends, and now they were less—but it was the only reply she could manage. Once back inside, Catherine fell asleep on the thick leather couch, a blanket wrapped around her.

The next day, first thing, Catherine took the train back to Denver and visited her storage unit. She intended only to grab her backcountry ski gear and cold weather clothing, but found herself distracted by all her other belongings. She looked through her clothing; it had a vaguely dusty smell from being cooped up so long. She peeked at some of the framed photos and art she'd had on the wall at her old place. In another container, she found storage drives with files of books, music, and research. It was strange to see it all packed up, without a home of its own. Suddenly, she recalled talking with Eshel about visiting her hometown, how she'd imagined showing him all this and introducing him to her father. A tear escaped her eye; but she pushed it, and its accompanying thoughts, aside.

After a few days of backcountry skiing with her dad, Catherine began looking for a job and a place to live. She considered contacting the Peloni Institute. But she decided to hold off until she figured out how she would explain why she'd abandoned the mission.

On Day 10, her phone rang. It was an unfamiliar number. She thought about ignoring it, but something made her remove the earpiece and put it in her ear.

"Hey. It's Snow."

She smiled. "Hey! Where are you?"

"Some island. It's hot here and I'm already sunburned. How are you?"

"Not bad. Been skiing mostly…"

"Listen, a few of us are making a New Year's run to London. Care to join us? We leave the day after Christmas, back by the second or third."

Catherine's smile faded. "Snow, I'm not returning to duty."

"Yeah, Tom told me. Don't worry about that. Just come have fun. It may be the last we see you for a long time."

She hadn't yet decided what to do with the remainder of her leave. London was never high on her list, but the prospect of going with Tom and Snow sounded fun. She agreed to it.

On the 26th, Catherine packed a few things for her trip. Four hours later she was on the Tube in London, heading to the hotel. Screens blared annoying ads for New Years costumes and cheap whiskey. Once reaching her stop, she emerged from underground into the chilly, damp London air. The entire city seemed to twinkle red, green, and gold with holiday lights, as bundled up people shopped and toured historic London.

She walked a relatively short distance to the hotel, a beautiful building restored in the old style, with a stone façade and paned windows. She entered the cozy lobby filled with the din of conversation, its guests lounging on couches or in chairs by the warm fireplace. A large Christmas tree stood in one corner, its bright silver decorations gleaming and its lights sparkling. As she looked around for the front desk, she heard her name.

Snow waved at her from a big chair. She spotted Tom, wearing a thick wool sweater like Snow's, and two men she didn't recognize. Tom strode toward her and gave her a tight hug. She was surprised at how happy she was to see them.

"You aren't pissed at me anymore, are you?" Tom said.

She shook her head.

Snow gave her a big hug and they introduced her to Rory and Miguel, childhood friends who now served in the Navy. They ordered her a dark beer, and for some time they sat near the fire and drank their beers.

"Let's get some dinner," Tom suggested. "The Gilded Carrot is the best pub in this city."

"I'll get us a cab," Rory said.

Snow shook his head. "No, man. We've been cooped up on a starship for eighteen months. We're walking." Rory and Miguel groaned but offered no argument.

Over the next few days they toured London, marveling at how the old world architecture of Buckingham Palace and Westminster Abbey contrasted with the towering angularity of the rest of modern London. They dropped in and out of pubs with names such as Hobbit's Nob and The Loathsome Dragon, where they drank beer and ate shepherd's pie and fish and chips. Then Tom convinced them to take a quick train to Bath, and a short time later they were sitting in Bath's hot pools.

Catherine gasped as she entered the hot pool, but found that she acclimated to it quickly. Tom sat down next to her.

"Isn't this awesome?" he said, heaving a happy sigh and resting his head on the edge of the pool. "You can barely smell the sulfur."

Tom rested with his eyes closed for a while. Catherine knew the silence was temporary, that Tom had something to say and was gathering his words. She knew Tom would try to talk her into returning to the mission. She dreaded the conversation, knowing Tom's capacity for persuasion was beyond that of anyone she'd ever met and more powerful than even her father's sternly rational arguments. However, Tom brought up something entirely unexpected.

"What the hell happened with Eshel?" he said. "I tried to get him to tell me, but he wasn't having it."

"I don't know what happened," she said. "He just ended it one day. He refused to give me a reason."

"Were you... were you in love with him?"

She looked down at her pale legs in the hot bath. "I guess I was."

"I don't get it... did you guys really never have sex, or do stuff?"

She gave him a look.

"Oh, come on! He dumped you. You can say what you want now."

She shook her head. "It's not that. He's cold to me now. He barely nods at me and keeps walking. That's what hurts."

"That's how he treats everyone, C. That's Eshel."

"That's not how he was with me."

Tom clasped his hands behind his head and leaned back again, beads of sweat forming on his forehead. "Maybe he just couldn't handle it... being close to someone, knowing they expect something from you." He closed his eyes for a time, until he spoke again. "You can't leave the mission, C. They'll never take you seriously again."

She shrugged. "Who cares? Steele forbids me to conduct side projects, Eshel isn't allowed to talk about genetics... I have no future with the Corps anyway."

"Look, I'm sure you've heard all the arguments from Jimmy, what it's going to cost you if you pull out now. So why not cross train? Why not get out of the labs, away from the whitecoats, away from Steele, and try something new? I'll put in a good word for you. And what about Suna... and Calyyt-Calloq?" He gestured around him. "These pools are nothing. On CC they have secret cave pools, hidden away from everyone. They're like nothing you've ever seen. You can only go there if you're invited, but I have a contact who can get us in. If you leave, you'll never see their deserts, learn more about their primitive culture, or eat moyyt-toq, which I'm told tastes pretty damned good if cooked right. CC restricts who can visit, you know, and they restrict what you do there. But if you're in the Corps, they'll let you see everything."

Catherine felt a stab of regret, but did her best to avoid showing it, knowing it would only fuel Tom's persuasive powers. She felt him studying her, looking for signs of weakness on her part.

"Hell," Tom went on, "we'll be stationed at Suna for months. There's so much to do there. You've got the volcanoes, the fires, the rivers of lava... and their kala." He smiled. "You definitely can't miss drinking their kala. It's better than they say. And, we'll be there during their sun season. It'll be too damned hot for Esh to handle, so you won't even have to deal with him." He had a look of great satisfaction, like he'd offered up a set of arguments that no one could refute.

Catherine sighed. "I can't stay on that ship to drink kala, Tom. My work is important to me... not just for me, but for my mom."

Tom nodded. He'd witnessed her mother's illness, had attended her funeral. He sat back again and closed his eyes, offering no other argument.

New Year's Eve, they took an evening sky tour of London on a floater craft. Floater crafts were slow and quiet, with lots of windows... perfect for viewing. As they talked among themselves and looked upon the city lights, their steward brought out a platter with 12 varieties of sashimi for them. Everyone but Snow ate the fish and washed it down with a bit of sake. When clearing away their plates, the steward—a man with ebony skin and lively dark eyes—asked them where they were from. When he learned that three of them were on mid-mission leave from space, he got excited.

"You are Space Corps?" he said in the thick accent of a non-Londoner. "How very interesting! What an honor! Are you scientists?"

Tom and Snow protested loudly and pointed to Catherine. "She's the scientist."

The steward turned to her. "What is your field, my dear?"

"Genetics."

"Genetics," he said in wonder. "How very fascinating. In my youth, when I came to London and began my education, I too wanted to become a space scientist and join the Space Corps. I studied geology. I longed to see the volcanoes of Suna, to study their unique geology. But, alas, I could not attend academy. My parents, my family… they needed me." He looked at her with wistful eyes. "Tell me… is Suna as beautiful as they say? Are the volcanoes as violent?"

Catherine felt her face grow hot. "We… I haven't been to Suna yet. I'm sorry."

"Have a seat, man," Tom said. "I'll tell you all about Suna."

And they sat, sipping their sake, as Tom regaled the steward with stories of Suna, including the time he'd "barely said two words" to a Sunai female before he was surrounded by four angry males. "It took some time, but promises of boxing lessons and some of my darkest beer calmed them down." He shook his head. "They got the last of my good stuff, too. I had to go without for the rest of the mission!"

Snow nodded with a wry smile, and the others laughed.

Finally, when the steward rose to resume his work, he seemed to realize something. "Was your ship the one that rescued the refugee? The one from planet Korvalis?"

"You mean Eshel," Tom said. "He's our friend. You want to see a photo of him?" When the steward's eyes grew wide, Tom looked around until he spotted one of the viewers used for business meetings. Snow stood up to help and, after a minute, a large image appeared on the viewer.

It was from Tom's birthday party: all of Tom's friends sitting at dinner while the Derovian host took their picture. Catherine felt a small fragment of sadness as she saw herself seated next to Eshel, a smile on her face.

The steward studied the image with great interest. "He does not smile. I am told the Korvali do not smile."

"True story," Snow said. "He isn't much for humor in general."

"He tried, a few times," Catherine said.

"How's he doing at boot camp?" Rory asked Tom.

"I don't know," Tom said, shaking his head. "He hasn't replied to my messages, which means they've restricted his privileges. Which isn't a good sign."

"It is very generous that you would trust this refugee," the steward said. "You call him 'friend' despite how many feel about his people. My family... we were refugees. Some did not like us. But others like yourselves... they showed us generosity." He turned to Tom. "Thank you for sharing your stories."

"Why don't you come have a drink with us?" Tom said. "My treat. We'll make sure you get home safely."

The steward smiled. "I know a place you will like. And please, call me Chima."

A couple of hours and many drinks later, they stood counting in an underground pub, surrounded by a horde of people with shades of skin and hair that ran the spectrum of the color wheel. The crowd shouted as a shirtless Miguel got up to 57 pull-ups before dangling from the bar, unable to manage another or to beat Tom's 64.

"Yeah!" Tom slapped hands with those around him.

A skinny, tattooed guy with hair in peacock spikes stepped forward. "Let me show 'ya how it's done, you bunch of pussies," he said in a twangy American accent. He jumped up to the bar and knocked out a nearly effortless 75.

Tom nodded, acknowledging his defeat with equanimity. "Not bad for a guy your size." He grinned.

Peacock gave Tom a look. "Size has nothing to do with it, you service kid dumbass," he said glancing at Tom's shoulder tattoo.

Chima spoke up. "Do not insult his service to his people. It is disrespectful."

Peacock scoffed. "Hey, fugee, I serve my people too. Without some bullshit tattoo about how I was raised all underprivileged and shit."

"Let's see how important size is now, you little fuck," Tom said, moving closer to Peacock. Before Snow, Rory, or Miguel could step in, Chima did.

"It is the New Year, my friends," he said. "Let us toast and enjoy the celebration."

Catherine, who stood aside, found her way through the tight crowd and put her hand on Chima's shoulder. "Let me talk to him, Chima," she slurred, gently nudging him aside. She turned to Peacock, whose aggression cooled slightly upon seeing her. "Hi," she said, giving him a smile. "You're kind of cute. And I love your hair," she said, gesturing to it. He looked at her, appearing unsure of what to say. And then she delivered a one-two punch to his face, knocking him sideways as a trickle of blood came from his nose.

Mayhem ensued. And she recalled nothing after that.

Catherine awoke to a sound and an irritatingly bright light that caused her to squint. Her back hurt. Her head hurt, too. Once she gained her focus, she sat up from her hard polymer bench and saw a very large woman with ratty hair sitting across from her, her head lolling forward as she slept. A uniformed man stood in the doorway.

"You're free to go," he said in a deep voice.

Catherine stood up slowly, her head pounding and her body stiff, and left the cell. She followed the guard until she saw the guys, who smiled at the sight of her. The area under Tom's eye had a purplish hue.

"You're lucky you're with the Space Corps," the guard said to them. "My son enlisted last year. This is your one and only free pass, mates. Happy New Year."

"Thank you. Sir," she managed to reply in a raspy, dry voice. The other men muttered their thanks as well.

As they left the station, Tom put his arm around her and laughed. She smiled.

When Catherine arrived at the airport in Washington DC, her father stood waiting for her. He accompanied her on the train ride back to the shipyards.

"What happened to you?" Jimmy asked, peering closely at her fading black eye.

"Nothing. Just a minor skirmish on New Years Eve..."

He sat back in his seat. "You're doing the right thing."

"I hope so, Dad."

"Be sure to visit the Fires of Tonaili when you get to Suna. It's a long hike, but it's worth every step."

She nodded.

When the train stopped at Headquarters, they hugged. As Catherine waited for her stop, her mind turned unexpectedly to Eshel. It was the first time she'd let herself think about all that had happened between them. She remembered their meeting for the first time, their training together, her drug-addled chat with him after the CCFs, their intimate encounters, their conversations, the sher mishtar, and the secrets they shared. Had she loved him? Of course. Had he loved her? Perhaps not. And what did it matter? Theirs was something without a future. They'd had a temporary alignment of interests, of needs, of curiosity, of willingness. Once fulfilled, such a thing would end.

Perhaps she was a fool for allowing herself to become emotionally entangled with him without having considered the ramifications of doing so. She didn't regret making that mistake. But she would never make it again.

CHAPTER 16

Virginia was dreary, rainy, and cold. Catherine always preferred the more extreme but drier cold of Colorado to the wet and drippy coast. She made her way through security, recognizing other crewmembers lining up to gain entry. The guards scrutinized her and checked her identification far more carefully than usual. She began to wonder what was wrong, until she realized she looked like a civilian, like she didn't belong. Crewmembers were typically expected to be in uniform when boarding the ship; Catherine still wore her civies.

Once aboard, *Cornelia*'s familiar odor of re-circulated air flooded Catherine with memories. It was a good feeling, which surprised her. After dropping her bag at her quarters and putting on her uniform, she walked to the starboard bar. Packed with officers, the place had the pleasantly noisy sound of vibrant conversation. She scanned the room for Tom's blonde curls. She didn't see him, but instead spotted Commander Yamamoto standing aside, as if watching over his crew. He looked right at her. She smiled a little, and gave him a salute. He nodded in return. She wasn't sure, but it almost looked like a nod of approval.

She found Snow's dark hair. Tom's head peeked out from behind Snow's, and both smiled at the sight of her. Despite having seen them just a few days ago, she walked over and hugged them. They slapped her on the back, made jokes about her putting her tail between her legs, and resumed swapping Thirty stories to see who'd had the wildest time. When anyone new entered the bar, everyone looked, as it wasn't unusual for crewmembers to return from the Thirty with one of three things: a new haircut or color, a bad sunburn, or an injury.

"Catherine!" she heard a feminine voice call out. She followed the voice and spotted a tanned Anka pushing through the crowd to get to her.

"How was Japan?" Catherine asked.

"Ehhh… we wound up in New Zealand," Anka replied with a grin. "Long story. What happened to your face?"

"Let me get a drink first," Catherine said, laughing.

Catherine and Anka fought their way to the bar and Catherine ordered a beer. The storytelling and festivities went on for the remainder of the evening. And, at 0400 the next morning, the entire crew back in their quarters or on duty, *Cornelia* left Earth.

Eight days later, Snow remarked during their poker game that the ship had dropped out of FTL. This time, however, they all knew why. Eshel would be returning from boot camp.

Since deciding to return to duty, Catherine thought a lot about what her father and Tom had said about training with the soldiers. The Corps strongly encouraged their officers to get experience in departments outside their usual areas as part of the Elective Training Program, unofficially known as cross training. The Corps especially liked when science officers chose to get soldier training because it provided a source of backup aid during emergencies or times of war. Those who completed the ETP were often promoted first due their broader skill set. And, ideally, the ETP fostered goodwill and under-standing between soldiers and scientists.

She set up a meeting with Commander Ov'Raa. When she arrived, Ov'Raa smiled at her and offered her a seat. His office was decorated with numerous images of Ovlon: the ocean, various plants and animals, and many Derovian people, who Catherine assumed were his family members.

"So you are interested in the ETP, Lieutenant! Excellent! We always encourage our scientists to learn new things! And what area interests you: Engineering? Operations? Administration?"

"I haven't decided yet, Sir," she admitted. "I wanted to learn more about the program first and make sure I'm eligible."

He nodded. "Yes, of course! You have a clean record, Lieutenant, and are not assigned to a 'sensitive' post, so you are quite eligible. The program would benefit greatly from someone with your strong background. The ETP requires a minimum six-month commitment, to be extended if the participant and his or her new CO desires. Participants must commit a minimum of four hours per week, beyond that required by one's duties. Once you identify where you want to train, you must apply to the program and obtain approval from your CO, the CO you will train under, as well as Commander Yamamoto."

Catherine nodded, thanked Ov'Raa, and left. She spent the next couple of days putting together her application. She ran it by Tom and her father before submitting it to Ov'Raa. The more she thought about it, the more it made sense, and the more excited she became. She wondered why she'd resisted the idea for so long, and looked forward to the opportunity to learn something new and make the next 17 months more tolerable.

Several days later, Ov'Raa called her in. He smiled at her as he clasped his thick hands together and rested them on his neat, organized desk. "Lieutenant Finnegan, we have reviewed your application to participate in our ETP. You are a most excellent candidate for the program and would be a truly excellent addition to the Operations team. However, unfortunately, Lieutenant, your request has been denied."

Catherine stared at Ov'Raa, momentarily at a loss for words. "Denied, Sir?"

"I'm afraid so, Lieutenant."

"Why?" she asked, feeling disappointment flood her. Had her decision to quit the mission angered Yamamoto? Did Marks dislike her? Did they not trust her because of her relationship with Eshel? It had to be the latter…

"Commander Steele did not offer his approval. The Commander feels that as the head of your genetics lab, your position there is of such importance that you could not spare time for the program."

Catherine felt herself grow angry. "Sir, he must be joking."

Ov'Raa offered a consolatory smile. "I'm afraid the Commander makes no joke." He paused. "I imagine you must be very disappointed."

Although Catherine had never minded the gentle, kind ways of the Derovians, at that moment Ov'Raa's words, and his look of pity, only made her angrier.

"Lieutenant, you are, of course, free to discuss the matter in greater detail with Commander Steele. However, this decision is not likely to change."

"Thank you, Sir," Catherine replied. She saluted and left Ov'Raa's office.

When Catherine arrived at Steele's office the next morning, she saluted and stood waiting, as usual. Steele turned from his viewer, appearing in no mood to talk about anything. But to her surprise, he motioned for her to sit down.

"Sir, I'm here to discuss my application for the ETP," she began. "I'm told you believe my position in the lab is too important to allow for cross training."

"That is correct, Lieutenant."

Catherine expected this response, and proceeded. "Sir, I… I take my position in the lab very seriously. However, I believe I can spare the time to cross train, and believe I have a lot to offer the Corps if I complete the program. I'm trained in the martial arts and come from a family with a military history—"

"Yes," Steele interrupted, waving his hand at her. "I reviewed your application, so there is no need to reiterate your qualifications."

"What I mean to say, Sir, is that I don't think my being in the program will impact my work or my duties. We will finish every project you assign us, even if I must work extra days."

Steele offered no reaction. "Lieutenant, you are the head of your lab. As such, you have extra responsibilities that the others do not, and you do not have the luxury of cross training for your own amusement."

Catherine sat there for a moment. "Permission to speak freely, Sir."

Steele hesitated before nodding.

"Sir, I don't think it's fair to be held back from a good opportunity that this organization encourages simply because I run my lab. That's essentially punishing me for all the years of hard work that earned me the privilege of running the lab in the first place."

"That is what you agreed to when you signed up for this mission."

"No, Sir, it isn't. With all due respect, I signed up for this mission to learn new things and to grow." She didn't go so far as to mention Dr. Edelstein or how dull her work was.

Steele's eyes narrowed. "If you mean to say that my assignments aren't up to your standards, I must warn you, Lieutenant, that I am perfectly willing to offer you more of them, leaving you even less time to pursue other goals."

Catherine knew that would be her only warning. She tried another tactic, and softened her tone. "I'm happy with the assignments, Sir. My point is that this opportunity would provide what I'm looking for and wouldn't harm the quality of my work. The new things I learn could even make me a better scientist, or could benefit the research group in other ways. Isn't that one of the purposes of the program?" She knew it was a stretch, but she was out of arguments.

Steele rolled his eyes. "Don't be absurd, Lieutenant."

"What's absurd, Sir?"

"You," he said. "If you were ever going to conduct science that is beyond the mediocre, whether under my command or not, you would've showed signs of it by now. The answer is no, and this conversation is done."

Catherine felt her face grow hot. She looked at Steele for several moments, stunned. "Did you just insult my work?" Before he could offer any response, she said, "Go fuck yourself."

Steele's angry expression turned to surprise. "What did you just say, Scientist?" Despite trying to sound threatening, even calling her by a moniker that was considered disrespectful to someone of her rank, he couldn't hide his astonishment.

"You heard me." She stood up, her hands clenched in fists, her heart beating quickly and adrenaline flooding her. She turned and walked out.

"You're not dismissed!" Steele bellowed after her.

Catherine kept going, heading back to the stairwell. She was too angry to do anything else. And she got no further than the second flight of stairs before two MAs stopped her. They escorted her to the first deck, passing several other crewmembers along the way, all of whom gave her a curious stare. Once at the brig, an MA entered a code and a door opened. She entered the tiny cell as the door shut behind her and made a latching sound.

She sat alone in the small, windowless room, the hum of the ship's engines more pronounced than ever. She began to deliberate over just how much trouble she was in. At best, she would face inquiry and a letter of reprimand. At worst, she would face the end of her career with the Space Corps. Whatever the outcome, she no longer cared.

After two hours passed, an MA entered Catherine's cell and cleared her to return to her quarters, where she must remain until she was served. Once escorted to her quarters, Catherine sat down to contact her father. But she hesitated; perhaps she would delay telling him until she had more information.

Legal served her the following morning; she was charged with violating Article 67 of the Space Corps Code of Justice—Disrespect of a Superior Officer. Until resolved, she would be restricted to her quarters, suspended from duty, and denied access to the VirNet and all ship networks, with the exception of her personal network.

Just before 1400, her doorbell sounded.

"What the hell happened?" Tom asked, his expression half surprise and half amusement. He turned a chair backward and sat down.

"How did you know?"

Tom gave her a dubious look. "Except for a couple of fights among drunken soldiers, you're the only person who's visited the brig since this mission started. Everyone knows. That, and Kovsky saw you being escorted and came and told us."

Catherine related the entire story, leaving out no detail. "Steele doesn't like me, okay. He gives me stupid assignments, alright. He prevents me from participating in cross training, fine. But he denigrates my work? I turned down a position at the Peloni Institute to come here and have my body of work insulted by that idiot? Hell, no!" She paused, giving Tom a look. "And if you tell me I'm overreacting, or that it's no big deal... like you did about Eshel... I'll kick the shit out of you."

"Easy, soldier!" Tom said with raised eyebrows. "Jesus. Unlike your breakup with Eshel, in this case I actually know the whole story, which means I can be more helpful. Get my drift?"

Catherine took a deep breath, trying to quell her anger. "Sorry."

"I didn't see this coming, C. Maybe it's my fault—I'm the one who kept pushing you to get some soldier training."

Catherine shook her head. "No. This was inevitable. I don't belong here. I should never have come back." She sat down and ran her hands through her hair. "The only thing keeping me here now is you and Snow. I love you guys, but it's not enough."

Tom sighed. "Don't give up yet, C. Yeah, you're gonna pay for saying that. But that asshole threw the first punch and that type of shit isn't tolerated anymore. The good thing is, since you pissed off Steele, you can still come work for me, or you could work for Snow, who said that O'Leary might be okay with it. I know it isn't what you want, but it's better than leaving." He stood up. "Let me see what I can find out. Until then, relax and don't do anything stupid. And don't be contacting Jimmy to say you're coming home."

Catherine chuckled. "Okay."

In the bridge ready room, Yamamoto sat down with Captain Ferguson and Ov'Raa, who read their documents about the incident between Commander Steele and Catherine.

Ferguson sighed and looked up from her pad. "So we've had our first Article 67 incident. Frankly, I'm surprised it took this long." Ov'Raa smiled at the Captain's comment. "If Steele wants a letter of reprimand, let's get it done quickly. We're still not far from home and a transport could retrieve Lieutenant Finnegan at relatively little cost."

Yamamoto shook his head. "I don't believe this warrants formal reprimand, Captain. Catherine's comment was disrespectful and insubordinate, but Commander Steele is not without blame. He offered a personal insult that was highly inappropriate. And from what I've heard, the Commander has a documented history of insulting his scientists."

Ferguson looked at Ov'Raa, as if waiting for him to corroborate Yamamoto's claims.

Ov'Raa nodded. "Yes, Captain, Commander Steele's record shows two documented incidents, although both occurred years ago…"

Ferguson put her hands up. "So? It's okay for her to tell her superior officer to go fuck himself because he hurt her feelings?"

Yamamoto shook his head. "Of course not. However, the Commander did more than hurt Catherine's feelings. He made a personal insult by denigrating her work as a scientist—"

"Maybe her work isn't up to par, Suko."

"Steele's reports indicate that she completes all her assignments satisfactorily. Moreover, I am told that Catherine turned down an offer from a renowned research institute in order to take this mission. Employment there is extremely competitive, only offered to those who show significant promise in the field. I'm told she's quite skilled."

"Let me guess," Ferguson said. "Eshel told you all of this?"

Yamamoto shook his head. "Eshel has said nothing. Tom mentioned the job offer, and the rest I got from the institute itself. They made it clear that with adequate funding they would still take her after the mission."

"Maybe they should take her now," Ferguson muttered, sitting back in her chair. "You want to forgo the letter."

"She has a spotless conduct record."

Ferguson gave a disapproving look. "You're quick to come to her aid again, Suko."

"It's my job to know the character of those on our ship."

Ferguson turned back to Ov'Raa. "Do you agree with the Commander's conclusions?"

Ov'Raa clasped his thick hands together, a pale blue flush coming over him. "I do not have all the information that the Commander does," he began, nodding to Yamamoto. "Yet I have noticed that Commander Steele can be quite… harsh." He smiled. "And I do not believe he fully supports the ETP. Records show that he hasn't allowed his subordinates to partake in it, nor has he allowed any soldier to cross train under his command." He paused. "I recommend, Captain, that we avoid formal reprimand and issue a warning to both parties, subject to more serious punishment if not heeded."

Ferguson smiled at Ov'Raa's magnanimity. "She insulted her superior officer, Commander. She must pay a steeper price than he does."

"Yes, Captain. A formal apology, then, for Lieutenant Finnegan. And probation."

Ferguson pushed out her chair. "Let Legal know what we've decided. Make sure those two stay out of each other's way for a while." She got up and left the ready room.

First thing in the morning, Catherine arrived at Steele's office to deliver her apology to Steele. The apology was brief but very formal, and would've made any old school brass proud. But everyone knew, perhaps Steele most of all, that she wasn't the least bit sorry for what she'd said. Steele listened to her apology with the same expression he always had when dealing with her; once she finished, he responded only by saying, "Get out."

At the lab, Catherine sat at her desk and looked over the results of some analyses that Varan had conducted. One of them didn't make sense. When she emerged from her office to ask Varan about it, he was talking animatedly with two other Derovians. She realized they were Coran and Dorel, two of Eshel's bunkmates. Upon seeing her, they ceased talking and stood straighter.

"Lieutenant Finnegan!" Coran said. "Hello to you!"

"Yes, Lieutenant!" Dorel chimed in. "Most excellent to see you!"

She smiled at the sight of them, reminded of Eshel's bafflement at their sweet natures. "Hi guys. It's good to see you, too. I just have a quick question for Varan." She showed Varan the problem. It turned out the report was missing a page, so he resent it to her. As she returned to her office, she heard shuffling footsteps approaching; when she turned, Coran and Dorel stood before her.

"Lieutenant Finnegan," Coran began, appearing unsure of himself. "We have a... special concern."

"About Eshel," Dorel said.

"Yes," Coran went on. "When Eshel first came aboard, he would... sometimes... make noise in the night—"

"Like Suzuki does when he has a nightmare," Dorel added.

"Yes," Coran said. "And, now, since Eshel has... has stopped visiting you... it is happening again—"

"But it is worse!" Dorel said. "We try to help him, but he will not let us!"

Catherine listened to the men, recalling Eshel's occasional nocturnal episodes. "He does that sometimes," Catherine replied quietly. "I don't know why. But I wouldn't worry... if he needed help, he would ask for it."

The brothers glanced at one another, appearing relieved. "Thank you, Lieutenant Finnegan," Coran said, waving goodbye as they left.

Catherine sat there for a few minutes, pondering yet another thing she hadn't understood about Eshel. A chirp snapped her out of her reverie. It was probably a message from Tom about her coming to the next poker game. It would be her first in a long time.

But the message wasn't from Tom. The message was encrypted, and it didn't indicate who'd sent it. Puzzled, Catherine began to attach her contactor to her network. Then she stopped herself. *Not here.*

Back in her quarters, she downloaded the message to her personal network, waited for it to pass scans, and began the decryption process. The message's encryption method was intricate, each step leading to another and another. It took her a significant amount of time to wade through the numerous, maze-like steps. She'd never seen anything like it.

Once decrypted, she saw that the message included a large compressed file. When she decompressed it, she found a long list of files, enough to fill her entire viewer. A quick glance at the file suffixes indicated that the files were emails, with the exception of two very large image files.

She opened the most recent email file: it was a message from Commander Steele, written to a Dr. Albert Vanyukov. Catherine thought she recognized that name, but couldn't recall why. A quick search on her viewer answered her question; Vanyukov was a professor and geneticist at Stanford University. A further search revealed that Vanyukov and Steele had done their graduate training in genetics together and were coauthors on several papers from decades ago.

December 2

Albert,
I have the files we need to move forward with this project. Let us speak more on the topic when I arrive on the eighth.

James

When Catherine checked the dates of all the emails, she saw that they spanned more than a year, the first one dating back to two Octobers ago. Just after Eshel boarded *Cornelia*.

Catherine read the next email, and the next, until she'd read them all. By the time she finished reading them, she knew exactly what was in those two image files. And opening them only confirmed her suspicions.

CHAPTER 17

Catherine projected the first image, zooming in, then zooming out, rotating it in one direction, and then the other. She ran the usual scans and found DNA alterations on chromosomes six, seven, and eighteen. There was a familiar pattern of changes to the epigenome. She called up the files from her previous scans; the results were identical. Just as she'd suspected, it was Eshel's genetic material, the same image from when Eshel had arrived on the ship.

The image contained unfamiliar black dots throughout. As she ran the remote over one of them, a small white shape popped up and disappeared. Confused, she moved her remote more slowly, stopping once the white shape reappeared. It was a note that briefly described the locus, with the letters AV. Albert Vanyukov. She realized the messages were annotations, and the image had more of them than she could easily count.

Steele and Vanyukov had been studying Eshel's genetic material since he'd arrived well over a year ago.

The second large file also contained an image of Eshel's genetic material, but the epigenomic changes were different. She examined the file date: it was more recent. They too must have figured out that they needed a second sample from Eshel to investigate the epigenomic alterations. But how did they get it? There was no way to know for sure... but Catherine would bet all the money she had that

Eshel hadn't given Steele that file. But then again, she didn't know Eshel as well as she thought she had.

She put such thoughts aside to focus on a more pressing question: who would send her such incriminating information?

Catherine examined the message more closely, trying to ascertain the encryption method and where it came from. Was it someone on the ship, or an outsider? Was it an individual, or an individual within a larger organization? Whoever sent it had scrambled the message's origin. And, unfortunately, she'd reached the end of her technical abilities. She knew a small handful of people who possessed the necessary skill to potentially solve this mystery. But there was only one she could trust.

"Catherine," said Patrick Holloway's voice.

"You busy?"

"Busy drinking," he quipped. "Did you need something?"

"Yeah. Come to my quarters whenever you're done. And keep it quiet."

She knew he wouldn't be long. Her secrecy would intrigue him. She closed all of her files and saved them to a portable drive. Ten minutes later, Holloway rang.

"I have a dilemma I can't solve," she said, motioning for him to pull up a chair.

"Oh, yeah?" he replied. His dark, curly hair was messy and his face a bit flushed from the alcohol, but he seemed coherent.

She pulled up the message. "I received a message that had the most complicated encryption I've ever seen. It took me almost two hours to get through it. Can you help me figure out who or where it came from?"

Holloway, now appearing more alert, took a look at her viewer. "I probably can. Or I can narrow it down to a list of suspects."

She turned off her viewer. "Before you look, you have to promise to keep your mouth *shut* about whatever you find. Do you understand?"

"I understand. Why? Is it sensitive information?"

"It could be."

She turned the viewer back on and Holloway studied the message. "Was the message sent to your main network or to your contactor?" he said.

"My contactor."

He put his hand out.

Catherine handed him her contactor and he synced it with her computer. He voiced a series of commands as the viewer filled with page after page of data that made little sense to her. He got a quizzical look on his face, and then chuckled. "Well, will you look at that…" He examined the output and called out a few more commands. "Normally I'd assume it came from someone on the ship, since it went to your contactor… but anyone who could do this could also make it took internal when it's not." After several minutes elapsed, he turned to her. "It definitely came from someone on this ship," he told her, rubbing his eyes. "Unfortunately, I can't tell who. They covered their tracks in a very obvious way, but it worked. My guess is someone with good program-ming skills, but not intel." He paused. "What is this message?"

Catherine pushed her hair out of her face and sat back. "I can't give you details. But it's a definitive sign our commanding officer is doing the very thing he ordered us not to."

Holloway knit his eyebrows, as if trying to recall the order she referred to. Then a look of recognition crossed his face and his eyes widened. "Something to do with Eshel? Is Steele working with Eshel?"

"I doubt it. Eshel never trusted him. But you're half right. Steele is working."

"Is he trying to reproduce Eshel's work?"

"I think so."

He scowled. "That old bastard! After the way he's blocked us from doing so?"

"You haven't even seen how he's threatened me about never touching those data, and how concerned he acts in front of everyone else about preserving Eshel's knowledge."

Holloway shook his head, running his hand through his messy hair again. "Balls to him! If he can do it, then why can't we?" he exclaimed, his cheeks red and his accent even more pronounced.

Catherine smiled.

"I'm serious," he went on. "Why can't we?" Then he stopped himself. "Did that message have any data?"

"No," she lied. She couldn't tell him what she had. It was the one thing that could cause Eshel to lose his asylum, and she couldn't risk that.

"Too bad." He paused. "Who could've sent this?"

She shook her head. "There are too many possibilities, really, especially after what happened with Steele and me." She stood up. "Listen, keep this quiet. If I find we have something to work with, I'll let you know."

Holloway nodded, a yawn escaping from him. "See you tomorrow."

Who sent it?

Her first thought was Eshel. Eshel would understand the significance of the project Steele was embarking upon in secret, and why it would be so important to her.

But Eshel couldn't be the source of the information, for many reasons. For one, Eshel had no way of knowing what Steele was up to. Steele was a jerk, but he wasn't stupid, and would know better than to let any clue of his intentions slip out to Eshel during their meetings. And while it was possible that Eshel had formed a trustworthy relationship with Steele, like he had with her, Steele and Vanyukov's email trail made it clear that the two scientists meant to keep their plans secret from all but one another.

Just as importantly, even if Eshel did somehow gain access to such information, why would he give it to her? Eshel no longer spoke to her, much less shared secrets with her. The rare times they crossed paths in the hallway near the mess or near the training studio, Eshel refused to acknowledge or even make eye contact with her. Eshel always remembered those who slighted him, and wouldn't forgive her hitting him.

But even if she ignored those arguments, which were adequate in and of themselves, there was one reason Eshel couldn't have sent her those files, one that trumped the others: for all his brilliance, Eshel lacked anything close to the knowledge or training to undergo such a task. Only those who'd worked in intel or those with highly developed technical skills had the know-how to hack into a highly protected research network, to use such advanced encryption techniques, to hide a message's origin from someone like Holloway…

Holloway. Catherine recalled their conversation long ago, when he'd first brought up their working together in secret. He shared the same frustration Catherine did with their work. He had the know-how to send her that information anonymously… with reasonable hope that she'd ask for his help. She shook her head, laughing. He probably also knew she'd be so grateful for the information that she couldn't hold it against him if he admitted the truth. If it were Holloway, perhaps he would confess at some point.

Catherine glanced at the time. It was late. She made herself a cup of tea and put her feet up on her table.

Perhaps she could work with Holloway. She could do it without him; but with him, they could work much faster. And with Steele and Vanyukov already ahead, working quickly mattered. What Steele and Vanyukov had in experience and access to Stanford's advanced labs, they lacked in stamina and innovation, two things she and Holloway had plenty of. Yes, it was risky. She'd worked day after day with Holloway for over a year—she knew she could trust him, that he'd bend the rules if it meant doing the science he wanted to do. But adding another person to the mix increased the probability of getting caught.

But what about Eshel? Friend or not, she couldn't do anything that put Eshel in danger of losing his asylum. And, friend or not, she could never reveal Eshel's secrets. Then she realized she didn't have to reveal anything—between the files she'd discovered on her network and the encrypted information she'd received, they had enough data to work with, none of which incriminated Eshel.

She recalled a conversation she'd had with Eshel at that very table. They'd talked of genetic engineering and cloning.

"Your people allow cloning, but not the cloning of humans?" he'd asked.

"Right," she'd said. "It was allowed once, but only experimentally and only by sanctioned labs. Even then it was a nightmare. The clones rarely survived gestation; the ones who did were usually dead within weeks, if not days. When the biocrackers began trying it, a black market developed for the clones and the technology to create them… it created this big political stink. The feds stepped in to sequester the clones but the human rights groups fought them on it… that ended any experimentation with human cloning on Earth." She paused. "Is it true that the Korvali don't clone?"

"Yes."

"Why not?"

"It is… disgraceful… to attempt to reproduce a sentient being in such a way. It is forbidden on Korvalis."

Catherine smiled. "No offense, Esh, but that seems a little judgmental coming from a people who engineer their own genomes at will."

Eshel shook his head. "It is not because we oppose genetic manipulation of that degree. It is because reproduction is highly valued on Korvalis. Due to our infrequent birth rate, a birth is an honored event. A manufactured person is shameful." He looked down for a moment. "It is difficult to explain. Sentient life has great value on Korvalis. Birth is celebrated. Death is honored. Murder is… very rare. My work… it was not only to survive my escape from Korvalis. It was intended to aid the survival of all those who would escape or who were captured by Elisan, drugged, and left in the remote territories to die."

"He does that to people, to your people?"

"To those who aren't Shereb, yes."

Catherine shook her head. "The work is extraordinary, Eshel. You would win the Nobel Prize for it, easily. It's already saved one life. Can Elan or the other Shereb scientists say as much?"

"That is another reason I developed it," he replied. "Shereb scientists spend far too much time and resources on stupid procedures."

Catherine pushed the memory aside and got ready for bed.

But she couldn't sleep. Her mind raced with too many thoughts. Finally, she grabbed her contactor and sent Holloway a message.

Meet me at my quarters tomorrow. 1900.

At 1902, Holloway rang.

"Here's how this will work," she began in her scientific tone. "You can't discuss any of this with anyone. *Anyone.* Do you understand?"

Holloway nodded. "I understand."

"This is a team effort, which means we share credit if the work produces fruit… and we share blame if we get caught. If we get caught, we'll be discharged and probably court-martialed. And if the brass doesn't punish us, the Alliance will. And if they don't, the Korvali will. Do you understand?"

He nodded.

"We'll work in the library, supposedly on a project in which I am mentoring you. Steele doesn't need to know, since we won't be using the lab.

"Why not the lab?" Holloway asked.

"I'm not allowed there after hours, remember?"

"Right. Why not one of our quarters, where there's more privacy?"

She shook her head. "Everyone will assume we're… involved. You're under my command, so we can't have that." Holloway's fair complexion blushed and he nodded in understanding. "Later, when it comes time for bench work, we'll have to get creative. Maybe we can work out a deal with Anka."

Holloway nodded eagerly. "Yes. Brilliant. But why the sudden change? Did your source send you more data, data we can use?"

She smiled a little. "Not quite. I lied to you. The message did include data. I wasn't ready to commit to this yet. And... I discovered I have all the files I'd generated when Eshel arrived. They'd saved to my network and I didn't realize it."

He grinned.

"Want to see them?"

"Do I want to see them, she asks!" Holloway cried.

She laughed and produced the files, letting Holloway take a good look. After being engrossed in the files for a few minutes, Holloway finally spoke up. "Extraordinary. Twenty-three chromosomes...!" He peered some more. "What the devil happened to his epigenome?" He turned to her. "Did you run a comparative analysis with a human genome?"

She hadn't. She was more interested in the engineering than in the similarities between human and Korvali genomes. Nonetheless, she produced a copy of her own genome for him to analyze.

"Extraordinary," he said. "They're more similar to us than I'd imagined. And I'd thought Stravinsky's work was rubbish!"

Dante Stravinsky, an evolutionary astrogeneticist who worked at the Peloni Institute, had published a paper theorizing that humans and Korvali may have a common ancestor. The paper generated much controversy. Unfortunately, without Korvali cooperation, there was no way to empirically test such a theory.

"Did Eshel ever offer an opinion on that topic?" he said.

"No. He's not allowed to talk about that stuff, remember?"

"And you two never talked in confidence?"

She shook her head. "Not really," she lied. "We both had too much to lose."

He rolled his eyes. "How can they continue to keep his knowledge stowed away indefinitely? Don't they understand how important it is?"

"No, they don't. Don't get carried away," she said. "I know it stinks, but there's a lot at stake here."

"Like what?"

"Like what would happen if Eshel gave away Korvali secrets. They'd find out and things would get ugly. He'd be in danger, we'd be in danger…"

"From what?" he cried. "From people who don't even have FTL technology?"

She shook her head. "You have to trust me on this one, Holloway. They're far more dangerous than you think. That, I know." When he tried to argue again, she stopped him. "Listen… you don't know anything. Remember those nine other refugees? The Korvali intentionally destroyed their water stores so they'd die a slow and painful death. They murdered Eshel's father because he opposed some of their leader's policies. And, I almost got sent home because Steele found out I told Eshel about the genetics of my mother's cancer. Steele is breathing down my neck and the XO has his eyes on me."

"Then why do you want to do this?"

"Because I'm not letting some bitter old scientist who doesn't know shit about modern genetics—or a bunch of soldiers who don't appreciate the value of science—stand in the way of progress! Steele doesn't care about protecting Eshel or the Korvali; he wants this information for himself." She paused, taking a deep breath. "Eshel and I… we had a falling out. But he trusted me. More importantly, he didn't trust Steele. We can't let Steele win, Holloway."

"Of course we can't let that bastard win. Even with Vanyukov on board, we can still kick the shit out them."

She smiled. "That's what I like to hear."

Catherine gave Holloway a long list of readings. They set a time to meet again and she sent him on his way.

For her, she would spend her time reviewing the literature on the body's physiological response to stress, particularly dehydration and starvation. Eshel and Othniel must have begun there. After all, to keep someone alive for an extended period of time without food or water, one would need to alter metabolic function and dramatically reduce heart and respiration rates, thus reducing the body's survival requirements. And if Eshel and his father could alter the Korvali epigenome to survive dehydration, she and Holloway could figure out a way to do the same in humans. And they would have to do it faster—and better—than Steele and Vanyukov.

Catherine woke the next morning to a bright light streaming into her quarters. Momentarily confused, she wondered if it were a hypnopompic hallucination, until she blinked a few times and realized she saw real, natural light. She got out of bed and went to her tiny window. Once her eyes adjusted to the sunlight, she saw rusty mountains along the horizon.

They'd landed on Suna.

CHAPTER 18

One either loves Suna… or despises it.
— Commander Valery "Val" Petrovsky, Space Corps, retired

In Catherine's experience, those who loved Suna remarked most upon its beautiful music, its spicy fermented kala, and the 19 moons that kept its shining planetary rings in line. Those who hated it complained about its violent volcanic activity, climactic temperatures that bordered on the inhospitable, the strangeness of the food, and, most of all, the inflated pride of Suna's males.

At the Academy, and from her father, Catherine had learned all about their past conflicts with the Sunai and the subsequent peace treaty, the latter of which had inspired the formation of the Alliance. The Sunai often took credit for the Alliance's inception, but those who did their homework knew it was the Derovians who'd convinced the Sunai to join with Earth and Calyyt-Calloq to create a coalition that could benefit them all.

A document from Administration discussed Sunai culture in detail, and Catherine shook her head at the Sunai being described as "passionate, competitive, and powerful." From what she'd learned, they were violent, sexist, and full of themselves. Their language wasn't difficult to learn (Eshel had told her it was easier than English), but the Sunai had numerous signals and customs they followed. And although knowledge of Sunai customs wasn't required for interacting with the Sunai, knowing them had its advantages.

Catherine only studied their most common customs. Other than her occasional dealings with their scientists, Catherine doubted she would spend enough time with the Sunai to justify more extensive study. From her perspective, Suna was a chance to get off the ship and explore a new place. And for that, she was grateful.

Yamamoto sat down in Ferguson's office. "What is it?"

Ferguson stood facing her window. "They're insisting on interrogating Eshel before he's allowed freedom on Suna."

"Who is?"

"Gronoi Okooii."

Yamamoto didn't answer right away. Gronoi Okooii was not only a Gronoi, second only to the Gronoio in rank... he was one of the most powerful Gronoi in Suna's military government. "I assume you put up a fight."

"You bet I did." She turned around, her face flushed. "But the Alliance supports their decision. And Headquarters backed them up."

Yamamoto let out a breath. He sat for several moments. "It's all bluster, Janice. We have what they want: control over Eshel."

"They can have the little shit, for all I care."

"Do not let the annoyances of the present make you lose sight of the future," he said. "If we can integrate Eshel, and bridge the gap with the Korvali, the possibilities are endless... for all, but especially for us. And the Sunai know that. Let them interrogate. Let them exert their influence. It won't change anything."

Ferguson didn't answer. But Yamamoto knew from her silence that she agreed with him.

"Did they insist on interrogating him without us present?" he asked.

"They tried to," she said. "I put my foot down. At least I got that concession. It's tomorrow, at sunset."

The next evening, Catherine followed Yamamoto as they left the ship and walked to the transport vessel that awaited them. She squinted at the intense sunlight as a wave of heat immediately enclosed her, a heat so powerful and so dry that Catherine felt her nostrils burn when she inhaled. They were told that 50 degrees, down from 65 during the day's peak, was on the cool side for Suna's sun season. She felt sweat accumulate on her torso after only thirty seconds of exposure.

Almost as powerful as the heat was the strange, pungent odor of the air. Catherine had heard about the smell, which emanated from the large shrubs that were indigenous to the volcanic rock and soil. Apparently, the abundant shrub grew only on that continent, as the rest of the planet had such harsh conditions that no sizable shrub or tree could survive.

As she entered the transport, relieved to be out of the heat, she felt several pairs of eyes on her. Ferguson sat next to Ov'Raa, who smiled at her in his usual way. Steele gave her his brief, withering look. Yamamoto had asked Catherine to attend the meeting with the Sunai, and she got the feeling her attendance was against Steele's wishes. Finally, from the corner of her eye, she saw one more person.

Eshel. He gave her a brief look with his sea eyes. She felt a momentary panic—the only remaining empty seats were next to him. Fortunately, Yamamoto stepped forward and sat down next to Eshel, while Catherine took the last seat.

As the craft gained elevation, Catherine peered out the window at the landscape below. Jula looked as modern as any city on Earth. Its tall buildings were surrounded by large mountainous volcanoes stained reddish-brown from the lava that, from time to time, surged down from the active peaks into the city. Once up high enough, Catherine could clearly see the system of viaducts that snaked through the city in order to accommodate the runoff after an eruption. Soon, Suna's brutal sun would begin its descent behind the peaks.

She spotted Suna's military headquarters from a distance, buried into the massive mountain and spreading out and around it like alluvium. Once they landed, uniformed men led them into the dark, cool mountain. They walked through the dimly lit hallways until they arrived at a vestibule. Two Sunai guards began scanning them one at a time, indicating when each passed the scan by putting a thick hand on a shoulder and urging them forward.

When Eshel's turn came, the guard moved to touch his shoulder. Eshel, anticipating the gesture, quickly dodged the Sunai's hand and spoke something in Sunai. The guard uttered an angry response and moved closer to Eshel. Just then, someone from the room behind the vestibule bellowed a command in Sunai. The guard immediately stood up straight and backed away from Eshel, letting him proceed.

Their meeting place was a windowless, cavernous room, somewhat dimly lit to accommodate Sunai ocular sensitivity and containing a large metal table shaped like a trapezoid. Behind the table stood nine Sunai in a shallow V formation, their rust-colored uniforms embellished with metallic decorations. All wore dark eyeshades.

The Sunai seemed even larger than Catherine remembered, with facial features that were strange… ugly by some accounts, striking by others. However, these uniformed men seemed different than the gruff gumiia who'd attacked her and Eshel.

The officer who stood at the V's apex stepped forward and introduced himself as Gronoi Okooii. He announced the rank and name of each of his men, beginning with those closest to him. Finally, he commenced the traditional Sunai welcome by extending his palm; Ferguson stepped forward and met it with hers. Ferguson appeared amusingly slight next to the Gronoi's bulk. They pressed their palms together for several seconds, until the Gronoi released his hand.

"Gronoi Okooii," Ferguson said, "you know Commanders Yamamoto and Ov'Raa."

The Gronoi met palms with Yamamoto and Ov'Raa, and then placed his large hands on Ov'Raa's shoulders. "Niri," he said loudly, his gravelly voice resounding through the cavernous room. "Most excellent to see you!"

Ov'Raa twittered a bit as he grasped the Gronoi's hands for the meron. "I hope your wives are well, Gronoi Okooii! And how are your children? Is your eldest a Gron yet?"

Gronoi Okooii raised his chin. "He will be very soon, Niri! Very soon, yes!" He released Ov'Raa and turned his gaze to Catherine.

Catherine felt herself stiffen, not knowing if she should offer her palm. But Ferguson went on to quickly introduce Commander Steele and Catherine before she said, "And, of course, this is Eshel."

Gronoi Okooii shifted his gaze to Eshel but did nothing, as if waiting to see what Eshel would do. Eshel, who wore his blue robe that day, stepped forward. He raised his palm. "Gronoi Okooii."

The Gronoi, appearing to approve of the gesture, raised his thick hand and met Eshel's. "You shall sit there," he ordered, motioning to the middle seat on the long side of the trapezoidal table.

Gronoi Okooii indicated for Ferguson and her crew to also sit on the side where Eshel sat. Catherine waited until the others chose their seats, taking the end seat next to Yamamoto. The Gronoi sat at the opposite short side of the table, while his officers took their seats on its angled sides, in the same order in which they'd stood. Two of them didn't sit, but instead took their places on either side of the door.

"I am pleased to have you and your crew here, female Captain. But it is not you I wish to speak to." The Captain's jaw tightened as the Gronoi turned to Eshel. "Private Eshel," he said, his voice resounding once again. "You are the first—and only—Korvali member of our Alliance!"

Eshel didn't respond.

"You have left the planet of your people," the Gronoi continued. "You now live among outsiders. You have enlisted in their Space Corps. You have even begun training to take position as an officer of respectable rank." The Gronoi paused. "Do you know, young Korvali, that the Sunai have found many Korvali ships, disabled and drifting in the darkness? Do you know that the Sunai have buried your homeworlders when they did not survive their journey to our home? Do you also know that we rendezvoused with your compatriot, Ashan, many sun cycles ago? That we, the Sunai, were the disseminators of Ashan's letter, that we were his protectors before his disappearance? Did you know all of this, young Eshel?"

Eshel still remained silent, likely knowing that the Gronoi hadn't finished.

"Yet," he went on, "when you leave your homeworld, when you seek protection from the Alliance, you don't seek help from those who have honored your people! You instead choose to live among the humans, to serve their Space Corps military, to repay a debt to them that does not exist!" He puffed up his chest and raised his chin a bit higher. "What is the meaning of this decision?"

"It is simple, Gronoi Okooii," Eshel said. "My physiology cannot tolerate the hot temperatures of Suna."

"Temperatures?" the Gronoi said. "Your concern is this trivial thing? We have many ways to protect you during our sun season! You would have the environmental conditions you require! You would have the food and drink you prefer! You would have an honored position among our superior armed forces! You would have all that you could want..." the Gronoi paused, "including permission to engage in the scientific research you so value!"

Catherine heard Yamamoto exhale. And from her corner of the trapezoid, she could see Ferguson shift in her seat. But Ov'Raa spoke first.

"Gronoi Okooii," Ov'Raa said in his sweetest voice. "The Space Corps did not prevent Eshel from sharing his knowledge of genetics. It was the Alliance's decision, decided through vote."

"This, I know," the Gronoi said, his expression still angry, but softened. "But had Eshel chosen to live among the Sunai, we would have persuaded the Alliance otherwise. We would have made them see."

Catherine watched the Gronoi, amused at his bravado, but also curious if there were any truth to his claim.

"Gronoi Okooii," Ferguson said. "You say that you would protect Eshel and any other Korvali refugees. Yet it was Sunai who attacked

Eshel on Derovia, on two occasions. The second time they had a weapon. How would Eshel be protected here even as a visitor, much less as a citizen?"

"The gumiia are an embarrassment to the men of Suna!" the Gronoi cried, waving his arm as his metallic decorations clinked together. "You find this garbage and bring them to me, and I will handle them." He paused, looking at Ferguson again. "You too, female Captain, must know the frustration of those who do not make your people proud."

Ferguson nodded. "I do, Gronoi. And we are glad to know that the men of Suna don't wish harm upon Eshel, despite his transgressions."

The Gronoi nodded, looking at everyone at the table. "We do not attack the Korvali. But the Korvali attack us! The Korvali ended the lives of eight excellent soldiers of Suna. Yet," he said, focusing on Eshel again, "you are here. You left your planet, your people, to live among otherworlders. Perhaps you do not trust the Sunai, trust that we will protect you, given this debt to us." He made a gesture with his hand. "Despite your lack of trust, and despite our being unwelcome on the planet of your Korvali people…. you are still, young Eshel, welcome on Suna."

The group seemed to let out a collective sigh, as everyone turned their attention to Eshel.

"Thank you, Gronoi Okooii," Eshel said. "It is my expectation that, someday, you and your people will be permitted to visit my homeworld."

The Gronoi raised his chin slightly. "Is this an expectation, or simply the wish of a young man full of ambitions?"

"It is my certain belief, Gronoi."

The Gronoi didn't answer right away, seeming almost intrigued by Eshel's claim. "I am told you did not know this… Ashan."

"I did not, Gronoi."

"But his writings, his words, they are true, yes?"

"They are true, Gronoi," Eshel said. "I would very much like to speak with Ashan, if possible. Do you know where he is?"

Catherine suppressed a smile. Only Eshel would be so audacious.

The Gronoi raised his chin again. "I know he would have a position of rank on Suna! Not as high as you, young Korvali, but a position of respect nonetheless!" He lowered his voice. "But he has fled. He chose to hide, like a coward, instead of letting us protect him. Some say he hides in the mountains of our uninhabitable regions... but most say he is dead. No Korvali can survive on his own here... even with your unique scientific talents." The Gronoi looked at Catherine. "You, geneticist. Lieutenant, yes?"

Catherine felt her stomach jump as the room shifted its attention to her. "Yes, Gronoi."

"Lieutenant, it is you who discovered the changes in our young Korvali's map of life, yes?"

Just as Catherine began to reply, Ferguson spoke over her. "Gronoi, Commander Steele will answer any questions about Eshel's genome or scientific abilities." She motioned to Steele.

The Gronoi turned to Steele. He asked only a couple of basic questions before he became uninterested and turned the topic elsewhere.

It was then that Catherine noticed one of the Grono. The second from Gronoi Okooii's right, easily in Catherine's visual field, made a slight gesture with his right hand. He placed it up on its side and oriented it in a way that pointed right at her. A moment later, his hand resumed its normal flat position. The Grono next to him made the same gesture, but more quickly, almost as if in response. They were signaling, like the anthropologists said they did, in a language only they knew.

Catherine felt her blood turn cold as she felt both sets of shaded eyes on her.

The lights dimmed suddenly, and the room seemed to quiet. Catherine glanced around uneasily until she saw the Gronoi remove his eyeshades. It was the gesture of goodwill. The other officers followed suit, while the two guards kept their shades on. They had big, amber eyes with enlarged pupils that seemed to encompass most of the eye.

The Gronoi adjourned the meeting, and the Sunai men stood aside as Ferguson and her crew exited the meeting room. As she waited for the others to exit, Catherine looked over at the Grono who'd made the hand gesture. He watched her with his huge eyes, his hairless head and physical bulk only reinforcing the effect of his unsmiling expression. Catherine scowled, staring him down until she was out the door.

You cannot intimidate me, Sunai. You don't know a powerful stare until you've known a Korvali.

"Ready to go?" Tom said to them.

In the early evening, Catherine waited at the ship's exit with Tom, Snow, Shanti, and Zander.

"Where's Middleton?" Tom said.

"He's coming," Zander said.

Catherine rolled her eyes. Much time passed before Tom agreed to let Middleton back into his poker game, with the agreement that Middleton would keep his hostility to himself. Catherine had expressed her disapproval, but Tom replied that her argument carried little weight given that neither she nor Eshel had attended a single poker game since before the Thirty.

"What about Eshel?" Shanti asked, glancing briefly at Catherine.

"He's banished to the ship for a while," Tom said. "Poor bastard can't handle this kind of heat."

Once Middleton arrived, they left for Jula's festival grounds, where the Sunai put on a music fest for *Cornelia*'s crew, on Gronoi Okooii's order. Music was a passion shared by all Sunai, regardless of sex or status. Her father and Tom didn't care for Sunai music, but Catherine liked what little she'd heard and looked forward to seeing it live.

And Snow... he'd talked of little else for weeks. The festival would begin that evening and continue until the morning, when the Sunai would retreat to their interiors and sleep through the day's heat. The following evening, business proceedings would begin.

They walked to the festival, which was surrounded by large stone formations that overlooked Jula below. With the sunset, the temperature had rapidly decreased to a more tolerable, but still quite hot, 38 degrees. But once they showed their badges and entered the grounds, the temperature suddenly dropped again, to something far more pleasant.

"Whoa," Snow said. "This is new." He looked around, searching for what Catherine could only assume was the source of the sudden temperature change. And he finally spotted them and pointed them out—devices that were only somewhat camouflaged in the stone formations that enclosed the grounds.

They walked past booths selling or offering lessons on countless musical instruments, some of which were strange and unusual, nothing like Catherine was used to. Snow slowed, wanting to stop at each place, but Tom urged him along, insisting they start with refreshment. They drank kala, a traditional Sunai fermented beverage, from clay cups. Catherine was surprised at how cool and refreshing the kala tasted, and how it managed to marry sweet and spicy flavors.

Sipping their kala, they strolled past several food booths as the smell of charred food and the now-familiar spice filled Catherine's nostrils. The smell didn't seem as strange anymore. Catherine followed Tom to get some of the Sunai cuisine, which Tom began to devour happily. She found that the spice tasted better than it smelled, and the dish, which appeared to be some kind of fleshy plant that reminded her a little of cactus, was tender and delicious. She gave Snow a bite—he scowled in disapproval—and offered some to the others, who were inspired enough to get their own.

They encountered several different areas where musicians performed—not on a stage, but on the grounds themselves, surrounded by those who chose to listen. They chose one group of musicians and sat down on low, comfortable cushions that protected them from the rocky soil. The musicians, both male and female, played stringed instruments as well as small curved wind instruments. When the music had vocals, all the musicians sang, and the music had a harmonious folky quality.

It was the first time Catherine had seen a Sunai female in person. Even photos of them were rare, mostly because it was considered an offense to take their photograph. While still displaying the striking facial features of the males, they were much smaller than the males, even delicate, with smoother skin. They had high voices and a distinctly feminine way about them, and wore white gowns made of wispy, soft material that covered all but their bejeweled hands and necks.

After a few songs, Tom got restless and talked Zander, Middleton, and Shanti into exploring more, while Catherine stayed with Snow to listen.

"It's strange here," Snow remarked.

She nodded. "I like it so far."

They listened, Snow never taking his eyes off the musicians as his hand lightly tapped to the music. After a long stretch of music, Catherine spoke. "You want to go try some of those instruments?"

Snow shook his head. "Maybe later."

Catherine got up and went to one of the music booths. She picked up a small seven-stringed guitar that caught her eye. Although difficult to communicate with the Sunai man who ran the booth, he seemed fine with her experimenting. He even showed her how to play a simple melody, speaking in his foreign tongue the entire time but placing her hands and rearranging her fingers in such a way as to yield the proper notes. Then he watched her play, correcting her finger placement when necessary until, to her relief, another customer required his attention. After practicing for a while, Catherine found she could reproduce the melody he'd shown her. She smiled.

Soon, however, she began to feel very thirsty. Suna's heat and spicy food had caught up with her and she had no more water in her canteen. She looked around for a place to refill it, but couldn't see one. She showed her bottle to the Sunai and spoke the Sunai word for water; he gave her verbal directions she couldn't understand, gesturing to a far corner of the grounds. Catherine walked to the area he'd pointed to until she finally located the water dispenser, with the circular blue symbol, on the other side of a stone formation.

She took a quick drink and began filling her canteen. Suddenly, she felt large arms encircle her, trapping her in their grasp.

CHAPTER 19

Catherine yelled out. Her captor only clamped down on her as he covered her mouth. "Be silent, nonaii!" he rasped at her, his breath hot in her ear. "Or I will silence you."

She let herself grow limp, staying still for a moment, and then she jammed her heel into his knee as hard as she could. And then again. The second time did the trick, as her assailant growled in pain and involuntarily loosened his grip. She delivered an elbow to his throat—but instead of disabling him further, he blocked her maneuver and grabbed her by her throat.

Her airway blocked by the Sunai's strong hand, Catherine felt panic descend upon her as she forced his arm to the right, making his fingers lose their grip on her neck. She let loose a series of punches to his throat and head, overwhelming his ability to block her, until he began to teeter. He fell to the ground.

She stepped back, gasping for air and reaching for her contactor. It was gone. She searched around her, seeing nothing on the dusty, hard ground around them. Then she spotted it—it lay next to the Sunai's hand. She leaned over and picked it up. As she put it back on, she saw that two more Sunai stood a few meters away.

"Stay away from me!" she shouted at them, hoping her attacker's unconscious state would serve as sufficient warning.

They didn't accost her, instead walking a bit closer and looking down with their shaded eyes at her assailant. As they spoke amongst themselves in Sunai, one of them kicked the body as he walked around it. Catherine realized she recognized him from the meeting with Gronoi Okooii. He was the Grono who'd made the hand gesture, who'd stared at her.

"Why are you following me?" she demanded.

He let out a growly laugh and looked at his friend. "She is an angry one, yes?" His English was quite good, and his accent strong but decipherable. The other, a look of amusement on his strange face, spoke his response in Sunai. "Lieutenant Finnegan. You recognize me, yes?"

"I recognize you." She looked down at the incapacitated Sunai. "He attacked me."

"Yes. We saw him follow you here. Who defended you?"

"Who defended me? I defended myself! He tried to take my contactor."

The Grono pressed something on his arm and spoke in Sunai. And in just a few moments a group of men in different uniforms arrived, which she recognized as police. The Grono barked at them in Sunai and they picked up her assailant and took him away.

The second Grono spoke. "This is not possible. You are smaller, weaker, slower."

Before he could react, she gently kicked him in just the right place to throw him slightly off balance. "Slower?"

She saw his counter-move almost before it began—and the one after that—and easily blocked them both. He looked annoyed. "You are still weaker," he said.

"Who cares, if I am faster?"

The Grono from the meeting began to laugh at his comrade. "You are a strange human female," he said to her. "Bold, yes? But you are... distrustful."

"I have reason to be," she said, massaging her throat. "It seems like every encounter I have with your people is a violent one."

"I know of the attack on Derovia, with the Korvali refugee. Gumiia trash," he added with a flash of anger. "They go to our sister moon because they are too inferior to serve Suna."

Before Catherine could respond, a wave of lightheadedness came over her.

"You need refreshment," he said.

She shook her head. "I have my water." She looked around for her canteen and found it lying near the water dispenser.

"I have something far better. Come." He took her arm and led her back to the festivities. At the first booth they encountered, the Grono gestured to the musician, who immediately picked up a large canister and poured a rusty liquid into a clay cup.

Catherine hesitated. But, curious, she took the cup and sipped the cold sweet beverage. It tasted like unfermented kala. She then drank half the cup and immediately felt better. "Thank you."

The Grono gestured again and the musician quickly refilled the cup, after which the Grono slipped something into the musician's hand. "The one who attacked you… he is what the humans call a 'biocracker.' He knows you are a scientist, that you associate with the Korvali refugee. He sought to gain access to your data. We have been tracking him for two sun cycles."

"Is that why the gumiia attacked us?"

He waved his arm dismissively. "These gumiia care nothing of science. They seek only to taunt the refugee. It is said they did not harm him because a female was present."

Catherine shook her head in amusement. "And you still believe that?"

The Grono grunted. "She smiles," he said in triumph to his comrade, who stood aside. "This is Grono Amui, Lieutenant. And I am Grono Amsala. You may call me Koni." They held up their palms.

It was a good sign when a high-status Sunai male shared his given name, rather than his rank and family name. Catherine eyed them, suddenly feeling silly for her defensiveness. She met palms with each of them. "Call me Catherine."

"Why do you enjoy the festival alone, Catherine?" Koni asked.

"My friends are here somewhere. I was trying one of the guitars before I went to fill my canteen."

"Ah, you play guitar!" Koni said, appearing pleased.

"I do not. I've always wanted to learn how."

"Then you shall." He called to the musician, and the musician again hurried over to attend to Koni. He spoke a few words before turning back to Catherine. "It is my gift to you."

Taken aback by the gesture, Catherine gave her thanks, unsure of what else to say.

"Catherine!" said a male voice.

She glanced over and saw Tom and the others coming their way. And with them was Eshel, taking a long drink from his canteen. Tom must have told Eshel about the temperature control and ordered a transport for him. She shook her head at Tom; she would explain later. She turned back to Koni, but Koni's eyes remained on her friends. They remained on Eshel.

As if sensing he was being watched, Eshel looked their way. He looked at her before shifting his eyes to Koni.

"We're glad Gronoi Okooii granted Eshel permission to visit Suna," she said.

Koni stared at Eshel for a moment before turning back to her. "The Gronoi forgives, even those who do not repay debts." He glanced at Grono Amui. "We must go. You will be contacted about this attack." He gestured above him and looked up briefly. "Enjoy the moons." And he and Grono Amui left.

After her lessons, Catherine looked up again at the night sky. The reflection from Suna's rings had faded and she could count eight moons.

A week later, Catherine's contactor chirped. Koni had sent her an invitation to hike to the Fires of Tonaili.

She accepted.

Once Catherine finished packing the things she needed for the hike, she headed to the ship's exit. The guard cleared her to leave, on the order that she remain with Koni. After the incident with the bioc-racker, the brass barred her from leaving the ship alone. She tried to argue, but Yamamoto gave her his strictest look, which she knew not to challenge. Once Koni saw her, he ended his conversation with Commander Marks and approached her.

"Catherine!" Koni said. "I am most pleased you will accompany me to the fires. Nowhere else will you see such beauty."

"Thank you for the invitation. My dad told me the fires were a must-see."

"Ah, yes! I have not met Commander Finnegan. He visits Suna before I am Grono."

They got into the transport ship, leaving just after sunset. When they arrived at the trailhead, it was still hot, but not so hot that Catherine couldn't withstand the hike as long as she carried plenty of cold water. As they hiked, Suna's moons, and the light they cast on its rings, illuminated their path. The hills looked like bell-shaped silhouettes all around them.

"Why did you make that hand gesture at me?" Catherine asked, demonstrating. "And why were you following me at the festival?"

"The gesture is the macai. It says I would speak to you. It is custom to acquaint ourselves with those who visit Suna for business. You were more interesting than the others, so I chose you. Also, on Suna, once one becomes Gron, then Grono, there is no opportunity for family. Our otherworld guests, they are our… amusement."

"But Gronoi Okooii has children. Ov'Raa asked about them."

"Gronoi Okooii is a Gronoi. When he was Grono, he had no wives, no children. To become Gronoi, one must dedicate all his time to service. On Suna, there is no… enlist for two years, enlist for four years. It is for life. Only the best become Grono, Gronoi, Gronoio."

"How old were you when they recruited you?"

"I was one of the only boys accepted after five sun cycles. That is nearly seven Earth years."

"And your father... is he a Gronoi?"

"My father? No, no. I do not know my father. When a boy is accepted, he no longer belongs to his family of birth."

Catherine followed Koni, rusty dust collecting on her boots as she sipped more of her cool water, wondering what it would be like to leave one's family at such a young age. "Does the Gronoi sit at the apex of the table so he can see all your signals?"

"He sits there because that is his place. A Sunai can see the signals of others from nearly any position. I can see you look down at the ground beneath you as you walk."

She looked at him in surprise. His eyes remained forward. "How many times did I just blink?"

"Three times."

She laughed. "Astonishing."

As they continued on, Catherine asked Koni more questions. Koni liked answering them; they seemed to make him feel important, rather than bothered or invaded. It was a refreshing change after having spent so much time with an otherworlder who was so guarded.

After hiking for quite a while, Catherine noticed that the heat had begun to intensify, turning her comfortable sweat into a profuse one. She spotted a strange glow over the dark hill up ahead. As they climbed the hill, she began to hear noises... popping sounds. Once they crested, they looked down into a massive bowl that glowed orange-red as little flares popped up here and there. Suddenly, a loud sound reminding her of an abrupt shift in air pressure startled her, and a massive flame shot up into the air.

"Holy shit," she murmured, backing up a little.

"Does that bring you joy?"

She nodded, watching the flames. "More than you can imagine."

"I can imagine much joy, Catherine!"

Catherine smiled. *I'm at the Fires, Dad! I'm here with a friend and it's beautiful!* Her smiled faded. "Koni… I'm sorry I was rude when we met. I… I'd formed a prejudice against your people."

He put his big hands on her shoulders in the gesture of friendship. "You shall not be sorry. You are a warrior. And a warrior, even a female warrior, must always be cautious."

Catherine looked up to count the moons.

"How many moons do you see?" Koni asked her.

"Ten."

"There are only nine," he corrected.

"Are you sure?" she asked, sure she counted ten.

"I am sure, nonaii."

They enjoyed the fires for a while, flares occasionally shooting up, although none as big as the first one she saw. But once she began to feel overheated, she backed away a bit and Koni suggested they return to the trailhead.

As they hiked back, Catherine splashed some of her cooled water on her face and on the back of her neck, feeling herself recover. Just then, she heard a loud noise. She looked back, wondering if it were another large flare, but when she heard it again she realized it sounded different. She stopped, looking around her in concern.

"It is the mountain," Koni said. "It will burst earlier than expected. We must go." He pressed a button on his sleeve and spoke in Sunai. Catherine turned to look up at the mountain. A massive ash plume billowed from the peak. "We must hurry."

They began to run. It took her best effort to keep up with Koni's pace as she ran downhill, keeping her eyes down to avoid tripping on the rocks. Sweat soaked her. The mountain sounded again, so loud that Catherine put her hands to her ears. Soon she saw lights ahead; the transport ship landed nearby.

Once inside the transport, they quickly gained elevation as Catherine peered out the windows. Bright, glowing lava spilled from the peak and rapidly descended the nearby mountain. She continued watching as the transport navigated through the rain of ash, hardly believing the violence of the eruption and the deafening noise. Soon she could see Jula below, its citizens scurrying for shelter as the encroaching lava eventually surged through the viaducts.

The ship took them to the other end of the city, away from the erupting peak, and landed near the base of another mountain. "The transport must not fly further," Koni said. "You are safe here, until the mountain is silent."

When they climbed out of the ship, a swarm of heat, gas, and ash engulfed her. She began to cough. Koni grabbed her and ushered her into a small door at the base of the peak, and soon they were inside, out of the heat and fumes. She looked around and saw a dimly lit, cave-like room with a large window overlooking Jula.

"This is your home?"

"Welcome," he said, raising his chin.

Koni's home, like most who lived in Jula, was built into the side of the hill, allowing for better insulation from Jula's extreme climate. It was cool, neat, and somewhat elaborately decorated, with numerous military decorations mounted on the main wall and a few musical instruments on a less prominent wall.

She checked her contactor, wondering why it hadn't alerted her to the eruption and ordered her back to the ship. The screen was black. "I think the heat disabled my contactor, Koni. They'll worry if I don't check in."

"I will contact your ship and tell them you are safe."

Once Koni contacted *Cornelia*, they sat down on cushions tucked into a nook that offered them a view of Jula. A minute later, a Sunai woman emerged and brought them tea. The tea was infused with an herb—not the herb that created Jula's smell and flavored the food at the festival, but a subtler, sweeter herb. Catherine commented on it.

"It is rare, from only the Kotui region," Koni said. "The Kotui are difficult, always rebelling against their neighboring people, always giving trouble. We stopped these rebellions. Now, they do not sell us spice." Koni drank his tea, appearing indifferent to the hot temperature that had already burned Catherine's tongue.

She put down her cup. "You've been so generous, Koni. I wish there was something I could do for you, in return."

He raised his chin. "There is."

"What?"

"I was Gron once. Now I am Grono. But I want to be Gronoi. I want wives. I want children. I want my sons to leave me after five sun cycles to serve Suna, for my daughters to have more sons." He paused. "If I know what another Grono does not, I will be Gronoi first." His giant pupils shrank slightly. "These... Korvali. They are mystery, hiding what they know, guarding their customs and expertise. You were companion to the Korvali refugee at one time, yes? You must know what others do not."

Catherine hesitated. That was one thing she couldn't give him. "I have no useful information about the Korvali. Eshel is... he was very secretive."

"Perhaps. But you will know how one must interact with these Korvali to gain their favor, their respect. This refugee chose you as his companion over others; you gave him something he valued, yes? Something your comrades did not give him."

Catherine, despite her willingness to share that kind of information, still wasn't sure how useful she would be. She took a deep breath, considering Koni's question. "The biggest mistake people make when dealing with the Korvali is that they expect them to be... to be what they're not. They say they understand them, and they recite those things we all know about the Korvali—that they don't like outsiders, that they don't share their scientific methods, that they don't like being touched—but then they get angry when the Korvali actually behave in those ways upon meeting in person. If you want to succeed with them, Koni, you have to do what even Gronoi Okooii has difficulty with—you have to accept them for who they are. Even when they anger you."

Koni grunted. She didn't know if he disliked her suggesting that Gronoi Okooii's handling of Eshel wasn't ideal, or if he simply found her counsel difficult to swallow. "But what of conversational themes, gestures or words to avoid, formal addresses…"

"I can tell you all those things. But they won't work if you don't take my first suggestion."

He grunted again, taking another swig of tea. "And you… you were able to accomplish this feat, to find no judgment in the ways of the Korvali?"

Catherine looked down, brushing a bit of ash from her pants. "Not always, unfortunately. But perhaps more than most."

They talked a while more, until a gonging sound reverberated through the room. Koni pressed a button on his sleeve and spoke in Sunai. Once finished, he turned to her. "I must go. A transport will return you safely to your ship."

And within minutes, the transport arrived.

"Thank you for a great day, Koni. I'll never forget it."

Koni beamed with pride. "You are welcome, Catherine!" He paused. "And because we are now friends, I shall offer you a warning."

"A warning?"

"A warning. It is a gift, because we are friends. Your male comrade, from the festival—he shall not trifle with a Sunai female."

Catherine grimaced. "I'll talk to him. Tom's just a flirt… he doesn't mean any harm."

"No. It is not Lieutenant Commander Kingston I speak of. It is the skinny one, the one with the markings on his arms."

Snow. "What has he done?"

"He was seen speaking to a female musician."

"That's it?"

"That is enough," he said sternly. "There is no warning for this—only punishment. But he is your friend, and you are my friend. If it stops, there shall be no consequences."

Catherine nodded. "Thank you for telling me. I'll speak to him."

Catherine sat in her quarters, examining the comparative analysis she'd run on both copies of Eshel's genetic material. The Captain had ordered the crew to remain aboard for a couple of days, until the Sunai had the volcanic ash contained enough to be safe for humans. Out her window, the setting sun offered an unusually brilliant sunset, casting an ochre glow throughout her quarters. When her door sounded, she put away her work.

Snow walked in, cup of coffee in hand, glancing around at her quarters. "You rang?"

"Pull up a chair."

Snow sat down and focused his dark eyes on her, looking for clues as to what she wanted from him.

"So," she said, "You've met a Sunai woman."

Snow's expression changed. He shifted in his seat, glancing down before he looked up at her again. "How'd you find out?"

"Grono Amsala told me. He offered me the chance to warn you first, before they punish you for it."

Snow rolled his eyes at the threat. Catherine expected that; Snow hated being told what he could and couldn't do, even more than Tom did. He got a dark look on his face.

"Do you have feelings for her?"

Snow scowled. "Don't say anything. Not to Tom, not to anyone."

She raised her eyebrows. "Tom doesn't know?"

"Not yet." He drummed his hands on the table to some tune that only he heard, then took his hands off the table.

"How did you meet her?"

"At the festival." Snow gave a rare smile. "At one of the booths. I tried a new guitar and we played together... she wanted to see my bass, so I brought it to her shop in Jula..." He shook his head. "I don't know how it happened. I'm always getting on Tom for this kind of shit, for getting involved with women without thinking about the consequences..."

"Can't you just... be her friend?"

He looked down again. "No."

Catherine sighed. "Then you'll have to be careful, Snow. You can't be seen in public with her. Find somewhere to go. I'll tell Koni you were only interested in… in a custom stand for your bass."

Snow looked up. "I owe you, C."

She smiled.

But Snow didn't get up. He drummed his fingers again. "How far do you go?"

"How far?"

"You know. How far do you take something… with an otherworlder?"

Catherine was silent for a moment, tucking her hair behind her ear. "As far as you want to."

"But what did you do… you know… about the physical stuff?"

She hesitated.

"You don't have to tell me," he said. "I just… no one else will understand."

She nodded. "We did what we wanted to do. And so should you."

"No regrets?"

"Maybe at first. Because he didn't feel the same about me. But not anymore."

"Maybe he did feel the same."

She shrugged.

Snow tapped his fingers again, before finally standing up. When she stood, Snow came over and put his arms around her. She hugged him back. Once he released her, he looked around her quarters. "You still haven't found anything for that empty spot?"

Catherine glimpsed at the photos on her bulkhead and the empty space that remained. "Not yet."

And Snow left.

February 12th

Hi Dad,

How are you? Has skiing gotten better? I know it's been a dry winter, but you'll probably get a good dump of snow come March, like usual.

Yes, I have found a Sunai friend. Believe me, no one is more surprised than I am. Don't get me wrong: they're still full of themselves and they always think they're right, and they have no women in their government, which is never a good sign as far as I'm concerned. (Criticize the Korvali all you want, but Eshel said they have as many females as males in their government). Anyway, I can hardly hold much against the Sunai; after that biocracker attacked me, Koni had him interrogated and wound up uncovering a whole group of them. They'd been tracking me, Eshel, and even Holloway, under the assumption that we had data they could use. What's worse is they had plans to steal some of Eshel's DNA—something strictly forbidden by the Korvali—but Eshel's inability to handle Suna's sun season has kept him ship bound, thankfully protecting him from them.

No, I haven't talked to Eshel since before the Thirty. Not that he's talked to me either. Part of me wants to break the ice with him, but what's the point? It's clear he has no interest in my friendship. He's focused on other things now and doesn't even play poker anymore.

I've taught Koni a few things about how to interact with the Korvali, as he believes such knowledge will aid his promotion to Gronoi. Like most Sunai, Koni doesn't much like the Korvali, mostly because of what happened when they tried to invade Korvali space. But I think it's more than that. When I told Koni the Korvali only touch their closest companions and don't kiss at all, Koni became indignant, saying that all species worth knowing show affection with the mouth and that the Korvali are "bloodless and passionless" and "colder than Suna's moon season." Although not entirely true, I admit that made me laugh.

The Fires of Tonaili and the eruption are still the highlights of this encampment so far. Since then, the intense heat has waned a bit and the hot winds don't bother me anymore. And I don't even notice the smell now.

Hope to hear from you soon.

Love,
C

CHAPTER 20

Eshel's contactor chirped. *Report to the Captain's office immediately.* He stood up and went to Tom's office. "The XO has asked for me."

"What'd you do this time?" Tom quipped.

"I do not know."

When he arrived at Ferguson's office, they asked him to sit.

"Eshel," Yamamoto said, "we have word that two Korvali government officials have arrived on Suna. They are here, in Jula, for diplomatic meetings with Alliance officials."

Ferguson leaned back in her chair and drank from her canteen. "Tell him the rest."

"These men requested to come aboard the ship, which we declined. But they want to meet with you."

"Are these the same men who visited previously?" Eshel asked.

"One is. The younger of the two—Minel. Do you recognize the other?"

An image appeared on the viewer: two Korvali men in blue robes, their hoods up over their heads.

"Yes. He also works for the kunsheld."

"Have you dealt with him personally?" Ferguson asked.

"I have not."

"We've organized a meeting with them," she said. "It will take place at Jula's headquarters, and Gronoi Sansuai has agreed to oversee the meeting. The Korvali have been difficult with the Alliance regarding your living among us and potentially sharing your knowledge. Perhaps the meeting will set their minds at ease."

"I doubt that, Captain," Eshel said. "But I will attend."

The following day, Eshel, in full uniform as requested, walked down the dark, cool corridor with Ferguson and Yamamoto until they arrived at a guarded door.

"Remove your weapons and devices," the guard ordered.

They did as they were asked. The guard scanned them and, to Eshel's relief, didn't attempt to touch him. When they entered the room, two Korvali sat on one angled side of the trapezoidal table. Eshel immediately made eye contact with Minel, and then the other. Both watched him. He'd forgotten just how powerful the gaze of his people could be.

They wore blue robes, their hoods removed from their heads and resting on their backs. Two containers of chilled water sat in front of them. Eshel considered commenting on their wearing the blue robe of the Shereb, rather than attempting to pose as members of the Guard. But he thought better of it, knowing the others would find such a remark insolent.

"You have arrived!" Gronoi Sansuai called out in his gravelly voice. "Most excellent!" He offered his palm to Ferguson and Yamamoto in greeting, and offered Eshel only a nod. "Captain, Commander, Private, you may sit here," he said, gesturing to three empty chairs at the other angled edge of the table. He introduced his officers, Grono Amsala and Grono Amui. Eshel recognized both officers from the music festival, where he saw them talking with Catherine.

Finally, Sansuai sat at the short side of the table and spoke. "Our Korvali neighbors requested this meeting. They wish to speak with Private Eshel first. You must speak in English. Then, we open discussion to all."

Minel began. "Eshel. You look well."

Eshel did not reply.

"How is your scientific work? Have you made progress?"

"You know I am doing no such work, Minel."

"So it is true," Minel said, sitting perfectly still in his chair. "You have not shared that which does not belong to the others."

"I have not."

Gronoi Sansuai spoke. "It is always the Alliance's position, Minel, that Korvali technology or knowledge shall not be shared unless the kunsheld himself approves both the content to be shared and those he wishes to share it with!"

The two men kept their eyes on Eshel. "And what work do you do now?" the other Korvali asked him.

"I have duties in the Weapons section. I also study, to learn more of the technology of the humans."

"And do you find the work to your satisfaction?"

"It is acceptable." He noticed a stirring among the Sunai officers. He knew such a lukewarm response about his service would seem disrespectful to them. But they could not understand. No Sunai could appreciate the true importance of science, of the work he'd been prevented from doing.

"And you have made friends among the others," Minel said. "One in particular, a female geneticist, seems especially worthy of your attention."

Eshel knew the Captain and XO would find such a comment unexpected, would wonder how the two men could know whom he'd befriended. But Eshel expected such an inquiry. "She helped me adapt to life among the others."

"Such an extended period of acclimation," Minel said, "for someone so intelligent."

"She said acclimation would take one Earth year. And that is how long I befriended her."

"Long enough to do the unspeakable?" Minel sneered in Korvali.

"Don't be disgusting," Eshel replied in Korvali.

"Do not speak your native language here!" Gronoi Sansuai bellowed, his voice resonating throughout the stone-walled room.

Minel didn't acknowledge Sansuai as he continued to stare at Eshel. Eshel turned to the Gronoi. "An apology, Gronoi." Sansuai raised his chin, then nodded slightly.

Minel spoke again, this time to Ferguson. "Captain, the kunsheld is still distressed that our citizen lives among those who are not his people. However, I believe such discomfort would be assuaged with information from yourself."

"What sort of information?" Ferguson said.

"First, evidence that he conducts no genetic research. Also, detailed information about his duties and training. And finally," he added, looking at Eshel briefly, "detailed information pertaining to the work of your own geneticist, Catherine Finnegan."

Before Ferguson could respond, Gronoi Sansuai spoke. "You will have this information, Minel."

Ferguson frowned. "With all due respect, Gronoi—"

"You will provide the information requested, Captain," Sansuai insisted. "You may contact Admiral Scott for confirmation on this decision." Ferguson said nothing more. He turned his attention back on the Korvali. "I believe it may be useful to come to an agreement. A covenant, if you prefer. When Captain Ferguson gives you the information you require, and your former countryman agrees to not share the technological secrets of his homeworld, you will meet with myself and other Alliance delegates to discuss terms upon which your kunsheld will join us and have a vote in how such important matters are handled."

Eshel watched the two Korvali closely, as did everyone else. They were silent for several moments. Then Minel spoke up. "We agree."

A pleased look on his face, the Gronoi turned to Eshel. "Do you agree that you shall not share any information that you have learned from your training on Korvalis?"

"I agree," Eshel said.

"And how do you seal your agreements?"

"That is private," Minel said. "However, for your purposes, we will drink water to the covenant."

Minel, his companion, and Eshel drank from their cups.

"Excellent." Sansuai turned to Ferguson. "Captain, you must gather this necessary information and send it to me by the sun's rise." He turned to the Korvali. "You will meet with us the day following. Do you have all the information you require?"

"Yes," Minel replied. "We are... satisfied." He looked at Eshel. "We shall offer Elisan your regards, Private Eshel."

Both Korvali men stood up. Sansuai quickly adjourned the meeting and let the Korvali exit first. Before Eshel, Ferguson, and Yamamoto left, Sansuai approached Ferguson.

"Captain, my curtness with you was for the benefit of the Korvali. You will provide them with the information, but you may omit that which is... proprietary."

Ferguson appeared satisfied with this. "You will have it, Gronoi."

"I think that went pretty well," Ferguson said, sitting down in her chair.

"As do I," Yamamoto said. "It was a step forward. I'm somewhat surprised they agreed to it."

"Why?" Ferguson scoffed. "They got the better end of that deal."

They looked at Eshel, who sat quietly.

"What do you think, Eshel?" Yamamoto said.

"I believe their commitment to that covenant was no more meaningful than the stupid way we sealed it," he said.

Yamamoto raised his eyebrows in surprise, and Ferguson's smile disappeared.

"Why do you say that, when they have nothing to lose from this deal?" Ferguson asked.

"They have nothing to gain from it, either, Captain."

"How so?"

"Elisan will never join your Alliance. Their request for that information is a decoy, similar to their pretending to be Korvali Guard when they visited previously. Their mocking questions, their referring to me as 'Private,' even their use of 'Captain,' are insults. They're plotting something, and I recommend great caution."

Ferguson looked unconvinced. "You said the same thing the last time they visited. It's been eighteen months and they haven't done a thing except harass the Alliance."

"That means nothing."

Yamamoto spoke. "How is this meeting any different than the one with Gronoi Okooii, where he grilled you and accused you of not repaying a debt to the Sunai? Did you suspect some ulterior motive on his part?"

"The Gronoi, like all Sunai males, sought to satisfy his pride. The Korvali care nothing of pride. They want to protect what they believe is theirs, and any niceties or meetings with the Alliance will change nothing."

Yamamoto sat for a moment, as if constructing his next question. But Ferguson spoke first. "Why is it mockery to call you by your title, or me by mine?"

"The Korvali place little value on titles or military hierarchy, Captain."

"And do you mock me by referring to me as 'Captain'?" Ferguson said.

"My referring to you as 'Captain' is doing as I am ordered to live among you, Captain, as Chief Selway taught me."

"You didn't answer my question."

"There is no mockery in my addresses, Captain."

Ferguson donned an expression he'd grown accustomed to. "But you believe as your people do, about the value of military hierarchy."

Eshel didn't reply.

"You may speak freely," Ferguson said.

"Yes, I do."

"That seems rather ungrateful, Private, considering that both the Corps and Sunai militaries have gone out of their way to protect you."

Eshel remained silent.

Ferguson glanced down at her electronic pad. "Dismissed."

Eshel's contactor chirped. He glanced at the message; the Korvali didn't attend the meeting that Gronoi Sansuai had organized with the other Alliance delegates. They claimed such an important meeting would require the presence of Elisan himself, who was unavailable at that time. Eshel felt a flicker of disgust, knowing such a meeting would never occur.

Eshel heard another chirp. Tom. *You coming?* Eshel replied yes and continued walking, feeling a sense of dread. He was going to a "party" for those Corps and Sunai persons who had collaborated during encampment on Suna, offering them opportunity to socialize outside of their work. Ov'Raa believed such an event allowed each culture to learn about the other and foster good relations between the two militaries. Corps crewpersons personally invited their respective Sunai associates to the party and were expected to play host for the evening.

The notion of fostering relations with otherworlders through such means seemed silly to Eshel, who believed that working with them would accomplish such a goal in a far more useful way. And unlike the Derovian need to socialize and help others, which seemed strange and unnecessary to Eshel but didn't bother him much, the overbearing posturing and competitiveness of the Sunai men irritated him beyond measure. No forced social event would change that.

When Eshel scanned the room, he saw Tom and Zander animatedly talking with several of the Sunai weapons specialists they'd worked with. Eshel could tell from Tom's appearance that he'd had a lot to drink. He then spotted Catherine and Holloway talking with their scientific collaborators, appearing to enjoy themselves. He felt a sudden discomfort. He needed to speak with Catherine, but knew that doing so was risky.

At that moment, Catherine split off from her companions and walked over to a table filled with food. He followed her and waited as she deliberated about what to select, finally choosing some charred meat. When she turned around, she appeared startled at the sight of him.

"Is it acceptable for us to speak?" he said.

"Yes," she replied, her brown eyes searching him, as if guessing what he would say.

Eshel hesitated before he went on. "I have two things I must tell you. The first is a message."

"A message?"

"Yes. One of the Sunai weapons officers has a friend who is Calyyt. This Calyyt knows the Calyyt you competed against in the CCFs. This officer claims that your competitor desires a rematch, believes quite strongly that he will defeat you, and will issue a formal challenge."

Catherine looked surprised. "A formal challenge? Only the pros do that."

"Perhaps some of this information is merely Sunai overstatement. However, I believe the rest is true."

Catherine tucked her long hair behind her ear. "I'll think about that." She paused. "What was the other thing?"

The other thing. "I am told that a biocracker attacked you. I do not believe this is unrelated to—"

Tom's loud voice interrupted them. "Finnegan! Can I borrow this guy?" He motioned to Eshel with a somewhat drunken gesture. "Marks wants us to show these Sunai our new targeting software. Now they'll see who's more advanced! Let's go."

Seeing Commander Marks standing impatiently in the doorway, Eshel looked at Catherine and quietly spoke two words to her in Korvali before he left.

After they'd finished with the Sunai, Eshel and Tom stood alone in Weapons.

"I'm headin' home," Tom said, yawning. "It's time to pack it in. You gonna study?"

Eshel shook his head.

"What are you gonna do?" Then a look of recognition crossed his face. "No, man. No. Don't go back and find Catherine. Just leave her alone."

Eshel said nothing, hoping Tom would back off.

"What do you want with her?" Tom said.

"Why are you questioning me?"

"Why are you suddenly so interested in her after all this time?" Tom said. "You didn't want her, but now that she's hanging out with the Grono she suddenly seems more interesting to you?"

He found Tom's invasive questions and absurd assumptions especially tiresome at that moment, but tried nonetheless to reason with him. "We were having a conversation I want to finish."

"Bullshit."

"I do not understand. You reproached me for not talking to her; now you reproach me when I do."

Tom ran his hand through his curly hair. He seemed agitated, as if too many thoughts pressed upon him at once. "You had her, Eshel. You had her and then you threw her away."

"I did not throw her away—"

"You did. And you didn't give a shit. I saw it, she saw it, and so did everyone else."

Eshel paused, gathering his thoughts. "This happened months ago, Tom. Why are you angry now?"

"I didn't say a fucking word when you two split up—which you know is hard for me—because it was a tough situation, and I know you hate too much questioning, and shit happens, and feelings change, and all that shit. But then you hurt her by shutting her out. And I see things, Eshel. I see how you look at her lately," Tom said, standing closer to Eshel and pointing at him. "I see the way your hackles go up anytime someone brings up Koni's name. And I saw the way you looked at her tonight. Don't try and deny it, Eshel. You may be smart, but I know people. You had your chance with her; now it's over."

"Why do you insinuate that I behave like a Sunai?" Eshel said. "And if I want to speak to Catherine, I will."

Tom shook his head. "Leave her alone, Esh, or I promise you I'll mess you up."

"Tom, you're drunk. You sound like Middleton."

"Fuck you," Tom shot back. "Don't ever compare me to him."

"Then stop blathering and make your point."

"My point is that you don't appreciate people, people who look out for you. I've shown you everything I know, given you access you shouldn't even get, and you act like it's nothing! Just like you treated Finnegan like she was nothing. And I know why: you come from this privileged world where they care more about genetics than they do about people."

Eshel finally lost his temper. "I don't care about people?" he said in a raised voice, stepping even closer to Tom. "I don't care? I care for my father, a good man and a brilliant scientist, who desired more freedom for us and a relationship with the outsiders. I still have visions of him, and have since the night I learned his life was stolen because of these desires. I care for my mother, who I do not know when I will see again. I gave up everything—my clanspeople, my work, my home—to come here and attempt to live among strangers who know nothing of my customs, who punish me for being unlike them. And you," Eshel pointed his webbed fingers at Tom, his voice lowered and his words measured, "you are a hypocrite for lecturing me about my behavior when your own stupid conduct has offended numerous people. I see things, too."

Tom glared at him, standing even closer to him, closer than he knew Eshel would tolerate. But Eshel didn't back down. He waited, his hands ready, for Tom to make his move.

But Tom did nothing. "You can unclench, you bastard. I'm not going to hit you. I've hit a lot of people… but you're my friend and I don't hit my goddamn friends."

"I still do not understand why you're angry with me."

"You're coldhearted, man."

"I don't know what that means."

Tom sighed. "You care about your father, your mother… but you don't care about us. It's like we're… we're just the means to help you get what you want. And once you get it, you're done. Like with Catherine…" He shrugged.

Eshel said nothing for several moments. "What you say about Catherine… it is untrue. I ended our romantic relationship for reasons I cannot share with you. But I did not hope to be embargoed from speaking to her."

"No one embargoed you, man."

Eshel relayed the story about Catherine slapping him.

"That's not an embargo, dumbass!" Tom cried, throwing his hands up. "She was angry at you! You went from treating her like she was the only person who mattered to you, to giving her the Korvali cold shoulder like you give the rest of us. Jesus, Eshel, you learn our weapons systems from front to back in a fraction of the time of anyone I've ever met, but you can't figure this out?" He shook his head.

"Relating to outsiders… it has been difficult for me," Eshel said coldly. "I thought you understood that." He broke eye contact with Tom and stood in silence. Finally, he turned and left Weapons.

As he walked, Eshel reviewed all that Tom had said. It was difficult to have Tom, who typically encouraged him in everything he did, suddenly criticize him so harshly for his conduct regarding Catherine, and even for his very temperament.

I cannot live among the others, Father. I have failed. They do not understand me, and I do not understand them.

He also felt residual anger over Tom's accusations about how he looked at Catherine, or his reaction to her association with Grono

Amsala. He attributed Tom's absurd comments to intoxication and lack of understanding of him. But as Eshel gave more consideration to the matter, he realized that the anger he felt was due to the fact that some of Tom's observations were correct.

However, such thoughts must be put aside for now. He still needed to speak to Catherine, and returned to the party to do so. But when he scanned the room, she was gone. It would have to wait until tomorrow.

As Catherine undressed, she pondered her conversation with Eshel that evening. How very strange that he'd speak to her after all that time, just to tell her what she would've found out anyway. And what was that second thing he'd meant to tell her? What he'd said in Korvali—two words roughly translating to "hidden information"—didn't make sense. Coming from Eshel, hidden information could mean anything.

She climbed into bed, feeling herself grow sleepy as her mind drifted back to their conversation. He'd mentioned her being attacked by the biocracker, that it was related to something… perhaps he wanted to ensure she still protected the genetic information she had about him, information that would prove highly valuable to a biocracker. She recalled him giving her the two storage drives, a blue one with a new copy of his genetic material, and a black one…

Catherine opened her eyes. The black one. The one he'd said to tuck away, in the event that something happened to him. She'd forgotten about it. Of course—he wanted to ensure she protected that information as well, as it probably contained sensitive information about the Korvali.

Although he'd told her not to look at it unless something happened to him, curiosity got the better of her and she got up, retrieved it from its hidden location, and viewed its contents. After doing so, she understood Eshel's warning; it contained intelligence that any non-Korvali military would love to get their hands on. Catherine carefully hid it away again and got back into bed.

A loud beep awakened Catherine. *Shit.* Chirps were fine, but beeps meant trouble. She glanced at the time: 0610.

"Yes, Sir," she said, not even checking who'd contacted her.

"Lieutenant Finnegan," said Yamamoto's voice. "Report to the Captain's office immediately."

"On my way, Sir."

As she quickly dressed, dread came over her. It didn't take a genius to figure out why they'd called her up. They'd found out about her project with Holloway. Steele was onto them. Her mind immediately went to Eshel. *That's* what he'd meant about hidden information. He'd found out something and meant to warn her.

As Catherine walked to Ferguson's office, she considered her defense… what she would reveal and how. She'd need to tell the brass about Steele's clandestine emails to Dr. Vanyukov, and produce them if necessary. They'd charge her with violating Steele's direct order and working with Eshel's DNA file, but Steele would face bigger consequences. He had more to lose, while her career trajectory with the Space Corps had turned out to be a dead end anyway.

Catherine could feel her palms sweat as she arrived at Captain Ferguson's office. When she saluted, she noticed their grave expressions. Both looked tired, like they'd been up all night. Ferguson was dressed down in pants and a Space Corps t-shirt, several strands of dark hair having come loose from her bun. Her blue eyes lacked their usual sparkle.

"At ease, Lieutenant," Yamamoto said. "Sit down."

Catherine sat down in the other chair, waiting for him to speak. But it was the Captain who spoke first.

"Lieutenant," Ferguson said. "Nothing we talk about here can leave this room. Do you understand?"

"Yes, Captain."

"Last night, the Command Center received an emergency signal from Eshel's contactor. When he didn't respond to contact, we sent Tom out with a crew to find him. They found the contactor... but Eshel's gone."

CHAPTER 21

Eshel's gone. Catherine was rendered speechless for several moments as she sat before Yamamoto and Ferguson, her mind sprinting from one thought to another. Last night, Eshel hadn't been trying to warn her to protect his data, or to protect herself from Steele... he'd known he was in danger. "They took him," she finally said.

A look of recognition made a fleeting appearance on Ferguson's face. She took a deep breath and flicked the escaped strands of hair away from her face. "Grono Amsala just contacted us. Sunai vessel logs show that a ship left Suna last night around the time of Eshel's disappearance. The same ship was detected at Station Ten."

"They're taking him to Korvalis," Catherine said.

"It looks that way."

Catherine turned to Yamamoto, eager to see a face that would comfort her. And that's when he spoke. "We didn't ask you here just to tell you what's happened. We have an interplanetary alert out for Eshel. It is imperative that we attempt to retrieve him, and the sooner the better. The Alliance has offered its full support. However, to do this, we must ask you some questions, questions you may find difficult to answer."

Catherine nodded.

"Based on your former relationship with Eshel, and your knowledge about him, do you have any reason to believe that his disappearance was planned by him in some way?"

"No."

"You believe he was taken by force."

"Yes. He knew this could happen."

"When Tom found Eshel's contactor, it lay on the ground, out in the open. There was no indication that any data had been downloaded from the device, suggesting that his abductor was not a cracker." He paused. "As I said, we must attempt to retrieve Eshel. However, to have the Alliance's support, we must do so without conflict. The ship carrying Eshel has too much lead-time on us and will enter Korvalis's atmosphere before we can catch up. Thus, we've discussed various methods of retrieval, each riskier than the last." He paused, leaning forward in his chair. "Catherine, do you have any information that could give us an advantage in this operation?"

Catherine looked at her mentor. She nodded.

"Not over my dead body, Suko!" Ferguson said.

"Janice…" Yamamoto began.

"We can't send a whitecoat to do a soldier's job!" she shouted, her face red. "She has no field experience! And I won't risk the life of a scientist and one of my best soldiers with this ridiculous plan, Suko."

"She has volunteered—" But Ferguson cut him off. "Let me finish, Janice," he hissed. She reluctantly stopped talking and let him speak. "She has volunteered, knowing the risks. So has Tom. An F-6 will get them to Korvalis in one day instead of three, giving them an advantage. The Alliance has made it very clear we're responsible for getting him back, and that we must do so without conflict. This is the only way to achieve that end. *We have no other option.*"

"Yes, we do."

He shook his head. "That will risk more lives, damage our relationship with the Alliance, and it could start a war with the Korvali. We cannot risk war." He paused. "I know you don't like Eshel, or trust him… but you know his character. He would not entrust those he cares most about to a foolhardy plan."

"How do you know he cares for them? He doesn't seem to care for anyone."

"I believe he does, in his own way."

"The Alliance has no goddamn business telling us how to handle this," Ferguson said. "They aren't the ones with the burden of protecting him."

"I agree. But they didn't ask us to take him under our protection, either."

"No. Headquarters did. And where are they now? Enjoying crab cakes on the Chesapeake Bay!" She gestured toward the window.

Yamamoto didn't respond. Although Ferguson's way of handling their difficult situation was different than his, he couldn't disagree with any of her sentiments.

Ferguson heaved a great sigh and ran her hands over her face. "I'll authorize this plan. But Tom should lead this op, not Finnegan. He's far more qualified."

"I tried that. Catherine insisted that it must be her."

Ferguson glared at him. "Who is she to insist?"

"She's the one with the information. I leaned on her, Janice. She would not relent. It seems she has something necessary for the operation to succeed."

"Like what? I want the details."

"So do I. But it's clear that Eshel is protecting something. And given who he is and where he comes from, are you surprised?"

"Tom hates not being in charge."

"Tom's wishes aren't what's important here. Getting Eshel back is. And we'll make it clear to Tom that if the op goes awry, he's authorized to take over."

Ferguson nodded absentmindedly. "We have a whitecoat rescuing a Korvali from the Forbidden Planet he escaped from, using methods only they know, while one of my best soldiers goes along as nothing more than a babysitter. All under my goddamn watch." She shook her head. "You can't make this stuff up. I hate this, Suko. I don't trust Finnegan. If it weren't for Tom, I'd kill this ridiculous plan."

"Unfortunately, this is one of those situations when we must relinquish some control," Yamamoto told her, knowing full well she would hate that answer.

Ferguson rolled her eyes. "Let me guess. Now you'll tell me there's no point in worrying about it, that worrying solves nothing, right?"

"Janice, it is extremely easy for the less worried person to lecture the worrier on the ills of worrying. I know Catherine better than you do. She's not a soldier, but she's a skilled fighter and tough in her own way. It isn't her character to embark on challenges she cannot handle."

"Well, Suko, it's your faith in her that I'm relying on. You haven't let me down yet." She walked to her window and looked out. "Why would Eshel entrust such information to her if they haven't been on speaking terms, especially after what he said about using her to acclimate to us?"

"I don't know. There are aspects to Eshel, and his people, that are a mystery to us all."

"How much do you want to bet he's shared more than this with her?"

Yamamoto didn't answer. He couldn't think about that now.

Catherine quickly climbed the stairs to the hangar deck, where Tom waited for her. He too was dressed in full field uniform. She wanted to tell him everything, just to share the burden with someone she trusted. But she couldn't. Eshel had made it clear to tell no one else what she knew.

"Do you have the units?" she said.

"Yup," Tom said, reaching into his pack. He retrieved six black devices and handed them to her. They were small, only a couple of centimeters in diameter. "Be careful not to lose them. You'll get five hours out of these. Six at most. Keep your eye on the light—it'll blink when it's getting low on power, about once per second, then faster once it gets really low. Change out when it's one per second. Don't take any chances." She put them into her pack and looked at Tom expectantly. "Oh," Tom said in recognition. He reached into his pocket and pulled out a larger flat, rectangular device. "Be careful with this one. It can do some damage."

Maintenance had just finished preparing the F-6 "Mosca" for launch. Snow emerged from inside it. "She's ready to go," he said. He'd spent hours making modifications to it, using the directions Catherine had given him. "Are you going to tell us what the modifications are for?"

"Yeah," Tom added. "And what are the little black devices for?" He glanced at Snow. "I tried one out and nothing happened."

"We have to go," Catherine said.

"Let me come with you," Snow said. "You don't have to tell me anything. But if something goes wrong with the Mosca…"

"Sorry, buddy," Tom said, slapping Snow on the shoulder. "Captain's orders."

Snow shrugged. "Worth a try." He came over and hugged Catherine. "Kick some ass."

When he released her, she looked over and saw Ferguson and Yamamoto enter the hangar bay. Both looked right at her; she saluted. She'd managed to convince them to send her to Korvalis. But she no longer felt the confidence she'd conveyed.

She turned to Tom and Snow. "Promise me, and Eshel, that you'll both keep quiet about what you've found out. Promise on your tattoos."

The guys looked at one another and touched their left shoulders, where each wore the emblem of military social services, and put their hands up briefly.

"Are you sure you're up for this?" Tom said, eyeing her. "I'm telling you, I can take the lead. I know how to keep a secret. Just say the word."

"I'm fine."

"We'll get him," he said, putting his arm around her. "I'm a soldier, C, and soldiers never leave a comrade behind."

As Catherine and Tom got into the craft, Snow left them and went to stand with Ferguson and Yamamoto behind the glass barrier. The bay doors opened. Catherine felt a bit lightheaded from the craft's motion, which felt quick and dynamic compared to that of *Cornelia*.

In the initial hours of their journey, they reiterated their plan again and again. They divided the operation into multiple steps, hashing out minimum and maximum time estimates for each step. The Captain and XO issued a time limit for the entire operation, at the end of which they must report back. They planned for every contingency and every what-if, including what to do if they were detected at any point. These conversations were helpful to Catherine. They must have helped Tom as well, as he repeated their plan multiple times and made her do the same. But after many of these repetitions, there wasn't much else to say.

So Tom, whose chatter often did much to ease tensions, told stories. He recalled memorable wins and losses from their many poker games, including the one where they wound up with Eshel's sick bay duty shifts. He talked of the brawl between him and Haus, and the one between Eshel and Middleton, and even the argument he'd had with Greta, who'd gotten angry when she asked to join his game and he told her that poker and romance don't mix. Catherine smiled at the memories, although they did little to ease her worry. And Tom noticed. "What's the matter?" he said.

Catherine shook her head. "How did this happen, Tom? I was just talking to him last night at the party. It was the first conversation we'd had in five months. At least until you showed up."

Tom let out a sigh. "Yeah… sorry about that. Eshel told me he wanted to go back and talk with you. He didn't?" She shook her head. "That's my fault, too."

"How's that?"

Tom's face clouded over. "We got into an argument. A bad one. I had a few too many… said some shit I shouldn't have. Not that he let me get away with it, believe me," Tom added. "But I gave him a hard time about talking to you."

"Why?"

"Because," Tom said defensively. "Because of everything that happened with you guys. I was trying to look out for you. I don't always let on, but I look out for you."

"I know you do."

Tom's jaw clenched. "I should've kept my mouth shut." He glanced at the time. "Get some sleep. You'll need to be rested for this."

"I can't sleep."

"Take this." He tossed her a small box. "When it wears off, you keep watch and I'll get a few hours in."

She took one of the pills and lapsed into a heavy sleep. But before she was asleep long, someone shook her. "Catherine. Wake up."

"What's wrong?" she said, her mind foggy. She heard music.

"Nothing's wrong. I gotta get some shuteye before we get there."

"How long was I out?"

"Six hours." He adjusted his seat. "If you see anything— anything at all—wake me up. Otherwise, give me five hours. Five, okay?"

After Tom drifted off, Catherine turned off the music and watched everything with vigilance, looking for the slightest problem. But none came, leaving her with her thoughts.

She looked out into the blackness, awed by the impressive velocity they were able to achieve in the F-6, while simultaneously struck by how slowly they seemed to progress when having to travel over such a great distance. People—that is, those who'd never gone to space—often remarked at how long it had taken to discover the Korvali. But from her own standpoint, it made perfect sense. There was nothing out here, no phenomena of any kind. Only the most tenacious would venture this far into nothingness.

Catherine tried to fill the time by thinking about her work with Holloway, about the progress they'd made. But all thoughts on that topic evaporated quickly. All thoughts of any kind evaporated quickly, except for those of Eshel.

Stay alive, Esh. We're coming to get you.

After what seemed an interminable amount of time, Catherine whistled to wake Tom up. They reiterated their plan several more times, identifying any remaining concerns and working out solutions for them. And just when Catherine thought she would go crazy if Tom said another word about it, a bright, shining mass came into view. The Gernoly star system. Korvalis's home.

She recognized the gleaming white from the long-range images that explorers had taken. Korvalis's cloud cover reflected its sun's light, making it easily visible from a great distance. The cloud cover didn't completely encompass the planet, however. As they drew closer, through openings in the clouds one could see the vivid blue of its massive oceans.

"We're near the boundary," Tom said, his eyes scanning the positioning system display. "Once we cross, eyes and ears." He entered a code into the console to deploy Snow's modifications.

They crossed. Catherine and Tom were silent, Catherine holding her breath, waiting for detection, for the sight of Guard ships, for any warning. They remained silent for several minutes, beyond the amount of time necessary for the Guard to detect and detain them. Catherine looked at Tom, and Tom at her. He lacked his usual grin, but she could see the excitement on his face.

How did you know how to do that, Esh? No geneticist knows such things.

"Shit," Tom said.

"What?"

"Two ships, heading our way."

Catherine saw the boxy, austere Guard station in the distance, as two clunky-looking ships moved in their direction. "Don't load weapons," she said, seeing Tom eye the weapons console.

The ships passed them. Tom smiled. "They're heading for where we crossed the boundary. They know something's up, but they can't see it."

The craft shook as they entered Korvalis's atmosphere. But just when it began to get too jumpy, they broke through. And after a brief period of good visibility, they entered the thick mass of clouds that temporarily blinded them and surrounded them in white. It made Catherine nervous. She glanced over at Tom, who looked calm, trusting his instruments to steer him in the correct direction.

After emerging from the clouds, Korvalis came in to full view. Among the vast oceans, muddy blue under the muted light of the clouds, there were verdant, hilly landmasses with outcroppings of dark gray rocky peaks. The land masses narrowed into countless peninsulas or broke off into clusters of keys, some of which were extensive in their reach. It was one of the most beautiful places Catherine had ever seen.

"The Forbidden Planet," Tom remarked. "Looks small. And wet."

Catherine nodded.

Tom glanced at his sensors. "No sign of pursuit. Give me the coordinates again. Read them out loud."

Catherine reluctantly took her eyes off the planet and read off the coordinates for the navigation system. The craft slightly shifted its heading, aiming for one of the larger landmasses that, from their view, still appeared rather small compared to the enormous seas sprinkled with keys and archipelagoes. As they got closer, Tom decelerated more, bringing the engines to a quiet hum.

They landed just south of Felebaseb, behind the cover of a thick wooded area. The Korvali couldn't see them, but they would hear them if Tom landed too close to the city. Catherine removed her contactor and put it aside. It would be of no use to her without the satellite network it relied upon. Instead, she donned a new instrument that Tom had loaned her to keep time and offer solar-based navigation. After Catherine checked her gear for the fourth time and got ready to leave, she and Tom reiterated their plan one last time.

"If you have any trouble—any trouble at all—come back here," he said. "You hear me? *Back here.* No matter what happens, we'll take care of it."

Catherine nodded.

"Promise," he ordered.

"I promise."

They started their timers. She hugged Tom, and he held her a little tighter than usual. She picked up one of the six black devices Tom had made and turned on the power switch, placing it in the chest pocket of her jacket before she zipped it shut.

As she exited the craft, she realized suddenly that she was, to her knowledge, the first non-Korvali to ever set foot on the Forbidden Planet.

Catherine quickly walked north toward Felebaseb, the cool, humid air refreshing her. It smelled moist, like rain, grass, and sea. After finding the hidden sun's location, she realized it was early morning. Once she entered the forest they'd hidden behind, it was almost as if the sun had set. The forest enveloped her, its dense dark trees with their tapered leaves towering over her and blocking the day's light. She glanced at her instrument to ensure she was still heading north. Soon, to her relief, Catherine emerged from the forest.

She went over the plan in her mind again, recalling the contents of the storage drive Eshel had given her. His tipping her off at the party, intended or not, had sparked her curiosity and given her the opportunity to prepare in advance. She recalled her dubiousness at Eshel's intricate, detailed rescue plan; she hadn't believed that the Korvali had the ability—or the sheer audacity—to snatch Eshel from under their noses. She, and many others, had been wrong. Eshel was right. He was always right.

Catherine felt sprinkles of rain on her hood as she looked toward Felebaseb, a compound with nothing but dull gray buildings that housed the Guard's corrections facilities. When she reached the door to the facility, she saw the security console next to it; it had a series of buttons, each with its own symbol. She pulled out the rectangular device Tom had made, aimed it at the console, and pressed the button.

Nothing happened. She waited a moment and pressed in again. Still nothing.

She felt a stab of anxiety. She examined the device more closely, discovering that it had a power switch. Once turned on, she aimed the device again and pressed. The electronic display went blank and she heard a click. *Holy shit. It worked.*

Slowly, Catherine opened the door and peeked in. She saw no one, so she tiptoed in and quietly shut the door behind her. She walked softly on the gray stone floor and headed toward the west wing, where the holding area would be. As she rounded a corner, Catherine halted when she spotted a group of Guardsmen protecting the entrance to the west wing. They stood quietly in their black uniforms, with their weapons belts on.

She waved her arm, daring the Guardsmen to see her. She was still far enough from them that she could flee back to the Mosca if her little black device didn't work. The Korvali were superior swimmers... but they couldn't run fast. The Guardsmen didn't see her. She slowly walked toward them, growing closer and closer, so much so that she could see their pale eyes as they looked right through her.

As Catherine approached the holding area, her heart began to pound. The anticipation of locating Eshel was more anxiety-provoking than anything she'd done thus far. She reached the first holding cell and looked through the window. It was empty. She walked further, to the next cell. Also empty. After passing several empty rooms, she approached one that had a gray-robed, hooded figure sitting inside of it, his long, thin webbed hand emerging from his sleeve. She felt the beginnings of relief. As she got closer to the cell window, however, she saw the figure's left hand. It had the spreading branches of the Osecal. It could not be Eshel.

She continued on, peering in all the remaining cells. Only two others contained a robed person. Neither was Eshel.

There was another possibility. After so little time, it seemed unlikely that they would've transferred him from the holding area to the prison. However, Eshel did say that, in some cases, trial and conviction could be swift. Catherine immediately headed to the prison, in the north wing of the compound.

Once she reached the north wing, she prepared to scramble the security door console until she realized a guard was coming. She stood aside, holding her breath again. He entered a code, opened the door, and Catherine slipped in behind him and then stopped, hoping to increase the distance between them.

The prison looked nothing like those on Earth. It had no bars, no strange echo, no creepy feeling. Instead, it looked more like a hospital, with pale gray floors and walls. It had many windowed doors, one after the next. It was scarcely populated and remarkably silent.

She peered in the first window, looking for Eshel, hoping to see his strong gaze meet hers. But then she had a realization—Eshel wouldn't see her with her device employed. Why hadn't that occurred to her before?

Catherine peered in one window after the next, the cells only large enough to accommodate two or so people. Many were empty. She scrutinized each prisoner, checking for any resemblance to Eshel. Most wore gray robes and, when visible, the branched marking on the left hand, rather than the magenta leaf. None were Shereb. She combed the prison from one end to the other, walking quietly in her sound-absorbing boots.

There was no sign of Eshel. He wasn't at either place he said he'd be.

CHAPTER 22

Eshel opened his eyes. All he saw appeared blurry, and his mind felt foggy. He tried to move, but realized he was bound to his seat. His first instinct was that he was on Korvalis. But once his mind cleared after a few moments, he recognized that he was on a moving ship. He didn't know the ship's origin, nor was there a window to offer any clues. But after a few minutes, he heard a deep, guttural voice from the cockpit, and then second one.

The two Sunai men spoke of a woman. One had outwitted the other the previous evening in gaining the attentions of a female; the other made it clear he would not give up his efforts to return her attentions back on himself. Eshel felt a wave of annoyance at the stupidity of their conversation.

He looked around for a way to free himself from his restraints, but found nothing that would help him. He noticed his missing contactor, recalling that he'd deployed its emergency signal. His hands were abraded, his shoulder ached, and his cheek hurt.

The two Sunai had approached him after he'd returned to the party; he would either leave the ship with them, or they would harm Catherine. After exiting *Cornelia*, he'd quietly dropped his contactor behind him; such a maneuver had some chance of going undetected by the impressive peripheral vision of the Sunai. As they'd approached a ship, Eshel, having no weapons on him, had defended himself using the only method available to him—his hand-to-hand training. He'd aimed for and broke both sets of eyeshades. However, before he could make his next move, he'd felt a brief pinch in his neck. He recalled nothing else.

The hum of the ship's engines changed. They'd decelerated, and Eshel realized they were getting ready to land. The copilot stood up and made his way back to Eshel.

"The bloodless one has awakened," the Sunai said.

The pilot landed the ship, turned off the engines, and joined his copilot, both observing him from behind new eyeshades.

"The black marking on his face is small," the pilot said. "You should have punished him more."

"I do not trust the Mutants to pay us if we damage him."

Eshel knew these were no gumiia. They were military. The two men removed his restraints and, each grabbing Eshel by an arm, yanked him up from his seat. Eshel grimaced at the pain that seared through his shoulder. The ship's hatch opened, and six Korvali Guard stood in their black robes, each gazing at him.

One Guardsman stepped forward and handed the Sunai something, fixing her eyes upon them. "Go," she said coldly.

The Sunai men grunted. The copilot turned back toward the ship, while the pilot lingered for several moments, meeting the Guardsman's stare. He finally turned and followed his comrade back into their ship. They started their engines, and the ship quickly rose and exited above them. The roof hatch closed, shielding them from the nighttime sky.

Two Guardsmen approached Eshel carrying a restraining device. They placed it around his torso, trapping his arms, and cranked the handle until it tightened. Eshel had heard of this device, but had never seen one. The Guardsman who'd ordered the Sunai to leave motioned to a small ship. Eshel climbed inside, as two other Guardsmen joined him. Once the ship left the bay, Eshel looked out the window at the darkness. Within minutes they were near the planet's surface, heading in exactly the direction he'd expected.

Just as they were to land, he felt another pinch in his neck. And everything went blurry.

When Eshel came to, he looked around him. He was lying down, unbound and unclothed. They'd taken his uniform. A gray robe, rather than a blue one, hung on a hook. He put it on, looking around him. The room contained a small bed, a desk, and a separate toilet. He tried the door: it was locked. When he looked up, he saw surveillance cells. With no window and no timepiece, he had no knowledge of the time.

He didn't know where he was.

Hours passed. And finally, the door opened. Eshel looked up, expecting to see Minel and continue their purposeless conversation in Jula… or perhaps even Elisan, the kunsheld himself. Instead, someone unexpected emerged.

Elan. He closed the door, his pale gray eyes examining Eshel closely as he stood unmoving for several long moments. Finally, he approached Eshel and put his cheek to his.

"You are returned," Elan said. He stepped back, his eyes running over Eshel. "They force you to wear the robe of the Osecal," he observed. He stood still, remaining silent for several more moments. "You are in danger, Eshel. I will exert my influence where I can, but I have little hope that you will be freed. Tell Elisan what he wants to know. Tell him about the technology of the humans. Tell him how you were able to survive your journey to the other worlds. Tell him *everything.*"

Eshel remained silent.

Elan looked around him, finally taking a seat at the desk. "Why, Eshel? Why leave your people, your work, your home… just to live under the rules of those who do not appreciate our science?"

"Some of them do."

"Not enough of them. It is said you were not allowed in their science labs. How could you not convince them?"

"How could they not convince Elisan, and your mother, to join the Alliance?" Eshel replied. "Such change does not happen quickly."

"That is no equivalent example."

"Isn't it? In both cases, each fears what it does not understand." Eshel paused. "Such a decision—to leave—was difficult, Elan. It is not my intent to be traitorous, or to reveal secrets to the others. But I believe, as my father did, that we, and our scientific abilities, cannot thrive in isolation."

Elan did not reply. Eshel knew he could not, that any support of such an idea wouldn't sit well with those who listened.

"Is Alshar well?" Eshel said.

Elan's cold expression softened. "She has grown quite tall. And she already shows impressive understanding of the science." He paused. "Your mother—she is well. I imagine she will be quite persuasive on your behalf."

Yes. Where his father was brilliant in his scientific innovation, his mother's many years of service in their assembly afforded her considerable power.

Elan stood up. He looked at Eshel once more, and left.

Eshel awoke to the sound of the door. This time, when he saw who entered, he felt an immediate revulsion.

Elisan, not quite as tall as Eshel and his hair faded with age, extended his arm, palm up, and slowly raised it. Eshel hesitated for a moment, then did as he was asked and stood up.

"Eshel," Elisan began in his disdainful tone. "How is it to return to your homeworld?"

Eshel said nothing in reply.

Elisan peered at Eshel for some time, as if he couldn't believe what he saw. "It has been a long time—1.84 years, to be accurate—since you have lived among us. Or do you calculate the passing of time in Earth years now?"

"Why am I here, Elisan?"

"You are here for the same reason I am, for the same reason we all are. You are here because you are Korvali, and the Korvali do not abscond from our homeworld, do not live among the others, and do not share our technologies with the others."

"You are at least partially wrong," Eshel replied. "I achieved two of those things you claim the Korvali do not do. Do you care to know which two?"

Elisan looked at him with unblinking eyes. "If you knew how your words will impact your future, you would be more cautious in how you speak to me."

Eshel relented. "I did not share my knowledge. I was forbidden to do so, even if I had wanted to. The others have informed you of this."

"Yes, we were informed. By so many. But why would I believe the words of the outsiders... or the words of a traitor?"

"Examine their publications. Their methodologies are as simplistic as they have ever been. You don't have to believe me; ask Elan to examine their work. He will find nothing of use."

"Perhaps. But this Alliance—they seek to exploit the knowledge of other worlds, to impose their rules, all with promises of protection and information exchange. They don't want exchange. They want to take, to dilute, to ruin what we have built, for their own gain. It is an insidious ploy for military societies to prey upon the intellectually advanced, hoping to control them."

"That is not the case."

"No? Then why do you wear their uniform? Why do you now speak with inflection? Why do you involve yourself with Catherine Finnegan?" Elisan sneered at the mention of Catherine's name. "Five hundred and seven outsiders available to you on that ship, and you align yourself with a geneticist. I do not pretend to have your skills with probability, Eshel... but do you not agree that such a choice was an improbable one, far beyond the vagaries of chance?" Elisan paused. "You do only what benefits you. You are like your father in that way. You didn't train to become such a proficient, just to dispense with it all."

Elisan sat, and gestured for Eshel to do the same. "You were difficult to reclaim, Eshel, at least with those bungling Sunai fools in charge of the task. I am told these gumiia were quite the objects of ridicule among their peers for having been scared off by this redheaded female! And the next time, when they found you alone at the water station after those unbearably primitive fights, they bungled it once again. It seemed they were unprepared for your newly developed combat skills, for your willingness to touch an outsider and use such primitive methods!" He paused. "And your special weapon—developed, I assume, with the help of this Space Corps? And you say you haven't succumbed to the Alliance's stronghold!"

"Such skills are a necessity offworld, Elisan," Eshel said. "It was not my desire to develop them."

"Yet it is interesting that this Catherine Finnegan knows these skills as well." Elisan was about to continue, but then stopped, his face growing colder. It was some time before he spoke again. "Such a defiance. Even if I did not punish you for your transgressions, for your traitorous acts... your people, the people of the Shereb clan... they will. They won't forgive this... abomination."

A strong sense of dread flooded him. They knew. They knew Catherine had been more than his friend. They knew he'd done the unspeakable.

"And this old man, this Commander you have conversed with," he said. "What do you say of him?"

"He is an idiot," Eshel said coldly. "His knowledge of the science is unworthy."

"Yes, of course."

"Again, Elisan, why am I here? It is clear you don't want to hear what I have to say."

"Be patient, Eshel. There will come a time, very soon, when we will listen to everything you have to say." Elisan stood up and walked toward the door. He then turned to face Eshel. "Perhaps some time in solitude, with no distraction, will allow you to recall all that you have learned in your extended stay among the others. And we will see if it meets our expectations."

Elisan left.

Eshel sat in silence, contemplating what he would say to Elisan and his aides. Elan had offered a veiled warning about the information they wanted most. However, there was only so much information Eshel had at his disposal, and only so much he was willing to share. And he sensed that no amount of information, no matter how powerful, would fully satisfy them. That's when he began considering ideas for escape. Unless Elan offered him aid, they would drug him and leave him in the remote territories to die. Without the drug to initiate stasis, the likelihood of his survival was slim. There was only one other option.

Catherine. Would she be inclined to help him, to implement the plan he'd laid out for her? Normally he would assume as much, that Catherine was less prone to behave with unnecessary levels of irrationality or to allow her anger to govern her decisions. But then his mind produced an image of Catherine, one so vivid that he could see the gold flecks in her brown eyes… her expression had seemed to show a combination of numerous emotions, as she'd delivered the blow to his cheek.

Even if Catherine would follow his plan, could she convince Captain Ferguson, who'd never liked or trusted him, to execute the plan? That too was difficult to predict. But even with Catherine's willingness and Ferguson's concessions, his plan had a flaw. A fatal flaw.

He was not where he'd told Catherine to look for him.

Even if Catherine and Tom infiltrated Korvalis, finding him would be nearly impossible. And if they didn't find him, the Space Corps would only have more violent alternatives available to them.

They would not risk brazenly disregarding the firm boundaries of the Korvali. They would not risk war with his people. The Alliance wouldn't allow it. And while Eshel wanted to hope for a solution, he knew one didn't exist. He knew that the risks to the Space Corps and the Alliance outweighed the rather small benefit of retrieving any refugee from his own planet, much less a refugee they didn't like, from a people they didn't like. He wouldn't either, if he were in their position.

And Eshel acknowledged the terrible inevitable—that he would never see the others again. He focused his mind on what he'd achieved during his time offworld: he'd followed through on a plan devised by him and his father, and created a small bridge between his people and the others; he'd taught the others more about his people, as Ashan had; and he'd left a piece of Korvali technology to Catherine, enough that someone of her intelligence could make use of it someday. It wasn't the legacy he'd hoped to leave, but it was a useful beginning.

Yet despite his best efforts, Eshel felt an emptiness descend upon him at the prospect of being separated from all that was outside Korvalis. To counteract the feeling, he focused on those things he would not, to use Catherine's word, "miss." He would not miss sharing such close quarters with boisterous, talkative bunkmates. He would not miss Suna's blistering climate and its insufferable males. He would not miss Captain Ferguson's needling him, Commander Steele's bumbling knowledge of the science, or Middleton's hatred. He would not miss Tom's inability to keep confidences, the strange foods they served on *Cornelia*, nor the absence of water for him to swim in. Life outside of Korvalis, as he'd been warned, had many shortcomings.

However, such an exercise did little to thwart the empty feeling, and Eshel's mind inexorably shifted to those things that would bring him regret. He would not see Earth, other than his very limited exposure at boot camp. He would not see Calyyt-Calloq or learn their complex language. He would not complete his education with the

Space Corps, or continue learning to pilot a T-1 "Pokey" with Tom. He would not play poker again, or drink rallnofia, or eat the pink berries from Derovia.

And his mind finally settled upon the thing that would bring him the most sorrow. He would not see Catherine again. A vivid image of her appeared to him, this time of her standing in front of him in the waters of Mellon, small cold bumps beginning to form on her sensitive skin. He would no longer train with her, talk with her, work with her, touch her. He kneeled on the ground and bowed his head down.

That night, after they brought his meal, he slept fitfully, tormented by visions of Catherine, of Tom, of the others.

And the following morning, Eshel prepared himself for what was to come.

CHAPTER 23

Terrible thoughts flooded Catherine's mind. He wasn't there. He could be gone, killed by his own people. They could have left him in the remote territories… but Eshel had said that would be highly unlikely, and that even if she found him, he'd probably be dead. He could be anywhere on Korvalis, and she had no means to find him. She could feel tears beginning to blur her vision; but somehow the adrenaline in her system dried them up.

After exiting the compound, Catherine stepped away from the entrance, feeling anger boil up inside her. She wanted to take her device and smash it against the stone wall. *Where the hell are you, Eshel??* She leaned against the wall and crouched down. *Think.* But her mind continued to race and anxiety began to build. She would drown in her own thoughts. She took several deep breaths and tried to remember everything Yamamoto had taught her. *Clear your thoughts,* he would say. *Don't try to think. Quiet your mind and let the answer come to you.*

It took every bit of discipline she had to follow her mentor's advice and stop trying to think of the correct solution. It was painfully difficult, as all she wanted to do was race to the next place where Eshel might be, to run from place to place, shouting his name, shoving everyone out of her way, until she found him. She closed her eyes, leaning up against the compound and breathing deeply. She forced out the inundation of thoughts, just to have them return with even greater force. *Stop trying so hard.* She let go of her thoughts, allowing them to swirl about her like a storm. Finally, the swirling began to wane and the thoughts became less forceful, until her breathing slowed and her mind cleared.

And it came to her. No people would go to such lengths, after so long a time, to retrieve someone like Eshel, just to kill him. It made little sense. He would be much more useful to them alive, at least for a while. It also made little sense to send him to prison like some rebellious, low status clansperson or some hated Osecal. No—he was Shereb. The Shereb would deal with him. He wouldn't be in Felebaseb, with the other prisoners. He would be where the Shereb were.

He would be at Fallal Hall.

Catherine arrived at the craft, breathless from running as Tom let her inside. "Take me as close as you can to Fallal Hall. It's west of here, about twenty kilometers." She pulled up the map and pointed. "You can land here."

Tom stared at her. "You want to infiltrate the palace, where their monarch lives? Come on, Finnegan! That's crazy! It's not even on Eshel's unlikely list."

"And that's exactly why they'd take him there… it's unexpected."

Tom shook his head. "We have no floor plan, no information about its security."

"I have a rough idea, based on what Eshel told me."

"Not good enough."

"Listen to me," she hissed at Tom, who backed away in surprise. "I know more about Eshel and his people than you do. You have to trust me on this."

"We didn't plan for this, Catherine! Without a plan, everyone's at risk, including Eshel."

"Then let's make a new plan."

"How? Without a floor plan we have no idea where to look, and randomly searching wastes time and increases our risk of detection.

And what if he's not there? We'll be down all that time and... we'll be done. We'll have to leave without him."

Catherine heaved a big sigh. "Tom, he hates their leadership, and they hate him. They hated his father, too. They're the ones with the power, with the means to have him kidnapped. They have him. I'd bet my life on it." She paused. "It's a far better bet than the remote territories."

Tom stood there for a few moments, considering her arguments. "Okay. I'll agree to this... on two conditions. One... we leave at least two hours to check the remote territories if we don't find him here." Catherine nodded. "And two... you tell me what you know. If I know more, I can come up with a plan for infiltrating this place."

She shook her head. "I can't do that, Tom."

"Do you want to find Eshel or not?" Tom said, stepping closer to her. "This is no time for your stubbornness, Catherine. You can't do this alone!"

"I have to, Tom! Eshel wanted it that way."

"Catherine, if they detect us, we're dead."

"I'm not being stubborn this time. Eshel isn't concerned about himself... he's trying to protect his people. The Corps, the Sunai... they still don't understand that the Korvali leadership are extremists, that a lot of other Korvali want to interact with outsiders. That's what they're fighting for. If what I know gets out, they'll be in danger. Eshel made it clear that he'd rather be left here than risk that."

"He doesn't have to risk it! I can keep my mouth shut."

Catherine looked at her friend for a moment. "If he believed that, you'd be in on this."

Tom's angry expression turned momentarily crestfallen at her comment. Then he rapped his hand on the bulkhead. "Alright... search the palace if you believe it's the best course of action. But I can't let you go without a plan. I'll do a flyover, high enough so they won't hear us, and take some images of the site. That'll give us more information, including the palace's dimensions. From there, tell me what you can about the place and we'll devise a plan. Time calculations haven't changed; you've got five hours on each device, six max, and you're down…" he glanced at his time, "about two and a half."

Tom went on, and Catherine listened, nodding at everything Tom said. After Tom sat down in the pilot's seat, within minutes they were in sight of Fallal Fall, a gleaming white stone edifice surrounded by sprawling grounds, all encircled by a large white stone wall. Northwest of the wall was a vertical cliff that descended into the stormy, roiling sea. Once they got their images, Tom scanned the grassy area near a forest and found no signs of humanoid life. They landed; and they made a new plan.

Catherine ran through the long grass, rain thumping on her hood and splashing her face. Fallal Hall was more than four kilometers from where Tom had set down. Dripping with sweat, she slowed to a brisk walk once she reached the outskirts of the capitol city.

The capitol—the epicenter of Korvalis and the seat of its power and influence—looked nothing like Felebaseb. It was a city of trees—tall, elegant creatures that lined the stone streets and offered protection to the white stone buildings tucked beneath their canopies. Catherine hurriedly walked through the streets, passing numerous buildings and crossing many streams. She saw its robed citizens walking or quietly tending their neat, lush gardens. She saw its sleek, quiet trains. And, in the distance, she saw the great Fallal Hall rise above all.

Once she reached the stone wall that surrounded Fallal Hall's grounds, she assessed whether she could scale it with the tools she had. She then decided that taking at least a few minutes to search for an entrance might be less risky. And she found one: a heavy wooden door that arced slightly to sit flush with the wall's curvature. She aimed the rectangular device at the security console; but instead of going blank like those in Felebaseb, it produced eight symbols.

She attempted to open the door, but it remained locked. She looked around her, reconsidering her plan to scale the wall. Then, something occurred to her.

The symbols. They looked familiar. And it dawned on her: each represented a DNA nucleotide. Eshel had shown them to her once. Catherine smiled. She managed to recall two of the four, which meant the display would read either TACCGTTA or TAGGCTTA. She chose the former; CCG was more common in the genome.

But what was she supposed to enter? She entered the same sequence of symbols, wondering if Eshel's device had caused the console to default to its password. Nothing happened. She tried the latter combo. It didn't work either.

Damn it. What the hell kind of response did they want to a string of DNA? Then she had an idea: the DNA analog, the sequence for the other strand of DNA that would make up the double helix. She entered ATGGCAAT, making sure she chose the correct symbols.

The lock released. Triumph flooded her.

Catherine peeked onto the grounds; once she saw no one nearby, she walked in and pushed the door shut. As she hurried through the great Hall's extensive gardens, she suddenly recalled the first time she'd met Eshel, when he'd reanimated in sick bay. The recollection was vivid, almost as if it had happened yesterday.

She began to see people—Shereb in blue robes, alone or in pairs, quietly walking in various directions. She went out of her way to avoid walking near them, until she finally arrived at the great Hall. After shaking the rain off herself and employing the device, the display producing another series of symbols. As she began to mentally translate them, the door opened suddenly.

Catherine gasped and quickly backed away to avoid colliding with the figures exiting the Hall. In doing so, she lost her balance and fell backward, her pack offering some cushioning before she quickly rolled to a kneeling position. She froze, hoping the tall figures, who'd put on their hoods in anticipation of rain, didn't hear her.

However, one of them halted and turned around. Catherine saw a face, but there was something different about the face—it had softer features, larger eyes. Catherine realized she was female. Her eyes searched the area, her gaze settling on Catherine. Catherine held her breath, trapped by the woman's powerful stare. *She sees me.* But the woman shifted her gaze, scanning the area again before she turned and resumed walking with the others. Catherine exhaled, her heart still pounding. She stood up, decoded the door, and entered a large foyer.

The first thing she noticed was a tranquil silence in the great Hall. Despite it being far busier than the correctional facilities, with tall robed figures coming and going often, there was no loud hum of conversation, no laughter, no chat-chat. Floor-to-ceiling windows let in light from the south. Most notably, the entire foyer centered on a giant, sprawling, gray-trunked tree whose branches bore only tiny, ashen leaves. The tree seemed almost familiar, but Catherine wasn't sure why.

She glanced at her instrument—just over 3.5 hours down. The light on her device shone steadily.

Beyond the foyer, Catherine found hallways and stairways leading elsewhere. As discussed with Tom, she would first search for the offices of the senior government: those in the assembly, their kunsheld, and the kunsheld's aides. Tom's images of the west side of the building showed large windows along the upper of the four floors and on the roof—living quarters. Eshel had told her that only the malkaris and her extended family lived in the building. Thus, the north or east sides must be where the kunsheld and assembly gathered, and the images did reveal a sizable ornate window facing east, suggesting one large room—a potential meeting place for their assembly.

And she found it. When she peeked into the assembly room, with its ornate crystalline window and its white stone benches in a circle around its center, she saw only a few people inside, sitting quietly. The surrounding areas also yielded nothing of interest, so Catherine returned to the foyer. When she checked her device again, her stomach jumped.

The device's indicator light blinked rapidly.

She quickly scanned the foyer for a place to hide, finding nothing but the thick trunk of the tree. As she hurried toward it, she glanced at her device again. The indicator light suddenly went out, leaving her visible to all. Two steps and she was behind the tree, obscuring her from those who came and went through the main door. She immediately pulled out another device and turned it on. She stood catching her breath as she reset her device timer.

Catherine glanced to each side, waiting for someone to look for her behind the tree. No one came. She saw only the window, revealing the gardens outside the foyer. In a dark cluster of trees she spotted moving reflections in the glass—people walking in one direction, and then the other, as they had been. Perhaps they hadn't seen her.

After only four hours, the device had either malfunctioned... or something drained its power. She had no way of knowing for sure until she tested her second one. Anxiety rose in her; she pushed it away.

She finally peeked around the tree. Blue robes still came and went.

Catherine put aside any remaining anxieties and resumed her search, glancing at her device frequently. She climbed the stone steps to the second floor and walked quietly through one of the hallways. Despite their high ceilings, the palace's hallways were narrower than those of the corrections facilities; moreover, she'd discovered that the Korvali maintained larger amounts of personal space when walking or talking with others than did humans. Both gave her less room to work with. Several times she had to wait for them to leave the hallway, rather than risk coming too close to any of them or to the building itself, where her device could cause visual distortions that would create suspicion.

The area was filled with sparse offices and windowed doors, inside of which many Korvali worked quietly. Some of the hallways and doors had signs. Her knowledge of the Korvali language was limited at best, so the signs were of little help. She carefully looked around, searching for any sign of Eshel or a place where he could be held. But after an extensive search, she saw no indication of Eshel's presence, or anything that would help her. So she returned to the foyer. A bit of sunlight streamed in the windows, giving the tree's small leaves a silvery shimmer.

All that remained was the third and fourth floors, and the laboratories in the adjoining buildings to the north. She glanced at the time: 5.5 hours down. She checked her device.

It blinked, once per second.

She uttered a silent curse as she hid behind the tree and retrieved her third device. Her mind began racing again as a dark dread came over her. She heard Yamamoto's voice again, telling her to quiet her mind.

One substandard device could be a fluke... but not two. The first device had lasted just over four hours, and the second barely 90 minutes. The first had spent most of its time at Felebaseb and outside Fallal Hall; the second spent all its time inside the great Hall. Perhaps something there drained the device's power. She needed to get out as soon as possible. Which meant she must resort to desperate methods if she were to have any chance of locating Eshel.

During her search, a paperboard box in one of the offices had caught her eye. It was actual paperboard—something she'd only seen in archival photos. She hurried back to the office, glancing around her to ensure no one was nearby. Removing her pack and retrieving her small knife, she cut through the box and kept a flat panel from it, her thin gloves preventing her from leaving evidence of herself. She found what appeared to be a writing apparatus. Just then, she heard something. Someone was coming. She took the panel and writing apparatus and tiptoed away to a quiet hallway.

She combed her memory to recall the Korvali symbols she needed. She didn't know all of them, nor did she have good understanding of Korvali grammar; therefore, she must limit her message to what she knew. Once finished, she went back to the foyer and propped the large piece of paperboard on a table, leaving it in plain sight of those who'd walk by.

The message said: ESHEL DIES.

She retreated to a spot that was out of the way but still near the door, and waited. She glanced at her device repeatedly. Several minutes later, two figures entered the foyer. Too engrossed in their own quiet conversation, they exited the Hall without noticing the sign. Two more figures appeared and left, with the same result. On several more occasions, more people passed, but no one seemed to notice the sign.

Catherine wondered if her idea was not only too crude, but utterly ineffective. *What's it going to take with you people? Do I need to shout Eshel's name just to get your attention??* If this didn't work, she could only keep up her fruitless searching until she ran out of time, leaving her with no other option but to return to the ship in defeat, with no chance of seeing Eshel again. Her sense of dread returned.

A group of young men approached from the other direction, removing their hoods. Perhaps the others, on their way out, had no reason to notice the table, whereas those coming in might. Sure enough, one of the men glanced toward the sign... but then kept walking. Catherine grew angry and uttered a quiet curse, until the young man looked back at the sign, this time stopping to inspect it.

He gestured at the sign and commented to the other men. The others halted, one of whom raised his eyebrows, much like Eshel did when something surprised him. They began talking. Catherine didn't understand what the men said, but the one with raised eyebrows gestured in a particular direction, up and to the left, and the others followed suit and looked that way. She also recognized the Korvali word for prison and the name Elisan, which was mentioned multiple times. When the young man gestured in that direction, he used a word that sounded like "kervasis." He picked up the sign, glancing around him, and he and the other men resumed walking.

Catherine took the stone steps two at a time to the second floor and headed in the direction the young Korvali had gestured toward, which was northwest. Many of the doors had no signs. Others did; but once translated, the words made no sense to her. She immediately went to the third floor.

More doors with no labels. Three people to avoid. Other doors with signs that, when partially translated by her, bore no resemblance to the word the young man had said. When she arrived at the end of a hallway, she found two more doors with identical labels on them. She attempted to translate the letters, but the word contained unfamiliar symbols. Skipping over the symbols she didn't know, the word bore a slight resemblance to "kervasis." She felt a surge of encouragement.

The two doors had no windows, and no other indication of what was behind them. As her heart began to pound, she chose the door on the left. After carefully decoding it and hearing the lock unlatch, Catherine opened the door and stepped in the room. Still holding the door, she leaned beyond the foyer wall and glanced around, her eyes adjusting to the darkness. The small room contained only a bed, a desk, and an adjoining room she couldn't see. To be thorough, she needed to check the adjoining room, which meant letting go of the door. She pulled a rag from her pack, scrunched it up, and carefully let the door rest on it. She rounded the corner; the room was a bath-room. It was uninhabited.

She grabbed her rag and quietly closing the door, turning her attention to the other door. It shared the same code as the first. When the door unlatched, she felt her heart pounding again as she gently pushed the door open. Immediately, she saw light. Someone was inside. Her breathing quickened as she slowly entered the small room, which appeared identical to the first one. The wall that separated her from the bathroom obscured her view. As she emerged from behind the wall, her hand still holding the door open, her throat tightened.

A hooded figure sat on the bed, leaned up against the stone wall, the hood obscuring the occupant's face. The figure sat perfectly still, its long webbed hands resting on its legs and a dark magenta marking peeking out from the left sleeve. She exhaled, hoping the figure would hear something and show a face. But it sat, unmoving.

She tried to swallow, her throat dry, as she gently shut the door. She approached the still figure, never considering what she would do if it weren't Eshel. Finally, she stood in front of the figure. And she reached out and gave the hood a tug, letting it fall back.

CHAPTER 24

Eshel's eyes opened at her touch, and he stared up at her for a long stretch of moments. Then, his cold, blank stare turned into something else, something that conveyed emotion. It was a look she'd never seen.

Relief engulfed her. Her throat tightened and her eyes burned as she felt tears begin to form. She willed them away.

Eshel looked up toward the ceiling. When she followed his look, she saw the surveillance cell.

But how could he see her? Her device was still engaged. Catherine immediately recalled the initial scan she'd conducted on Eshel to follow up Vargas's medical scanner results: four altered genes… two involved in visual processing, two with a regulatory function. Had he genetically altered his vision?

She made a face, pointing to her device and shaking her head, then gesturing toward the door.

Eshel stood up and walked into the bathroom, motioning for her to follow him. He pointed at her feet. She pulled Eshel's pair of sound absorbing boots from her pack and he put them on. She gave Eshel one of the black devices Tom had made; he examined it briefly, turned on its power, and placed it in a hidden pocket.

She decoded the door, opened it, and took a look around. The hallway was empty. They emerged from the room and Catherine closed the door behind them before heading toward the exit. Eshel grabbed her arm, urging her to follow him in a different direction. Several times, they waited for others to pass before proceeding. They descended a smaller staircase and walked down a quiet hallway to a door.

Once outside, Catherine let out a breath as she glanced around. She turned to Eshel. "You can see me."

"Yes, I can see you." They stood looking at one another. Finally, Eshel walked closer to her and put his cheek to hers, holding the back of her head. Catherine, not expecting the gesture, did the same as Eshel held her for longer than he ever had.

When they separated, Catherine spoke. "Are you okay?" He looked tired and his upper cheek had a dark mark, like someone had struck him.

"I am unharmed."

"We need to go," she told him, looking at the time, then at her device. "The devices don't hold a charge for nearly as long as they should. Something at Fallal Hall is draining their power."

"How much time has elapsed?"

"Six hours, forty-one minutes."

"Tell me where you were with each device, and how long each lasted."

After giving him a quick rundown, she followed Eshel, noticing all that she'd been too preoccupied to notice previously. From this side of the great Hall, one could see the ocean beyond the white stone wall, tiny islands dotting the horizon. As Eshel led her through the gardens, she looked in awe at the extraordinarily large trees with branches that hung down, much like a weeping willow but larger and leafier. Some had benches under the canopy; others had canopies so dense that one couldn't see the tree's thick trunk. Small streams meandered in every direction, the bottom of each lined with a magenta moss-like substance. Small, white stone bridges allowed one to cross the streams. Pairs of robed Korvali sat on the benches, talking quietly amongst themselves. In the distance, she saw a series of tall white sculptures in a row, each appearing to have some symbolic meaning.

It no longer rained and the sun made an appearance, causing everything to glisten. Another glance at her instrument told her that Eshel headed east, not south. But she said nothing, trusting that Eshel's less direct route had some benefit that was unknown to her. They came upon another large willow-like tree, its crown so massive that Catherine couldn't see around it, and its dense-leafed branches so long that their tips reached the ground. Eshel stopped and looked around. Suddenly, he took her arm and led her between the branches, until they stood completely hidden under the tree's canopy.

Eshel faced Catherine, gazing at her. But he said nothing.

"What's wrong?" Catherine asked him, concerned. When he hesitated, she put aside her concern for time and stood silent, waiting for Eshel to speak. If Eshel had something to say, it would be important enough to warrant delaying their goal a bit longer.

"I know that time passes, that we must not waste it," he began, recognizing her urgency. "I ask your permission to leave you and complete an important task. It may take two hours. I will meet you at the craft."

"What? What important task?"

Eshel hesitated.

"This isn't the time for secrets, Eshel," she said. "I won't repeat it."

"I must gather the remaining evidence regarding my father's murder."

"Now?" she cried. She shook her head. "It's too dangerous. I don't know how long these devices will last. You risk detection."

"I believe I know what drains their power, and how to avoid it. I will know for sure by how long this device lasts." He placed a webbed hand over his pocket. "If you give me one spare device, I will have enough time. This leaves you with a spare, which is more than enough to protect you."

Catherine took a deep breath. "Eshel, I know this is important to you. But every moment we linger vastly decreases our chances of success. At some point, they're going to realize you're missing," she added, gesturing back toward the great Hall.

"My captors will not discover my absence for some time."

"They had you under surveillance!"

"They knew I could not leave, and did not watch me closely. I once went into the toilet room for numerous hours, just to test them, with no repercussions. And they won't bring my meal until the evening."

She felt herself grow more agitated. "Eshel, a lot of people are waiting for confirmation from me, including Tom, who's probably losing his mind by now." She pointed to the south, where Tom waited in the craft. "Do you have any idea how many resources are being used to protect you, how much effort so many people have gone to for you? Do you know how difficult it was for me to convince them to let me do this? Why do you put me in this position? If something happens to you, after I already found you... Eshel, I couldn't live with myself! And the more we blather about this, the more time we waste on our devices."

Eshel reached over and turned off the device she held in her hand, and then his.

"What are you doing?" Catherine demanded in a hushed voice, looking around her.

"Please be calm, Catherine. I am saving power. No one can see us in here—"

"God damn you, Eshel! This is my operation! You asked me to do this, and I did. And I'm getting back on that fucking ship, right now, with or without you."

Eshel stood silent for several moments. Finally, he spoke. "I will come with you. And if we must go now, then we will go." He found the switch to his device and turned it on. He looked at hers. Once she turned hers on, he exited the tree's canopy and headed south.

Catherine followed him in silence, walking rapidly to keep up with him. It had begun to rain. The light in the gardens darkened and, soon, heavy water drops pelted against her hood. Suddenly, the rain came down in a deluge and the wind thrust it sideways, making it nearly impossible for her to see anything as she tried to focus on Eshel's gray robe in front of her. She felt a hand grab her arm, and suddenly the rain ceased but for a few drops, and the wind was still. They stood beneath the canopy of another one of the trees.

She coughed, wiping the water from her face and rubbing her eyes.

"Turn off your device," Eshel said, removing his hood. "We must let this storm pass."

Catherine frowned, taking off her pack and shaking the water off her jacket. She sat down at the foot of the tree, facing away from Eshel, and checked the time and her device. They still had time. They would be okay. She calmed herself, putting her anger out of her mind.

"Catherine."

"What?" she replied without looking at him. A drop of water hit her nose.

"Why are you angry?"

"You're coldhearted, Eshel. That means—"

"I know what it means."

Neither spoke as the rain poured down outside their protective tree. Catherine's memories of Eshel coldly ending their relationship, and barely nodding at her in the hallway, came flooding back.

"Tom also said that," Eshel finally said.

"Said what?"

"That I am 'coldhearted.'" He paused. "Perhaps it is fair for Tom to say that. He does not know my... feelings, as you call them, because I do not share them with him. But you... you shouldn't call me that."

"Why not?" She turned to face him.

"I shared much with you, Catherine. Things I have shared with no one. And do you believe I would make such a request if I didn't care for others?"

She sighed and turned away again.

"What do I not understand?" he asked.

"Everything," she said, leaning back against the tree. "You're not coldhearted about your father, or your loved ones. But you don't care about the rest of us. Including me."

"I don't care about you?" he asked, anger in his voice. "It is you who hit me, who ordered me to never acknowledge you, who did not speak a word to me for months. Who is coldhearted?"

Catherine stood up and faced Eshel. "You severed our relationship, Eshel, with no warning and no reason. I could accept that, but then you nodded at me in the hallway like I was some stranger! I did your damned sher mishtar and kept your secrets and took interest in what mattered most to you. And what did it earn me other than being disregarded by you, than being treated like some outsider you care nothing for? Even now, I'm here, running all over Korvalis looking for you—you weren't where you said you'd be and you wouldn't believe how I managed to find you—and all you care about is your own agenda!"

"That is not all I care about."

She ignored him. "Tom told me you said, after a couple of drinks, that sexual contact with otherworlders is not only taboo, but an abomination," she said, her voice shaking. "Then I recalled how many times you kept telling me to never share what we did, and how strange you looked the first time we…" She trailed off. "That was far worse, Eshel, far worse than your cold treatment. I let you into my private world, and you lied about it because you were ashamed." Overwhelmed, she backed away, making her most valiant effort to relax the constriction in her throat and avoid crying.

"Why does your voice sound that way?" he asked, looking at her with concern.

"Is it true? Is it an abomination for your people to have sex with outsiders?"

"Yes."

She felt sick to her stomach. She turned away, knowing Eshel could never understand how she felt.

"Catherine—"

"Don't talk to me."

"Catherine," he said. "I will speak. And you will listen to me."

It was the angriest she'd ever seen him. She turned back around.

"The Korvali do not believe in comingling with outsiders," he said. "It is forbidden to share information with others, to touch others, to live among others. Sexual contact with others is especially taboo because it is... private... and because it can result in offspring, which is... it is not done. The Korvali value genetic and scientific fidelity. It is who we are."

"Then why did you involve yourself with me? I would've been happy to be your friend, to respect your traditions. It was *you* who initiated the sharing of information, the touching, and everything else."

Eshel's angry expression faded. "I chose to share with you because I trusted you, and you only. And I did so because I wanted to. I didn't expect to want to. I resisted the desire for some time. But, what seemed impossible, even unthinkable, with time became... something I desired."

Catherine felt some of her own anger dissolve. "Then why did you say those things to Tom?"

"It was the most effective way to silence Tom on the topic."

"Why? Why not tell him the truth?"

He hesitated. "He has no respect for the privacy of others."

"You weren't ashamed to have been with me?"

He hesitated again. "At first, yes," he admitted. "But with time, no. Do not ever believe I consider our interactions repulsive, Catherine. You were important to me. You still are."

"Then why did you end our relationship?"

He looked around him. "When we arrived at Station 3, I received an encrypted message from Elisan, relayed through the Sunai. It was a collection of images of you and I on Derovia, even in Mellon.

They'd been watching me… watching us." He paused. "I could not risk your life, my life, or that of my family. I had to refocus on my purpose and make it clear, to all, that you were of no importance to me other than helping me adapt to life among the others."

She felt a chill go through her. "Did you tell the brass?"

"Yes. For them, a series of images was not adequate evidence of my suspicions. Nothing was."

"You couldn't just tell me all of that?"

"No."

"Why not? You told me other secrets. Why is this any different?"

"Because it is," he told her, his tone colder. "And what would be different if I had told you? You know, or you don't know, either way the result is the same—I could not engage with you."

"The result is not the same, Eshel!" she cried. "If I'd known the truth, I wouldn't have gotten angry with you! And I wouldn't have had to bear the pain of believing that you didn't care for me."

A look of understanding crossed Eshel's face. Then his expression clouded over. "You aren't the only one who bore pain, Catherine. I am not human. We do not casually sever personal bonds the way humans do."

"You did."

"I didn't. The difficulty I experienced was nearly unbearable at times. And it did not help to see you with Grono Amsala, or to see you working with Ensign Holloway, as we once had."

All her remaining anger drained from her. Eshel had seen much.

Eshel went on. "When you stood above me at Fallal Hall, I thought I hadn't yet awoken and was seeing a dream vision. I had accepted that my life was coming to an end, and all my plans with it." He paused. "We will leave Korvalis; I will perform my duty to my father in the future.

Catherine said nothing. Eshel's expression was as it always was, but he looked different somehow. She walked over and hugged him. As he put his arms around her, she felt his warmth penetrate her in the cool, damp air.

"The storm has passed," he said. "We can leave."

Catherine realized he was right. The pounding rain had ceased, and the sky seemed to brighten. She walked over to her pack, glancing at the time again. Almost seven hours down. But she hesitated.

"What is wrong?" he asked her.

"Why did you want to deal with your father's murder now, given our circumstances? It's not like you to take that kind of risk."

"Do you believe I would make such a request if I hadn't considered the risks, if I didn't believe the risks were trivial? If so, then we have another misunderstanding to resolve."

Catherine gave a half smile. He had a point. Eshel never made important decisions without carefully ensuring the odds were heavily in his favor. "Can you do what you need to in two hours?"

Eshel raised his eyebrows. "I believe so."

"And if you can't?"

"I will abort the operation and rejoin you at the craft."

"Can you do that, walk away?"

"Yes."

"Then do it," she said. "Do it now."

"I will need some of your supplies, including your pack."

She shook her head. "I'm coming with you."

CHAPTER 25

Eshel looked through Catherine's pack, taking out each item and arranging it neatly in front of him. He repacked it all, placing one of the devices in his robe pocket.

They reengaged their devices and emerged from the tree's canopy. Eshel walked north again with Catherine just behind him, past Fallal Hall and out beyond the white stone wall. They entered another garden, surrounded by more large stone buildings, where Eshel stopped.

"Stay here," Eshel told her.

Eshel strode toward the white building, crossing a tiny stone bridge that spanned a burbling creek. He glanced at the small tree he passed; it had grown since he'd last seen it. He employed his device, input a code into the console, and entered.

He saw no one as he walked quietly past the atrium filled with a dark pond and pink-flowered vines that crept up the glass. He continued walking until he reached another room, brightened from the light streaming in through the glass roof.

There, at her desk, stood his mother. Having heard the door, she kept her eyes toward the front room, her hand in her pocket, ready to defend herself. Eshel disengaged his shell.

His mother, startled, stared at him with the gray eyes of a Shereb. They approached one another as he pressed his cheek to hers. Eshel's mother, almost as tall as he, kept a warm hand on his head. When she let go, she spoke. "You have escaped."

"Yes."

"What is this technology that obscures you from my view?"

"It is a combination of Korvali and human technologies," Eshel said.

His mother's expression changed. He knew she was intrigued by the idea, but also bothered by his mingling their expertise with that of the others. "You shouldn't linger, Son. They will look for you here. You must go east."

"No. I have... another way." Eshel paused. "Once they know I am gone, you will be in danger. You must leave this place, and you have only two hours to do so. You know where to go?"

Fashal examined him for a moment. "I will clean your traces. They won't know you were here. There is no need for me to hide."

"There is."

She watched him closely, a glint of recognition in her expression. "You are going to identify the one who murdered your father."

"He cannot receive punishment without evidence."

"There isn't enough time to find Elisan's aides. They are too many."

Eshel paused before revealing the truth. "Elisan's aides did not kill Father."

Her eyebrows went up. "Who did?"

"One of the malkaris's sons. And only one of them is capable of such an act."

Fashal's face paled as she looked away momentarily. "Ivar."

Eshel paused. "I will need some of Father's supplies." She showed him where she'd hidden Othniel's things and Eshel rummaged through it all and found what he needed. As he prepared to leave, his mother stopped him.

"When you obtain the necessary evidence, give it to me. I can ensure his exposure and punishment better than you can."

"No," Eshel said. "You must leave here. I will handle this." He again pressed cheeks with his mother, reengaged his device, and left.

Without a word, he led Catherine back into the walled garden and back to Fallal Hall. The rain came down upon them once more. Once inside the great Hall, Eshel led them up stone steps to the fourth floor. He put his hand out and Catherine immediately gave him the rectangular device. He entered the code and opened the door, just cracking it and peering inside. Once inside, he carefully closed the door and returned the device to Catherine.

Visions of the past flooded him. Disgusted, he did his best to remove the images from his mind.

Eshel walked down the large hallway, squinting at the light from the rooftop windows high above them. Once arriving at a doorway, he stopped. When Catherine handed him the device again, he decoded the door and entered. No one was present. He moved on to the next one. No one was there either. As they continued down the hallway, he began to hear voices. Eshel followed the voices, passing another doorway and stopping at a fourth. The voices grew louder, echoing off the white stone that surrounded them. Eshel decoded the door and peeked in. Then he turned, grabbed Catherine's arm, and pulled her in quickly.

Eshel and Catherine stood in the alcove of Ivar's apartments, out of visible range from almost anyplace within the large living quarters. He glanced back quickly to ensure Catherine was ready, and he emerged from the alcove.

Two young males in blue robes sat at a stone table, talking among themselves—Moeb and Vashar, the younger of the malkaris's four sons. Their eyes were a pale gray, and their short hair had just enough red in it to make them stand out from the populace. Rain pattered on the ceiling of the living area, its tinted glass casting a bluish hue over the room. The large window on the far side of the room offered a spectacular view of the sea.

Eshel walked slowly, making his way around the table, glancing around him carefully. Once behind Moeb, he passed his father's scanner close to him. After running only briefly, the instrument indicated that Moeb's DNA didn't match the sample his father had secretly collected from his murderer. He looked around, wondering where Ivar was.

Eshel moved on to Vashar, passing the scanner close to him. As the instrument began scanning the image, its processing time taking considerably longer than had Moeb's sample, Eshel waited, recalling that the smaller instruments functioned more slowly. But as it went on, Eshel began to wonder if the instrument would yield an unexpected result, that young Vashar would be capable of such treachery on his own. Perhaps his father was less suspicious of Vashar and more likely to walk alone with him, where Vashar could deploy his weapon. But just as Eshel began to accept this speculation as possibility, the scan halted. Vashar's DNA didn't match.

He glanced at Catherine and motioned for her to stay near the door while he went to search the apartments for Ivar. Catherine waited, attentive and calm. He had strongly opposed her request to accompany him, but she'd insisted. Now, her presence brought him solace.

Before Eshel got far, he heard a voice from around the corner. Ivar walked in, singing and throwing grain at his brothers, both of whom leveled a few curse words at him. They were words Eshel never used, even at his most angry, and words his mother and father had forbade him to use. Eshel felt himself grow angry at the sight of Ivar. Two steps… two steps and he could engage Ivar, choke him, watch him perish, and walk out the door with Catherine. But Eshel made no move. He must obey Doctrine and pursue justice properly.

Eshel attempted to scan Ivar as he walked by, but he was too late and didn't get an adequate reading. Ivar paused his walk again, continuing to toss the grain at the others. Eshel made another attempt to scan him, but before he could, he bumped into a large potted plant whose prickly tips stabbed him in his side. He gasped.

Moeb turned around and looked right at him. Eshel froze, and then slowly backed away from the plant. When Moeb's eyes still focused on the area near the plant, rather than on him, he relaxed slightly. He glanced at Catherine, who'd advanced a couple of steps toward them. Moeb ceased his staring and refocused on Ivar.

Eshel recovered himself and waited, hoping Ivar would be still or sit down. And soon, Ivar ceased his grain assault and took his place at the table. Eshel continued his pursuit, making sure to avoid the spiny plant, and scanned him.

Eshel glanced at Catherine. She waited only for his sign. He looked back at the scanner, waiting for it to process the information. Ivar's scan took even longer than Vashar's had, which only confirmed Eshel's suspicions. He'd longed for this moment, to follow through on what he'd begun before he had to abandon his investigation and leave Korvalis. Finally, the scan finished.

Ivar's scan didn't match.

Eshel studied the readout more closely, making sure he'd read the result correctly. Although uncommon, such an instrument occasionally malfunctioned and simply needed to be powered down briefly. Eshel turned off the scanner, waited a few moments, and turned it back on. He scanned Ivar again, deaf to Ivar's cold voice and blind to all that was around him, and he waited. It yielded the same result.

Ivar didn't kill his father.

Eshel stood motionless, wondering what had gone amiss. Did the scanner no longer function? Not likely, as it wasn't that old, and the estimated match percentages for the other boys fell into the expected range for sibling DNA. He went through every memory he had of his investigation before leaving Korvalis, attempting to identify the source of his mistake. Then, a horrible, sickening dread came over him. He stood there, still frozen, trying to adjust his mind to the unthinkable.

He saw movement from the corner of his eye: Catherine, gesturing to him. She pointed at her device. He snapped out of shock, stepping around the table where the young men sat talking. They quietly left the apartments and Catherine changed her device. That left them only one spare.

Eshel looked around, the feeling of dread still nearly overwhelming. Seeing no one, he turned to Catherine to check the time. He felt her watching him, waiting for explanation. But he avoided her gaze, leading her out the door, down the stairs, and outside again.

The light rain sprinkled upon them, and Eshel was overcome by sudden visions from the past. He stopped and knelt down, hoping they would subside. He barely heard Catherine speak his name. The visions ceased, enough for him to recover and keep going. "One last stop," he told her.

Again they traversed the gardens, Eshel walking swiftly and Catherine jogging a little to keep up with him. He led her into another building and proceeded down endless labyrinthine hallways, dark and in shadow, with no windows and many closed doors. There were few people around. Familiarity washed over him as he quickly navigated the place in which he'd spent so much time.

And then he stopped. "I will not need your assistance here. Please wait until I come out."

"Check your device," she said.

He did; it blinked, once per second. He changed it, glancing at Catherine. "Do not worry."

As Eshel stepped into the laboratory, another series of strong memories flooded him—memories of his father, of their colleagues. The clearest one was of the schematic Eshel had made, outlining his plan, the one where he would manipulate his own epigenome and survive his escape. But despite the familiarity of the place, this wasn't his lab.

It was Elan's lab.

Eshel proceeded to the back room. It was silent, except for the quiet hum of the computers. And there, in the back, sat a man in a blue robe. Eshel observed his friend, the one he'd played with as a child, sat with during their schooling, discussed science with, swum countless waters with… who'd given him the codes to their apartments, attended Othniel's rite of death, and whose daughter he'd played with. Eshel silently walked to where Elan sat, examining the code he'd written, presumably for his next project. He scanned him.

He watched the display, the slow processing of the scanner attempting to make a DNA match. Finally, the scan halted and the scanner's display lit up, offering him the result he'd expected from Ivar. He stared at the display for a moment before putting the scanner back in his pocket. He continued looking at Elan, who worked silently, who would've begun work early that morning, after a swim, and would probably stay until well into the evening. Eshel, standing a mere meter away from where Elan sat, disengaged his shell.

"Elan."

Elan turned, his expression one of surprise. "How did you get in here?" he said, standing up and facing Eshel, his gray eyes making contact with Eshel's. "Did they release you?"

"I know you killed my father, Elan," Eshel said, staring Elan down. "I know you deceived me. I want to know why."

Elan hesitated, his expression changing slightly. "You are my friend, Eshel. But it is my duty to protect Korvalis. Your father was a traitor. If I did not kill him, another would have."

"I don't want to know why you believe he deserved to die. I want to know, *why you?*"

"You know why."

"I want to you to tell me."

As Elan gave him a chilly look, he no longer looked like the friend he'd known throughout his life. "Because you would not suspect me."

"You are correct, Elan. I never suspected you."

"How did you find out?"

"You are cunning. But my father was more so."

Elan raised his eyebrows. "You will not reveal your subterfuge? It does not matter. No one will believe the evidence of a traitor. Even if they do, they can do nothing."

"I do not need them to," Eshel said.

"Oh? You will attempt to leave us again, to flee and live among the outsiders?"

"Yes," Eshel said.

And before Elan could react, Eshel retrieved the weapon he'd taken from his father's cache, quickly injected Elan's neck without touching him, and immediately backed away.

Elan, stunned by the attack, put his hand to his neck. He found the micro-syringe and pulled it out. He stared at it, as if attempting to decipher how it worked. But it was too late. Elan began to stagger, and soon slumped to the floor. He started to convulse. Eshel, unable to bear any more, looked away.

Once Elan's body remained still, Eshel faced him again, watching the limp corpse of his friend lie motionless on the laboratory floor. He knelt down, taking a deep breath to control the sick feeling he had, and came very close to vomiting. He calmed himself. After a few moments, Eshel retrieved the tiny syringe from Elan's hand, careful to avoid touching him. He retracted the needle, put it in his pocket, and exited the lab.

"Did you get what you needed?" Catherine said, her expression concerned.

"I did. We must leave."

Eshel set to walking again, his pace even quicker than before. Catherine followed him, winding through the numerous quiet hallways, until they reached a door that led them outside to the gardens. They pulled their hoods over their heads as rain fell upon them. They headed south, through the gardens, beyond the curved door of the white stone wall, and away from Fallal Hall. About halfway to the craft's location, Eshel stopped walking. He turned and looked back at Fallal Hall in the distance, its white stone rising above all, gleaming through the rain.

It was time... time for them to return home.

CHAPTER 26

After sitting alone in the quiet for hours, Catherine finally saw Station 10 in the distance. Tom dozed, and Eshel had been asleep for some time. She whistled.

"What," Tom said groggily, as he sat up.

"We're in range."

Catherine sent an encrypted message to the Captain: *Mission accomplished. ETA: 3:12.* Tom slowed the Mosca and pulled into a vertical structure, landing on one of the shielded platforms near the top, designed for smaller ships. He got out and gave a few commands. Catherine watched the robotic arm find their fuel tank and latch onto it. When Tom came back in, he walked past Catherine to where Eshel sat, newly awakened.

"Esh, why'd you put Finnegan in charge of this operation?" he said, pointing at Catherine. "And why'd you give her all the intelligence, and leave me to sit by like an idiot? I'm a soldier with a lot of field experience—I'm trained to do this kind of shit!"

Eshel, visibly surprised at Tom's sudden outburst, sat up. "Why are you angry? The operation was successful."

"That's not the point! Do you have any idea what it was like for me to sit and wait for all those hours with, no offense," he glanced back at Catherine, "a whitecoat in charge?"

"Only Catherine had the necessary knowledge to do this, Tom."

"Don't give me that shit! You weren't even where you said you'd be. It's damned lucky she found you in that place. If you'd trusted me with more intelligence, I'd have been more helpful and the op would've been far less risky." He ran his hand through his curly hair. "You don't trust me, man. And that pisses me off, considering all I've done for you."

Catherine could see Eshel starting to get angry. But he took pause before he finally answered. "I have not adequately shown... what is the word...gratitude, for all you have done for me. I am sorry for that." Tom deflated a little, glancing at Catherine again. "You are correct. I do not trust you, as I do Catherine, for many reasons. And you are not one who keeps secrets."

Tom shook his head vigorously. "I can keep secrets when they're important. For example, when you gave me that bioweapon casing for my birthday, I know you had others made. I know you probably used a bioweapon on those gumiia assholes after the CCFs. I have contacts, Eshel. I know things. And I never said a word to anyone, because we can't always look out for you and you deserve to defend yourself any way you can against those vest-wearing goons." He stood, hands on hips, looking at Eshel. "So... what it's gonna take for you to trust me?"

Eshel stood up. "If you share with nobody what you learned during this operation—nobody at all, including the Captain—you will have earned my trust. Until then..." Eshel bent over and removed his shoes. He began pulling his robe over his head, taking it off altogether and setting it on his seat. He stood completely nude.

Catherine gasped. Tom looked shocked... and uncomfortable.

"It is forbidden to allow any outsider to see a Korvali unclothed," Eshel said. "Only Catherine has seen me this way. I deceived you about not engaging in physical relations with her, for reasons I will share with you at another time." He put his robe back on.

They heard a noise—the robotic arm detaching itself from their craft. Tom left and paid for the fuel. When he returned, his expression was serious. "Hey, man... thanks for everything you said." He

laughed a little, shaking his head. "I didn't need to see you naked...
but I appreciate the meaning of the gesture. Look... I'm sorry too,
for some of the shit I said... you know, that night after the party."

"Thank you," Eshel said.

Tom grinned. "Say 'thank you' to the Captain. This trip cost a
fortune!" He rapped his hand on the bulkhead. "Alright... let's go
home!"

Once moving again, Catherine brought Eshel a cold canteen and
ran a medical scanner over him. "How do you feel?"

"I am fine."

"Then why do you keep putting your hand on your shoulder like
it hurts?"

Eshel gave a tiny frown. "It has ached since the Sunai detained
me."

"Let me look." She felt around until he flinched, and then scanned
his arm. "Your rotator is torn. Take this," she said, rummaging
through the medical kit and retrieving a painkiller. "Be still." She
made some adjustments to her device and ran it over Eshel's shoulder
while Eshel grimaced in pain. "When we return, go to sick bay to
make sure I didn't miss anything."

"How do you know this?" he asked, puzzled.

"I learned a few things after working a few extra sick bay shifts,
thanks to someone beating me in poker."

Eshel gave a tiny smile.

They reached *Cornelia* several minutes before their ETA. Tom docked
the craft and woke Eshel, who'd slept most of the way home. The
three of them gathered their things as the bay door shut.

Eshel approached Catherine and Tom. "Before they question us,
I want to speak," he said. "On Korvalis, before Catherine found me,
I believed I would not see either of you again. It was an unpleasant
feeling." He paused. "I am grateful to you both."

"We love you, buddy," Tom said, slapping Eshel on the back. "We'd do it a thousand times over. With me taking the lead, of course," he added with a grin.

Catherine elbowed Tom. "You're welcome, Esh."

They heard knocking, so Tom opened the hatch. Ferguson and Yamamoto stood with pleased expressions, and Koni and Snow stood behind them. Catherine, Eshel, and Tom saluted.

"At ease," Ferguson said with satisfaction, the gleam returned to her eye. "Welcome back, Eshel. And good work, you two," she said to Catherine and Tom.

"Thank you, Captain," they replied.

Snow slapped hands with Tom and gave him and Catherine a hug. He hesitated with Eshel, until Eshel held out his hand for Snow to shake.

As Snow talked with Eshel and Tom, Koni approached her, his eyeshades protecting him from the bright light of the hangar bay. He placed his hands on her shoulders. "I am happy to see you safe. How are you, nonaii?"

"Relieved. And tired."

"When you are rested, I have much to tell you." He looked over at her friends, his gaze settling upon Snow. "Your comrade listened to your warning, yes? He has not consorted with our females."

Catherine nodded. "Glad to hear it."

Snow had done plenty of consorting with one particular Sunai female, in secret. On their long journey back to *Cornelia*, Tom told her that Snow finally confessed his feelings to him. Envy aside, Tom had not only managed to keep his mouth shut, but he helped Snow continue the liaison by offering up creative ideas for sneaking around.

She disliked lying to Koni, especially when he'd done so much for her. But she'd done things for him as well, and would continue to. And she now understood what the old Space Corps adage meant about choosing your long-term mission companions carefully. She knew who her close friends were, who would always have her loyalty.

"Listen up," Yamamoto said. They quieted down. "Snow, remove the Mosca's modifications."

"Yes, Sir," Snow said.

"Eshel, Tom, Catherine... head to the bridge ready room for debriefing."

"Yes, Sir," they replied.

Eshel sat in Ferguson's office, finishing up his debriefing.

"Visiting your mother," Yamamoto went on. "And gathering evidence of your father's murder... why did you take such risks, considering the consequences of detection?"

"They stole my father's life, Commander. It was important that I attempt to remove my mother from danger. As I told Catherine, I believed the risk of detection was low, and that is the only reason I made such a choice."

Yamamoto nodded. "I believe I speak on behalf of the entire command when I say you showed tremendous prudence in planning your own rescue in advance, and foresight in developing a plan that avoided unnecessary mess."

"Thank you, Commander. I am... grateful... that you and the Captain were willing to adopt the plan," Eshel replied, hoping they would appreciate his use of that word.

"You told us the information you revealed to Elisan about our organization and our weapons systems. Do you recall anything else you told them that we need to prepare for, such as our store of bioweapons or our information systems?"

"I revealed that you have bioweapons. I told them the weapons were very simple in nature, using only non-engineered microbial agents."

Ferguson frowned. "How do you know anything about our bioweapons?"

"I don't. But with Elisan, it is better to confabulate an interesting lie than to reveal a dull truth." Eshel didn't mention that he'd seen their bioweapons stores before, thanks to Tom, and that his visual memory allowed him to recall many specifics. He knew the weapons were more sophisticated than he'd let on to Elisan. Eshel hoped that Elisan would come to underestimate the resources he had access to with the Space Corps.

"And the information systems?"

"We had not fully discussed that topic before Catherine arrived. They know nothing of concern."

"And I assume they questioned you about how you survived your escape?" Ferguson said.

"Yes. I said I had killed the other escapees with a bioweapon so I could survive on the little remaining water left, a deception I would prefer to remain secret."

"You would have them think of you as a murderer?"

"In order to hide my scientific innovations, yes."

"But didn't they detect your genetic changes, like Dr. Vargas did?" she said.

"It was Catherine who discovered the changes, Captain, not Dr. Vargas. They detected them. I lied about what they were for."

"And they believed that lie?"

"Probably not," Eshel said. "But they have too little information with which to prove me wrong."

Ferguson nodded in understanding. "What would've happened if Lieutenant Finnegan hadn't found you? Would Elisan have kept you as prisoner indefinitely?"

"No, Captain. Once they believed I had run out of useful information, they would have killed me, assuming I did not escape first."

"Escape? Where would you go?"

"There are places one can hide on Korvalis, Captain."

"And Elisan... he admitted to orchestrating both gumiia attacks on Derovia, and that more attempts to kidnap you never took place because you stayed onboard the ship to avoid the heat?"

"Yes."

Ferguson glanced at Yamamoto. She sighed and sat back in her chair. "Well, Eshel, it appears your suspicions were correct."

Yes, they were. Perhaps you will listen to me in the future, Captain.

"Grono Amsala was able to ferret out the two Sunai who abducted you," she went on. "They're dissidents from another province, in cahoots with Elisan. They stole the uniform and decorations of a Grono and infiltrated the party." She gave a half smile. "Perhaps now Gronoi Okooii will consider your debt paid to the Sunai."

"Perhaps."

Ferguson took a swig from her canteen. "Knowing that anything you say here is classified, do you believe that Lieutenant Finnegan competently carried out your plan as you laid it out?"

"Yes, Captain," Eshel replied without hesitation.

Ferguson got up and walked around to the front of her desk, standing closer to where Eshel was seated. "Do you still believe she was the best choice for taking point in your rescue, considering that she's not a soldier and not trained for such operations?"

"Yes."

"Why? Because the operation was successful?"

"No. It is due only to her exceptional inventiveness that Catherine was able to find me."

"Exceptional inventiveness," she said, glancing at Yamamoto. "That's high praise for someone whose methods included a paper-board sign."

"She would never have found me without it. None of your soldiers, with their combat training, could have achieved such a result. Nor could they have infiltrated Fallal Hall without detection."

"Is that why you chose her?" Ferguson said. "Because she's not a soldier?"

"I chose her because I trust her, Captain. I won't have my people pay for the evils of Elisan and the malkaris by revealing weaknesses in Korvalis's defenses."

Ferguson said nothing for a moment. Then, she nodded. "We're glad to have you back safely. You're dismissed."

Eshel saluted, and left.

Yamamoto sat down in the Captain's office. "Anything yet from the Korvali?"

"No. I'm sure they'll contact us through some mysterious means, sometime between tomorrow and three months from now," Ferguson said, rolling her eyes. "Has Grono Amsala reported any progress with the investigation?"

"A little," Yamamoto replied. "The two men who abducted Eshel have provided more information about their scheme, in exchange for leniency in their punishment. They claim the Korvali approached them and offered them technological information they could sell to Sunai scientists. It seems the two men hadn't yet sold the information."

"If the Grono gets his hands on that information, let's have Eshel look at it. And make sure Tom and Finnegan don't let Eshel out of their sight. If the Korvali are still hunting him, we need to make sure he isn't dangled out like a piece of meat."

"We cannot hide him forever."

"I know. But until we leave Suna, we can't take any chances." Ferguson leaned on her chair's arm, chin resting in her hand. "Were you as confident as you let on that this would succeed?"

"I was confident in Catherine's ability to handle the task. However, I admit I didn't have high hopes that they would find Eshel."

"She got lucky, finding him."

"Luck favors the prepared, Janice. Tom admitted he was pretty impressed with her."

She stood up and looked out her window. "I didn't think a scientist could impress me. Now two of them have." She turned back toward him. "Tom did a great job, as usual. He prefers taking point, but I'm glad he was forced to only oversee this one. It's good training for when he takes command someday."

Yamamoto shook his head. "I don't know if he's command material."

She smiled. "He will be. When he grows up a little." She paused. "Looks like Eshel got to him, too. I hoped he'd have more intelligence for us."

"Me too. I think it's safe to assume the devices altered their EM emissions to something the Korvali eye cannot detect."

Ferguson nodded. "Tom said Eshel made him destroy the evidence before they returned. Probably figured we'd try to confiscate it."

"Can you blame him? If such information got out, Korvalis would become vulnerable to invasion."

She sat back down. "These people aren't stupid. Once they realize Eshel's back with us, they'll put two and two together. Whatever Eshel's trick, it'll only work once." She paused. "Hopefully once is enough."

Two days later, Yamamoto received a message. The message was from the Korvali, relayed through the Alliance. He sat down to read it. Once finished, he immediately stood up and left his office.

A short while later, Yamamoto went to Ferguson's office. He waited for her reaction, but she merely sat down and looked at him.

"What's wrong?" she said.

"Did you not receive the message from the Alliance?"

Her eyes narrowed as she scanned her mail again. "I don't see it. It must be delayed again." She sighed. "What does it say?"

"They've heard from the Korvali. They're angry. They claim that Eshel's removal without their permission was an act of war, and that we must return him immediately. They view him, or claim to view him, as one of their citizens, thus making his retrieval illegal and in defiance of the Alliance's promise to leave them be."

"How do they know we retrieved him?"

"They know our F-6 was sighted at Station 10, twice," he said. "And they have the paperboard sign." He paused. "Most damning, they claim that Catherine appeared briefly on their palace's surveillance. Eshel mentioned that was a possibility."

Ferguson grimaced. "They'd assume it was us with or without that evidence." She tapped her fingers on her desk. "We've tried to accommodate these people, Suko. We've banned Eshel from even discussing genetics, we've given them what they've asked for, and Eshel's gone out of his way to protect them. Yet they still engaged in this sneaky plot to snatch him! There's nothing else we can do." She shook her head. "Let's set up a meeting with Admiral Scott. Then we'll talk to the Alliance." She stood up to leave.

"There's another issue," Yamamoto told her. "And you won't like it."

Ferguson turned to look at him.

"The malkaris's firstborn has been murdered. He was found dead on the very day Eshel escaped Korvalis. The Korvali have formally accused Eshel of the murder, and—"

"They'll say anything," she said, waving her hand at him. "They accused him of divulging their genetic secrets too, and he hasn't."

"This time it seems they're correct. I asked Eshel about it. He admitted to the murder."

Ferguson slowly sat down, silent for a moment. "There's going to be another murder, Suko. I'm going to throw that Korvali idiot into space."

Yamamoto didn't reply.

"Get him in here," she said.

Eshel glanced at the empty chair after he saluted the Captain and XO.

"Do not sit down, Private," Ferguson said. Eshel remained standing. "Did you murder your monarch's eldest son?"

"She is not my monarch—"

"Answer the question!" she shouted.

"I did, Captain."

Ferguson gave him a stony look. "I hope you enjoyed your time with us, Eshel."

CHAPTER 27

As Eshel took his seat in the softly lit, cave-like room, everyone grew silent as they turned their attention to him. He sat alone, separated from the others, watched by those who listened from one side of the room, and those who would decide his fate on the other.

He saw new faces, as well as those he'd met previously. Gronoi Sansuai stood speaking with Tallyn, and Ov'Raa gestured in sign language to an unfamiliar person—an earless, black-eyed Calyyt called Toq. Another Sunai stood with them—an interpreter, offering aid to Ov'Raa's limited skills with the Calyyt language. Finally, an older human male stood aside: Admiral Scott. Each delegate wore a sash with the Alliance insignia.

"Let us now begin," Gronoi Sansuai said, his gruff voice echoing in the large stone meeting room. The Alliance delegates took their seats, but the Gronoi remained standing. "This hearing will determine whether Eshel, of the planet Korvalis, who is a refugee under our Orion Interplanetary Alliance, shall suffer punishment for the murder of his malkaris's primary son." He gestured to Admiral Scott, his decorations clinking together. "The Space Corps will allow the Alliance to decide on this case, and on Eshel's punishment. The delegates have reviewed the complaint from the Korvali, Eshel's report of the killing on Korvalis, and other information pertaining to this case. I will now question the refugee." He turned to Eshel. "You freely admit to killing this Elan, this Prince of Korvalis. Tell us why you performed this act."

"He murdered my father, Gronoi Sansuai. I gathered scientific evidence to prove his guilt. Then, as allowed by the sher keltar, I killed him."

"What is this 'sher keltar'?"

"It is an ancient rite, older than the Age of Industry, and even older than the Age of Agriculture. When murder transpires, Korvali Doctrine permits a genetic relative of the murdered one to reclaim his or her lost years by stealing those of the murderer."

"It is for revenge, yes?"

"No, Gronoi. The sher keltar is my right, and my duty, as a Korvali."

"If that is so," Gronoi Sansuai said, "why does this Elisan seek punishment?"

"Not all clans observe the rite. Some prefer more... modern methods of justice. The family of the malkaris believes it is above Doctrine. It is one of many ways they are corrupt. But Doctrine says nobody, even the malkaris herself, is beyond the sher keltar."

"Your former clan, this Shereb clan... they do not observe this rite?"

"They do not."

"Then how did you learn of it?"

"From my father. He is of unique heritage, a descendent of the Shemal, a primitive clan that resides in the remote territories. Like all primitive clans, the Shemal adhere to old traditions."

Gronoi Sansuai glanced at the interpreter, who rapidly communicated the proceedings to Toq. "Tell us, Eshel, about your father's death."

Eshel hesitated, preparing himself. He shouldn't share such information. But he knew the consequences of not sharing would be worse than the discomfort he felt at that moment. "After being invited to dinner with the malkaris and her family, my father was found dead in the gardens of Fallal Hall. A bioweapon killed him. A friend had discovered my father's body and contacted my mother, rather than the Hall Guard. My mother, in the cover of darkness, performed a thorough search of the body, including genetic scans. Such efforts are often futile; Shereb assassins rarely touch their victims—it is considered beneath them to do so—and they make sure to avoid shedding DNA. Once finished, my mother's friend contacted the Hall Guard. The authorities completed their investigation; upon finding no useful evidence, they closed the case.

"In her search, my mother found a hidden device. The device, which my father had secretly developed, allowed him to surreptitiously scan the DNA of any person who attacked him. However, the device, while small enough to easily hide, also has reduced power and storage capacity—the scanner saves only one image at a time, and the person whose sample is collected must stand very close to the scanner.

"I set aside my work and began investigating the murder. When I downloaded the data from the device, it contained an image. The image had poor resolution in some places, but it still contained enough DNA to conduct a match. However, when I examined our database for a match, I found none. Such a result meant only one thing."

"What did it mean?" the Gronoi said.

"That someone related to the malkaris performed the murder. The only DNA samples unavailable to Shereb scientists were those of the malkaris and her first- and second-degree kin. This also violates Doctrine."

"What happened next?"

Eshel had gathered all of his father's belongings, systematically searching through each and every item. And he found what he'd hoped to—Othniel's logs. His father had kept detailed logs of all his dealings with the malkaris's family, Elisan and his aides, and the other Shereb scientists. Eshel had found his father's obsessive log-keeping a waste of time. But when Eshel searched the logs, he found what he sought.

Othniel had secretly collected DNA samples from the malkaris's kin, using the very technology he'd created, and had hidden the files. Othniel never mentioned the samples to him; he must have collected them after they performed the sher mishtar, when Othniel revealed everything about his logs, his new scanning device, and his ideas for Eshel's escape. Othniel kept the device with him at all times and would scan the DNA of any suspicious person who tried to isolate him from others.

"And this… analysis," the Gronoi went on. "It gave you the result you sought?"

"No, Gronoi. The images of the ruling family were also poorly resolved in some areas, making full identification impossible. However, I narrowed the list of suspects to four: the murderer was one of the malkaris's four sons. Unfortunately, that day I received an offer to leave Korvalis and could not pursue the case further." He paused. "When Catherine freed me, I took the opportunity to scan the four suspects with a superior instrument and finish my investigation."

"And how were you able to gain such information without detection?"

Eshel paused. "I cannot share such information, Gronoi."

Gronoi Sansuai raised his chin. "That concludes my questions for now."

The Gronoi sat down and gestured to Admiral Scott, who stood up and walked closer to where Eshel sat. He stood with his arms behind his back, his sharp eye and aged face looking around the room, and then at Eshel.

"You stated, Private Eshel, in your report of what happened on Korvalis, that you performed this rite after Lieutenant Finnegan found you."

"Yes, Admiral."

"So she was an accomplice."

Eshel felt a sting of regret. "She was not. She knew nothing of my intent to perform the rite, only that I needed to gather evidence."

"And how did you kill this… prince?"

"I cannot share that information, Admiral."

"This is no time to be secretive, Private," Scott said.

"Doctrine states that others shall not witness the sher keltar or know the method of death."

The Admiral paused, as if considering his next question. "You no longer live among the Korvali. Why did you choose to do this rite?"

"The sher keltar is my right as a Korvali. Judgment for such an act is not the domain of the Space Corps or the Alliance."

"One could say you gave up such rights the day you sought asylum with us."

"I disagree, Admiral. I am always Korvali, whether or not I choose to live among your people. And even if I had forsaken these rights, they were mine again when I was abducted and taken to Korvalis."

Admiral Scott stepped closer to him. "We have a problem, Private. If you're a Korvali citizen, you may perform such a rite. But as a Korvali citizen, you cannot leave Korvalis or live among us, and we cannot protect you or go to such lengths to retrieve you as we did."

Eshel fell silent. He hadn't considered such a perspective.

"Private, do you have evidence that this rite is legal?" Admiral Scott asked.

Eshel hesitated. "I do not." He heard a small murmur in the room. "I attempted to obtain such information through review of the documents pertaining to Ashan's escape from Korvalis. However, I found no evidence of the rite's legality."

"Maybe the law doesn't exist in your Doctrine," Admiral Scott suggested. "Maybe your father believed it because his primitive relatives taught him of it."

Eshel felt his anger rise, and made considerable effort to refrain from insulting the Admiral. "My father would never teach hearsay, Admiral. He showed me the pertinent Doctrine."

"I see." He paused. "With all due respect, Private, this rite seems barbaric for a people who look down on militaries and hand-to-hand combat."

"Murder is rare on Korvalis, Admiral. We have a lower birth rate and a smaller population. Life has great value there." He paused. "Perhaps the sher keltar is barbaric. But no less so than the murders that occurred during your former wars with the Sunai." Eshel knew, even before the Admiral gave him a surprised look, that such a comment was risky. But it was the truth, and if they were to still accept him, they must tolerate his beliefs, just as he must tolerate theirs.

Admiral Scott glanced at the other delegates. "No further questions."

Toq stood up next. While older, his compact, muscular build and quick movements reminded Eshel of the CCFs, of the sudden aggression the Calyyt were capable of. He signed his questions, the interpreter translated them, and Eshel answered them. During this process, Eshel began to recognize the structure of the Calyyt language, which he could see was as complex as he'd been told. He hoped for the opportunity to learn further; but if discharged from the Space Corps, such opportunity was unlikely. The only other possibility was under the service of the Sunai, but he couldn't allow himself to consider such a terrible prospect yet.

Toq's questions, as well as those of the gentler Tallyn, were less probing and did not, in his opinion, do further damage to his case.

Sansuai spoke up. "Are there more questions for Private Eshel?"

The delegates said they had nothing more.

"Let us take a short recess," the Gronoi said.

After the four delegates retreated to a separate room, Eshel remained seated. Catherine and Tom approached him and spoke in hopeful terms. However, he could tell by their expressions that they didn't feel the optimism they spoke of. When they'd learned of what he'd done, they'd gotten angry, but not as angry as Ferguson had, especially after he explained that knowledge of the sher keltar shouldn't extend beyond one's family.

The door opened and the four delegates sat down at their table. Sansuai spoke. "After discussion among the delegates, we agree that Eshel, citizen of the planet Korvalis or not, may be entitled to perform such a rite and murder his father's murderer. It is not for us to decide whether this act is acceptable. Until the Korvali join our Alliance, we shall have no say in how one Korvali treats another Korvali, on Korvali territory."

Before Eshel allowed himself to entertain any notion of relief, he sat quite still, waiting for the rest of the Gronoi's speech.

"Yet, there is the problem of documentation. We lack evidence that such a rite exists, that this rite is part of Korvali Doctrine, or that Eshel remained within the bounds of this Doctrine! If Eshel were not under this Alliance's protection, such a concern would be no domain of ours! But as a member of our great Alliance, Eshel's conduct toward even a fellow Korvali shall be scrutinized. My officers have made many attempts to receive confirmation from the Korvali about this sher keltar, through many persuasive means. The Korvali claim this rite is no longer practiced and no longer part of their Doctrine."

The room seemed to quiet.

"At conclusion, this leads myself and the other delegates to choose whom to believe. Shall we believe the Korvali government, who failed to keep the covenant they agreed to on my own planet, in my own meeting?" The Gronoi's decorations jingled as he gestured emphatically. "Or shall we believe the words of one Korvali," he motioned to Eshel, "who left his homeworld, and whose own leaders believe him dangerous?" He paused. "With no further evidence, we can only conclude that Eshel must receive punishment for his offense against this Prince of Korvalis. We shall deliver the details of such a punishment by the sun's rise."

Eshel sat alone in the cool, dark room. He'd requested to stay behind. Gronoi Sansuai had honored his request, requiring only that one guard stand near the closed door. He knew Catherine and Tom would want to talk to him. But he could not face them.

He'd considered the punishment he could incur, the basis of which he'd learned from examining prior cases where an individual from one Alliance planet had killed a citizen of another Alliance planet. However, no such case involving the Korvali, a non-Alliance people, existed. Viewed one way, the Alliance gained from his inclusion, as one Korvali served as the seed that would eventually bring more Korvali to the Alliance's table. But viewed another way, his presence among them only antagonized his people, leading them to consider, as with his rescue, the benefits of such a thing relative to the costs.

Without evidence, it was his word against Elisan's. It disgusted him that his word should have equal value to Elisan's, particularly for an act such as the sher keltar, which, on Korvalis, would be supported by all but the malkaris and Elisan's band of corrupt supporters. But he could hardly blame them for their unwillingness to believe him. To choose his word over Elisan's would be to choose merely out of loyalty, or some other irrationality. He didn't want punishment, but he could accept punishment under such circumstances.

And there was no punishment he couldn't endure when he weighed against it the justice of having done his duty. The length of punishment would prove small when compared to the number of years he'd taken from Elan. An image of Elan standing with Alshar flashed before him. The visions had already grown fewer with each day since the sher keltar. He cursed Elan for his stupidity, for his duplicity, for his amorality.

Why, Elan? Why did you not let Ivar perform the murder? Now your mate has no mate, your child has no father, and you have put our people in further jeopardy by allowing Ivar to become malkaris someday. Even you, with your treachery, must understand the disservice you've done to Korvalis by creating opportunity for Ivar to gain more power.

But Eshel realized that, perhaps, he was the stupid one for refusing to see Elan's true nature.

Eshel returned his thoughts to his punishment. That he would incur punishment was expected. But it was still unclear whether the Space Corps, who postponed any decision until after his trial, would allow him to continue serving in their organization. Leaving Korvalis for the first time, leaving those who mattered to him, had been difficult. Now, he feared he must face such difficulty again. The Sunai would use their powerful means of persuasion to implore him to live among them; but under no circumstances, other than having no other option, could he allow that. He would live among the humans on Earth, if they'd have him, and begin all over again.

Much later that day, the guard opened the door. People filled the seats until the four delegates and the interpreter emerged from the other room.

"Let us begin!" Gronoi Sansuai said loudly, as everyone quieted down. "Out of respect for the organization that Private Eshel belongs to, Admiral Scott will announce the verdict of this hearing."

Admiral Scott stood, his arms behind his back once more, and addressed the room. "Only hours ago, Gronoi Sansuai received a transmission from Sunai officers in Jula. They found evidence for this… this sher keltar… among the sealed documents pertaining to Ashan's escape." He paused, and the room grew even quieter. "This source fully supports Private Eshel's claim to commit this act of murder. It doesn't specify whether the Doctrine applies to a citizen who has escaped and sought refuge elsewhere. However, the Korvali forced Private Eshel to live among them again, suggesting that they consider him their citizen. Therefore, Eshel acted within his rights, and furthermore will face no punishment and no loss of his asylum."

Admiral Scott paused again, looking at Eshel. "However, from this day forward, if Private Eshel continues to live among us, and to remain enlisted with the Space Corps, he must formally revoke his Korvali citizenship and the doctrinal rights that come with it. He will no longer have rights to Korvalis or its customs, under any circumstances." He turned to the other delegates. "These proceedings are adjourned."

As the silence broke and people stood up from their chairs, Eshel saw only the smiling faces of Catherine and Tom as they approached him.

CHAPTER 28

"At ease, Lieutenant," Yamamoto said. He motioned to a chair.

Catherine sat, looking at him in that hesitant way she always did whenever he requested an unplanned meeting with her.

"Catherine," Yamamoto began. "We've reviewed your recent operation to retrieve Eshel from Korvalis. We've interviewed yourself, as well as Eshel and Tom. Your handling of the operation, which had many tactical challenges, was impressive. That is Eshel's opinion, Tom's opinion, and, from the standpoint of one who oversaw the operation, my opinion."

Catherine's expression turned to surprise, and she blinked a couple of times, as if searching for the correct response. As she started to speak, Yamamoto put his hand up briefly before he continued. "Everything we discuss from here forward is classified. I imagine you are used to that by now." She smiled and offered her consent. "Would you be interested in providing a unique service to the Space Corps?"

"What kind of service?"

"You would complete special operations, assigned by myself, when your services are needed. The operations would typically involve information gathering and thus would, in most cases, prove somewhat less dangerous than the one involving Eshel's retrieval."

Catherine's eyes widened, recognizing what he referred to. All those in the Space Corps, even the scientists, knew about Clandestine

Operations Officers, or COOs. Most of what they knew was false, but they knew COOs existed and that their identities were kept secret. "Really?" she said.

"Really. You will undergo a trial period, to ensure you're a good match for such a position. However, you have a cluster of traits that make you a good candidate. An obvious one is your superior self-defense skills. Another is your ability to work independently. You perform well under pressure, and you show a capacity for improvising in difficult circumstances. However, until recently, I had no knowledge of how you would perform in the field. As the Captain pointed out, you are a scientist, not a soldier, and thus an unconventional choice to serve in this capacity." He paused. "Your position as a senior scientist offers more advantages, as we can place you in a variety of settings without raising the suspicions that a soldier would."

"How... how much time will this involve? What about my post?"

"If you choose to take this role, you must maintain your role as a scientist. However, to release you from some of those duties, I will enroll you in the ETP under the Operations Department, reporting to me. In effect, you will be cross-training."

"And I would work alone?"

"Alone, or with one other. This person will train you."

"Who is this person?"

"You must commit to the position to find that out."

"Who would know?" she asked.

"Other than myself... only the Captain."

"And the Captain is okay with this?"

"She took quite a bit of convincing."

He'd had to pull for Catherine. He needed one more COO—someone who could work with scientists, with people his soldiers couldn't relate to. He'd had a few other candidates in mind, but Catherine had qualities they lacked. Her sign-making ploy showed an ability to innovate even when under stress. She hadn't leaked

Eshel's secrets to her superiors, her father, or even to her closest friends; that showed she was above the need for social approval or the pressure to accede to authority, both of which were crucial in a COO. Her ability to convince someone like Tom Kingston to modify their rescue plan showed an ability to bend the rules and persuade when necessary. And, from his standpoint, her willingness to risk her career by standing up to Commander Steele's insult, and to risk her neck by facing a Calyyt in the ring... those actions showed sheer, uncompromising guts. He shared none of this with Catherine. She needed to prove herself first.

"Are you interested?" he said.

"I am."

He gave a nod. "There are two caveats, Catherine. If you make this commitment, you will receive training and access to information about our organization—and others'—that you cannot share with anyone, anytime, under any circumstances. You will swear an oath to protect this information—any breach of this oath will have severe consequences associated with it. To some extent, when you take on this role, you gain certain privileges, but forsake others." He paused. "The other caveat is Eshel. I know you and he share a number of secrets and an important history, more than you admit to. And it's clear to me that, on some level, you and Eshel still share something that is beyond friendship. Do you see where I am going with this?"

"I think so, Sir."

"I'm not asking you to reveal that which Eshel has already shared with you. However, if you choose this role, you can no longer keep Eshel's secrets. You must choose your allegiance to the Space Corps over your allegiance to Eshel." He paused. "Is this something you can do?"

Catherine hesitated for a moment. Then she leaned forward in her chair. "Yes, Sir. I can."

And with that, Yamamoto put out his hand. "Welcome aboard."

"Lieutenant Finnegan a COO," Ferguson said, shaking her head. "I never would've predicted it."

"I believe she will do well," Yamamoto said. "She has different skills than the others."

"To say the least," Ferguson said, laughing. "She's a whitecoat, for God's sake! Can you think of any COO who wasn't a soldier?"

"None comes to mind," Yamamoto admitted.

She shook her head again. "You have real vision, Suko. Her knowledge of genetics, her intimate relations with Eshel, her recent intelligence with the mission, even her friendship with Grono Amsala... And hopefully, over time, her loyalty to us will outstrip whatever remaining loyalty she has to Eshel."

"You still doubt him."

"Not as much as I did. But just because he chose to give up his citizenship doesn't mean he isn't still Korvali. He's just as much a liability as he is an asset."

Yamamoto nodded, standing up. "I agree. I will continue to keep my eye on him." He paused, looking at her. "By the way, Janice, I believe you owe me a bottle of red tefuna."

Ferguson eyed him. "How's that?"

"Nearly eighteen months ago, after the Korvali visited the ship, you bet me Eshel wouldn't last with us. Under my calculation, you lost."

Ferguson gave a half smile, a twinkle in her blue eyes. "You got me there. One bottle of red tefuna, coming up."

"Make it a bottle from five sun cycles ago," he said. "It's a better vintage."

And he left.

Catherine headed to one of the private ready rooms on the fifth deck. Who was this other person, the one who would train her? Would it be someone she knew? Would it be a man or a woman? Yamamoto would consider this person carefully. It would be someone experienced, and someone the brass trusted. It would most certainly be a soldier, and someone Yamamoto believed would be a good influence on her.

Just before 1300, Catherine buzzed the door. When the door opened, she walked in. And there, in the middle of the room, a grin on his face, stood Tom.

CHAPTER 29

Saturday, Catherine finished her morning training class. Still a bit tired, she holed up in her quarters for the day to get some rest. She read, slept, and even turned down Tom's invitation to play poker. But at almost 2330 hours, her door sounded.

Eshel. He walked in, out of uniform, holding only his canteen. "Is it too late to speak?

She shook her head, turning off her reader and joining Eshel at her small table. "Did you come from Tom's?"

"Yes."

"Good game?"

Eshel cocked his head slightly. "I won a good sum; although I no longer need it."

"Why's that?"

"I was saving for a transport to Korvalis. To perform the sher keltar."

"So your abduction saved you a lot of money." She grinned.

Eshel smiled, sitting in his usual still way, patiently waiting for their small talk to complete so he could proceed. Once it did, he began. "Catherine," he said. His tone sounded cold and formal, but belied some emotion underneath. "I wanted to express my gratitude for your execution of my rescue plan. I know I already did so, but I wanted to again... " He paused, as if considering his words carefully.

"I doubted that you would come for me, that the brass would allow it… that such an endeavor would be worth the risks."

She looked at him with a softened expression. "You have a lot to learn about us."

"Yes," Eshel said. "Tom also said that." Eshel composed himself and switched to a less personal tone. "I informed the Captain and XO that your handling of my retrieval was superior. I doubt they appreciate the difficulty of the task." He paused. "It occurred to me, during the debriefings, that we have shared our experiences on my homeworld with the Captain and the XO, but not with one another."

Catherine hesitated, wondering if such a discussion would violate her promise to Yamamoto. But it wouldn't. The mission—and what they shared during it—had occurred before agreeing to her new role. So they swapped stories.

"I have questions," she said afterward.

"Ask me anything."

She smiled at his answer. "What's the history behind that silver-leafed tree in the foyer at Fallal Hall?"

"The tree is an ancient koshac tree, and one of only a few left of its kind. The Osecal erected Fallal Hall around it, when they ruled. The malkaris allows no one to grow more of them. The branched marking on the hand of the Osecal… it is a symbol of this tree."

"That's why it looked familiar," she said, nodding. She grew more serious. "When you took me to the fourth floor of Fallal Hall… the one throwing that rice-like stuff, that was Ivar, wasn't it? You thought he was the murderer… but his DNA didn't match. And that ruled out everyone… except Elan."

Eshel nodded, almost imperceptibly, his face growing pale. "You shouldn't know that. No one should. I did not believe Elisan would publicize the murder, as it meant revealing that Korvali borders can be breached." He shook his head. "I would call him stupid… but to underestimate him would be even more foolish than underestimating Elan."

Catherine nodded. To fool Eshel was no easy task, and Elan had done so for years.

Eshel went on. "I do not know if Elan deceived me because he was skilled at deception, or because I was blinded by our bond."

"But wasn't Ivar the bad seed among them?"

"Yes. Elan admired my father's work, was always a trustworthy person. He had much to lose—his work, his mate, his daughter. Ivar had none of that. Ivar is like Elisan—he is merciless, and lacks good understanding of our science. Elan—and others—believed that Ivar conspired to murder him, so Ivar would be malkaris when their mother died." He paused. "Now, I do not know what is truth, and what is deception."

"You looked so pale afterward. Did your father warn you that it would be so difficult?"

"Performing the sher keltar is necessary. What is difficult, as you say, is severing the bond we shared."

"How?"

"It is as I explained on Korvalis, under the tree. The Korvali form bonds with... with what you would call loved ones. To sever that bond results in significant... difficulty."

"What kind of difficulty?"

"Nausea. Difficulty eating. And strong visions of that person that recur, often for many months."

"How strong?"

"It is as if the person is really there."

"What happens if you're at work and you get one of these... visions?"

"I ignore them. But they generally occur during sleep."

A look of recognition crossed Catherine's face. "Is that why you'd wake up at night, breathing funny?"

"Yes."

"How long do the visions last?"

"It depends on the strength of the bond. Because my bond with Elan had diminished after my leaving Korvalis, those visions have already begun subsiding. But I still see my father." He paused, gazing at her. "And until you found me, I still had visions of you."

Catherine's face fell. She blinked a few times before shifting in her seat. "I'm sorry," she said, her voice a whisper. "I should never have hit you."

"Do not concern yourself, Catherine. The visions were due to our broken bond, not your striking me."

"But still. If I'd known—"

"You could not know. I am at fault, for involving myself with an outsider without fully considering the consequences."

Catherine nodded faintly. "Eshel, I hope we can put all of that behind us, and be friends again. Like we used to be."

Eshel's eyes studied her. "That is your preference… friendship."

She nodded. "I think you'd agree it's the best way, for us."

Eshel was silent for a minute. Finally, he said, "I would agree."

He stood up to leave, pushing in his chair. Catherine stood up as well. As Eshel headed toward the door, she realized one could easily see her photos, mounted on the bulkhead. And that meant one could easily see the open spot, once filled with the art Eshel had given her. She cringed, holding her breath, resolving then and there to find out who had it and get it back. Fortunately, Eshel didn't appear to notice the missing painting.

Just as he was to leave, he turned to her. "There is something you should know. It is important, but you cannot repeat it."

"Don't tell me," she said suddenly. Eshel raised his eyebrows. "I was warned about sharing more information with you."

Eshel's eyes narrowed. "Warned by whom?"

"By those in charge."

"This is not a new secret. It is something you already know, and the piece I will share is one you must know, for your benefit."

Catherine relented, offering her consent.

"I sent you the encrypted files regarding Steele's activities with Dr. Vanyukov," Eshel said.

Catherine gasped in surprise. "So that *was* you!"

"I advised you not to trust him. Now you know why."

She shook her head, unsure what shocked her more: that Eshel pulled off such a stunt without anyone knowing, or the reminder that Steele had clamped down on her and thwarted her progress so he could exploit the information for his own gain.

"He greatly disliked our being involved," Eshel went on. "And he seems to dislike you for other reasons, similar to the way that Middleton dislikes me."

Catherine had another thought. "Wait. There was a second image file among the stuff you sent me. Did you give him an updated copy of your genetic material?"

Eshel raised his eyebrows again. "Do you believe I would do that?"

She shook her head. "That worthless asshole. Taking a sample from you without your permission... that in itself is a huge violation! We need to report him!"

"No," Eshel said.

"No? Why not?"

"His deceptions offer us useful leverage, allowing you to continue making progress in secret without complaint from him." He gave her his hardest look. "I cannot have my work exploited by inferior scientists, Catherine. You must prevail. And you must do so without my assistance."

"I'm on it, Esh. I've already made quite a bit of progress. But you should know that I brought Holloway on to help." She felt a pang of guilt as Eshel's expression turned colder. "Are you angry?"

"Of course I am angry."

"He's very smart. And trustworthy. With him, we can work twice as fast."

"I know. It is only that you should be working with me, not him."

"That's my preference, too, Esh." She cocked her head in curiosity. "How the hell did you do that, anyway? Where did you learn such skills?"

"My sources," he replied. And he turned and left.

April 3rd

Hi Dad,

I just started my training in the ETP. So far, so good. I'm as surprised as you are that I report to Yamamoto. After 22 months on this ship, I admit he still intimidates me. I've learned a few things from Tom about our weapons systems, including all the bioweapons, which has been really interesting. And if Steele's angry about the decision to release me from some of my duties, I haven't heard about it. Which is fine with me.

I just received a formal challenge for a rematch with the Calyyt I competed against in the CCFs. Eshel had warned me that my opponent would offer the challenge; it looks like he was right. The match, if I accept, will be several months from now. That gives me plenty of time to train, but we don't know if we'll still be encamped on Suna by then. If we are... I may take the challenge. I'll let you know what I decide.

Get in some more skiing before the snow melts.

Love,
C

CHAPTER 30

Catherine's contactor chirped. *Poker. Tonight. 2100. Bring kala.* Catherine smiled. Tom's request for kala—instead of beer—meant he was feeling festive and wanted to make it a long evening.

At 2100, Catherine arrived at Tom's quarters. It was the usual suspects: Eshel, Snow, Middleton, Zander, and Shanti, each carrying enough kala for him- or herself, plus a little extra. They sat down and played, their pot of money spread among them and shifting from person to person over the evening, but never really settling upon one clear winner.

And after many hours, multiple games, and a several cups of kala, Tom stood up. "I want to make a toast," he announced. Everyone quieted down. "You know the old saying in the Corps: choose carefully who you associate with during the first six months of a long-term space mission, as those people will become your closest friends for the next three years, if not for the rest of your life." He looked around him. "For better or for worse," he grinned, "I consider you people my closest friends, and I'm glad to know you." He held out his metal cup. "To friendship."

"To friendship," everyone said, as they drank to the toast.

"And," Tom went on, "To poker… the only game worth playing."

"To poker!" they cried, putting up their cups.

He looked at Middleton. "I want to toast Middleton, who loves the Ace rag and gives me his money more often than he wants to."

"Bullshit!" Middleton cried, but smiled and said "here, here" along with everyone else, and took a sip of his drink.

"Third—or is that fourth?" Tom shrugged. "To Zander, who managed to master the Sunai hand greeting and, recently, won enough money from me to buy himself a new girlfriend."

Everybody laughed as Zander gave a sheepish grin. "Here, here!"

"And to Shanti," he said, looking at her with a smile, "who finally learned to bluff an occasional hand without the entire table knowing it."

There was more laughter, and Shanti, a grin on her dark face, gave Tom a smack.

"Here, here!"

"And to Snow, who managed to go where few human males have gone… with a Sunai woman!"

Snow shook his head and waved dismissively at them, but still raised his cup.

"Here, here!"

"And to Catherine, who's the best woman I've never had sex with, and who's *finally* taking my advice and cross-training with the soldiers." He grinned and pointed at her.

Catherine shook her head, laughing.

"Here, here!"

"And last, but never least," Tom said, "to Eshel." He looked at Eshel. "You're not a goddamn thing like me and I don't understand you half the time, but I can say with all honesty that life on this ship wouldn't be the same without you, man."

Eshel raised his cup and gave a small smile. "Thank you, Tom."

"Here, here!"

"To another fourteen months!" Tom said.

"To another fourteen months!" said the others, clinking their cups together one last time.

And they all sat down, and played another game.

Thank you for reading *The Refugee*!

If you would like to be notified when I finish the second book in the *Korvali Chronicles* series or when I'm going to make an appearance at an event (such as a Comic Con), please sign up for my email list at the bottom of my home page. Don't worry: these emails will be infrequent!

Also, book reviews mean the world to authors like myself. If you feel like leaving a review on Amazon, I would be very grateful!

ABOUT THE AUTHOR

C.A. Hartman is an author who specializes in near future science fiction. Recovering from her years as an academic scientist, she's refocused her overactive, analytical mind on creating and appreciating thought-provoking stories with memorable characters. She recently released her novel *The Refugee,* the first book in a series that chronicles the fallout that occurs when an alien scientist escapes from his oppressive, xenophobic planet and comes to live among humans on a starship.

Hartman loves film as well as books and enjoys in-depth film analysis. She strongly prefers films that utilize memorable visual style as well as intelligent characters and storytelling. Bonus points if the film has a good psychological component. Some of her favorites include *Inception, Blade Runner, The Matrix,* and Hitchcock films. And although she prefers sci-fi, she secretly loves good fantasy and has spent many an hour re-watching *The Lord of the Rings* trilogy.

A graduate of the University of Colorado (CU), Hartman earned her PhD in Behavioral Genetics and worked as a scientist at CU for 11 years. Living in Denver with her husband, she enjoys hiking, camping, and traveling to faraway places.

Check out Hartman's books, blog, and events at 5280Press.com. You can also find her on Twitter: @5280_SciFi.

28339077R00197

Made in the USA
San Bernardino, CA
28 December 2015